King of the Air and Sea

King of the Air and Sea

Marnie White

LOST
COAST
PRESS
Fort Bragg, California

Lost Coast Press
155 Cypress Street, Fort Bragg, CA 95437
800 773-7782, publishing@cypresshouse.com
Book design and production by Cypress House

Publisher's Cataloging-in-Publication
Names: White, Marnie, 1946- author.
Title: King of the air and sea / Marnie White.
Description: First edition. | Fort Bragg, California : Lost Coast Press, [2025] | Interest age level: 010-018. | Summary: Inspired by the real-life exploits of the author's grandfather, who was a sailor, balloonist, and aviator at the turn of the 20th century, King of the Air and Sea is an exciting, fun-filled tale of two teenagers, Oliver and Jack, who in their adventures together solve mysteries, learn that life is not all fun and games, and discover that part of growing up is taking responsibility for your own actions.-- Publisher.
Identifiers: ISBN: 978-1-935448-49-5 (print) | 978-1-935448-50-1 (ebook) | LCCN: 2024917118
Subjects: LCSH: Teenagers--Juvenile fiction. | Sailing ships--History--Juvenile fiction. | Balloonists-- New York (State)--History--Juvenile fiction. | Airplane racing--United States--History--Juvenile fiction. | Biplanes--United States--History--Juvenile fiction. | Responsibility--Juvenile fiction. | Disguise--Juvenile fiction. | CYAC: Teenagers--Fiction. | Sailing ships--Fiction. | Balloonists--Fiction. | Airplane racing--Fiction. | Responsibility--Fiction. | Disguise--Fiction. | LCGFT: Action and adventure fiction. | BISAC: YOUNG ADULT FICTION / Historical / General. | YOUNG ADULT FICTION / Action & Adventure / General.
Classification: LCC: PZ7.1.W4456 Ki 2025 | DDC: [Fic]--dc23

Printed in the USA

2 4 6 8 9 7 5 3 1

First edition

Dedicated to all who dream of adventure and are
young at heart

"Fair Winds and Following Seas."
—Anonymous

Part 1

Greenhorn at Sea

Chapter 1
Escape

"Oliver! Wake up, boy! I've warned you before about daydreaming. This is the third time today I've caught you looking out that window. Hold out your hand!"

"Huh? Sorry, Mr. Strong what did you ask me?" Oliver said, a blank expression on his face.

"Okay, boy, I've had it with you. Hold out your hand."

"But Mr. Strong, I was only—"

The sting of the ruler's slap on Oliver's palm jolted him back to his senses and he sat straight up.

Turning to face the class, Mr. Strong repeated the question: "Now, can anyone in this classroom tell me why we celebrate Columbus Day?"

Only one student raised her hand, a girl who bounced up and down on her seat in anticipation. Mr. Strong sighed because Louise was always the first to put her hand up. "Okay, Louise, tell us why—"

Suddenly, there was a loud bang, similar to a gunshot, and the sound of people running, shouting, and a horse whinnying outside on the street.

"Uh… wait just a moment, Louise," Mr. Strong said as he rushed to the window to slam it shut and block out the din. As he reached the window, there came an earsplitting sound of vehicles crashing into each other. A man yelled obscenities: "Damn yer hide, mister! That confounded contraption of yours scared my horse and nearly caused a serious accident. Why, I oughta—"

Hearing another loud crash, the entire class rushed to the windows to see a brand-new 1908 Model T Ford whiz down the street, spewing clouds of black exhaust. As the automobile raced out of town, the driver squeezed the bulb attached to the klaxon horn—ah-ooh-ga, ah-ooh-ga!

Oliver used the diversion to slip out the classroom door; his presence wasn't missed.

At age fourteen, Oliver was of average height. Slim and wiry, he had muscular arms, thick brown hair, and shiny dark eyes with long black lashes. He was good-looking, and many a young lady in the town had her eye on him, but Oliver wasn't interested just yet. Instead, he spent his spare time reading books about magic, and the Popular Mechanics magazine that told him how to fix things.

As Oliver meandered toward home, he couldn't help thinking about the nasty argument he'd had with his father the past evening. Out of disgust, Oliver kicked a rusty tin can in his path. Oliver's father had confronted him again about being late for his after-school job at Symon's Foundry, which meant Oliver had to work overtime and be late for supper. Being late for supper had upset Oliver's mother. "Oliver, if you are going to be late," she said, "I cannot keep your food from getting cold."

"Mary! Stay out of this! I'll handle it! Go tend to the other children!" Oliver's father said angrily. Oliver's mother responded by escaping to the kitchen.

In the Victorian Era, unless the family was wealthy, a wife's role was limited to tending to the household chores and her children's needs. The man of the house was in charge of everything else, including discipline of the children.

In the heat of the argument, Oliver's father had shouted, "You're nothing but a bad egg, Oliver. It's high time you started to grow up and act like an adult!"

Oliver had yelled back at his father, "You- you nincompoop! You've never cared a damn about my feelings."

His father, eyes narrowed, had yelled back, "No son of mine speaks to me that way and gets away with it! Get out of my sight, boy! I don't want to see hide nor hair of you 'til you can grow up and show me respect!"

Oliver's father, Isaac, wasn't so much hurt by the angry words Oliver had yelled at him, but Oliver had challenged his authority and made him feel as though he had lost his power as the family patriarch.

"That's fine with me!" Oliver yelled back, and stomped out of the room. When Oliver arrived back at home after leaving the school, he immediately ran upstairs to his room, filled his knapsack with an extra shirt, toothbrush, a copy of the latest issue of *Popular Mechanics,* a book on magic, a deck of playing cards, and a small bag of marbles. He shook his head, muttered to himself, rushed back downstairs, and slammed the door behind him with a loud *bang!* He hadn't even stopped to say goodbye to his older brother, Theodore, his sister, Phoebe, and ten-year-old little brother, Stanley, who stood in the foyer, his mouth agape.

Chapter 2
The Golden Lady

It was the evening hour, and the streets were deserted except for a tired-looking horse pulling a hansom cab, and a vagrant whose arms were wrapped around a streetlight as he mumbled to himself about the recent 1906 earthquake in San Francisco and the imminent end of the world. Oliver had just one thing in mind, which was to get as far away from his father as possible.

It began to drizzle, and cloud cover masked the stars and moon and made the light of the street lamp cast ghostly shadows. With his knapsack slung over his shoulder, Oliver trudged along until he reached Lake Union near the Port of Seattle. A chill wind made him shiver, and he turned up the collar of his thin coat.

When he arrived at the wharf, a pale sun had broken over the horizon. The air reeked of tarred rope, salt from the briny sea, and a mix of foul odors. A flock of gulls swooped overhead. The quay buzzed with men who wheeled handcarts and loaded cargo onto an old sailing ship. The ship was a three-masted, full-rigged schooner with square sails; it was built for speed rather than capacity. These days, most investors and clients wanted their cargo carried by the fast and reliable steamships. Several of them, moored along the pier, rocked gently on the incoming tide.

At the prow of the old ship, Oliver noticed a freshly painted wooden figurehead of a beautiful lady with streaming golden hair. She wore a flowing white skirt, and her breasts were exposed. Oliver would hear later that it was believed by sailors that a woman's bare breasts would shame the stormy seas into calm. Around the figurehead's waist was a golden girdle, and on her head a crown studded with red, blue, yellow, and turquoise glass jewels. The fake gems reflected light and cast colorful prisms on the water's surface. Oliver had read that figureheads were supposed to protect ship's crews from harsh seas and safeguard them on their journeys. He imagined the figurehead as magical and alive.

On the side of the ship's black hull, painted in gold letters, was the name *Amphitrite.* Oliver remembered reading that in Greek mythology, Amphitrite was the queen of the sea and the wife of Poseidon. Later, when Oliver became a member of the ship's crew, he learned that since many of the sailors could not pronounce her name, the ship became known as the *Golden Lady.*

The dockworkers, absorbed in their work, created a din; they yelled orders, swore, talked loudly, and rolled barrels loaded with provisions up a ramp onto the deck of the ship. They didn't notice Oliver as he crouched behind one of the larger crates on the pier.

The deckhands manned a crane with block and tackle so they could swing the heaviest cargo boxes onto the deck of the schooner. Once on deck, the cargo was lowered into the ship's belly.

Oliver took a chance and crept onto the opposite side of a crate that was being loaded. He quickly grabbed hold of one of the ropes attached to the sling, just as the crane hoisted the box onto the deck. As the crate hit the deck, Oliver jumped off and scurried behind a box marked PREMIUM BISCUITS. He then snuck down the companionway ladder to the hold where he crouched between some barrels. It was a tight squeeze, but Oliver didn't dare move until the sailors had left.

Two of them were in the hold, spreading boxes and barrels evenly along the sides of the hull so the ship would have a proper trim. The old sailor was girthy and had a weathered face with a grizzled chin. The younger sailor was a tall Black man with broad shoulders, muscular arms, and wooly hair.

Oliver noticed that the two seemed to get along well regardless of race. He would later learn that on a ship, sailors were not treated unfavorably because of their race, skin color, or origin, but were judged on their nautical skills and whether they could obey orders.

"In her prime, this ship musta been a grand lady, Stubs," the younger mariner said.

The other replied, "That she was, Mr. Jones. She was one o' the last great clipper ships built by the famous Donald McKay in New York City. In her heyday she made regular runs from New York to the California, Oregon, and Washington coasts, transportin' supplies, gold seekers, missionaries, and immigrants."

In her earlier days, the ship's bill of ladin' boasted fine silks, blue willow dishes and hemp from China; aromatic spices from the Spice Islands in Indonesia; leather hides from California that were headed to the shoe and trunk factories in New England; bolts of gingham and calico, ribbons, buttons, ladies' fans and other frippery; copper pots and kettles; coffee beans and sugar cane from the Sandwich Islands, and fine Cuban cigars. These days she's lucky to transport a load o' lumber. One thing in her favor, she was never a slave ship or opium runner.

"I remember the last real moneymaker was durin' the Klondike Gold Rush of 1898. What a gay time that was! We sailed from Seattle to Anchorage, Alaska, with enough supplies to choke a horse. Aboard were adventurous young lads, old-time miners, gamblers, barkin' sled dogs, horses, and ladies of the evenin', all with the gold fever, anxious to seek their fortunes."

The old man chuckled. "Them ladies of the evenin' was some-thin' else. For half a poke of gold, they was willin' to show their drawers to any rovin' eye, includin' a reverend. Yep, them were the days!"

"Ten years ago, when Cap'n bought the old gal, she was leakin' like a sieve and startin' to list to one side. Woulda sunk, too, afore she was a mile from shore if he hadn't forked over a boatload o' money to have her made seaworthy again.

What the cap'n don't know is the crew's been caulkin' and patchin' her with tar, hemp, and lead goin' on the past couple o' years. Truth is, in some places her hull's worn so thin the tar paper and copper are showin' through. She's like an old woman I once knew who tried to make herself look younger by dyin' her hair and usin' a lot o' makeup to hide her blemishes," the old man said with a laugh.

The beefy young sailor said, "Some say Cap'n Matthews is plain crazy to sail this old ship all the way home to New York City, but I guess he has his mind made up, and once the old man's made up his mind, there ain't no goin' back, even if it means decidin' 'tween the devil and the deep blue sea."

"All I can say is that the cap'n is a stubborn old fool, and I wish we weren't makin' this trip, especially since we still gotta go around the Horn at the tip of South America 'cause the government insists on draggin' its feet to finish that new canal they're buildin' across the Isthmus of Panama. I read in the paper that President Roosevelt is doin' his best to speed things up, but the French, who started the project, is balkin' at things," the old man said.

"The scuttlebutt is, once we get to New York, this ship's gonna be dismantled by breakers who'll strip her of all her metal fastenin's and fittin's, then burn her or put her on the block to be made into a storehouse along the Hudson River. Just hope she don't keel over durin' a storm before we get there. One huge swell washes over her bow and we're goners," he said, with a shake of his head.

"Yep, the *Golden Lady* is on her last legs, but so am I, so I guess it's too late to divorce myself from her now. All I can say is, may we have fair winds and followin' seas," the old man said.

"I hear Cap'n had to scour the town for a crew who'd sail on her. Word is, he was offerin' a ten-dollar gold eagle to any man who'd sail with him for the entire passage. That's nearly a month's wages. Still, weren't many sailors who wanted to sign on for such a long haul. Some of the men that come aboard this mornin' looked a little unsavory, if ye ask me. One was so tipsy he barely made it up the gangplank. Another was talkin' to himself."

"I hear tell Cap'n's been down on his luck lately, and nearly broke. Not much business for an old sailing ship. Most traders want to use them new steamers to carry their cargo. Mind ye, I'm only tellin' ye this 'cause ye're the first mate, so don't be spreadin' it around. Trouble is, Cap'n can't find enough investors who want to risk slappin' down their hard-earned money on this old ship. Most of 'ems afraid the old gal won't make it around the Horn again," the older man said.

"So, Cap'n says we'll be makin' a few side trips to pick up extra cargo, to earn enough money for the long trip around the Horn. First stop is Mendocino to pick up lumber, then San Francisco, then Honolulu, where we're pickin' up a load o' raw cane sugar that we'll offload at the new Hawaiian sugar refinery in a town called Crocket, near San Francisco. We'll also be loadin' pineapples from the Dole Pineapple Company on the Island of Lanai."

"Maybe we'll find some sailors in Hawaii who'll be willin' to sign on for the long journey to New York City," the first mate, Jonesy, said.

"Aye, even I have doubts 'bout goin' that far, but don't want to let the cap'n down. It's gonna be a long shot, and we'll need a deal of luck to get to New York City," Stubs replied. "Cap'n Matthews and I been goin' on ten years, and there ain't a man alive I'd trust more to get us to New York in one piece. Besides, if the cap'n hadn't begged me to come aboard, I'd still be sittin' in a rockin' chair on the porch of the Old Sailor's Home, twiddlin' me thumbs. Would ye believe it? That son of a gun threatened to shanghai me if I didn't come with him. I swear, Jonesy, Cap'n practically got down on his knees and begged me to come. Said he'd pay me top wages if I'd be cook again, which I'm holdin' him to. Promised me the only time I'd have to break my back was when he needed all eight stalwarts to help turn the capstan when we haul anchor. Besides, Cap'n says he needs me to teach the nubs a thing or two. Not many sailors today got the guts and know-how to run a sailin' ship like the *Golden Lady*. Thing is, they don't know how much fun they'll be missin'," the old sailor said with a chuckle.

"Well," said Jonesy, "we best quit our jawin' and get a move on. Cap'n wants all this cargo labeled and loaded this evenin' so's we can haul away on the first tide. We'll be pickin' up supplies from some local ports, then on to Hawaii."

Chapter 3
Discovered

It was near midnight before the two sailors finally finished stowing the last of the cargo and climbed the ladder to the upper deck. Oliver had sat so long behind the crates that he felt pins and needles in his legs. After he'd rubbed them and stamped his feet, the circulation came back and he was able to stretch his legs. Suddenly, the ship lurched violently. Oliver could only guess that it was headed out to sea.

The damp chill of night penetrated Oliver's lanky body. His teeth chattered, and he continued to rub his arms and hug his legs to try to keep warm. He hoped he wouldn't get seasick from the ship's constant rocking. He nearly choked on the bile that rose up in his throat, caused by the foul odors of tarred rope, rotting cabbage, bilge brew, dried fish, and animal dung. The old timbers creaked and groaned, and from the other end of the hold he could hear the pitiful cacophony of live chickens, sheep, goats, and pigs.

The dim light that came through the grating above allowed Oliver to pass the time reading the labels on the huge pile of barrels and boxes crammed into the hold. There were barrels of biscuits, flour, salted beef and pork, peas, cheese, butter, salted fish, potatoes, rum, ale, molasses, onions, tea, coffee, and many other staples. Reading the labels made Oliver hungry.

In another section of the hold were numerous barrels of water, stacks of lumber, bricks, nails, tools, and sheets of tin. *With so much cargo and supplies aboard,* Oliver thought, *the ship must be destined for a very long journey.*

As the night wore on, Oliver grimaced as he felt what he thought were rats running over his ankles, and heard the hum and crunch of many insects that scurried near his feet. He had been up since dawn. With the constant rocking of the ship, drowsiness finally overtook him. He slept, head on his chest, and woke every so often to the sharp strike of the ship's bell tolling the hour, the jingle of the rigging as it swayed in the wind, and the muffled voices of the sailors on watch.

It was still morning when Oliver woke with a start. He felt a gnawing in the pit of his stomach and was extremely thirsty. Surely by now the ship was far out to sea. Cautiously Oliver crawled from his hiding place behind the barrels. His legs were stiff and wobbly, but he managed to get up. Just as he stood, he lost his balance and fell against a barrel marked APPLES. Oliver started to pry the lid off the barrel, but a cold hand with skeletal fingers suddenly clamped down on his shoulder. The sailor's voice squeaked and broke as he shouted in Oliver's ear, "Aye, I got ye now, ye dang scallywag!" Oliver tried to wriggle out of the man's grasp.

"Where you think ye're goin'? Think ye can stow away on this 'ere ship and eat our apples, do ye? Well, ye got another think comin', 'cause the cap'n don't take kindly to stowaways, and nobody gets away without earnin' their keep!"

The sailor grabbed Oliver by the collar and dragged him up the narrow ladder to the deck above. Oliver struggled to free himself, but the sailor only let out a nasty laugh and hung on tighter.

On the deck, Oliver was nearly blinded by the sunlight. After a short time his eyes became accustomed to the brightness and he was able to take a better look at the sailor who had discovered him. The young man appeared to be only a couple of years older than Oliver, but it was hard to tell because he was short for his age, scrawny, and had slumped shoulders. His face was pitted and his sinewy long arms hung to his sides. He also dragged his right foot when he walked. He wore faded blue overalls that looked like they had once belonged to a much bigger man. His black greasy hair was tied back with a thong, and he reeked of cooking grease and sweat that smelled like onions.

Suddenly, Oliver heard a shrill bosun's whistle and was promptly marched along the deck to a spot where he was told to stand at attention in front of an older gentleman who was seated at a table fastened to the deck. Oliver figured he must be the ship's captain because he wore a blue uniform with brass buttons. Though his jacket appeared to have been recently brushed, it showed signs of wear around the collar and cuffs. The man had a neatly trimmed salt-and-pepper mustache and beard. He removed his hat and bowed to Oliver, exposing a patch of baldness at the back of his head. Wisps of hair fluttered in the breeze.

In front of the captain was a plate of fresh-baked sourdough bread, a bowl of savory-smelling beef stew, a wedge of cheddar cheese, and two apples. The captain didn't look up at the youths; he brushed cigar ashes from his stew and proceeded to eat his meal. He tore off a hunk of the bread and sopped up the rich gravy, then sliced a piece of cheese and apple. Using his knife like a fork, he picked up the slice of apple and put it in his mouth. He chewed the tasty morsel for a long time, as if stalling for time before he swallowed it.

The captain then pushed back his chair, patted his full stomach, and said to the cook, "Ahh, that was one delicious meal, Stubs! I should be offerin' ye double pay."

The captain then wiped his mouth on the back of his hand and stood up. All the while, Oliver and the other youth waited patiently. The captain stared at the young man who had captured

Oliver. "Well, Mouse, ain't I told ye before, I don't want to be bothered when I'm eatin'!"

"But sir, I was down in the hold, lookin' for a barrel of butter for yer biscuits, when I seen this 'ere stowaway hidden behind a…" Mouse stopped midsentence as Oliver again tried to kick him and wriggle out of his grasp, but Mouse just held on tighter. "If I had my way, I'd feed this stowaway to the sharks!" Mouse said.

The captain stood up, stabbed the knife into the table, and said, "That'll be enough, Mouse! It ain't yer business, it's mine, so ye can just get your bony arse back to the galley!"

Mouse narrowed his beady eyes, gritted his teeth, and sneered at Oliver, then turned and slunk off toward the galley. Before he'd gotten very far, he turned and hissed over his shoulder at Oliver, "Ye better be lookin' over yer shoulder, boy, 'cause one of these days I swear I'll get ye back for this!"

The captain shook his head and muttered, "That son of a gun, always stirrin' up trouble. Can't learn to leave well enough alone."

He cut another slice of cheese and apple, and inquired of Oliver, "Now, boy, who might ye be?"

"My name is Oliver, sir. I'm an orphan and was apprenticed to a cruel and stingy foundry owner who beat me, so I ran away. When I saw your ship getting ready to set sail, and heard some sailors saying it was the first ship to leave, I stowed away."

In a gruff voice the old captain said, "A likely story; one I've heard before, and I don't believe a word of it, so tell me the truth!"

"Uh- uh," Oliver stammered.

"Don't lie to me boy, or ye'll be paid out by the bosun with a rod come next mornin'. There's two things I detest: One is lyin' and the other is thievin'. You run away from one of them wayward homes for boys? Or did yer family throw ye out? And what made ye choose my ship to stow away on? Why didn't ye choose one of them new steamers? And don't think I didn't notice what ye're wearin'. Them's mighty fine duds for an orphan, and ye don't look like ye're starvin' none, even if ye've gone without food for a few days."

"Oh, but I'm telling you the truth, sir. I really am an orphan who…"

The captain picked up the other apple like he was going to eat it, and Oliver's mouth watered. The captain stabbed the apple with his knife and held it up under Oliver's nose. "You want this apple, boy? Ye got two choices to prove to me that ye're worthy of it. Ye can climb the mast to the top or ye can walk the plank," he said teasingly.

Oliver thought, *Gadzooks! I could fall to my death either way.* "Uh… sir, I think I'll take the lesser of two evils and climb the mast."

The captain shaded his eyes and looked skyward. "See that small platform up there, boy? It's called the crow's nest. If ye can climb that riggin' to the top o' the mast where that platform is by the next sound of the quartermaster's bell, I'll not only give ye this here apple but ye can have as much bread and cheese as ye can eat. We're too far out to sea now to put ye to shore, and I could use a personal steward, but first ye gotta prove yerself.

Oliver looked at the apple, then up at the small platform atop the mast. The platform looked a mile high, but Oliver was so hungry he could have eaten the rats that had scurried over his ankles in the night. At that very moment, a gray cloud passed overhead and cast a shadow over the sun, which made the captain look skyward again.

"Storm's brewin', so ye better start climbin', boy," he said. As the captain looked up, Oliver seized the moment and used sleight of hand to make the apple magically disappear into his jacket pocket. When the captain looked down, he was amazed to discover that the apple had vanished before his very eyes. He smiled and let out a belly laugh. The few crewmembers who were watching also laughed.

"Well, I'll be a monkey's uncle if that don't take the… seems we've got ourselves a magician or perhaps a thief among us, men." The sailors laughed again as if on cue.

The captain addressed Oliver, "I gotta hand it to ye, boy, makin' that apple disappear was a good trick, but it won't merit ye goin' without punishment. Pilferin' food and bein' a stowaway are capital offenses and won't be tolerated, so I demand ye climb!"

Oliver felt the apple in his pocket, narrowed his eyes, and looked up at the crow's nest. His stomach flip-flopped and growled. He was so hungry it felt like his navel was stuck to his backbone, and at that moment he would do anything for food.

Well, what ye waitin' for, boy? Start climbin', or it's the plank with ye!"

Oliver didn't know what speed and agility it took to climb aloft into the rigging, but he had no choice. Before he began the climb, Oliver took a big bite of the apple and put the rest back in his pocket. He then removed his hat, shoes and socks, and rolled up his pant cuffs. He closed his eyes for a moment, took a deep breath, and began to ascend the rigging, hand over fist. He didn't dare look down, but kept climbing until he reached the small platform at the top of the mast. When he reached the crow's nest his heart was pounding. He was breathing hard, and a cold sweat had seeped down his brow. On the platform, Oliver lay face-down and rested momentarily until he heard a bell ring and the men below cheered in recognition of his successful climb to the top. Later on, Oliver would learn that the ability to climb the rigging at lightning speed was a source of pride for sailors.

Suddenly, a strong wind swayed the mast back and forth, and Oliver had to cling to the edge of the platform with claw-like fingers in fear that he would be swept to his doom. He peeked cautiously over the edge. Below was the blue-gray ocean, and above puffy gray clouds. Numerous gulls swooped overhead. Oliver felt like he was on top of the world. From his high perch, the sailors below looked like toy soldiers busily going about their work as they mended sails, coiled rope, swept and swabbed the decks, and moved cargo. He could see the captain and the man called Stubs wave their hats at him. The captain yelled, "Ye can come down now, lad! Ye've earned yer meal and then some!"

The crew stopped work and looked up. Without warning, a barrage of screeching gulls dive-bombed the crow's nest. Oliver crossed his free arm over his head to protect his eyes. As he did so, a bird called a wandering albatross swooped down among the mob of gulls, which scattered at the sight of the very large bird. To Oliver's surprise, the albatross landed on the edge of the platform as if he owned it, and let out a loud mooing sound. The few remaining gulls flew off. Oliver swatted at the albatross with his free hand.

"Go away, you good-for-nothing critter! There's not enough room for the two of us on this platform," Oliver shouted. He continued to swat at the bird with his free hand, but it nearly made him lose his balance and topple over the edge of the platform.

At that same moment, the apple slipped out of Oliver's pocket and plummeted to the deck far below, smashing into a pulpy mess. Oliver thought, *If I'd fallen, that could have been my head.* He took another swipe at the creature and yelled," Go away, you dumb bird! You nearly got me killed!"

As Oliver slowly climbed down the mast, the gulls came back and once again circled overhead. The albatross took flight, dived into the swarm, and scattered them in all directions. It then flew in circles just above Oliver's head, squawking, as Oliver continued to descend. When he got to the deck, his hands were raw and bloody from the rope, but the jubilation of making the climb had numbed his pain.

Chapter 4
Spike the Albatross

Seeing Oliver's scraped and cut-up hands, Stubs, the old cook, daubed them with a rag soaked in warm water and vinegar, an old remedy used to disinfect wounds. He then wrapped them with strips of cloth.

"Ouch, that stings!" Oliver complained bitterly.

"Sorry, boy! "Them ropes gave them soft hands of yers a beatin'. I know it hurts, but the more ye climb the thicker yer skin will git. For now, try keepin' yer hands clean."

Stubs then introduced to Oliver his old friend, the albatross, who was standing on the table eating a crust of bread, "Oliver, meet Spike the wandering albatross."

"We've met," Oliver replied, puckering his mouth.

"Lad, Spike and me have been friends ever since I found him a few years back. At the time, he was just a fledgelin'. He'd injured his wing and couldn't fly, so I patched 'im up. Guess he never forgot. Ever since, Spike follows the ship in her travels. When ye was up on the crow's nest, Spike weren't tryin' to attack ye. He was protectin' ye from the gulls, like ye was one of his chicks. Some o' them unruly gulls can be mighty cold-blooded."

The albatross seemed to know what Stubs was saying and nodded his head up and down. Stubs fished in his apron pocket for another crumb of bread and held it out to the albatross. The bird timidly approached, then snatched the scrap of bread from the old sailor's hand and gulped it down. He then flapped his huge wings and flew out across the sea.

Stubs yelled, "Hey, Spike, is that any way to accept a hand-out, ye ungrateful gooney?!"

Oliver strolled to the rail to watch the albatross fly off and to look at the sea. For as far as he could see, there was no land in sight, only sparkling blue-gray water. The sun had begun to set and a reddish-orange glow reflected on the water. It looked like the flesh of a half cut cantaloupe as it slowly sank below the horizon. The old saying, "Red sky at night, sailor's delight, red sky at morning, sailor take warning," popped into Oliver's head.

The captain leaned back in his chair and puffed on his clay pipe. He turned to the cook and said, "Stubs, I think I'm a bit old for this kind of initiation," referring to making Oliver climb the mast.

"Cap'n, a greenhorn climbin' the mast is tradition. If ye hadn't held up yer part of the bargain, ye'd have lost faith with the crew, and they'd think ye was gettin' soft," Stubs said with a smile.

"Well, maybe I am gettin' soft in me old age, but I guess it was okay, 'cause the boy lived to see another day. Perhaps with proper trainin' he could become a good sailor. Maybe even become my personal steward," the captain replied.

"Aye-aye, Cap'n! Ye could use a good steward, since Mouse ain't worth a plug nickel."

Captain Matthews pushed back his chair, tapped the remaining tobacco from his pipe on the heel of his boot, put on his hat, and headed to his cabin.

The captain hailed Mr. Jones, bosun and first mate, through the ship's speaking tube. "Mr. Jones, the sun is settin' and we'll shove off at first light. Try to find a safe place where the lad can sleep the night without bein' bothered by the rest of the crew.

And tell Stubs to get him some supper. Oh, and one more thing: tell the boy I expect him to bring me dinner tomorrow at 1200 hours. If he's goin' to be me personal steward and a member of this crew, he's got to earn his keep and learn to obey orders like all the rest."

Chapter 5
Meeting Jack

Oliver woke the next morning to someone violently shaking him. "Wake up ye dirty mangy yellow dog! Hear them bells ringin'? Well, them bells mean it's goin' on 1200 hours, high noon to ye landlubbers, and the cap'n's waitin' for his dinner," the boy said.

Oliver was barely awake and still groggy. "Is it time to wake up, Ma? My stomach hurts and I don't feel like going to school today."

The boy shook him again. At first Oliver thought the ringing sound came from his alarm clock back home, and blindly reached out to shut the thing off. He then stretched, gave a cat yawn, and swung his legs over the side of the bunk.

"Aye, it's time to wake up, ye sorry nub. The rest o' the crew has already started their day's work. Cap'n will make ye sweep the decks twice over with a short broom if ye don't show a leg! Only payin' passengers is permitted to remain in their bunks after the mornin' watch."

Standing over Oliver was a lad about the same age. He was two inches shorter than Oliver, with tanned skin, and a smattering of gold freckles across the bridge of his nose. His hazel eyes were framed with long black lashes that gave him a slightly feminine look. He wore a knitted navy-blue seaman's cap, faded overalls, a crewneck sweater, peacoat, and Wellington rubber boots. In his hands was a folded pile of similar clothing, on top of which lay a tray of food.

The boy cleared his throat to make his voice sound deeper, and he put the clothes down on the bunk. "Ahem. I found these clothes in the slop chest. Thought ye might need 'em. Those fancy duds ye're wearin' would git ruined in no time on this ship. Thought ye might also be hungry, so I brung ye a mug o' hot coffee and some burgoo—what you landlubbers call porridge."

Oliver stared at the boy with blinking eyes and, not knowing what else to say, said, "Gee, thanks!"

"And heads up, boy, today is washday, and Mrs. M. said to bring yer dirty clothes to her after ye eat. Ye'll find her at the stern, bent over a washtub. "Oh, almost forgot. Stubs, the cook, is also askin' for ye. Ye'll find him in the galley. Just look for the small house forward on the deck, the one with black smoke curlin' out o' the stovepipe. If ye don't earn yer keep on this ship, ye may not eat."

The boy turned to leave. "I gotta go now. I'm needed elsewhere."

"Uh, wait a minute! What's your name? And who's Mrs. M?"

The boy gave Oliver an annoyed look and said over his shoulder, "Name's Jack, and I already know who ye are. Ye're that stowaway Mouse found yesterday, and Cap'n took a likin' to. If ye think the cap'n's gonna do ye any favors 'cause he made ye his steward, ye're mistaken.

"And Mrs. M. be the cap'n's new wife. Guess she's okay, but a little uppity if ye ask me. I think I've answered enough of yer questions, boy. Gotta get back to swabbin' decks. Oh, and just so ye know, I ain't no wet nurse. Ye'll be wakin' yerself up from now on, and gettin' yer own porridge."

Oliver suddenly felt the urge to relieve himself. "Hey, Jack, where's the water closet on this ship?"

"Crew ain't got one. We either go over the side or use a slop bucket or the jardines. The only commode on this ship is in the cap'n's cabin. He had Lee the carpenter build it special for his wife. Guess you'll have to use the jardines like the rest o' the crew."

"What's a jardine?" Oliver asked.

Jack laughed. " 'Jardines' is a fancy French word for 'gardens'. Course they don't smell like a flower garden, less yer growin' stink cabbage. That's just some fool Frenchman's joke. They's seats with holes in 'em that hang over the railin' at the ship's bow, the head of the ship. That's why some sailors call a toilet on a ship the head. Can't miss it, just follow yer nose.

"Oh, and if ye're needin' a wipe, there's some old hemp fibers in a tin can hangin' by a bale on a nail. Or if that ain't refined enough, ye can use crumpled-up pages torn out o' the Monkey Ward catalog. Prob'ly won't be necessary, though, 'cause the sea spray does a good job o' washin' yer backside when it blows up through the hole," Jack said with a teasing laugh. He saw the disgusted look on Oliver's face and said, " But I guess for now ye can use the slop bucket in the corner, yer Royal Hiney. Then ye better look sharp, 'cause Stubs don't take it kindly if ye keep the cap'n waitin' for his dinner. "Gotta go now!" Jack said, then turned and hurried out the door.

What a strange fella, Oliver thought. He quickly changed into the clothes Jack had left for him. The pants were high-watered, and he had to cinch the belt around his waist a couple of notches.

Oliver took a swig of the coffee and nearly choked. The brew was bitter and strangely sweet, something like the cough medicine his mother used to give him. He decided to pass on the coffee and gobbled down the porridge. It was the consistency of glue and had no flavor, but at least it satisfied his hunger. Oliver quickly removed the bandages and stared at his badly scraped hands. Home, school, and the work he did at the foundry were easy compared to what he had to look forward to on this ship. He headed out the door.

Chapter 6

First Day

As Oliver walked toward the stern of the ship, the air was fresh and the warm sun felt good on his back. He observed the crew, busy as ants, as they mended sails, climbed the rigging, swept the decks, and shifted cargo. Two other nubs were bent over the railing; they threw up, and then walked back and forth on the deck in hopes of relieving their nausea. Oliver was grateful that he wasn't seasick.

Oliver found Mrs. M. at the rear of the ship, bent over a tub of soapy water and vigorously scrubbing a shirt against a washboard. Her hair was covered with a strip of pink cloth, and little wisps of her blonde hair blew in the gentle breeze. She looked up when she heard footsteps, brushed back the wisps with a damp hand, and stared at Oliver, who saw that she was much younger than the captain, perhaps in her mid-twenties.

"Oh, you must be the boy they found yesterday. I told Stubs over an hour ago to have you bring me your soiled clothes so I could wash them. As you can see, I'm almost done with the washing."

"Uh, sorry, ma'am. I just now woke up."

"Oh, all right, boy. I forgive you the lateness, but from now on you'll try to be on time. Most of the crew has been up since dawn, including me—oh, beg pardon, I'm Sarah Matthews, Captain Matthews's wife. What might your name be?"

"My name is Oliver. Jack told me you and the captain were just married."

"That's right. I guess you could say this trip to New York City is our honeymoon. Well, now, since the wash can't hang itself, perhaps you could help me hang it over the yardarms. Then you'd best be getting back to your other duties."

Oliver helped Mrs. M. hang the clothes, and got ready to leave.

"Nice meeting you, Oliver."

"Same here, ma'am," Oliver said, removing his cap.

Mrs. M. thought, *Nice boy, and he's got manners. Perhaps Jack could learn a thing or two from him.*

Oliver headed to the galley, entered, and addressed Stubs the cook, "Sir, my name's Oliver. Jack said you wanted to see me."

The cook was sucking on the stub of a cigar and appeared to be a mite tipsy. "Pipe down, boy. I knows who ye are, and I ain't the cap'n," the old man said. "What kept ye? Don't tell me, I know, ye first had to see the missus 'bout washin' them clothes ye was wearin' yesterday, and ye're that stowaway Cap'n made climb the riggin'. I patched ye up afterwards. Course, I'd had a few too many swigs o' me pain medicine by then, so me memory's a bit rusty. Confounded miserable pain!" Stubs said as he rubbed his lower back.

Oliver didn't really want to hear about the old man's ailments.

Stubs continued to smoke the stubby cigar while he stirred a steaming pot of stew. Occasionally an ash from the cigar fell into the stewpot. Oliver thought, *The cigar stub is how the cook must have got his name.*

"Ye hungry, boy?" Stubs asked. We're havin' boiled fish for dinner."

"No, sir. Jack brought me a bowl of porridge."

"Hear Cap'n made ye his steward. So here's yer first assignment: take Cap'n his dinner," Stubs said. He handed over a tray that held a thick-rimmed mug of the bitter coffee Jack had brought Oliver, a plate with two pieces of boiled fish, some salt beef, cheese, and a biscuit. Several hours had passed since Oliver had eaten the bland porridge Jack had brought him. Even so, the food on the cap'n's tray didn't look very appetizing.

"I asked Mouse to bring Cap'n his dinner earlier, but as usual, the boy made some weak excuse 'bout havin' to fetch somethin' for the bosun, so looks like ye're it, boy! Ye'll find the cap'n in his cabin 'bout now." Oliver hesitated and stared at Stubs for a moment, a frightened look on his face.

"Well, whatcha waitin' for? Take Cap'n his dinner, and ye better be lively 'bout it, 'cause he don't take kindly to havin' his dinner cold."

Still, Oliver hesitated.

"Boy, Cap'n may seem a mite rough around the edges, but he won't bite. Just make sure ye git on his good side right away or ye'll never hear the last of it."

"What about the way he treated Mouse?"

"Never ye mind 'bout Mouse. Whatever the cap'n dished out to that boy, he had it comin'."

"I just want to know why Mouse treated me so badly, and why does Jack have a chip on his shoulder?" Oliver asked.

"We can talk 'bout that later. Ye better git a move on and take this here tray to the cap'n," the cook replied.

Chapter 7

In the Captain's Cabin

Oliver managed to find the captain's cabin at the stern of the ship. On the door was a brass plaque embossed with the letters "CQ," for Captain's Quarters. Oliver knocked, and a raspy voice said, "Enter." Oliver pushed the door open with his elbow and stepped into the cabin. For a moment he stood in awe.

The captain's stateroom was the largest on the ship. The windows at the stern let in a gray light, but Oliver was able to see that the cabin was finely paneled with teak and mahogany. It featured a berth wide enough to accommodate the captain and his wife. Beneath the bed were built-in drawers. Against one wall was an aqua-colored seaman's chest with the letters "WSM," for William Sebastian Matthews, painted on the side.

An armoire with a beveled oval mirror in the door was attached to the opposite wall. The closet door was ajar, and inside it Oliver could see a freshly laundered captain's uniform, a clean white shirt, and a lady's high-necked satin dress with a ruffle at the bottom. In a corner of the cabin was a private water closet, complete with a marble sink and commode. Oliver remembered Jack saying the water closet was specially made for the captain's new wife. In another corner was a comfortable-looking chair with an ottoman. On it sat a lady's sewing box and a book. Next to it was a small table with two chairs. In the middle of the room was the captain's desk, on which numerous books and sea charts were scattered. Shelves on the walls held maps, a nautical almanac, a clock, and a brass instrument. Forehead furrowed in deep thought, the captain was bent over the desk, using a pencil, compass, and ruler.

Oliver stood holding the food tray. He cleared his throat to get the captain's attention.

"Ahem. I brought your dinner, sir."

"Just set it on the small table and leave, boy," the cap'n said without looking up. "I'm in the middle of plottin' our course and can't be disturbed." Oliver set the tray on the table. As he did, he noticed a framed photograph, the size of a formal visiting card, of a pretty young woman in a high-necked white lawn dress trimmed with lace, and a picture hat with a silk flower on it.

"Is that a photograph of your wife?"

"Boy, I said don't bother me! I've got to finish plottin' this course so I can discuss it with the mates. Perhaps we can talk later," the captain said, when ye to come back to clear the dishes. I don't hanker to rats and vermin comin' in here. Oh, and tell Stubs I'll be eatin' me supper in the saloon this evenin', as I'm meetin' with some of the mates afterwards."

Before Oliver left, he took a quick peek over the cap'n's shoulder at the nautical chart he was working on. "Sir, is that the route we'll take to New York City? While I was hiding in the hold I heard a sailor say we'd be sailing around Cape Horn. Is that true?"

"Aye, but before we start the trip, we'll make a few stops along the way to earn extra money for the trip. Now didn't I just say don't bother me when I'm takin' a bearin'? Begone with ye, boy, afore I..." the cap'n said, looking sternly at Oliver.

"Yes, sir, but you can't blame a fella for being curious as to where this ship is headed."

The cap'n gave Oliver a half-smile. "All right, if it's the only way to get ye to leave me be. Our first stop is Mendocino, California, to pick up a load of lumber that we'll be deliverin' to

San Francisco. After that awful earthquake and fire, them San Franciscans is in need o' lumber and supplies.

"Yes, sir. I saw some lumber and bricks when I was in the hold, and heard some of the sailor's talking."

Then we'll head to Hawaii to get a load o' sugar for the C&H Sugar Refining Company. We'll also pick up pineapples from the Dole Pineapple Company on the isle of Lanai. A greengrocer in San Francisco has contracted with us to deliver them.

"Then, if we make enough money deliverin' the cargo, we'll head south along the coast o' California to the town of San Diego, then down the coast of Baja, Mexico, to Valparaiso, Chile, then the tip of South America where we'll round the Horn. That'll be the most treacherous and difficult part of our journey 'cause we'll be crossin' from the Pacific Ocean to the Atlantic. The *Golden Lady* has done it before, and I have faith she can do it again. From there, we'll sail up the East Coast of the United States 'til we reach New York City. With a good tailwind, I estimate it'll take us a hundred twenty days to get there. That answer yer question?"

"Yes, sir." Oliver thanked the captain and started out the door, then turned and said, "I was just wondering, sir, what is that brass instrument on the shelf over there? I like to find out how things work."

The captain looked at the instrument. "That's a sextant. It's used to find the angle between the horizon and a heavenly body such as the sun, moon, or a star, to determine latitude and longitude. Seein' that ye show so much interest, and ye seem to be a smart lad, how 'bout we meet tomorrow when the sun is high overhead and I'll show ye how to shoot the sun."

"Really, sir? I'd like that! Thank you, sir. Well, I better be getting back to the galley before Stubs raps me on the head and throws me overboard," Oliver said with a slight laugh. He thought, *Stubs was right. For an old man who's supposed to be a grouch, the captain's not so bad.*

Chapter 8

Mouse and Jack

When Oliver returned, Stubs was alone in the galley. Seated at the table, he sucked on the stub of a cigar, sipped from a mug of coffee, and stroked an orange cat that sat in his lap. The cat purred loudly.

"Me and the cat are just takin' a break," he said.

In a box near the stove, four squirming kittens were piled on top of each other.

Stubs looked at Oliver. "I see ye brought the cap'n his dinner okay. Hope he didn't growl at ye too much. Cap'n don't like to be disturbed when he's porin' over them charts."

"No, the captain and I got along fine. He even offered to teach me a few things about navigation. Say, Stubs, is now a good time to talk about Jack and Mouse? I'd like to know more since I'm to work with them."

Stubs got up and the cat wandered over to her kittens. "Found the cat and her babes this mornin'. Must have come in durin' the night. They'll make good mousers and keep down the swarm of rats on the ship," Stubs said.

"Say, do you think I could have a cup of that coffee?" And could you put a couple of spoonsful of sugar in it?" Oliver asked, recalling the bitter taste of the coffee Jack had brought him.

"Sure thing. Help yerself to a cup, pull up a chair, and we can talk," Stubs said. He took a flask out of his pocket, poured a shot of amber-colored liquid into his own mug, and said, "Well, ye see, Mouse is his own worst enemy. He holds a grudge against the cap'n, and ye'll prob'ly be next once he hears the cap'n made ye his steward and offered to teach ye navigation. Knowin' Mouse, he'll be hell-bent for revenge, so I'm warnin' ye, watch yer backside.

"Cap'n don't take kindly to the boy, 'cause he's a slacker. Cap'n calls him a squeaker, 'cause his voice cracks and he's always complainin' and shirkin' his work. That's how he got the name Mouse. His real name is Mortimer Sanderson. Some of the crew call him a Jonah—they think he brings bad luck, but I don't believe it. If it wasn't for Mouse bein' the cap'n's first wife's nephew, Cap'n woulda got rid of him long ago.

"I suppose Mouse had good intentions when he first come aboard. His ma and pa pulled some strings to get him apprenticed as a midshipman when he was around twelve years old. He done okay 'til one day, while climbin' aloft, he got his foot caught in a ratline and nearly tore it off tryin' to get loose. He lost three toes—that's why he has that limp. He weren't any good at climbin' after that, so Cap'n took pity on him and gave him a job helpin' in the galley, but as I said before, Mouse ain't worth a pisspot."

"And what about the boy named Jack who brought me some clothes and my breakfast this morning. What's his story?" Oliver asked.

"Same as the rest o' the idlers: helpin' me in the galley, mendin' sails, coilin' rope, swabbin' the decks, tyin' rope knots, and playin' games o' chance. Dagnabbit, I may as well tell ye the truth, 'cause ye're gonna find out sooner or later, though Jack's gonna hang my hide from the nearest yardarm for tellin' ye!"

"What?" Oliver said.

Well, besides bein' a good all-round sailor, Jack is the cap'n's daughter from his first wife. Her real name is Jacqueline Fiona

Matthews, but everybody, includin' Cap'n, has always called her Jack."

"There was a photograph of a young lady in the captain's cabin," Oliver said.

"The one with the big hat? Yep, that be Jack. Wouldn't know it, would ye, the way she acts and dresses on this ship? That picture was taken a year ago before she was to attend some boardin' school back East. Jack's dreadin' having to go back to that school once this voyage is over. Says she hated every minute of it. Cap'n shoulda known she'd be a duck out of water at that school, but the cap'n's new wife insists that Jack learn to be a proper young lady. Between you and me, I think sendin' Jack back to that school is just an excuse for the cap'n's new wife to have him all to herself. Jack and Mrs. M. don't always see eye to eye.

Once ye git to know Jack, ye'll see she ain't as tough as she puts on. Actually, she's a pussycat and all the sailors like her, but if ye wrong her, look out! She can be a real hellcat!" Stubs said with a chuckle.

"Ye see, Jack takes after her real ma, who wasn't as fussy 'bout bein' a lady, and like Jack, she loved the sea. Cap'n used to take her with him all the time on voyages 'til she was in the family way, but the birth was too much for her and she was never well after that. Then she got real sick. Never complained, mind ye, even on her deathbed. Cap'n never shoulda taken her on that last voyage. Still blames himself for her death. I told the cap'n it weren't his fault. She even tried to tell him herself, but he wouldn't listen." With a sad smile, Stubs said, "The face on the ship's figurehead was made in her image."

"If Jack's ma was anything like the figurehead, she must have been real pretty," Oliver commented.

"That she was. She and the cap'n loved each other very much. When she died, Jack was still a baby. We was way out to sea when it happened. After we give her a proper seaman's funeral, Cap'n was distraught. He didn't want nothin' to do with the babe for some time. The nearest port was a long way off, so the crew sort of adopted the little girl and took turns bein' her mama. She was a small thing at first, and we kept her bed next to the stove in the galley so she'd stay warm at night. Since she had no woman's breast to clamp onto, we fed her condensed milk mixed with warm water and molasses. We put it in a vinegar bottle with a tit made from the corner of a dishrag.

"Like I say, the crew took a real likin' to the babe and looked after her. All of us had a turn at changin' and washin' her nappies and gowns. Hung 'em up on the yardarms to dry. If another ship come by and seen all 'em dainty whites flyin' in the wind, they'd think we was pirates tryin' to surrender," the old man said with a laugh.

"When Jack got a little older, she ate watered-down porridge, and she gummed hard crackers 'til her teeth come in. When she cried 'cause her gums and teeth hurt, we rubbed 'em with rum to ease the pain, sang seaman's shanties, and bounced her on our knees. There weren't a sailor aboard this ship that didn't take a likin' to that little girl. No siree! She made us feel like a real family. She still does. I feel like I'm her grandpa!" Stubs said, a tear in his eye.

"When Jack got older we learnt her to tie knots, climb the riggin', set sails, coil rope, sweep the decks, just like the rest of us common sailors. The ship was her playpen. By the time she was six years old, she could scramble up the riggin' like the best o' us sailors. Playin' the part of a common sailor is what makes Jack happy.

"Only bad thing is, Jack picked up a few nasty habits along the way, such as actin' like a Tasmanian devil whenever she couldn't get her way, barin' her teeth, snarlin,' and wavin' her fists. One day, the first mate bought her a frilly pink Sunday go-to-meetin' dress and a right pretty straw bonnet that tied with a bow under her chin. She was pretty as a china-head baby doll in a storefront winda'. Then, suddenly, she like to throw a fit to end all fits. Teared off that bonnet and stomped on it like she was puttin' out a fire or killin' a rat. Rollin' on the deck and screamin' bloody murder 'til the cap'n come along, stripped her down to her skivvies, and drenched her with a bucket of cold seawater to stop her squallin'. Don't think Jack's ever wanted to wear a dress since, 'cept when she was made to at that straitlaced girl's school. The first mate, Jonesy, knowed how to read, write, and do ciphers and taught her some. I guess I won't mention what else she learnt."

"Like what?" Oliver asked, though he kind of knew.

Oh, I guess it won't do no harm. Ye see, a sailor's life aboard ship for months at a time can get pretty dull. There's times when they got nothin' to do. To fill the time, many sailors bet on cards or dice or any other game o' chance. Jack took to gamblin' like she had nothin' better to do to while away her time. She also learnt to swear a blue streak when she was just a wee kid. Course it weren't really her fault, always bein' around sailors, but the cap'n's new wife frowns on gamblin' and swearin', and has tried her best to cure Jack of those bad habits. At least Jack doesn't drink, or the Mrs. would have another thing to harangue her about. But I'd be the first to say, if ye ever find yerself in trouble or need a hand, Jack's got yer back, so, it'd be a good idea to make her yer friend. She could probably use a friend about now, I expect.

"About six months ago, Cap'n went and got a new wife much younger than himself. Name's Sarah—Mrs. M., the crew calls her."

"I know, I met her," Oliver added.

"After she and the cap'n was married and Sarah come on the ship, all hell broke loose for Jack. Ye see, the new Mrs. Matthews is determined to make a lady out o' Jack, if it's the last thing she does. And Jack don't want no part of it. If it was up to Sarah, she'd have the cap'n and her livin' in one o' them fancy decorated gingerbread houses back East. And, Jack goin' back to that prissy finishin' school. Don't git me wrong: Mrs. M. ain't a bad person, she just don't understand ye can't make a silk purse out of a sow's ear. She needs to cut Jack a little slack.

"I gotta admit Mrs. M. has her good points. She does the cap'n's laundry and isn't a bad cook. Once in a while, on special occasions, she'll come in the galley and make the best cookies sprinkled with sugar and cinnamon; calls 'em snickerdoodles. Cap'n and the crew eat 'em up faster'n she can bake 'em."

Oliver smiled, "Thanks, Stubs, for telling me about Mouse, Jack, and Mrs. M. It explains a lot. I kinda know what Jack's going through. She reminds me of my own fam—"

Stubs picked up on Oliver's last sentence and yelled, "Good Gawd, boy! Don't let me catch ye bein' a liar. Ye said ye was an orphan. There's nothin' the cap'n hates more than a liar and a thief." Stubs raised an eyebrow, a questioning look on his face.

"I'm not lying. I am an orphan! My family all died three years ago from scarlet fever, except me." Oliver crossed his fingers behind his back and hoped Stubs would believe him.

"Next thing, Jonesy wants ye and Mouse to swab the decks. Here's your mop. Mouse will be waitin' for ye outside."

"Aye-aye, sir!" Oliver said, saluting.

Oliver looked puzzled. "Uh, Stubs, this mop has a short handle. I thought swabbing the deck with a short handle was punishment."

"It is. Guess the first mate thought climbin' the mast weren't good enough punishment for bein' a stowaway, stealin', and lyin' to the cap'n. As first mate, Mr. Jones is second in command, so best ye get on his good side too and not give him any cause to make ye do somethin' different.

"'Sides, usin' a short-handled mop, ye won't miss any bit of dirt under the spars. And boy, don't be doin' any o' that salutin' stuff to me. We ain't in the navy, and I'm just the cook. Here, put this in yer pocket for later." With a grimy hand, Stubs gave Oliver an apple and some ship's biscuits. "Salt from the crackers helps if ye feel seasick."

"Thanks, Stubs, but so far I feel fine," Oliver said.

Stubs gave him a quirky, toothless smile as if to say, Wait 'til we get a rough sea.

Oliver took the mop and thought, *There are a lot of things I'll have to learn if I want to survive as a sailor.*

Chapter 9
A Lesson In Navigation

The next day at midday, Oliver met the captain on the quarter deck. He was holding the same brass sextant Oliver had seen on the shelf in the captain's cabin.

"Ahoy there, boy! I was wonderin' if ye was gonna take me up on teachin' ye to navigate," the captain said, screwing up his right eye to get a good look at the sun through the small telescope on the instrument.

"Ye know, boy, afore they had this instrument, early mariners who sailed out of sight of land used what was called a cross-staff—'cause it looks like a Christian cross—to find the altitude of the sun. The term "shootin' the stars" comes from holdin' the cross-staff up to yer eye with one hand and holdin' the transom, the crosspiece, with the other, somethin' like a man with a bow and arrow takin' aim at his target. In this case the target be the sun or a star. Ye slide the vertical piece along the staff so ye can see the sun over the upper edge of the transom while ye align the horizon with the bottom edge."

"Uh, Cap'n? You lost me with holding the cross-staff," Oliver said with a puzzled look.

The cap'n handed him the sextant. "Perhaps ye'll learn better if ye do it yerself. First ye hold the instrument vertically and shoot the sun with it, like this. Sight the horizon through the telescope alongside the mirror to get the image of the sun.

That's it. Now, move the index arm like this, 'til the image of the sun appears to be sittin' on the horizon. Then sight the horizon through the part that's not silver on the horizon mirror. You can then read the altitude of the sun from off the scale on the arc, which is in degrees on the bottom o' the instrument's frame."

"Now that ye found the latitude, next ye want to find the longitude. Many shipwrecks have come from not findin' longitude. Then ye need a good ship's clock and the correct time, GMT, meanin' Greenwich Mean Time. You need to remember: 15 degrees of longitude is the same as one hour o' time. That gives ye the longitude of 8 degrees, 15 minutes west of Greenwich."

Oliver still looked confused. "Uh, sir, can you go over the part where ye shoot the sun again? Ye lost me back in Greenwich."

The captain chuckled. "Well, it's a little difficult to understand the first time ye do it, and there's a lot to remember, but if ye keep practicin', by the twentieth time ye should be able to get the gist of it. I could use a smart boy like ye to help me with the navigation. I'm also willin' to teach ye about plottin' a course, about charts, and how to use the binnacle and compass, if ye're willin'. Maybe one of these days ye can spell me at the wheel."

Oliver smiled. "I'd really like that, sir. Can we do this again sometime?"

"Aye, me boy, but first ye better practice shootin' the sun with this," the captain said. With a fatherly smile, he took out of his peacoat pocket a small carved wooden cross, which he called a transom. Attached to the piece of wood was a cord with several knots.

About a thousand years ago, the Arabs used this sort of cross to find their way home. Before leavin' their homeport, an Arab sailor would tie a knot in a cord so that by holdin' the cord with his teeth, he could sight the North Star along the top of the cross and the horizon along the bottom. To return to his homeport, he'd sail north and south as needed to bring the star to the same altitude he'd observed when he first left home, and then he'd sail down the latitude. Each of the knots represented one degree per 36 minutes, which is about the width of your index finger," the cap'n explained.

Oliver thought that was too much information all at once, so to be polite he just nodded and smiled at Captain Matthews.

Chapter 10

Mendocino Village

"Look for landmarks, lad, so's we can get our bearin's," the captain yelled to Oliver. "Up on top o' them bluffs there should be a tall redwood tree with a white flag."

As the ship slowly sailed the coastline in search of Big River, where the village of Mendocino was situated, a thick fog crept in, masking the outline of the shore. Suddenly, it became very still, except for the occasional call of a gull and the roar of the crashing surf. A chilly, damp mist penetrated Oliver's peacoat and made him shiver.

The captain looked concerned and took the helm, then ordered Oliver, "Go a aloft with a torch and telescope, lad! Scan the shoreline for any signs o' the lighthouse at Point Cabrillo. If we're close, ye should see her beam soon. And listen with your ears, boy—many a ship has been wrecked off them rocky shores. Also, see if the red and green sidelights and the arc light atop the masthead is burnin' bright."

Oliver answered, "Aye-aye, sir. All the lights are okay."

Taking the torch and telescope, Oliver scrambled aloft and scanned the shoreline. From the rocks off the nearby town of Casper, he could hear what he thought were sea lions barking. The fog lifted slightly and he was able to sight the beam from the lighthouse station near Russian Gulch.

"The opening at Big River should be just ahead, sir. We're about two miles out and closing fast," Oliver shouted.

"Mr. Jones, I want ye to take a soundin'. We need to know how deep the ocean is here," the captain commanded.

"Aye-aye, Cap'n."

"And Mr. Jones, hold the anchor a-cockbill 'til I give the signal to drop her. After that, ye'll take the helm—and mind ye, steer a straight course to the shippin' point."

"All hands on deck!" yelled Mr. Jones from the quarterdeck. Mr. Harris, the second mate, who was standing on the fo'c'sle relayed the cap'n's order to the crew through a speaking trumpet: "All hands on deck—includin' Stubs, Mouse, Jack, and Oliver!"

Every man aboard the *Golden Lady* rushed up on the deck, as did Jack, Oliver, Mouse, and Stubs. All of the seamen ran to their appointed stations to await further orders.

The captain's voice boomed, "Ready—about! Keep her a good full, so she's got plenty o' headway. We're buckin' a heavy head sea lads, and don't know whether she can stay against it!"

The first mate relayed the captain's orders: "Mr. Harris and Mouse, ye'll be stationed on the fo'c'sle to work the head sheets and bowlines and the fore tack. Jack and Oliver ye'll work the main tack and bowline. Mr. Wang, ye'll see the lee fore and main braces is ready for lettin' go, and stand by to let go the lee main braces. Put one hand to let go the weather cross-jack braces, and with the other ye'll haul in the leeward. Mr. Lee and Stubs'll work the foresheet. Once ye've all done yer part, station one or more of ye at the spanker sheet and guys, then the rest o' the crew'll be at the weather main braces."

Mr. Jones relayed the instructions to the crew: "Haul down the foretopmast staysail, ease down the helm, and raise the foresheet! When we're within a hair's breadth o' the wind's eye, let go the main tack and sheet, lee braces, after bowlines, and mainsail haul!"

"Helm's alee! Let go the jib sheet and foresheets. Raise tacks and sheets! Mainsail haul! Let go and haul!" the captain shouted into the wind at the top of his voice. "She's fallin' off too fast! Vast bracing!" he hollered.

"Vast bracing!" relayed Mr. Jones.

"Clew up the fore and main topsails, put the helm down, haul down the jib, and flatten in the spanker! Make sure the anchor's off the bows, Mr. Jones, and hung by the cat-stoppers and shank-painters! Stand by to give her chain and drop anchor!"

To Oliver, all the nautical terminology the captain and first mate shouted to the crew seemed like a foreign language, but he mimicked every movement Jack made, and together they completed their part of the task. When it was finished, Jack smiled at Oliver and slapped him on the back. "Ye done well for a nub, Greenhorn!" she shouted above the wind.

The captain gave the order that all hands, except for a chosen few, would help load the lumber onto the ship, which would, he said, depart on the next incoming tide.

From a warehouse on the shipping point a large boom jutted out. Attached to its end was a pulley through which a stout cable was threaded, and the loose end, which had a hook on it, was ferried out to the ship where it was attached to the mainmast. Stacks of lumber were loaded into a sling, and with the help of a winch, slid along the cable to the ship's deck, where the men unloaded the stacks either into the ship's hold or chained them to the deck to keep the lumber from rolling off the ship in rough seas. The work was backbreaking, and by the time they had finished, the tide had begun to come in.

Jonesy approached Jack and Oliver, who were not needed to help with loading the lumber. "Good job, lads, helpin' with our approach and lowerin' the anchor! I'd say ye both earned a bit o' shore leave, but ye better hurry. Mind ye, be back at the point in two hours when we set sail. Ye can catch a ride to shore

aboard that bench swing they slide along the cable to load passengers and cargo."

Jack and Oliver smiled at each other and climbed aboard
the swing. They hung on tight to the guidelines as the swing slid
quickly along the cable, skimming the wave crests to the bluff
beyond. It was a thrilling ride—Oliver felt like he was flying, and
imagined that he was part of a squadron of pelicans soaring in
formation along the shoreline. When the bench swing reached
the point, a millworker on the bluff caught the bench and stead-
ied it so they could hop off. Oliver and Jack scrambled up the
bluff to the main street in town.

On the cliff, many stacks of raw redwood lumber were
waiting to be transported onto ships bound for San Francisco.
Behind the stacks were the lumber mill and warehouses, and two
new metal smokestacks, taller than the mainmast of the ship,
with plumes of white smoke curling out of their tops. During
the 1906 earthquake, the old brick smokestack had collapsed.
A steam train called the Skunk transported the logs from the
woods to the mill in Fort Bragg where they were processed into
lumber and shipped to San Francisco.

At the shipping point, the land was almost completely bare
of vegetation with the exception of the many stacks of lumber.
Large piles of scrap wood, hills of sawdust, old pieces of cable,
dark spots on the ground where oil and chemicals had been
spilled, links of heavy chain, eye bolts embedded in the ground,
rusty tin cans, and even a workman's castoff leather boot lay
strewn about the yard.

In contrast, farther down the bluff were the millworkers' New
England-style houses, white-washed white with gingerbread trim
and shutters painted black and dark green, reminiscent of the
homes and buildings back in New England where many of the
millworkers hailed from. Farther up the hill, Oliver could see
some grander homes with picket fences around their spacious

yards. He commented to Jack, "Those larger houses must be where the lumber barons live."

Almost every house, hotel, and building in Mendocino had a water tower attached to it or nearby. In the back and front of a good many of the houses and hotels were vegetable and flower gardens to supply the townspeople and hotels. Oliver and Jack could see cabbage, carrots, beets, and onions growing. The warm sea air was scented with the honey-like smell of sweet alyssum and fresh-cut pine and redwood logs.

Across the main street Oliver counted a half dozen hotels, several brothels, boarding houses, and a slew of saloons. On a side street there was a Chinese Taoist temple and a Chinese laundry with a clothesline stretched across the street to a building on the opposite side of the road. Pinned to the line, freshly laundered sheets and clothes flapped in the wind. Above the buildings, Oliver could see the steeples of two churches.

On a street farther up, Oliver spied on the top of a bank building a painted white wooden carving of Father Time with his scythe and a maiden. With further inspection they saw at the crest of the building the Freemasons' symbol of a compass and ruler with a "G" in the center.

"Let's first head for that mercantile over there with 'em storefront windows. I wanna buy Stubs a birthday present," Jack said excited about being in a town.

"Tomorrow is Stubs's sixty-fifth birthday, and the entire crew is buyin' or makin' gifts. Startin' at the dinner hour there's gonna be a gammin' to celebrate," Jack said, racing toward the store.

Oliver doggedly followed Jack. A sign over the store entrance read, JARVIS-NICHOLS MERCANTILE. Written underneath in gilt letters were the words IF WE DON'T HAVE IT, YOU WON'T FIND IT ANYWHERE!

"What's a gamming?" Oliver asked Jack.

"It's a party where the entire crew gets together, and there's a lot o' food and drink, games of skill, gamblin', music, and dancin'."

Oliver stood outside the store and stared at Jack.

"Well, what ye waitin' for? Let's go in," Jack said eager to spend her money in the store.

"Aah, Jack, I ain't got any money," Oliver announced, turning out his pockets. Jack sort of frowned, then grinned at Oliver and flipped a small leather pouch of coins tied to her belt.

"Well, that's okay, 'cause I got enough for the both of us. Been savin' me wages for over a year now, and won a boatload off Mr. Wang last night," Jack said. She fumbled with the drawstring to her poke, then pulled out two Morgan silver dollars. "See?"

Oliver stared at her. "I can't take yer money, Jack, 'cause I've no way to repay you. Back home, I'd have to work a couple weeks at the iron works to make that much, and since I was a stowaway I'll probably never earn enough on the ship."

"Sure ye will! By the time we get to New York City ye'll be rollin' in dough."

"But New York City is near three months away," Oliver retorted.

"That's why I want to give ye the money now, so's ye won't have to go beggin' from the other lads, like Mouse does. Where's home, Oliver?" Jack asked nonchalantly, trying to catch Oliver off guard. He stared at the ground and didn't say anything. Jack placed a hand on his shoulder. "It's all right if ye don't want to tell me."

"All right, Jack, I guess it's okay if you pay for my purchases, but next time it's my turn to treat you." *If I ever get enough money,* he thought.

The two young people then entered the store.

Chapter 11

Inside the Mercantile

The Jarvis-Nichols Mercantile was loaded to the gills with a variety of goods. Oliver and Jack stared at the overstocked shelves. The room held a hodgepodge of copper and cast-iron pots, ladies' corsets, men's and women's clothing and hats, high-topped shoes, a wicker baby carriage, bisque-head dolls, a high-wheel bicycle, and bolts of brightly colored gingham and calico cloth. Hung on the walls were washtubs, scrub boards, horses' harnesses, two-man saws, and kerosene lanterns. On a nearby shelf were boxes of nails and various carpenter's tools. Oliver nearly tripped over a coil of hemp rope on the floor.

In the middle of the room were barrels of soda crackers, green apples, and fat dill pickles. Near the front door was a barrel full of brooms, shovels, and garden rakes. On a display rack next to the barrels were colorful packets of Burpee's vegetable and flower seeds.

At one end of the counter sat a fancy brass "National" cash register. On its top was a brass sign that read AMOUNT PURCHASED. Next to the register were tall jars of peanuts, pickled eggs, jellybeans, and jawbreakers. Oliver wished he had a penny to buy a jawbreaker. On the shelves behind the counter were tins of canned fruit and vegetables with brightly colored labels, red and gold cans of coffee beans, Ball and Mason canning jars, and boxes marked SUGAR, CINNAMON, NUTMEG, and SALT.

Mounted on the opposite end of the counter was a tall Enterprise-brand cast-iron coffee grinder painted red and gold. On each side of it was a flywheel. Attached to one of them was a crank handle, and under the grinder was a little drawer to hold the ground coffee.

After the recent storm, the crew had spent hours untangling and coiling rope. Seeing the coffee grinder gave Oliver the idea to make a rope winder that would keep the ropes straight and save the sailors time. The reel would have a flywheel on each side of a long spindle. One flywheel would have a crank handle to turn the spindle, which would have hooks spaced along it to attach the ropes. A longer rope would be attached to a smaller rope with a quick hitch knot. The loop on the end of the knot would be placed over the hook on the spindle. When a sailor cranked the handle, the wheels would turn and the ropes would twine around the spindle. To release the ropes from the spindle, all a sailor had to do was pull the ends of the hitch knot and the ropes would fall apart. To hold the reel in place, a cradle could be made that would fasten to the deck so it wouldn't tip over. Oliver was sure the ship's carpenter could help him design and build the rope winder.

Next to the counter was a barrel that still had its straw packing in it. Nestled in the straw was a set of pretty blue willow china dishes and teacups.

"My mother had a set of dishes and cups like those, once," Oliver said to Jack, remembering the table set for Sunday dinner.

Jack tried again to catch Oliver off guard: "Yer mother? I thought ye said ye was an orphan."

Oliver quickly caught himself, "I am! My mother died from consumption a few years ago."

"Ye said yer entire family died of scarlet fever," Jack replied.

"They did, except for my mother. She died later."

Seeing Oliver cringe, Jack didn't want to push the subject any further.

While Jack browsed about the shop looking for the perfect birthday gift for Stubs, Oliver warmed his hands at a potbellied stove that stood in the center of the room. Near it were several captain's chairs and a pile of well-read newspapers.

Suddenly, Oliver froze. One of the newspapers was the Seattle Star, dated two weeks prior. It was laid open to the PUBLIC NOTICES page, where he spied a notice with the title YOUTH MISSING. Oliver looked around for Jack, who was in another section of the store seeking a birthday gift and wasn't paying any attention to him. The notice read:

YOUTH MISSING

Boy, age 14, dark brown hair, height 5'8", brown eyes; last seen wearing tan trousers, white long-sleeve shirt, light brown tweed jacket, and gray newsboy's cap; possible runaway. Foul play suspected. Contact: Investigator Edgar Holland, c/o Seattle Star, Washington.

Oliver quickly balled up the page, lifted the stovetop lid, and stuffed in the paper, which instantly caught fire.

From across the room, Jack yelled, "Say, Oliver, I think I'll buy this bowler hat for Stubs. His old one's gettin' pretty shabby. I think he'd like it. What ye think?"

Oliver appeared to be in a trance and didn't reply.

Jack carried the hat to the clerk behind the counter. Oliver came over and, seeing the bowler, said, "I'm sorry, Jack. Yes, a hat would be a great gift for Stubs!"

"Oliver, ye look like ye just seen a ghost. Are ye okay?" Jack asked looking concerned.

"Yeah, yeah, I'm fine. I tried one of those dill pickles in that barrel over there and I guess it didn't set right," Oliver said making a sour face.

Addressing Jack, the clerk said, "You got good taste young man. This hat costs two dollars and would look smart on any fine gentleman."

"Two dollars?! Why, that's highway robbery!" Jack yelled. Luckily there were no other customers in the store to hear her.

"The hat costs two dollars, take it or leave it! It's a genuine billycock, come all the way from Christy's Hat Shop in London, England. Ye can't find another like it anywhere. Boater and bowler hats are the latest fashion in men's headware," the clerk said.

"I'll take it," Jack said, and poured the contents of her poke onto the counter. The clerk counted out $2 and pushed the remaining coins back to her.

"Oh, rats! I forgot the sugar and cinnamon Sarah needs to make Stubs's favorite dessert of baked apples and sugar cookies. If I don't bring back them spices, she'll skin me alive."

The clerk took a tin off the shelf and took out three sticks of cinnamon. From a large sack he scooped a mound of white granules into the plate atop a scale.

Jack didn't notice the stamped letters C&H SUGAR COMPANY on the sack and said, "Hey, that don't look like the kind o' sugar our cook uses. You sure it ain't salt? The only kind o' sugar our cook uses is brown lump sugar that ye got to grind," she said.

The clerk smiled. "I can guarantee this is real sugar. It's the latest rage. It's called pure cane sugar from Hawaii that's already been refined and ground to particles at the C&H Sugar Refinery in the town of Crockett near San Francis—"

Oliver interrupted, "Say, Jack, the cap'n told me we'd be makin' a delivery of raw sugar to that same sugar factory."

The clerk appeared annoyed at the interruption, but continued his spiel: "Once the sugar is refined it turns white. Housewives love it because it saves time and is better for bakin', and they can make white cakes with it. You only need a couple of teaspoons to sweeten your coffee."

Remembering the nasty taste of molasses in his coffee, Oliver shouted, "We'll take five pounds of the stuff!" He and Jack watched as the clerk scooped more of the sugar onto one of the plates of the balance scale, until the amount of sugar equaled the weight of the five-pound stone on the opposite plate. The clerk then poured the sugar into a cloth bag and tied the top in a knot.

"Will you be wantin' anything else, boys?"

As Jack was about to pay for the cake ingredients, Oliver stared at the shelf above the clerk's head. "Uh, sir? How much does a cigar cost?" he asked, thinking he might gift Stubs a cigar for his birthday.

On the shelf were several boxes of cigars, plugs of chewing tobacco, and tins of cigarettes. One of the tins had a blue and black drawing of a sailor on the lid. Underneath were the words PLAYERS NAVY CUT CIGARETTES. Oliver thought Stubs might like one of those tins because of the picture of the sailor, but Stubs only smoked cigars.

Oliver said, "Sir, I'll take one of your best cigars."

"I thought you said you didn't have any money," Jack said.

"Please, Jack, I promise to pay you back when I get paid. I can't go without giving Stubs a present."

From the top shelf the clerk pulled out a red, white, and blue tin of soda crackers with the name PREMIUM BISCUITS printed on it. Behind the tin was a dusty cardboard cigar box. The clerk reached for the box, dusted it off with his feather duster, and set it on the counter in front of Oliver and Jack. On its lid was a picture of a pretty Hispanic lady who wore a blue dress with fine lace around the neckline. Above the image was written LA FLOR DE GARCIA Y VEGA, FINE CIGARS SINCE 1882.

"Been savin' these for a special customer of mine, but he ain't come in here for some time now. These cigars was once favored by many an aficionado, but the current economy bein' how it is, most men prefer the cheaper ones."

He opened the box and looked inside. "Hmm! Only three left. Thought I had more than that. Oh, well." He picked up one of the cigars and ran it under his nose to savor the aroma of cherry-flavored tobacco. Then he held the cigar under Oliver's nose so he could smell its sweetness. Oliver sneezed.

"Since there's only three left, tell ye what, fella: I'll let ye have all three for seventy-five cents. That's just twenty-five cents each."

"Seventy-five cents for three old cigars?! What kinda flim-flam are ye tryin' to pull here, mister? What's so good about those cigars that they cost so much?" Jack said, feeling like she was being cheated and hoping to get the clerk to lower the price.

Oliver spied a notation in the lower lefthand corner of the cigar box. "Says here, 'The cigars herein contained are made of the world's finest tobacco, skillfully aged and blended with a hint of sweet cherry flavor and at an affordable price of only eighteen cents each.' "

The clerk narrowed his eyes and said, "Eighteen cents is the price if you buy them direct from the company. For your information, these Cuban Cherry Delights are hand rolled and come all the way around the Horn from an island called Cuba in the Caribbean.

"I know where Cuba is," Jack interjected.

The clerk sneered at her and continued his pitch. "And the factory that makes these burned down awhile back, so you can't get them anymore. Twenty-five cents is my price, take it or leave it! If ye want the box it'll be another dollar," he said.

"Another dollar?! Now ye're really gettin' me dander up! Tryin' to charge me extra for a dusty old cigar box that ye'll probably just throw away," Jack said, getting hotter under the collar.

"Jack! Keep your shirt on! The man has to make a profit somehow!" Oliver said, trying to calm her.

The clerk again stared at Jack and said, "These cigar boxes are a premium. They're in high demand by the ladies in town 'cause of the pretty gold letterin' and pictures on 'em. Whenever I have an empty one, all I have to do is put the word out. They come runnin', and they bid to see who gets it. They use the boxes to keep their trinkets in," he said, grinning.

Seeing Oliver's disappointment at the cost of the cigars and the box, however, the clerk softened and said, "Well, seein' that these have been sittin' on that shelf for over a year, suppose I sell the three of 'em to you for twenty-five cents apiece, and I'll throw in the box for free. Besides, the last time I let them ladies bid on one of 'em cigar boxes, I near had a riot on my hands."

"Thank you, sir, thank you. You don't know what this means to me. Jack, will you pay for them? I promise to repay you later," Oliver said, remembering he had no money.

The clerk said, "What do you kids want with stogies anyway? Ain't yer mamas ever told ye that smokin'll stunt your growth and make ye turn green around the gills? On second thought, I think I should keep these cigars," he said, just to see their reaction.

"Hey, we struck a bargain," Jack replied. "Besides, them cigars ain't for us. We're both sailors on the ship *Golden Lady,* and the hat and cigars are for our cook, Stubs, whose birthday is tomorrow. We just wanted to buy him somethin' we know he'll like."

"Did you say his name is Stubs and he's the cook on the *Golden Lady?* Several years back a sailor named Stubs who was a cook on that same ship come in and bought these same cigars and a couple of peppermint sticks. We got to talkin, and he told me all about his excitin' adventures at sea," the clerk said with a smile. "If he's the same sailor, tell the old geezer Henry Jarvis sure enjoyed hearing his stories and wishes him a happy birthday."

Oliver was becoming impatient and wanted to leave. "So, Mr. Jarvis, are you going to sell us the cigars or aren't you?"

"Yes, yes," the clerk said.

Jack poured the contents of her poke onto the counter. "This enough money to cover everything?" she asked. Mr. Jarvis counted out the coins and said, "You're a dollar short."

"Aw, rats! That's all the money I got, 'cept for a coin I been savin' to…" Jack fished in her pocket. "If I give ye this gold coin, will it cover the balance?"

Jarvis's eyes opened wide when he saw the coin. He picked it up and examined it closely, noticed how newly minted it was, felt its heft, and touched it against his teeth to see if it was real. "Where'd ye get this coin, boy? Never seen one like it before. Is it some kinda foreign coin?"

Jack hesitated. "If I tell ye, are ye gonna think any different of me? Ye see, I won it off a sailor last night, playin' cards. I don't know what it's worth, but I took it 'cause I figured I could drill a hole in it, put a string through the hole, and wear it round my neck as a good-luck charm."

Jarvis gasped. "Don't do that! Don't put a hole in this fine coin. You'll only lessen the value. Handing it back to Jack, he said, "This coin could be worth a lot more than you think. If I'm right, it'll cover all your expenses, includin' the bowler hat, spices, and cigars, with enough left over to buy each of ye an ice cream at the pharmacy."

Oliver tried to get Jack's attention. "Psst. Jack, if that coin is worth as much as he thinks…"

Jack didn't hear a word Oliver said, and immediately slapped the coin down on the counter.

"By the way what was the name of the sailor ye won this from?" Mr. Jarvis asked.

"I didn't get his name," Jack said, trying to protect the sailor and herself from getting into trouble, because the captain didn't hold with gambling on his ship, even though it was common practice for sailors to gamble.

"It's just, with the way prices of goods is goin' up every day, and thieves comin' in here robbin' me blind, I can't trust nobody.

Why, just before you two showed up, a scruffy-lookin' youth with a pocked face and a limp come in, wearin' clothes similar to what you two got on—'cept they hung on him like a scarecrow. He browsed around for a while, read one of the newspapers quiet as ye please, then asked to see some pocketknives."

Oliver suddenly thought, *If it was Mouse, maybe he read the 'Missing Youth' ad.* He could only hope Mouse wouldn't think it was him.

The clerk went on: "Showed that young man where the pocketknives were kept, and trusted him to look through the lot while I continued with my dustin'. Lo and behold, if that thievin' nipper didn't steal one of them knives and sneak out the door. He was so quiet, I didn't even hear him leave," Mr. Jarvis said, shaking his head.

"Sounds like somethin' Mouse would do," Jack said.

"Did you say mouse? Where?" asked Jarvis, looking over the floor.

"Jack screamed, "Eek! A mouse! There he goes, behind that barrel o' crackers. Now he's under the counter," she said, stifling a laugh.

Jarvis grabbed a broom and swept under the counter, "Goddamn varmints! They come in the store when it gets cold out. Guess I'll deal with it later." Jack and Oliver had a hard time not laughing.

Jarvis wrapped up their purchases and handed the parcels to Jack. He then looked Jack and Oliver up and down carefully, opened his cash registrar drawer, and handed the change from the gold piece to Jack.

Oliver kept his eyes on Mr. Jarvis and couldn't help but notice that he only pretended to deposit the gold coin in the till, and instead put it in his vest pocket. When Mr. Jarvis's back was turned, Oliver snuck two penny jawbreakers from one of the jars on the counter. He thought, *My taking a couple of penny jawbreakers is nothing compared to cash theft. But I guess*

Mr. Henry Jarvis and his partner can do as they please, since they own the store.

Suddenly, Oliver and Jack were startled by two blasts from a steam whistle. "Excuse me, sir, what in heck is that whistle for?" Oliver asked.

"It's the four o'clock whistle. Quittin' time at the mill. Loud, ain't it?" the clerk said with a grin.

Jack tugged on Oliver's sleeve, "C'mon, Oliver! Our two hours is up and we got to get back to the point before the ship leaves!"

"Hold it one second, you two! Here's a couple of peppermint sticks for your friend Stubs. Tell him Henry Jarvis of the Jarvis-Nichols Mercantile in Mendocino says happy birthday!"

"Thank you kindly, sir, for all your help. We'll surely stop in your shop next time our ship is in port," Oliver said, taking off his cap and bowing to Mr. Jarvis.

Outside, Jack chastised Oliver for being so polite. "What's with all the sappy yes sir and no sir, and thank you, Mr. Jarvis? The way ye was talkin', I was afraid ye was givin' us sailors a bad name. We seamen got a reputation to uphold, ye know."

Oliver's mood suddenly changed. "Oh, give it a rest Jack! I just didn't want to give him the wrong impression, that's all, and, as far as bein' a real sailor, I'm far from it. I'm not even a real cabin boy yet. I'm nothin' but a thievin' stowaway who snitched two jawbreakers when Jarvis wasn't lookin'. That should prove to you that I'm no better than Mouse, so, leave me alone!"

Oliver backed away from Jack and put one of the jawbreakers in his mouth without offering the other one to her.

"That's a nice how-do-ya-do, Mr. Genteel! After I give ye the money to buy those cigars for Stubs," said Jack releasing her hold on Oliver. "And don't think ye're not indebted to me for buyin' them cigars either. I aim to collect one way or another. And what's got your craw all in such a dither?"

"Fine! All I want is to be left alone and to head back to the ship," Oliver yelled, and stomped off ahead of Jack. She stood for a moment, wondering what Oliver's problem was and what had him so ticked off. Oliver walked on ahead toward the wharf. Suddenly, Jack threw a well-aimed pebble at the back of his head. He rubbed the spot and continued walking. Jack threw a small stone that hit Oliver square in the back. He turned to face his assailant and narrowed his eyes. "What the hell?! Dagnabbit, Jack, if you hit me with another pebble, I'm gonna—"

"Ye'll what? Run off like a rat abandonin' a sinkin' ship? Quit yer bellyachin', Oliver, and tell me what's really botherin' ye. Runnin' away from your problems won't solve them. I swear, if it's 'cause ye're scared ye can't make it as a sailor, ye're damn wrong. I seen the way ye've takin' to sailin' these past couple o' weeks, and ye've proved to all of us, includin' the cap'n, that ye got the guts to make a darn good seaman! If you don't come back to the ship with me this minute, ye're nothin' but a yellow-bellied dog, and ye can just say "Fair winds and followin' seas" here and now!" Jack pursed her lips and a tear rolled down her cheek.

Oliver didn't dare tell Jack that he was afraid the authorities would find out he was the runaway described in the newspaper, and that if they caught up with him, he might be beaten and thrown in jail. He also feared what the captain and his father would say and do, so, he let Jack go on thinking his moody behavior was just because he was scared of being a sailor.

Still, after hearing Jack's plea, a smile crept over Oliver's face. He couldn't help laughing at her antics and stubbornness. "Stubs was right," he said to her. When you want something, Jack, you're really good at getting your way. I'll go back to the ship with you and try my best to be a good sailor. Like you told me when I first met you, if I want to eat and have a place to sleep, I've got to earn it." He thought, *On the ship, there's less chance of being discovered by the law.*

"Now ye're talkin', sailor boy!" Jack said, giving Oliver a friendly nudge.

Chapter 12

The Gamming Celebration

The next day the gamming party was held to celebrate Stubs's birthday. The entire crew supped on boiled fish and split pea soup, washed down with a swig of ale or rum. For dessert they ate baked apples and Mrs. M's sugar and cinnamon cookies.

After dinner four sailors brought out their musical instruments. One sailor had a concertina, one a flute, another a fiddle, and a fourth a banjo. They played lively sea shanties such as Blow the Man Down and Spanish Ladies. Since the ship would soon sail to Hawaii, one crewmember suggested they sing the boisterous shanty Rolling Down to Old Maui. Originally an old whaling song, it had been sung by sailors ever since it first came out around 1850. Often sailors would change the lyrics to suit their own circumstance.

> It's a damn tough life, full of toil and strife, we sailors undergo;
>
> And we don't give a damn when the gale is done, how hard the winds did blow;
>
> 'Cause we're homeward bound from the Antarctic ground with a good ship, taut and free;
>
> And we won't give a damn when we drink our rum with the girls of Old Maui.

> Rolling down to Old Maui, me boys, rolling down to Old Maui

> We're homeward bound from the Antarctic ground

> Rolling down to Old Maui.

On the deck, several sailors, including Jack, danced the traditional seafaring dance called the sailor's hornpipe. Jack took Oliver by the arm and tried to get him to join in, but Oliver was all feet and catawampus, and the two of them fell down in a heap, laughing.

After the dance everyone sang *Happy Birthday* to Stubs and presented him with their presents. Most were made by the sailors in their slack time. There was a carved meerschaum pipe of a captain's head, a charcoal drawing of the ship, and a belt made by square knotting. When Stubs held up the belt, the crew laughed because everyone on the ship knew Stubs was very much in need of a belt, as he was always hiking up his pants over his protruding belly.

After Jack gave Stubs her gift of the bowler hat, he modeled it for the crew. He looked very dapper in his new hat and it gave the rowdy crew another excuse to whistle, clap and throw stones in the sea. Oliver then gave Stubs his gift of the three cigars and the peppermint sticks. Oliver kept the cigar box for himself. Stubs was pleased with the cigars and immediately chewed off one of the cigar ends, lighted the cigar, and blew a couple of smoke rings.

The captain's wife addressed the party: "Now for the pièce de résistance we've all been waiting for! May I present to you "Revilo the Magician!" known to all of us as Oliver, who has promised to amaze us with his awe-inspiring magic tricks!" With a flare, Revilo threw Mrs. M.'s cloak over his shoulders, and bowed to the crew, who clapped, cheered loudly, and threw more stones into the sea.

Revilo stepped up in front of the table where the captain and Stubs were seated. In one hand he held the cardboard cigar box and in the other a marble. He opened the box to show everyone that there was nothing in it.

"I'm now going to place this marble in the box and make it disappear before your very eyes," he said.

The sailors watched intently as Revilo put the marble in the box and closed the lid. Then, carefully holding the sides of the box, he shook it back and forth, creating a rattling sound to show the audience that the marble was inside. He spoke the magic words "Abracadabra, Alcazar," and tapped the box with the tip of Mrs. M's parasol, then opened the box and showed everyone that the marble had indeed magically disappeared. Amazed, the crew clapped and hooted, especially the captain and Stubs.

"For my second trick I will need the assistance of a lovely lady. Mrs. M. will you please assist me?" Revilo asked, bowing to her. Mrs. M. was pleased to assist; she stepped forward and curtsied to the audience. Everyone cheered and whistled.

Revilo then placed nine playing cards on the table in three rows of three. He blindfolded himself with a bandana, then asked Stubs to pick out a card and whisper to Mrs. M. which one he had picked. Revilo then removed the bandana.

"Oh, dear," said Mrs. M. "With all the excitement, I've plum forgot which card Stubs picked. Now, just give me a moment. Ah-ha, I think I have it. Placing the tip of her finger on a card, she asked, Was it this one?"

"No!" Revilo replied.

Mrs. M. placed her finger on another card. "Was it this one?"

Revilo wrinkled his brow and tapped his index finger against his chin as if thinking hard. "Yes!" he exclaimed, with a shout the entire crew could hear. The sailors went crazy, whistling, clapping, and tossing stones into the sea.

For Revilo's third trick, he produced a white cotton bag and a hardboiled egg. He turned the bag inside out to show the audience that the bag was empty. He then placed the egg in the bag and showed them the lump it made. He said the magic words, turned the bag inside out with a quick jerk, and the egg had disappeared. The audience was amazed. Revilo and his assistant, Mrs. M., bowed to the crew, and the sailors clapped, whistled loudly, and threw yet more pebbles into the water.

The captain then stood up. "Well, folks, I hate to break up a great party, but it's now goin' on 1600 hours, and duty calls. Jones and Harris have promised to take the next watch so the rest of you can continue to party 'til the sun starts to go down." The crew let out a loud cheer, and Jack immediately joined one of the gambling games.

Chapter 13

Sugar and Pineapples

At high tide, The *Golden Lady* set sail for the Hawaiian Islands, and with a good tailwind, arrived on the Big Island within two weeks. Captain Matthews gave the order that none of the crew was to go ashore because they were all needed to load the sacks of sugar onto the ship. Only the captain and Jonesy, the "super" in charge of cargo, went ashore.

On the wharf, a gang of barefooted, bare-chested, brown-skinned natives carried sack after sack of raw cane sugar to the end of the pier, where the ship's crew hoisted the sacks onto the ship by block and tackle, then lowered them into the hold.

It was hard work loading the sacks of sugar onto the ship and the hot Hawaiian sun beat down on the natives and crewmembers creating sticky brown beads of sweat on their bodies as they passed the sacks hand over hand onto the ship and down into the hold. Once the sacks of sugar were in the hold, they had to be sealed in oil cloth, and placed in crates to protect them from moisture and vermin.

As the natives and sailors carried the woven cotton sacks, every so often one of them would burst open at a seam and leak a trail of light-brown molasses laced with unrefined sugar crystals that made the wharf and the ship's deck slippery and sticky. The men carrying the heavy sacks often slipped and fell in the gooey muck. At the end of three days, they had completed the tedious task of loading and stacking the sugar and were looking forward to rest and relaxation, but the captain was adamant that there would be no shore leave and that they would set sail for the island of Lanai on the next tide. There the crew would have another tiring task: loading crates of green pineapples aboard from the newly opened Dole Hawaiian Pineapple Company, owned and operated by James D. Dole.

"Captain Matthews," he said, shaking the captain's hand, "I am most grateful that you accepted our contract to transport our pineapples to San Francisco. No other shipping company has been willing to take our cargo since my cousin, Sanford Dole, smeared our good family name in 1893 when he tried to overthrow Queen Liliuokalani." James Dole further explained, "In that same year, the minister of Hawaii proclaimed Hawaii a US protectorate. This caused quite a stir among the native Hawaiians, who tried to restore Queen Liliuokalani to power but did not succeed. Since that failed attempt, the natives have not trusted the new government, and there have been several hostile uprisings. Many of the natives are still restless, and the cargo of pineapples and sugar are both perishable, so it would be wise of you not to delay your journey back to San Francisco."

When the work of loading the pineapples was done, the crew was again hot and sweaty, and reeked of the odor of fermenting pineapples. The captain suggested they dive into the warm ocean waters to wash off the stench and stickiness. Immediately, the crewmembers, Jack and Oliver included, dived overboard. The warm seawater soothed their tired muscles. Oliver floated on his back gazing at the azure sky, and Jack swam nearby. She spied a green sea turtle paddling toward the shore where she would make a nest and lay up to a hundred eggs. Once they were laid she would head back to sea, leaving the eggs to incubate in the warm sand. Approximately two months later the eggs would hatch and the baby turtles would have to fend for themselves to reach the water. During that dangerous journey, many a seabird would swoop down and snatch an easy meal of baby turtles.

Oliver and Jack both dove down a few feet where a multitude of colorful fish tickled their feet. There were yellow and rainbow-colored angelfish, yellow and blue tang, and myriad others. A multicolored parrotfish swam in and out of the asparagus fern-like seaweed. The Hawaiian ocean was very much alive and magical.

Jack and Oliver decided to swim ashore. As they lay on the sand and warmed themselves, Jack said, "The sea turtles lay their eggs onshore and bury them in the sand. Let's gather some for Stubs. The eggs are soft-shelled and taste better than chicken eggs. Stubs eats his raw, but I like mine slightly boiled."

Jack found a nest, gathered up the eggs, and tied them in her shirt so she could swim back to the ship with them.

Looking through his telescope on the *Golden Lady,* Jonesy spied a humpback whale. Her calf swam alongside her. Suddenly, through two blowholes at the top of her head, the mother whale spouted gallons of foul-smelling vapor in a plume that rose fifteen feet into the air. It smelled like a nasty fart combined with the odor of fermenting fish. The offensive stench took Jones's breath away and left a bad taste in his mouth.

Without warning, Jonesy saw a pod of fast-moving, voracious killer whales heading straight for the humpback and her calf. Like most mothers, the humpback would fight to the death if necessary to protect her baby.

Upon seeing the Orcas bearing down on the humpbacks, Jonesy shouted through the speaking trumpet, "Now hear this! "Get out of the water, now! All crew and passengers will return to the ship immediately!"

Oliver, Jack, and the other crewmembers wondered why the alarm had been sounded. In the water near the beach, many of the native dockworkers were also washing off the stickiness of the pineapples. Seeing the humpback's spout and the pod of killer whales speeding toward the whales, Jack and Oliver swam as fast as they could toward the ship as the natives scrambled to reach the shore.

Back on deck, Oliver asked to use Jonesy's telescope. Through it, he saw how lush was the island vegetation. A pungent odor of pineapple juice and the fragrance of plumeria flowers carried on the gentle trade wind. Oliver wished he could have stayed longer to swim and lie on the island's warm beach.

After all the work of loading the sugar sacks and pineapples and the cleanup afterward, the captain ordered that the *Golden Lady* set sail for the whaling village of Lahaina on the isle of Maui.

In the town plaza of Lahaina, Oliver and Jack sat under a sixty-foot- tall tree that had many prop roots hanging from its branches. The tree cast a delicious cool shadow, like a giant umbrella. Looking up at the tree through its numerous hanging branches, Oliver said aloud for anyone to hear, "I've never seen a tree like this before. What's the name of it, and what are all those brown and black birds roosting in its branches?"

An old native Hawaiian sitting in the shade of the tree heard the boy and said, "The tree is a banyan dat was planted many years ago in honor of da town's first Protestant mission, and dem noisy birds is mynahs. Ye can teach a mynah to talk and mimic sounds, just like a parrot."

Later, Oliver and Jack toured a church called the Hale Aloha, or House of Love. A plaque read that the church was built in 1858 as a tribute to God for sparing the town of Lahaina from a bad outbreak of smallpox on Oahu.

Next, they visited the old prison on Prison Street that was built during the reign of King Kamehameha III to lock up rowdy sailors who didn't go back to their ships at sundown. The Hawaiian name for the prison was Hale Pa'ahao, which meant "stuck in irons house."

Tired of looking at old buildings, Jack looked at the sun to see what time it was. "C'mon Oliver! The sun is startin' to set. If we don't get back to the ship soon, we'll be locked up in irons."

Chapter 14
Mr. and Mrs. Sanders

From the ship's railing, Oliver stared at the sea. A small skiff rowed by two strong natives was making its way toward the ship. The captain peered at the skiff through his telescope. In the bow of the boat sat a white man in a rumpled linen suit. He anxiously waved a battered straw boater hat. Next to him sat a woman who the captain assumed was his wife. She wore a filmy white lawn dress with a high-necked collar, and on her head sat a wide-brimmed traditional Hawaiian-style hat called a *pāpale piko'ole,* woven from the leaves of a coconut palm or pandanus tree. The crown of the hat was cut open at the top, and around it was a wilted flower lei.

In the stern of the boat sat two Catholic nuns, wearing traditional habits consisting of black long-sleeve robes, a belt, rosary with crucifix, a mantle, cape, and white wimple that framed the nuns' faces underneath a black veil. One of the nuns appeared to be in her early twenties, and the other much older.

Through his telescope, Captain Matthews again looked at the man in the linen suit. After he'd made the skiff fast to the *Golden Lady,* the man stood up in the boat, shielded his eyes from the sun, and yelled up at the captain, "Ahoy there! My name's Sanders. I am a planter, and I have what may be a profitable proposition for you!"

"State your business, sir, or shove off! This ship is leavin' on the next tide," the captain yelled back.

"Well, I was hoping my wife and these two kind sisters here, and two native oarsmen and myself, could take passage on your ship to return to San Francisco. I have the money in hand for our voyage, but I would feel more comfortable telling you our story if I could come aboard," the desperate-looking planter said.

Hearing that there might be a chance to earn extra money, the captain hollered back, "Permission granted!" He then ordered Mr. Harris to lower the rope ladder over the side.

The man climbed the ladder to the deck above. Red-faced and panting from the heat and the climb, the man continued his story. "Ever since the coup against Queen Liliuokalani, there have been several native uprisings, causing white planters like myself and my wife to live in fear for our lives. The same goes for the nuns. For months now we've been waiting for a ship to take us to San Francisco."

Without being invited, the planter's wife and the nuns climbed up the ladder, each carrying a valise. The two oarsmen followed; each carried a heavy trunk. As they reached the top of the ladder they heaved the trunks up onto the deck. One of the trunks landed with a thud and a clinking sound as it hit the deck.

"Careful with those trunks, sailor!" yelled the planter. "In one of them trunks is an expensive silver tea set and china tea-cups that once belonged to my wife's mother. My wife never travels without them. It would break her heart to see that set smashed. The other trunk contains the sisters' Bibles and the trinkets they hand out to the natives and lost souls."

The planter immediately reached out to shake Captain Matthews's hand. "Captain, you can't imagine how overjoyed and relieved my wife and I were to hear that your ship was in port. We'd almost given up on being able to leave this island and go back to the States. Your ship is the answer to our prayers.

"In the past year, several American planters and their families, both native and white, have been killed or have had attempts made on their lives. Their homes have been plundered, and their coffee, pineapple, and sugarcane fields trampled and set afire. If my wife and I hadn't left our plantation when we did, we could have been next. A band of hostile natives burned down the church near our home. That's why the sisters are with us. When we heard your ship was in port we abandoned our plantation and have traveled these past four days to reach your ship before you set sail.

"Please, sir, take us with you, I beg of you. "The native oarsmen have worked for me for the past several years, and I trust them wholeheartedly. Their loyalty lies with the United States and not on the side of the renegades. Because of that, they too fear for their lives. They both know the sea, and would make able-bodied seamen if you would be willing to take them on as members of your crew.

"As I said, I have the money to pay for our passage. Recently, we sold our plantation to a neighboring planter, lock, stock and barrel. His wife is a native Hawaiian and related to the royal family, so they will not be harmed. He paid me half of what my property is worth, but that doesn't matter. All we want is to get away from this stinkin' cesspool."

Sanders drew a heavy pouch from under his coat and poured out several newly minted silver and gold coins to show that he had the money.

In a hushed voice, Captain Matthews said to the man, "Sir, put yer money away! Ye never know who may be dyin' to get his greedy hands on it!" *Includin' me*, the captain thought. *If I had all that money, I'd have enough to finance our entire trip to New York City.*

Captain Matthews said to Mr. Sanders, "Okay, the four of you are welcome to sail with us to San Francisco, and I could use two more crewmembers, but if you choose to sail any farther on my ship, it will cost you more!

"There's just one problem: I'm afraid we cannot accommodate ye in the way ye're probably accustomed to. This is a cargo ship, not a passenger ship, but if ye don't mind roughin' it a bit, I'm sure the first mate, Mr. Jones, and second mate, Mr. Harris, won't mind givin' up their cabins for a fortnight, the time it should take us to git to Frisco. Will ye, Mr. Jones and Mr. Harris?" the captain said with a commanding look at the mates. Jones and Harris both grinned and nodded their heads.

"And 'til we get to San Francisco, Mr. Jones, Mr. Harris, and Oliver can bunk with the rest o' the idlers and seamen in the fo'c'sle. Jack says she can sleep in a hammock on the quarterdeck, since ye'll also be needin' the saloon.

"Unfortunately, the cabins are small, and have only a single bunk, washstand with wash basin and pitcher, and no commode, just a slop jar. As for a chair, table, and dresser, the seamen use their sea chests or trunks. At least the cabins are snug and will give the ladies some privacy. Since each cabin has only one bunk, you will have a choice of sharin' the bunk, or one o' ye will have to sleep on a mattress on the floor or in a hammock. I cannot guarantee that ye'll not be visited by rats and vermin durin' the night. This is an old ship, and many rats and other pests live on her."

The younger nun spoke up, "Sir, when I was a novice at the church, I would wrap myself in my one thin wool blanket at night and sleep on a cold stone floor. I'm sure sleeping on the floor of a cabin with a mattress would be a luxury in comparison."

The captain replied, "To keep the rats and insects from crawling over their bodies, the crew collect the urine from the goats and pigs. When it turns to ammonia, we mix it with water and soap and place a bowl of it where rats and mice have been seen. The ammonia acts as a poison to rodents. For a more fragrant method, my wife dabs peppermint extract on her body.

Rats hate the smell of peppermint and stay away. I will have our cook give you a bottle."

Mr. Sanders said, "Speaking for the entire party, we are just grateful that you have agreed to take us with you. I'm sure we can all endure a few inconveniences," he said. He looked at his wife who made a sour face.

Captain Matthews nodded. "We will be leavin' early tomorrow mornin' as soon as it reaches high tide. With a good tailwind, it shouldn't take us more than two weeks to get to San Francisco, but it could take a bit longer, dependin' on the weather. Since you don't have yer sea legs yet, for your safety, I ask that ye stay in your cabins 'til we're out to sea. The boys will bring ye yer meals."

Chapter 15

The Detective

Early the next morning, just as the *Golden Lady* was about to depart, another skiff, rowed by two native Hawaiians, raced to the ship. Also in the skiff was a white man in a lightweight linen suit—not as refined as the planter's—and a derby hat. The man blew a whistle and shouted up to the mate, "Stop the ship! I have urgent business with the captain!"

Captain Matthews looked over the side. *Oh, no, not another dang landlubber askin' for passage!* He yelled, "Who might you be, sir, and what gives ye the right to keep us from weighin' anchor? State your business or begone, and be quick about it! With this risin' tide, we've no time to waste!"

The rope ladder was lowered over the side and the man climbed aboard. He was breathing hard, and drops of sweat ran down his face. He removed his hat and wiped his bald head with a white handkerchief.

"Captain, I'm a detective working undercover for the United States Hawaii Protectorate, and I have it on good authority that a man in a white suit similar to my own, and a straw boater hat, was seen boarding your ship last evening. Accompanying him were two nuns and a woman posing as his wife. I believe the man robbed the Bank of Hawaii of nearly $50,000 in newly minted silver and gold coins. The gold commemoratives were minted in honor of Liliuokalani, the last queen of Hawaii.

"Although the gold coins are legal tender, they were not minted for general circulation, only for major investments and business transactions. The silver dollars are also legal tender, and can be used for everyday transactions in which they are passed from person to person, which makes them much harder to trace. The only thing we can count on is that some merchant may think they are counterfeit and alert the police.

"Recently, several of these coins have surfaced, and we have reason to believe that the bank robber is aboard your ship. Further evidence has led us to believe that he is not working alone, but is part of an wide ring of international thieves."

The captain looked the self-proclaimed detective up and down and said, "Sir, I don't know ye from Adam. You have given me quite a story, but you could be a criminal yerself, even though ye say ye're a detective. As captain o' this ship I must safeguard me crew, family, and any passengers who take passage, and if ye hadn't noticed, a lot o' men on this island wear linen suits and boater hats and fit the description o' the man ye're accusin' o' bank robbery. As far as two nuns boardin' the *Golden Lady*, that is true. Now, will ye show me some form of identification, or must I have ye thrown off the ship?!"

The man searched in his pocket, then hesitated. "Uh, I was in such a hurry to get to your ship that I must have left my badge on my desk at the office," he said.

A likely story, the captain thought. *Is this buffoon a robber himself and just pretendin' to be a detective so he can get his hands on the planter's money? Then again, what if this so-called detective is tellin' the truth and Sanders did rob the bank? Then, as captain of this ship I could be accused o' harborin' a criminal, and that could cause further delays for me and the crew.*

The contracts the captain had signed with the sugar and pineapple companies had strict clauses stating that the documents would become null and void if the cargo was not delivered by end of the month. The captain was counting on the money from those deliveries to further finance his trip to New York. He thought he had no choice but to lie, so he narrowed his eyes and said with authority, "No, sir! No man o' that description has come aboard, only two nuns and two oarsmen. Under normal circumstances, I wouldn't be takin' them nuns as passengers, 'cept I owe the Church a favor for blessin' me ship."

"Sir, if ye haven't noticed, our business is to transport cargo, not passengers. Since ye can't prove who ye claim to be, as master of this ship I order ye to leave immediately!"

The two beefy Hawaiians who'd come aboard with Mr. Sanders crossed their arms over their chests as a warning sign to the alleged detective to come no farther. The man stumbled backwards, then scrambled down the ladder.

The captain ordered, "Weigh anchor!"

Chapter 16

Mouse Gets His Revenge

During their first few days en route to San Francisco, the weather remained mild and balmy with a whisper of trade wind. Only the two nuns were seasick, and spent most of the time on their knees in their cramped quarters, saying Hail Mary's.

In the evenings and over supper, the captain and his wife, Sarah, enjoyed visiting with the congenial planter and his wife Abigail. The women found they had certain things in common. Both had grown up in New York City and had patronized the same shops. Abigail said her father was a banker; Sarah lied and said her father was a successful businessman.

On the third day out, Stubs complained to Oliver and Jack about his painful lumbago and about having to make special dishes for the Sanderses, because the crew's regular meals weren't palatable enough for their highbrow tastes, and because the captain wanted to impress the couple. The nuns were used to plain food and didn't complain. The problem was that they insisted on marking the canonical hours with prayer four times each day, which cut into the dinner hour.

The first and second mates heard all kinds of complaints from the crew, which the captain chose to ignore. Jonesy vented, "I knew things wouldn't be the same once that planter and his wife and 'em nuns come aboard. Yesterday, Wang, the carpenter, was asked to make a canvas canopy out of one of the spare sails

73

on the quarterdeck so's the sun wouldn't burn the ladies' delicate skins. The sun never bothered the cap'n's wife afore—if it was hot out, she just put on a big hat. As for the nuns, they don't need protection from the sun, 'cause they's already covered up in 'em black and white penguin suits they wear. All I can say is, be prepared to batten down the hatches, boys, 'cause this storm is just startin' to brew!"

Stubs predicted things would get worse, and grumbled, "If one of us sailors says a single cussword or takes the Lord's name in vain, Cap'n's all over him like fleas on a dog's back, which is damn hard for a sailor, since swearin' comes natural to us. Cap'n's makin' us feel like it's a cardinal sin to swear and that we oughta have our mouths washed out with lye soap. Every night he's been makin' us nonbelievers say a prayer afore we eat our supper and hit the sack. Says it's to appease our poor souls, and it wouldn't hurt none of us to have a little religion in our lives. I've got so sick o' thankin' the Lord for every bite I eat, I been takin' me meals on the bench in the fo'c'sle. The thing is, that bench is now gettin' crowded with the rest o' the crew, and I'm thinkin' 'bout eatin' me supper topside."

"When we reach San Francisco and it comes time for them nuns to disembark, all of us so-called heathens'll get down on our knees, lift our arms to heaven, and praise the Lord," Stubs said. Jonesy, Jack, and Oliver let out loud belly laughs.

On the fourth day out, dark clouds with streaks of rain were seen on the horizon. Within hours a fierce tropical cyclone hit the *Golden Lady.* The wind whipped the sails, and gigantic waves rose up and crashed over the bow making the ship roll violently. Mr. Harris, the second mate, was at the helm when the storm struck. Thunder boomed and streaks of lightning flashed overhead. Slanted rain and sleet pounded the ship. "It's a hurricane!" Harris yelled.

Mr. Jones blew his bosun's whistle to alert all hands to batten down the hatches, secure the cargo, and make sure the passengers were in their cabins.

The storm lasted three days, and by the time the weather improved, the *Golden Lady* was nearly 200 miles off course, which put her behind schedule by a week. The captain was in a foul mood, worried that he would not make his delivery of the sacks of raw sugar to the C&H Sugar factory on time. He was also concerned that the pineapples would rot before he could deliver them to the greengrocer in San Francisco. The captain stormed into the galley where Oliver, Stubs, Jack, and Mouse were taking a break, and demanded, "Mouse, git yer Jack Nasty-Face down in the hold and check on the sugar and pineapples. After this storm it'll be damp down there, and I don't want moisture and mold gettin' to 'em."

When the captain left, Mouse whined, "Why can't Oliver do it? Cap'n's always orderin' me around! Mouse, do this! Mouse, do that! Mouse feed the animals! Mouse, take out the slop jars! Then there's Stubs. Mouse, fetch me some water. Mouse, I need more coal for the stove. And all the while, this foul weather is makin' my foot ache somethin' awful!"

Oliver pantomimed playing a tiny fiddle. "Okay, Mouse, I'll go check on the sugar, pineapples, and animals, but don't think I'll be taking over any more of your duties." He thought, *I'm only doing this 'cause it was Cap'n's orders, and I don't want another row with Mouse.*

As Oliver headed out the door, Stubs called out, his words slurred, "B-boy, b-best ye be careful g-g-goin' down that la-ladder. W-w-with this damp weather, she can be m-m-mighty s-s-slippery!" Since early morning, Stubs had been lacing his coffee with what he called his rheumatism medicine, which was known in sailor lingo as "shakin' a cloth in the wind," meaning he was drunk.

Oliver put on his oilskins, grabbed a lighted lantern, and crept down the slippery ladder to the hold. It was damp and cold, and bilgewater had pooled on the lower deck. The nauseating odor of fermenting pineapples mixed with rotting cabbage and animal dung hit him square in the face. Oliver pulled his coat collar over his nose. He held the lantern high and cautiously sloshed through the foul water to the cargo of sugar and pineapples. He lifted an edge of one of the oilcloths that covered the sacks of sugar. As far as he could see, the sacks were dry and no moisture or mold had gotten to them. He found a crowbar lying nearby and opened one of the crates of pineapples. A few were on the verge of getting overripe, but none were spoiled. Oliver figured he could report to the captain that the cargo would be okay until the ship reached San Francisco.

Oliver could hear the pitiful bleating of sheep and goats coming from the orlop, a small room next to the hold where extra cables, sails, and ropes were stowed. The room was partitioned off as a pen to house the live chickens, pigs, goats, and sheep. When Oliver reached the animals, it looked like they hadn't been fed and watered for several days. He felt sorry for the poor beasts and proceeded to pitch fresh hay into their manger, fill up their water buckets, and scatter scratch for the chickens. The sheep and goats immediately followed him to the feeding and begin to chomp on the hay. They were friendly, and rubbed their heads against Oliver and nudged his body. He noticed that they had bald spots and sores on their heads, legs, and backs, where they had scratched themselves raw against the hull.

Suddenly, Oliver felt an intense itch on his head and torso and the creepy feeling of bugs crawling all over him. He wondered if the animals had lice. Back when he was in school, some kids had gotten lice and had to have their heads shaved and scrubbed with tar soap. Grabbing the lantern, Oliver raced up the ladder to the galley. In the light of day, he discovered that he was covered from head to toe with voracious biting black fleas. He jumped up and down, trying to rid himself of the parasites, then ripped off his clothes, down to his skivvies, and threw them on the deck.

Seeing Oliver so miserable from the infestation, Stubs grabbed a bucket of seawater and threw it over him. The cold salt water stung Oliver's body where he'd been bit, so the cure felt worse than the itchy bites. Stubs then ordered Jack to lower the bucket over the side for more seawater. She raced back with a bucketful and doused Oliver again, but he still felt the fleas crawling in his hair and biting him.

"Again, Jack!" Stubs ordered. Eventually, after several more drenches, the fleas were killed and the intense itching subsided.

All this time, Mouse was laughing his head off. His pleading for Oliver to go down in the hold in his stead had been a ruse to get back at Oliver for getting him in trouble with the captain that first day, and for becoming the captain's steward. Mouse knew all along that the warm tropical air and rain would make the fleas in the hold hatch out in multitudes. Mouse had deliberately neglected to feed and care for the animals so that Oliver would see how hungry they were and feed them.

Oliver hated Mouse at that moment, but knew that if he did anything to get back at him, Mouse would only find another way to torment him.

"Try some of your own medicine, ye low-down, scheming, batter-brained son of a—! You knew all along the fleas were hatching! See how you like cold saltwater thrown on you!" Oliver grabbed a bucket of saltwater and threw it at Mouse, who managed to jump out of the way. Jack's mouth flew open because she didn't think Oliver had it in him to stand up to Mouse. Mouse just continued to laugh, swigged the last of his coffee, walked out the galley door, and slammed it behind him.

Chapter 17

Frisco

Under favorable wind conditions, the old sailing ship cut the waves like a warm knife cuts butter. She averaged 4 to 6 knots and left a foamy white trough in her wake. At that rate, she could sail 250 miles per day and reach San Francisco within a fortnight. Stubs was right: the old *Golden Lady* still had gumption. The storm delayed their arrival at the Port of San Francisco by only a week.

As they neared the California coast, the captain let Oliver try his hand at the wheel. There was a steady moderate breeze, and the captain gave the order to set the flying jib.

"Steady as she goes, boy! Watch them rocks and keep her full and by!" he ordered.

Oliver felt the wind and sea-spray on his face and tried his best to steer in the direction the wind was coming from. It took great effort to keep the wheel steady and the schooner on course. As soon as Oliver was on the money with the compass, the ship would suddenly veer to starboard and he would overcompensate with the wheel to get her back on course. It took a strong hand and several turns of the wheel to steady her. Luckily, the captain was right beside Oliver to make sure he didn't get into trouble.

They soon reached the Carquinez Strait, where they had to skirt around several islands and huge rocks before they could anchor near the small town of Crockett. There they delivered the sacks of sugar to the C&H Sugar Company, then set sail for San Francisco to deliver the pineapples.

As the ship slowly sailed the coastline in search of the small opening to San Francisco Bay, a thick fog rolled in and masked the shoreline, making it nearly impossible to see the land. Suddenly it became very quiet, except for an occasional shrill call of a seabird. A chill dampness penetrated Oliver's peacoat and made him shiver.

The captain looked concerned, and ordered, "Go aloft, boy, with a lantern! Use yer eyes to scan for any signs o' the lighthouse off Point Bonita. Use yer ears as well! If we're close, give the signal by flashin' your light. Also, see if the red and green sidelights and the arc light atop the mast are all burnin bright."

From the crow's nest, Oliver searched through the thick fog for signs of life. He figured they were nearing land because he could hear a dog's bark. The sound was sharp, like that of a small terrier.

"I think I hear a dog barking," Oliver yelled to the captain.

"Could be seals on Seal Rock. Sometimes they bark just like a dog. That's why they call 'em seadogs," the captain yelled back.

"No, it's a real dog, sir. I can make out his outline on the point. Down the shoreline a few miles is a bright light. It must be from the lighthouse."

"Good work, boy! Mr. Jones, have the crew stand by to lower the cockboat to take us ashore so's we can hire a pilot to guide the ship through the bay. Ye can come down now, lad!" At the captain's order, Oliver gingerly climbed down the rigging.

"Uh, Cap'n, can I go with you in the cockboat? I want to thank that dog personally for showing us the way," Oliver asked, a smile on his face.

"Well, I guess, ye've earned yer shore leave, boy!" the captain said proudly, and patted Oliver on the back.

Jack suddenly appeared behind Oliver. "Sir, can I go too? I promise not to make trouble. Perhaps I could help with the rowin'."

"Well, all right, the two of ye can go, but ye best look sharp and mind what I say," the captain said. Behind his back, Jack and Oliver snuck a smile at each other, like two excited schoolboys.

"Mr. Jones, lower away!" the captain ordered.

The skiff was lowered and the captain, Oliver, Jack, and the first mate scrambled in. Jack and Oliver each grabbed an oar, while Jonesy took the tiller. The captain took the seat in the center of the boat. "Mr. Jones, head her toward the shoreline, where Oliver thinks he spotted the dog. Its owner must be near and about."

Jack and Oliver rowed steadily toward the point where they thought the barking had come from. As they neared shore they could hear the barking again. They headed the boat straight toward the direction of the dog.

"Mind the rocks, boys! And come in slow," the captain warned. Jack and Oliver slowed the boat by shipping their oars and letting the cockboat drift shoreward. As they neared the beach, they hopped into the shallow water and together managed to drag the boat onto the shore. The captain and first mate scrambled out and helped them haul it farther up.

Suddenly, a small terrier jumped from the cliff into Oliver's arms and licked his face. This so startled him that he almost dropped the dog. Its ribs were showing and its front right paw was swollen and bleeding, as if he'd been on the sharp rocks for a long time.

"Cap'n, this dog is hurt and starving. Could we take him back to the ship with us? Stubs could patch him up, and he could be the ship's watchdog. I think he's a Jack Russell terrier; they're good ratcatchers," Oliver said, hoping the captain would assent.

"We already got two watchdogs," the captain replied, grinning right at Jack and Oliver.

"Very funny, Cap'n! Please, sir, if we leave the dog here he'll starve to death. And this dog has earned his freedom by leadin' us to shore," Jack said.

"Please, Cap'n?" Oliver chimed in.

Captain Matthews looked at Oliver and his daughter and saw that a strong bond of friendship had formed between them. He sighed, "Oh, very well. But make it quick, afore I change my mind. And it's your plates the dog'll be eatin' off when rations git low."

"Thank ye, sir," Jack and Oliver said in unison, smiling.

"Mr. Jones, this place is deserted. Best we head for the lighthouse or old Fort Point."

The four sailors shoved the cockboat back in the water. This time, Jonesy and the captain took the oars while Jack manned the tiller. Oliver sat in the center of the boat holding the dog, which shivered with the cold. Oliver put the dog beneath his peacoat and held it to his warm chest. Within minutes, the dog poked his head out, licked Oliver's cheek, and let out a sharp bark.

Jack laughed. "Look, I think he wants to say 'thank-ye' for savin' his life and takin' him with us."

"Perhaps he'll make a good sailor and learn to say, Aye-aye, Cap'n!" Oliver said with a smile.

The current had picked up, the sea became choppy with whitecaps, and the air grew colder. Jonesy and the captain pulled hard on the oars, while Oliver and Jack searched through the dense fog for the beam from the lighthouse.

Suddenly the captain shouted, "Light ho! Over there, Mr. Jones! We'll have to stake the skiff to the rocks, as the current is too strong for the anchor to hold."

Upon reaching the shore where the lighthouse stood, Jonesy and the Captain shipped the oars and jumped out of the skiff. While the captain held the boat by the painter, Jonesy used a sledge hammer to pound a large metal eyebolt into a nearby rock. He then threaded the painter through the eye of the bolt, and tied a Flemish knot to hold the boat firmly. The captain told Jack and Oliver to stay with the dog while he and Jonesy went up to the lighthouse to find someone who could help them hire a pilot to guide the *Golden Lady* into the mouth of the bay.

Even with a tug, it would not be easy to maneuver the big ship through Raccoon Straits, past the fishing village of Sausalito, and Angel and Alcatraz Islands, to the Hyde Street Pier in the heart of San Francisco.

It was cold in the boat and the wind had picked up. The little terrier shook and burrowed his nose into Oliver's coat. Every so often the dog would poke his head out through the collar as if playing peek-a-boo, and then let out another sharp bark. This made Jack and Oliver laugh, which strengthened their growing friendship and warmed their souls.

"Hey, Jack, I'm glad the cap'n said we could keep this dog. Maybe we can share him and both take care of him!" Oliver shouted over the wind.

Jack smiled and shouted back, "I'd like that! Ye know, Oliver ye're not half bad for a landlubber!" she said, giving him a friendly shove.

"Say, how about we give the dog a name? If we name 'im, that means we have to keep 'im, Oliver said. "Oh, and Jack you don't have to pretend anymore. I know you're the captain's daughter; Stubs and Sarah told me. I promise to keep your secret and treat you like one of the boys if that's what you want, and it doesn't matter to me that ye like being a sailor. I guess I like being a sailor too. What say we name the dog Hershel?"

Jack screwed up her face. "What kinda name is Hershel for a dog?"

"It was my grandfather's name," Oliver said, looking sad.

"I was thinkin' of a real dog's name, like Poochie, Butch, or Rover," Jack suggested.

"Those are too common," Oliver said. "Hey, why don't we name him Frisco after the Port of San Francisco?"

"Say, I like that name," said Jack. "He's frisky and he's from Frisco."

The little dog poked his head out of Oliver's collar again and barked in agreement. He then barked louder, alerting Jack and Oliver that the captain and Jonesy had returned. Jonesy quickly untied the painter, and both he and the captain got in the boat. "Heave ho, lads, and make for the ship! I was lucky to hire a tow that'll guide us through the strait and won't take us for every last nickel."

Chapter 18
The Tow

The powerful tug *Goliath,* black smoke swirling from her smoke-stack, plowed through the ever-increasing whitecaps toward the *Golden Lady,* whose billowing sails swung her into a last lap toward the pilot boat. As they neared the village of Sausalito, tug and schooner met. A turbulent wind, dense fog, and the constant heaving of the sailing ship made it difficult to throw a towline. *Goliath* zigzagged side to side and tried several times, but as the wind increased, the sea owned the schooner.

Mr. Jones stood on the deck ready to catch the towline. On the fifth try he grabbed it, nearly falling overboard. All hands, including Jack and Oliver, held fast to the end of the line and together managed to tie her off. A cheer from the crew echoed across the water. The *Golden Lady* was in tow!

The tug made steady progress, cutting the churning water as she swerved through the narrow Raccoon Strait, careful to avoid the rocks. High on the hills overlooking the town of Berkeley was a tall redwood tree, which acted as the tug's beacon. As the tug continued to chug across the ever-roughening waters of San Francisco Bay toward the Hyde Street Pier, the shrieking wind battered the ship and made their progress even slower. Sprays of seawater surged over the bow of the tug, and the *Golden Lady* beat to windward on the strength of the west-running ebbtide.

Their progress was slow, and to work the ship into port they had to wait to go forward on the flowing tide. After several exhausting hours, the two boats finally neared the pier.

The size of the ship and the high waves made it impossible to tie up at the wharf, so the captain ordered the crew to drop anchor 300 feet offshore. They would have to use the cockboat as a tender to get the passengers and cargo to the beach.

The captain was concerned about leaving the ship unguarded, so he ordered, "Men, there'll be no shore leave while in port. Exceptions will be made for passengers and mates—and that's if the weather turns fair, perhaps tomorrow. That includes Oliver and Jack." The pair smiled at each other.

"I also want a full watch tonight in case any wharf pirates are lurkin' about, just waitin' to steal the ship's gear and riggin'. Even though it's been a couple o' years since the earthquake, I hear tell some people here are desperate for money and won't think nothin' 'bout stealin' an egg right from under a hen."

That evening the passengers were told to stay in their cabins and the entire crew was on watch, including Oliver. Oliver was paired up with Jonesy, the first mate. As the two of them circled the quarter deck for the third time, Oliver spied something floating in the water near the ship. The floating bundle gave off a foul, nauseating stench of rotting meat and the sickly sweet smell of decaying fruit.

"What is that terrible odor, Jonesy?" Oliver asked holding his nose.

"Hell's bells and buckets o' blood!" Jonesy sang out. "It's a goddamn floater!"

A floater was waterfront lingo for a floating dead man.

"Ye're not a real sailor 'til ye seen one," Jonesy said to Oliver. Now I guess ye are. I've seen three in me years at sea. The Barbary Coast isn't far from here. It's a plague of opium dens, crimpin' joints, saloons, brothels, and gamblin' houses.

Often, unsuspectin' sailors wander into one of those dives, get slipped a Mickey Finn, and are robbed, beaten up, and shanghaied. Next thing ye know, the poor saps wake up on a ship far out to sea where they have to serve on some long voyage against their will and may not get home for years. I've heard some cap'ns pay crimps, the devils that do the kidnapping, up to seventy-five dollars a head to get able-bodied seamen to serve on their ships. I'm tellin' ye, Oliver, many an innocent lad has met his fate that way. I hear the Eagle Saloon is one place ye wanna stay away from."

"I promise to never go in that saloon or any other like it," Oliver said. "So, what do we do with the floater?"

"Nothin'! 'Cause Cap'n don't want no trouble with the authorities. We've got worry enough as it is if that planter, Mr. Sanders, turns out to be a robber. The only thing we can do is shove the poor bastard off with a gaff and hope the tide takes him out. Cap'n plans to be in Frisco just long enough to unload the cargo o' buildin' materials and pineapples and pick up a few supplies. He's also hopin' to hire a few nubs to fill out the crew afore we start our long journey to New York City.

The next morning, when Oliver and Jonesy's watch ended, without taking his clothes off, Oliver collapsed onto his bunk and slept for several hours. While he slept, some of the crewmembers loaded the pineapple crates onto a freight wagon to be hauled to the produce shop. There the grocer inspected the pineapples. Many of them had begun to go bad. The odor of fermenting pineapples permeated the shop's storeroom.

"*Cazzo!* Pineapples bad! I no can sell these if bad. Contract say pineapples must arrive in good condition by end of month, not month and a half. If pineapples not good to sell, I not pay you for delivery, capiche?"

The captain looked desperate and practically begged the grocer, "Please, Signore Rossi, not all the pineapples are bad. I really need the money to continue our trip, and the crew will skin me alive if I don't pay 'em. Can't ye see yer way to givin' me even half the cost of shippin' these goods?"

The greengrocer sighed. "I pay you one third, no more. Then you leave!"

As the captain left the shop with the money, the disgusted greengrocer said under his breath, *"Buona liberazione!"*

Chapter 19

Port of San Francisco

Oliver rolled out of his bunk sleepy-eyed. He dressed quickly and made his way through a dense fog to the galley where he knew Stubs would have coffee brewing. When Oliver entered the galley, Stubs and Jack were seated at the table chatting. Their hands were around their steaming mugs to keep them warm. Mama cat seemed to sense that the dog was hurt and left him alone. Stubs had bandaged his front paw and given him food and water. Now the dog rested comfortably on a pile of old rags.

"Mornin', Oliver. Hot coffee and porridge are on the stove. Help yerself," Stubs said with a yawn.

"Is it still morning?" Oliver said, rubbing his eyes.

Oliver poured himself a cup of the bitter brew, added several spoonsful of the new refined white sugar, and sat at the table. Frisco stood up, stretched his back legs, bit at a pesky flea, and trotted over to Oliver. He barked a friendly greeting, wagged his tail, and settled down at Oliver's feet.

"Guess he's claimed ye as his master," Stubs said. Oliver reached down and scratched the dog between the ears.

Oliver rubbed his arms, "Brr! Sure is cold and damp this morning."

"For cryin' out loud, Oliver! It's cold enough to freeze the balls off a brass monkey!" Jack exclaimed, hugging her coffee mug. Oliver looked aghast at Jack as if she had just said a mouthful of vulgar swearwords. He turned to Stubs, "What's a brass monkey, and what's the matter with Jack this morning?"

"As if ye didn't know," Jack retorted.

"Jack's afraid if some of the crew find out he's a girl, they might start to treat her like one and not accept her as their equal," Stubs said.

Oliver shook his head "What a crock! Jack's one of the best sailors on this ship. Besides, true friends don't turn their backs on each other. I made a promise not to tell anyone she was a girl, and I'm keeping it!"

"See, Jack? I told ye Oliver could be trusted," Stubs said.

Jack spat on her hand and reached out to shake Oliver's. "I'm sorry, it's just that—"

"I understand," Oliver said, accepting the handshake.

"To true friendship!" Jack said, and lifted her mug of coffee as if making a toast. After their handshake, Oliver wiped Jack's spit off his hand. Seeing that, Stubs burst out laughing and slapped his knee.

"It coulda been a blood oath," Stubs commented.

"And if ye wanna know what a brass monkey is, it's a tray that held cannonballs on old warships. When the weather got real cold, the monkey would shrink and make the cannonballs fall off," Stubs explained.

"Oliver, after ye been on a ship for a few months, ye'll get used to the sailor lingo; but that don't go to say that Jack couldn't wash her mouth out every so often and start actin' more like a lady," Stubs said, giving Jack a toothless grin."

Jack took a swipe at Stubs. "Ye been talkin' to Mrs. M., ain't ye, Stubs? Give it a rest, will ye?" she said with narrowed eyes. "Say, Oliver, Stubs has asked me to go ashore to fetch a package for the cap'n. Wanna go along? Maybe we could tour the town afterwards. Jonesy and Harris'll be rowin' the nuns ashore as soon as the fog lifts, and if we hurry, Cap'n says we can hitch a ride with 'em."

"Maybe I should hear firsthand from the cap'n or he'll think I'm jumpin' ship," Oliver said.

Stubs looked at Oliver. "If ye're lookin' for the cap'n, he left early this mornin' in the cockboat to see if he could hire more sailors. That bluestockin' planter and his wife was with him."

"What's a bluestocking?" Oliver asked.

"From what I hear, the word come from when a Victorian lady once invited a gentleman to a party she was hostin' and he didn't wanna come 'cause he had no nice clothes to wear. The lady told him that for all she cared, he could come in the ugly blue stockin's he was wearin'," Stubs replied. "Cap'n mentioned he thought ye and Jack should go to town together. If ye ask me I think he wanted Jack to have a chaperone. Since the earthquake there's been a lot o' thieves and unsavory characters in San Francisco lookin' for a handout. Oh, and Cap'n mentioned he wants ye to pick up a package for him at a place called Ming Kwon's Herbal Apothecary Shop in an alley off o' Stockton Street in Chinatown. While ye're there, ye can pick up some herbs for me that I use to ease me lumbago. Oh, and some ginger candies. The nuns and that planter and his wife used all I had when they didn't have their sea legs."

Stubs handed Oliver a scrap of paper with his list of items. The paper was old and yellowed.

Jack looked annoyed. "Anythin' else, Stubs?"

"Nope, that should do it."

Stubs took an old tin tea box off the shelf and poured the contents on the table. In it was a handful of assorted coins, some American, some foreign; a used candle, a sliver of soap, and a couple of corks. Two of the coins were newly minted shiny silver dollars. Stubs handed them to Jack. This should cover all of it."

Noticing the newly minted coins, Oliver asked, "Where'd ye get the new dollars?"

"Ain't no secret. That planter fella give 'em to me, for makin' all them special dishes for his wife." Jack raised an eyebrow.

Oh, and if there's any change left over after ye make me purchases, treat yourselves to a bit o' chocolate at the Ghirardelli Factory at North Pointe. 'Sides chocolate, they make mustard, so ye might buy a small pot. Cap'n likes mustard with his ham. Hear the factory weren't damaged in the earthquake or fire and is open for business."

"As far as treatin' us to confections, Stubs, ye can keep yer money," Jack said. I know for a fact Cap'n don't pay ye enough to be spendin' yer hard-earned money on chocolates for us. I still got a few coins o' me own," she said, taking a small leather pouch from her jacket pocket. She turned over the two silver dollars in her hand, and put the coins and the list in her coat pocket.

"Well, ye two best be goin'! Jonesy and Harris ain't gonna wait all day. Them nuns is in a hurry to get to the old St. Mary's Catholic Church that's bein' rebuilt after it was gutted by the fires. Heard they burned so hot they melted the bells and the altar. If ye're lookin' for Cap'n, he left early this mornin' with Sanders and his wife in the longboat," Stubs said.

Jack and Oliver didn't care where the two nuns and Mr. Sanders and his wife were headed, as long as they didn't return to the *Golden Lady.*

As Jack and Oliver made their way to the skiff, Jack said, "With all them errands Stubs and the cap'n want us to run, we won't have time for chocolate or anythin' else."

"Maybe that's what the cap'n had in mind," Oliver replied.

With the two oarsmen and the nuns and their trunk of Bibles, the small skiff was packed and rode low in the water.

"Looks like you're pretty crowded. Maybe we should wait 'til you get back," Oliver yelled to Jonesy.

"We won't be back 'til high tide, so ye better come along now. 'Sides, the sisters won't mind squeezin' over a bit, do ye, Sisters?" Mr. Harris said, giving one of them a friendly smile. The other moaned under her breath.

"Jack and Oliver scrambled down the rope ladder and toppled into the small boat, rocking it violently. With their added weight the boat sank even lower, the water nearly reaching the gunwale.

"Maybe we should throw that big trunk o' yers overboard," Jack suggested, addressing one of the nuns.

The older of the two looked sternly at Jack and put her hand on the trunk, rocking the boat even more.

"I'll have you know, young man, that trunk contains two dozen much-needed Holy Bibles. After the disaster, there are many people in San Francisco who, unlike yourself, would give their eyeteeth to have them. Perhaps you should think about taking one. Ye might learn a thing or two about manners and respect," the nun said, sitting up straight. Jack looked at Oliver, and both of them stifled a snicker.

From atop the ship, Mouse narrowed his eyes as he watched Oliver and Jack. As the skiff got underway, he gave a sinister sneer.

At the Hyde Street Pier, Jonesy and Harris tied up the skiff, unloaded the nuns' trunk, and helped the two women climb up the slippery wooden ladder to the pier. Jack and Oliver followed. They waved goodbye to Harris, Jones and the nuns, and hurried to the Powell-Hyde Street cable-car line at Powell and Market Streets, where Jack bought two roundtrip tickets to the stop at Grant Street.

The cable-car's gripper threw a switch and the car turned around on a turntable in order to head in the opposite direction. Jack and Oliver climbed aboard. The car was crowded and there was only room to stand, so they curled their fists around a leather strap that hung from the roof of the car. The conductor clanged the bell and shouted, "All aboard!"

As he engaged the cable, the car jerked and Jack was thrown forward, bumping into Oliver who stood in front of her. The car then slowly crept north along Powell Street until it sped up. The conductor yelled, "Hang on tight" as they swerved around a hairpin turn at breakneck speed. The brakes squealed, and the cable car zigzagged back and forth and shook on the tracks. The conductor warned his passengers to not lean out because the tracks ran close to where several wagons and automobiles were passing by. With the wind in their faces, Jack and Oliver hung on tight and enjoyed the thrilling ride.

From the car. they could see Coit Tower, Alcatraz Island, and the bay. The car passed Union Square, through the business area, and up Nob Hill. Up and up it continued. At the crest of the steep hill, the conductor brought the car to a stop and two more passengers got on. The conductor then changed gears, clanged the bell again, and the car crept down Russian Hill toward Fisherman's Wharf. From there it was just a block up California Street to Grant, the main street in Chinatown. As the car neared Grant Street, the operator pulled back on the brake handle; sparks flew as the car slowed down and came to a screeching halt. Jack and Oliver and several other passengers quickly hopped off the car near two new buildings constructed right after the quake, called Sing Chong and Sing Fat.

"Whoo-ee, that was some ride!" Oliver said, his face red from the wind and excitement.

"Yeah, 'bout as much fun as that cyclone we was in," Jack said. When the car flew around that corner, I thought I was gonna heave me breakfast."

Oliver said, "Now where's that alley where the Chinese herbal shop is supposed to be?"

"Stubs said it was just down the street aways. C'mon! We better run 'cause we ain't got much time to buy Stubs's herbs, pick up the cap'n's package, then catch the cable car to North Pointe where the chocolate factory is, afore we have to meet Jonesy and Harris back at the pier," Jack said in one breath.

As they ran down Grant Street, Oliver and Jack passed shop windows that had skinny plucked chickens and ducks with their heads still on hanging from hooks. Outside one of the shops, a multitude of flies swarmed around baskets filled with dried shrimp, dried octopus, dried seaweed, rice, and many things they couldn't identify. Another store window had firecrackers, statues of Buddha, miniature pagodas, jade rings, and several small boxes wrapped in red crepe paper tied with gold ribbon.

"Say, look at that cute ceramic cat with his paw facin' down, like he's wavin' to us," Jack said.

"Yeah, I've seen one of those before. The Chinese cook at the orphanage had one and told me they're called Lucky Waving Cats. The Chinese and Japanese believe they bring good fortune to whoever owns one. That's why so many stores, restaurants, and businesses have them in their windows or on their counters," Oliver said.

"If I have enough money left over after purchasin' the stuff on Stubs's list, I think I'll buy me one o' them cats, so it'll bring us good luck on our journey to New York," Jack said.

Oliver raised his eyebrows, shook his head, and thought, *Why should I care if you waste your money on a dumb ceramic cat 'cause you're superstitious and think it'll bring us good luck?*

"Here it is," said Jack as they came to the Chinese apothecary shop. A small bell over the door tinkled as they entered. The only light that illuminated the shop came from a small dirt-encrusted window high up on the wall. The dusty ray of sunlight pulsated with dust particles.

Once their eyes adjusted to the dim light, Oliver and Jack were awed by the myriad items in the shop. Crammed on shelves and counters were jars filled with dried herbs, repulsive things afloat in brine, dried chicken's feet, and other strange-looking objects. One jar looked like it contained human eyeballs. Each jar had a label in Chinese writing, so they could only guess what was in it.

Upon hearing the tinkle of the doorbell, an old Chinese man in felt slippers shuffled into the room from behind a curtain at the back of the store. He wore the traditional long-sleeved dark dress favored by Manchu men, and gold-rimmed spectacles that slipped down the bridge of his nose. From the top of his scalp, a long braided queue hung down his back while the front portion of his head was shaved.

"My name Kwon. I help you buy?" he said.

"Uh, yeah. Our cook wants us to buy some herbs and pick up a package for Captain Matthews of the ship *Golden Lady*," Jack said, handing the clerk the yellowed paper with Stubs's list.

"You from sailing ship come in yesterday from *xia' wei yi*—Hawaii," he said.

The clerk pushed his glasses up on his nose, and held the list up to the light. He then handed the paper back to Jack and said, "You read. Eyesight and English not so good."

Jack took a quick look at the list and handed it to Oliver. "Maybe you should read it, Oliver. Stub's scratches is hard to read."

Oliver knew that Jack's reading and writing skills were limited, and promptly read the list of items to buy. "I think it says turmeric, feverfew, and ginger."

"Chinese herbs for pain. In Chinese, *Jiang Huang, Xio Bai Ju, Jiang*. Herbs for you?"

"No, for our cook," Jack said.

"You wait here. I get herbs and package for captain." The old man disappeared through the rear curtain.

Again, Oliver looked at the paper the list was written on. In the lower righthand corner he noticed a small drawing in faded red ink, and the Chinese characters 黃龍. Oliver thought the drawing looked like a dragon or a sailing ship.

"I can't tell what this drawing is. Can you make it out?" he asked Jack, handing her the piece of paper.

"Why do ye wanna know? It's just an old scrap Stubs had lyin' around. Paper ain't cheap, so he's always savin' scraps to write on." Jack focused on the drawing. Could be anything.

If ye're so curious, why don't ye ask the clerk. Maybe he knows," she said.

When the clerk returned with the packages, Oliver showed him the drawing and Chinese characters and asked, "Can ye tell us what these characters and the drawin' mean?" he asked.

The old man took the paper, pushed his gold-rimmed glasses back up on his nose, held the paper up to the light, and squinted at the Chinese writing and symbol. He suddenly gasped as if frightened. "Mean golden or yellow dragon. Chinese symbol for wealth, power, harvest in New Year. Also sign for secret society called Tong. Very bad people! Run prostitution ring, gambling houses, drug trade. Steal money, drug sailors, shanghai, put on ships. Also make shopkeepers pay money. Best you stay away! Could also be name of Chinese restaurant, Chinese junk, *Golden Dragon,* hee-hee!"

Or, Oliver thought, *some Chinese man's interpretation of the Golden Lady. Was she used in the past to smuggle illegal goods in and out of the country?*

The old man handed the list back to Oliver, along with the captain's package and the herb packet for Stubs. The captain's parcel was heavy and lumpy, wrapped in brown paper and tied with a string. Jack wondered what was in it, but didn't ask.

"You want to know why package for captain come to Kwon's shop? I tell you. Long time ago, before captain have his own ship, Kwon and captain come from China on same ship. Captain and Kwon become friends. Ever since, when captain go to sea and have no place to send packages, he have them sent here. Kwon keep packages for captain 'til he come to San Francisco," Kwon said with a grin.

Kwon then handed Jack and Oliver three more packages, each wrapped in red tissue paper with a gold ribbon.

"What's this?" Jack asked.

"Gifts for you to celebrate Chinese New Year! Sticky rice cakes, wife make. Called *nian gao.* Mean grow higher in prosperity, not get drunk on Chinese wine, hee-hee! Also in package, firecrackers—go boom!—and Good Luck Cat."

Oliver and Jack thanked the old man for the gifts. Then Jack paid him for Stubs's herbs with one of the two silver dollars he had given her. The clerk held the coin up to the light, turned it over, and bit the coin to see if it was real. Where you get new dollar? Man come in earlier with same coin. Maybe fake."

Before Oliver could answer the man's question, the small bell over the front door tinkled, alerting the clerk that two men dressed in commoners' brown suits and bowler hats came into the shop.

Jack gasped and whispered to Oliver, "I'm pretty sure one of 'em is the same man who posed as a detective in Hawaii, and tried to come aboard 'cause he thought Mr. Sanders robbed a bank.

The clerk stared at the two men, and looked nervously around the shop to see if there were any other customers. The men approached him, said something to him, and then left.

The clerk looked scared; he shuffled to the front door, flipped the OPEN sign to CLOSED, pulled down the shade, and locked the door. He then turned to Jack and Oliver and said, "You go now, to alley out back. Must hurry! Maybe police come. Kwon not want trouble."

Jack and Oliver hurried through the curtain to the back door that led to the alley.

"I wonder what those two men said to make him so afraid, and why he wanted us to leave in such a hurry?" Jack said.

Jack and Oliver walked to the end of Grant Street to catch the cable car. From where they stood, they could see the newly constructed Ferry Building with the clock tower at its top. Oliver could make out that the hands on the clock were pointed to quarter of four. Soon the clock would chime the hour, and Mr. Jones and Mr. Harris would be awaiting them at the Hyde Street Pier.

"Whatever it was, we can't worry about it now. According to that clock we should be heading back to the wharf to meet Jones and Harris," Oliver said.

"Too bad! Guess we won't be gettin' any chocolate after all," Jack replied.

They raced down street to the cable-car stop. As they climbed aboard the car, Jack noticed a familiar-looking man and woman board the car.

"Oliver, ain't that the planter and his wife that was aboard our ship?" Jack whispered.

"So what? Maybe they're just touring the city and wanted to ride a cable car."

The conductor clanged the bell and the car began to move. Jack and Oliver took no further notice of the couple. Soon the car reached the end of the line at Powell Street. From there they ran to the pier. Unknown to Jack and Oliver, one of the men who had come into the herbal shop was following them. Jonesy and Harris were waiting in the skiff. Just as Oliver and Jack reached it, the same man ran up and said, "Sirs, you must take me with you to your ship. It's very important that I talk with your captain. It could mean life or death!"

"Okay. Ye made it just in time! Tide's gettin' high and we gotta shove off," Harris said. The man got in the boat and sat on the middle seat next to Jack.

Harris was on deck when, a half hour later, the other cockboat came alongside with the captain and Mr. Sanders and his wife in it.

Harris raised his eyebrows and thought, *What in the heck do those overbearing snobs think they're doin', comin' back here? Dang! Now Jones and I have to move back to the fo'c'sle with the idlers.*

Chapter 20

Hotel del Coronado

Once back aboard the *Golden Lady,* Oliver and Jack presented Stubs with the herbs, the New Year's gifts wrapped in red tissue, and the plain-wrapped package for the captain. Jack kept the one that contained the Lucky Cat to give to him personally.

It took nearly four days to sail down the coast from San Francisco to San Diego. When the ship arrived there, the captain surprised the crew by announcing that they would be in port for a week, and those of them who were not on watch would be allowed to go ashore after loading extra barrels of water and supplies.

The captain took Stubs, Jones, Harris, Jack, and Oliver aside and told them that his wife and he would be spending the week at a posh hotel called the Hotel del Coronado for their honeymoon. He didn't tell the crew that Mr. Sanders had offered to foot the bill for their stay at the expensive hotel in exchange for passage for his wife and him to New York City, and that in addition, Sanders had agreed to pay the captain double the amount for their passage from Hawaii to San Francisco.

The captain had jumped at the agreement because he desperately needed the money to complete the trip. Also, he thought a honeymoon at a fancy hotel would delight Sarah. He hadn't gotten half of what he'd expected for the lumber he'd brought, because every mill along the coast was selling lumber to buyers in San Francisco, so the price had plummeted. Also, the green-grocer had given him only a third of what he'd hoped to get for the pineapples.

Stubs thought the arrangement with the planter sounded too good to be true. He didn't trust the slimy Sanders and his pseudo highbrow wife. Maybe they were swindlers and bank robbers after all, and only using the captain to make their escape from the law.

Over breakfast the next morning, Stubs shared his concerns with Jack and Oliver: "I couldn't sleep last night thinkin' we gotta do somethin' to help Cap'n get out of this bad state of affairs. I believe Sanders is a crook, and I don't trust him as far as I can throw an anchor, and at my age that ain't very far. Cap'n's so desperate for money to finance his trip to New York he's willin' to take money from a criminal. I tell ye, we gotta do somethin' to stop the cap'n from windin' up in jail!"

"I've been thinking," Oliver said. "What if Jack and I go to that hotel? We could disguise ourselves as Cap'n and Mrs. M.'s servants. Lots of them rich people bring their help along with them and stay for weeks at a time. We could warn the captain, and maybe persuade him to contact the police if we can some-how prove that planter really did rob the bank in Hawaii. From the San Diego pier, Jack and I can take the ferry to Coronado Island. Jack, you got any girls' clothes you can wear?"

"Sure, I still got that fancy dress and hat I wore for that photograph was taken of me afore I was shipped off to school. And you could wear the shirt and pants ye was wearin' when ye stowed away on the ship. Sarah washed and ironed 'em, and they're hangin' in the cap'n's closet."

"Sounds like a good plan, boys! And if we expose them rob-bers, maybe there's a fat reward that the captain can use to finance our trip to New York," Stubs said.

Carrying the sack of clothes, Jack and Oliver climbed down the ladder to one of the skiffs that waited to pilot the crew ashore.

Seeing the sack, Jonesy kiddingly yelled to Oliver, "Days too fine to be doin' laundry, Oliver!" Oliver just laughed.

"I have enough money to buy our ferry tickets to Coronado Island," Jack said to Oliver, showing him a purse. Won it all in a poker game last night."

Before they boarded the ferry to Coronado, Jack and Oliver changed clothes to blend in with the servants of the rich. It was a sunny day, the sea was calm, and they enjoyed the ferry ride. A number of small fishing boats were in the bay, and they watched gulls screeching overhead as they followed the boats. Oliver wondered if Spike the albatross was nearby. Suddenly, a big seabird swooped down and landed at Oliver's feet.

"Why, if it ain't our old friend Spike after all. Come to say ahoy, have ye?" Jack asked the bird.

"Likely he's just looking for food. Maybe if we get in trouble we can use him like a carrier pigeon. We could tie a message to his leg and have him fly back to the ship for help," Oliver said teasingly.

"Say, that might not be a bad idea. If we ain't careful and get caught, we may have to do just that," Jack said, teasing back.

At the landing to Coronado Island, several complimentary carriages, each drawn by a dark horse with a red plume attached to its aristocratic head, waited for passengers to carry them and their luggage to the hotel.

"Going to the hotel? asked one of the coachmen. Step this way, madame, sir." He opened the door to an elegant brougham, a lightweight, horse-drawn carriage. Jack lifted her skirts like she'd been taught at the girls' school and stepped in. Oliver followed. The seats inside the carriage were covered with plush red velvet. Jack leaned back against her seat and felt like a fairytale princess.

The coachman clicked his tongue and the horse slowly plodded up the road to the Hotel del Coronado. As the coach approached the Victorian hotel, Jack eyes popped at its grandeur.

With its round turrets and lacy white gingerbread trim, the hotel appeared to be an enchanted seaside castle.

"Looks like a fancy wedding cake to me," Oliver said.

The coach stopped under the portes cocheres, the overhang in front of the hotel, where a footman opened the coach door. A porter stood near the fancy carved doors to the hotel. "Welcome to the Del Coronado Hotel and Seaside Resort. May I take your luggage?"

Jack handed the porter the burlap sack stuffed with their old clothes. The man took the bag and held out his hand for a tip. Seeing the hand, Jack shook it and grinned. They then entered the hotel. Jack was still in awe at its splendor, and turned around and around to look at everything.

"Don't do that, Jack, you'll draw attention to us," Oliver said.

Jack came out of her trance. "Oh, I'm sorry, suh. What was y'all sayin'?" Jack tried to imitate a southern belle to disguise her uncouth sailor's talk, but wasn't doing a very good job of it. The porter wasn't convinced. He'd heard many a false accent from guests. Oliver quickly leapt to Jack's rescue.

"Sir, you'll have to excuse my wife. She's still awestruck by the grandeur of your hotel. She's from Savannah, Georgia, and sometimes slurs her words."

"I understand, sir. We get guests here from all over the world, some with accents much more difficult to understand."

When the attendant was no longer in earshot, Jack said to Oliver, "Your wife! What was that all about?"

"Well, I couldn't just say 'my girlfriend.' In this place, they might get the wrong idea," Oliver said.

"Are you kidding? I bet half the men here ain't with their wives," Jack replied.

The attendant opened the double doors, which had oval-shaped inserts of etched and frosted glass that was beveled around the edges. "Right this way, sir and madam," he said.

Remembering how she was taught to walk like a lady at the girls' school, Jack smiled and followed the doorman to the main desk, Oliver right behind her. At the desk, the doorman addressed the clerk who stood behind a long marble-topped counter.

"This couple say they are the servants of Captain Matthews. Should I show them to his suite?"

"No. Even though they are Captain Matthews's servants, I'm sure they'll understand that for the protection of our guests, they must wait in the lobby or the atrium until the Matthewses return.

"Uh, I believe Captain Matthews left a note. Let me see," the clerk said, and took a note from one of the rows of cubbyholes behind him. Oliver noted that beneath the box from which the clerk had taken the note was the room number 308, which must be the captain and Sarah's room number.

The note says, "If anyone from his ship should come looking for him, they should wait in the lobby because Captain Matthews and his wife will be in the theater watching the silent moving picture *The Great Train Robbery.*

"Oliver said, "Sir, we just left his ship. I'm sure he was referring to us."

The doorman said excitedly to them, "If you haven't seen the film already, you should go see it. It's about a gang of outlaws who rob a steam locomotive at a station out West and flee across the mountains. A posse finally catches up with them. Gilbert M. "Bronco Billy" Anderson, whom I once saw in vaudeville, is the star of the movie."

"Edwards, that's enough! I don't care a rat's ass about that picture show. While you've been jabbering about it, a long line of guests has been waiting to be checked in and are getting hot under the collar, so go back to your duties before one of them demands to see the manager!"

Jack whispered in Oliver's ear, "Can ye ask the desk clerk if there's a public washroom in the lobby? I gotta go bad."

Several wealthy guests in the line were impatiently tapping their feet and asking what was the holdup. Suddenly the man in line behind Jack and Oliver skirted around them and stepped up to the desk.

"Ahem. My name is John Jacob Astor, and I have been waiting for over a half hour to check in. What is going on here? I demand to see the manager! I'll be giving this hotel a bad name if you do not check my party in soon."

The desk clerk's face turned a bright red and he said apologetically, "Yes, Mr. Astor. We are happy to have you and your party as our guests and will check you in right away!"

The clerk turned to Jack and Oliver and waved them off. "Since you will not be checking in at this time, I need to ask you to please step aside."

Oliver whispered to him, "Just one more question, sir. Is there a women's washroom in the lobby? My wife has to go real bad!"

Agitated, the clerk said, "Yes, yes, in the lobby next to the telephones. Now will you please leave so I can help our paying guests?"

Oliver and Jack backed away from the desk and walked to the lobby where Jack asked a snooty-looking lady seated on a settee where the telephones were. She pointed to three booths on her left. From the ceiling near the booths hung a blue-and-white porcelain sign that read BELL TELEPHONE COMPANY. A man in one booth vigorously cranked the handle on a wooden box attached to the wall. A tube with a rounded black end protruded from the box, and a mellow-sounding woman's voice came from the tube: "This is the operator. How may I connect your call, sir?"

The man hollered into the tube, "Get me the police! I'm a guest at the Coronado Hotel, and someone has just picked my pocket!"

At that moment, Oliver came up to Jack and asked, "What are you doing eavesdropping on that man's conversation? I thought you had to use the water closet?"

"I do, but I was curious how that machine in the booth worked. I've never seen a telephone before. That man was saying someone picked his pocket."

"I'm not surprised! In a swanky hotel like this, wealthy people are like chickens just waiting to be plucked," Oliver replied.

Next to the telephone booth were two doors. On one of them was a brass sign that read WC WOMEN; on the other, WC MEN. Jack entered through the door that said WC WOMEN. Like the lobby, the room was brightly lit with electric lights. Against one wall stood a row of white porcelain sinks, each with two white porcelain knobs, one of which read, in black letters, HOT, and the other COLD. Behind each sink was a mirror. On the opposite wall were several stalls. Jack walked into one.

In the middle of the stall was a porcelain bowl with water in it. On top of the bowl was a smooth, round wooden seat. Jack assumed that you used the device like a Jardine. She managed to hike up her cumbersome skirt, pulled down her pants, and sat. While she urinated, she looked around. Attached to the bowl was a pipe that ran up the wall to a box, and hanging from it was a long chain that reached all the way down to her. On the end of the chain was a handle. After she'd finished, Jack pulled the handle and heard a sudden whoosh just below her. Like a scared rabbit, she jumped up from the seat and looked into the bowl and thought, *Works just like a Jardine when the sea is rough!*

As she came out of the stall a matron handed her a white linen towel and put her hand out for a tip. Jacked looked at the towel and said, "Don't need it. Already wiped my hands on some o' that tissue paper that was on a roll.

Chapter 21

High Tea

Back in the lobby, Jack and Oliver sat at one of the small round tables. A waiter in a black cutaway coat and tails with a tea towel over his arm walked toward their table and asked, "Miss, are you and your gentleman friend waiting to be served high tea?"

Jack stammered, "Uh- uh, what? We didn't order any tea."

"Miss, afternoon high tea at the Del Coronado is always complimentary. You do not have to pay anything, unless you want to leave a tip. Today, you have a choice of Earl Grey, Darjeeling, Assam, Ceylon, chamomile, lavender, or mint. Or, you may have lemonade or iced tea if you prefer. The Del has an icemaker."

Jack hesitated, then smiled at the server. All these fancy things were new to her.

"I'll have whatever he's havin," she said, looking across the table at Oliver.

"We'll have the Earl Grey," Oliver said, as if he ordered tea every day.

"Wise choice, sir. It is our most popular."

The waiter asked them to push back their chairs so the serving boy who accompanied him could put a spotless white linen tablecloth, fine painted china plates with gold rims, silver spoons and forks, and two bone china cups with saucers on the table. The boy shook out a white linen napkin and placed it on Jack's lap. After he'd left, Jack tucked the napkin under her chin.

The server soon arrived at their table with a silver tea set, creamer and sugar bowl, a small plate of lemon wedges, and a three-tiered serving stand. On its lowest level was a selection of dainty square sandwiches, the crust cut off, filled with chopped olives, sliced cucumbers, and a tangy salmon spread. On the second level were scones served with clotted cream, marmalade, and raspberry preserves, and on the topmost level were tiny cakes with pastel-colored frosting, each topped with a dainty rosebud made of frosting. Jack asked the waiter what the little cakes were called. "These, miss, are petits fours. The other desserts are filled creampuffs sprinkled with powdered sugar, and an array of bite-sized cookies."

Placing another white linen napkin on Jack's lap, the waiter asked, "May I pour for you, miss?"

Jack and Oliver watched in awe as the server poured the tea through a strainer into the china teacups. He then left them to enjoy their afternoon tea. Both were starving and dug into the magnificent spread. Jack took two of the dainty sandwiches and crammed them into her mouth, then immediately spat them onto the plate in front of her. She wiped her mouth on the back of her hand. "What the devil? Who'd put chopped olives and cucumbers in sandwiches?! If Stubs made these, the crew would think he was tryin' to poison 'em."

She took a sip of tea to freshen her palate. "Yuck! This tea is worse than bilgewater. Smells like it too!" she said, making an ugly face.

Oliver laughed, then said, "Shh! Someone will think you're 'new money' and haven't got any manners."

Irritated, Jack said, "I can be a lady if I want to. I may not have been listenin' when they was teachin' Latin and proper grammar at that school for young ladies, but I learnt how to hold a fork and knife!"

Oliver laughed again.

"Oh, ye think it's funny, do ye?"

Oliver munched on one of the sandwiches filled with smoked salmon spread and held one out to Jack. "Maybe you'll like one of these fish sandwiches, or try a scone with cream and marmalade. They may be more to your liking."

As they enjoyed the high tea, Jack looked around the room. Crystal chandeliers hung from the ceiling. In various niches near the beveled and stained-glass front windows were small tables and chairs, settees, and wingback chairs. An oil painting of bathers on the beach and one of a mounted hunting party in red coats, with hounds running ahead, hung on the walls. In front of the huge fireplace sat two plush wingback chairs.

On one side of the room were French doors that led to an atrium full of short palm trees, flowering shrubs, exotic orchids, and other tropical plants. Butterflies flitted among the flowers, and they could hear the calls of tropical birds in cages.

A couple who looked like Captain Matthews and Sarah walked through the doors from the atrium into the lobby. Oliver stood up. "Psst! Cap'n, over here!" he called, trying not to draw attention.

The captain and his wife came to Jack and Oliver's table. "Jack, is that you in that getup? I didn't recognize you. Why, you look just like yer ma. Coarse ye could do with a better hat." How did you two get in here?"

Jack grabbed the napkin from under her chin and gulped the food in her mouth, "We told 'em we was yer servants. Ye'd left a note at the desk sayin' if anyone was to come from the ship lookin' for ye, they was to wait in the lobby, so they believed us. Then this waiter come along and give us this free tea and food."

"Sir, we need to talk to you," Oliver said. "Stubs told us to come here 'cause he was afraid that planter and his wife were blackmailing you or coercing you into taking them with you to New York. There's something damn fishy about them two."

"I agree," Captain Matthews replied. "But that crook Sanders got his hooks into me by offerin' to pay for this grand honeymoon in exchange for passage to New York. He also said he would pay double. Hell, I could be arrested and indicted for harborin' a fugitive if he did rob that bank in Hawaii. Mum's the word 'til we find out more about the robbers. That means we play innocent and let the police in New York handle it."

"After two days here, maybe Sarah might fit in with this highbrow society, but to me it's all a big folderal and gives me a bellyache! Sarah, I refuse to be a part of it anymore! Let's leave this highfalutin place now!"

"I agree with ye," Jack said. She stood up and let the napkin on her lap slip to the floor.

"That's me daughter!" the captain said with a smile. "Let's make haste back to the ship!"

Sarah looked disappointed and said to her husband, "Dear, you did enjoy that moving picture show about the train robbery."

Chapter 22

Sarah's Story

The next day, Sarah asked Jack to come to the captain's and her cabin. Jack hoped Sarah wasn't going to give her another lecture on minding her Ps and Qs and how to act like a lady. When Jack arrived, Sarah motioned for her to sit next to her on the bed.

"Jack, I know you think I've been priggish about your being a lady and all. Last night, the captain and I had a talk that turned into an argument, and we decided that if being a sailor is what makes you happy, we are both for it. I promise not to nag you about it anymore—at least until we get to New York," Sarah said with a smile.

"I must confess, though, I didn't grow up being prudish, as you may think. When I was young, my father was a dockworker, and my mother washed clothes to make extra money. There were seven children in our family, four boys and three girls. I was the eldest. When I was thirteen, my father died in an accident; a block and tackle hit him. After that, Mother tried her best to feed and care for us on her own, but it wasn't enough. When I turned fifteen, she told me it was time I made my own way in the world.

"I found work as a scullery maid for a rich family who lived uptown. The lady of the house thought she was better than everyone else. She was always tellin' the staff she didn't care for our common ways, and that we'd better mind our Ps and Qs or we'd be out on the street. I guess some of that snobbishness rubbed off on me, and in turn I passed it on to you. I'm sorry. Anyway, as I said, your father and I want you to continue being a sailor if it's what pleases you. That's all I want to say on the subject."

"It *does* make me happy," Jack replied. "I don't want to do anything else. Bein' a sailor is all I know. I love the sea, and the people on this ship are my family. May I be excused now?" she asked, squirming on the bed.

"Not just yet, Jack. I'd like to tell you how I met your father. The lady's husband where I worked owned several warehouses on the wharf. He had goods that needed to be transported, and he contracted with the captain to take them on his ship. They had a lot of things to discuss beforehand.

"The lady of the house held a dinner party one evening, and invited the captain. The headmistress told us to be on our best behavior and to treat all their guests with respect. The lady, being short-staffed at the time, asked me to help serve the meal. I was nervous and feared that I would make a mistake. When I asked the captain if he wanted more gravy on his mashed potatoes, some of the gravy dripped off the ladle onto his white shirt. I was mortified, and scared that I'd be let go."

"I was very apologetic, and said so to the captain so the lady of the house could hear: 'Oh, I am so sorry, sir. Come into the kitchen and I will do my best to take out that stain.' The lady didn't scold me, and tried to make light of the incident. The captain excused himself from the table and followed me into the kitchen, where I dabbed at the spot of gravy with a towel dipped in soda water. The captain smiled at me and asked my name. 'Sarah,' I said shyly."

" 'Well, looks like there's no harm done, Sarah. Look—the spot is nearly gone!' he said. Then he put his finger under my chin and lifted my head up. Our eyes met, sparks flew, and my heart thumped. It was love at first sight. Later, he told me that he had the same feeling. I was taken aback, and asked myself, *Why would a man of his stature, and much older than I, be interested in a lowly scullery maid?*

"The captain was determined to see me again, and pretended he had to discuss more business with the man of the house regarding the transport of his goods. Often the captain would use the tradesman's entrance in the scullery in hopes that I might answer the door. Sometimes he lingered in the kitchen after talking with the master, hoping to talk to me. On one occasion, the captain asked if I would take a walk with him along the shore on my next day off. He said he had something important to ask me.

"As a scullery maid, I worked six days a week from dawn to dusk, sometimes longer, with half days off on Sunday. In my time off, I'd walk along the seashore, watch the children play on the beach, and feed the gulls scraps of stale bread.

"Your father would sometimes meet me there and we'd sit on a log and talk. One day he told me he would be leaving at the end of the month to go on a long voyage. He was talking about the trip to New York. He said he didn't want to leave me, and proposed marriage then and there. He said we could get married the following Sunday. I jumped at the opportunity to leave my job and the dreary life I lived, and said yes, even though I wasn't sure at the time that I was in love with him, and that it wasn't all just a childish fantasy.

"The lady of the house didn't want to lose me; she told me I was being foolish, and that the captain would leave me in some port, in the family way and penniless. As you know, that was not true."

"I've heard enough," Jack said. "I'd like to go now."

Sarah grabbed Jack's arm. "There's just one thing more you need to hear. I'm going to have a baby, and when the time comes, I could use your help. Please don't tell anyone. I haven't even told your father yet."

Instead of being happy about having a baby brother or sister, Jack jumped up from the bed and said to Sarah, "A baby?! Now I've really gotta go!"

Chapter 23

The Sanderses Return

Back on the ship, Jack was teaching Oliver how to tie a bowline knot with a piece of rope.

"First ye gotta form a loop near the end of the line; next, ye run the end of the line back through the loop; then ye run the line around the standin' end and back through the smaller loop. Now, ye grasp the end and pull the knot tight. That's how ye tie a bowline," Jack said, proud of knowing how to tie the sailor's knot.

Oliver tried his best to follow Jack's instructions, then grasped the end of his rope and pulled. The knot fell apart. "Guess I skipped the part about running the end of the line back through the loop. Show me again, Jack. Say, look! A boat's coming alongside."

Jack peered over the railing. "It's them damn Sanderses again. Thought we was rid of 'em for good once we left 'em at that fancy hotel. Cap'n was hopin' they'd change their minds 'bout sailin' with us to New York."

Seeing Jack looking down at them from topside, Mr. Sanders shouted, "Lower the ladder, boy, and make quick about it! I got business with your captain, and the sun is beating down something fierce on our heads. Well, hop to it!"

Jack yelled down at him, "Hold yer horses, mister. We wasn't expectin' ye to come back, not after—"

Annoyed at the delay, Sanders shouted back, "Get the captain! We struck a bargain and I mean for him to keep it, even if he and his wife didn't stay at that hotel the entire week!"

Hearing that exchange, Jonesy said under his breath, "Rats! Harris and I will have to give up our cabins again."

Jack and Oliver lowered the ladder, and Mr. Sanders and his wife climbed aboard.

Jonesy addressed him: "Cap'n can't be disturbed right now. He's goin' over his charts and plottin' our journey. I'm the first mate. How can I help ye?"

The planter pushed Jonesy aside. "Get out of my way, boy! The only person I want to see is your captain!"

Being spoken to that way made Jonesy hot under the collar. Used to being treated with respect, he didn't like being called 'boy.'

Jonesy retorted, "Ye can't just go bargin' around this ship like ye own it!"

"Well, if your captain doesn't repay the money I paid for him and his wife to stay at that fancy hotel, I may just *be* the new owner!" Sanders said angrily.

Hearing the commotion, Captain Matthews yanked open his cabin door and stormed onto the deck. "Hells bells, what's all the racket about?"

It's Mr. Sanders, sir. He's insistin'—"

"Mr. Jones, I'll handle this, the captain said. "Mr. Sanders? I thought we'd seen the last of ye."

Sanders yelled, "You thought *what*, Captain—that my wife and I would be long gone by now? You're not getting out of our bargain that easy. I paid in advance for a week so you and your wife could honeymoon at that expensive hotel. Even if you didn't stay the entire week, I expect you to keep your part of the deal and take my wife and me to New York!"

"Mr. Sanders, that hotel was too highbrow for us. Also, ye haven't paid me a nickel for takin' ye from Hawaii to San

Francisco and then to San Diego, so I think we're even. Now, ye're demandin' I take ye all the way to New York? Ye got some nerve, Mr. Sanders!"

"Now wait just a minute! I promised to pay ye; I just haven't got around to it yet! I've had other things on my mind, and it's just a matter of finding a bank that will exchange some of my money."

The captain thought for a moment. *If he promises to pay me what he owes, perhaps I should let him and his wife back on the ship.* "All right, Mr. Sanders! Ye can come aboard, but what about that other couple?" he said, pointing to a second boat that was tying up. "Ye don't expect me to take them too?!"

"They missed the steamer that was to take them to Valparaiso, Chile, where they would meet another steamer that would take them on to New York. Unfortunately, to meet the steamer at Valparaiso they had to have left two days ago. They've checked with all the steamship lines, but your ship is the only one leaving before the end of the month. They promised to repay me if I booked their passage."

"Ye what?! Ye offered to have me take them to New York? Takin' on more passengers weren't part o' the bargain, Mr. Sanders. If any new passengers is comin' on my ship, they gotta deal with me direct."

Sanders hesitated, then said, "Uh, I believe he said his last name was Astor."

"Astor?" Captain Matthews thought, *Does Sanders think me such a dummy as to not recognize the name of one of the wealthiest families in America? Astor was probably the first rich man's name that popped into Sanders's head, and it's all a ruse. The idiot!*

The captain stared at the so-called Mr. Astor, who had removed his expensive-looking jacket, bow tie and high paper shirt collar, and had rolled up his sleeves to his elbows because of the sweltering heat. He wore a Panama hat similar to the one

President Theodore Roosevelt had worn when he visited the Panama Canal.

Mr. Astor's wife was dressed in a long, lightweight cotton skirt and lace-trimmed white lawn blouse. On her head was a huge straw hat with a large artificial flower. She held a white eyelet parasol to shade her from the sun.

The captain thought, *These people may be dressed to the nines to fool me, but in no way are they the Astors. The Astors woulda traveled with a fleet o' servants and a boatload o' baggage. This pair is prob'ly in cahoots with Sanders.*

Captain Matthews feared that if he did not let all four passengers come aboard, they would cause trouble, and perhaps alert the authorities, which he definitely did not want. He also needed the money.

"All right, Mr. Sanders, all right! The four of ye can book passage, but this time ye gotta pay me in advance for all o' ye, plus the money ye still owe me for takin' ye from Hawaii to San Francisco and San Diego. Passage on the *Golden Lady* ain't free."

The captain thought, *Can't trust anyone these day, especially them as claims to be rich.*

Sanders huffed, but reached for the money pouch that hung from his belt. The captain looked around. "Not here, man! No offense, but I can't trust anyone these day, even me own crew. If one of 'em got wind that ye had a lot o' money on ye, we might find ye with yer throat slit the next mornin'. Once ye get yer trunks aboard and we're out to sea, come to my cabin and we can settle up." He had only mentioned to Sanders that he might be murdered to scare him into paying.

"Our trunks are pretty heavy, Captain. My wife brings everything but the kitchen sink when we travel," Sanders said.

"I remember from the last time ye come aboard," the captain replied. "Mr. Harris, have the crew bring the block and tackle, a cargo net, and a wheelbarrow.

Sanders wasn't kidding. One of the trunks must have weighed a ton; it took four crewmen to haul it up on deck where it landed with a loud *clunk!* "Ma'am, what ye got stowed in here, lead bars?" Mr. Harris joked.

"You could say that, she replied with a smirk. I never go anywhere without my mother's silver tea set, serving trays, and silverware. The trunk also has some souvenirs that I picked up in our travels. Please do be careful, won't you?"

Once the ship had weighed anchor and the passengers were settled in Harris's and Jones's cozy cabins, Mr. Astor and Mr. Sanders strolled to the captain's quarters and knocked.

"Come in, gentlemen," the captain called out.

In the cabin, Mr. Astor started to pull a wad of bills from his wallet.

"Stop right there, Mr. Astor. Don't want no paper money, only coins. Many of me crew come from foreign lands and don't know what to do with paper money. They'd use it to wipe their arses. Ha-ha! Besides, where we're headed, American paper money is worthless."

"But- but I haven't got any large coins," Astor sputtered.

"Never mind, my friend. Put your money away," Sanders interjected. I still have enough coins stashed away to pay for all four of us and then some. Captain, you'll have to wait while I go back to my cabin. It'll only take a minute," Sanders said, and hurried out.

Sanders came back to the captain's cabin with a bulging pouch. He removed a handful of silver and gold coins from it, and stacked them on the captain's desk.

A good many of the silver coins were tarnished, and looked as if they'd been in circulation. Mixed in with them were several shiny silver dollars and three gold coins that looked newly minted. One of the new silver dollars rolled off the desk onto the floor. The captain picked it up and examined it closely. It was a new Morgan silver dollar, with the profile of Lady Liberty on one side, and on the reverse an eagle on an olive branch and what looked like a quiver of arrows.

"Where'd ye get these new coins, Mr. Sanders?" the captain asked.

Sanders hesitated. "I'm not quite sure. Perhaps they were given to me as change when I paid the bill at the Del Coronado Hotel. Also, my wife bought several items before we left Hawaii, a few in San Francisco, and yet more here in San Diego. The coins may have been given to her in change."

"Hmm! I'll accept 'em as part payment," the captain said.

After the two passengers had returned to their cabins, the captain put the silver coins in his safe. He then picked up a gold coin he was going to give to Sarah. It was very shiny, as if brand-new. On one side was the image of Queen Liliuokalani. He knew it was Liliuokalani because he had seen a painting of her at the Iolani Palace in Honolulu. On the reverse side of the coin was an engraving of a lei.

Chapter 24
Nature's Calamity

By late afternoon the next day, dark rainclouds hung in the sky, and drifts of frothy foam fluttered like seabirds in the increasing wind. The captain told Sarah and the four passengers to stay in their cabins.

Suddenly, a furious gale called a cyclone struck the *Golden Lady*, and Captain Matthews, fearing for the ship's safety, made a run down the coast in hopes of finding a safe haven where they could wait out the storm.

The ship made little headway against the shrieking wind and the sheets of torrential rain that drove it back. The *Golden Lady* could carry so little sail that she wouldn't work to windward. The squalls came on thicker and faster, and the ship rolled side to side, now up, now down, with a frightening. The sheets snapped in the wind, and ropes and rigging clanged against the masts and yardarms with the sound of church bells ringing. The wind had reduced some of the canvas to shreds, and the captain ordered that all sails be snuggly stowed. Under bare poles, the ship scudded before the wind.

In contrast to the cold and the howling of the wind, the galley was cozy and warm from the heat of the stove, and there was the inviting smell of hot coffee brewing. Oliver was practicing his knot-tying, and Mouse was asleep on the opposite side of the small table, his head resting on his arms. The shrill whistle from the teakettle broke the silence, and Mouse lifted his head with a jerk. "Aye-aye, Cap'n! I'll get to it right away!" he mumbled.

"Oliver, Mouse! The two of ye take this pot o' coffee and some mugs to the crew on deck. I expect they'll be mighty grateful for a cup about now," Stubs ordered.

Oliver set down his knots and reached for his oilskins, which hung on a hook near the door. He gave Mouse a poke. "Come on, Mouse! Stubs wants us to take this coffee to the crew." Mouse yawned, rose reluctantly from the table, and put on his own oilskins.

Even with the coffeepot between them, it was no easy task to make their way over the slippery wet deck. Mouse and Oliver staggered along and more than once nearly slipped and fell. They reached Jonesy who was stationed on the deck. Oliver poured a cup of the hot brew and handed it to him. Jonesy cupped his hands around the thick mug to warm them, and took a sip. "Ahh, thank ye, boys! Just what I needed to warm me insides. Awful weather we're havin'!"

The boys moved on to the next sailor, and finally made their way to the helm where the captain stood, his clenched white hands gripping the wheel. "Here's coffee for you, sir," Oliver said. With the ship's rolling, some coffee sloshed from the mug as Oliver handed it over.

"Bad storm, boys! Been sailin' these waters nigh on forty years and never seen it this bad."

"Cold too, Cap'n. "Me fingers is numb to the bone and me ears is near froze off," Mouse complained, pulling his knitted cap farther down over his greasy hair.

"Captain, if the weather gets any worse, do ye think we'll have to dump a load of cargo overboard?" Oliver asked.

"Not if I can help it, lad. If we have no choice but to jettison cargo, it'll mean a huge loss o' money. I'm counting on deliverin' a load o' lumber and bricks to Valparaiso, our next port o' call. Even with the money them passengers give me, it won't be enough to cover our entire trip to New York. This storm is gettin' worse. We need to find a cove big enough to hole up in 'til it passes. Oliver, are ye game to take my spyglass and make yer way to the bowsprit to keep a lookout? I can barely make out what's ahead of us from here."

"Aye-aye, Captain," Oliver said, leaving Mouse to take the half-empty coffeepot to the rest of the crew.

"That's a good lad, Oliver! Mouse, you continue your rounds with the coffee," the captain said with a stern look at him.

"Aye-aye, sir, but this here pot is mighty heavy for just me to carry," Mouse said.

The captain gave Mouse a look as if to say, *Ye damn slacker, I should give ye somethin' heavier to carry!* Mouse was too tired to balk at the order, but when the captain's back was turned, Mouse shot a jealous glare at Oliver and moaned under his breath, "How come Oliver gets to do everythin', and I always get the grunt jobs?"

Captain Matthews clamped his hands firmly onto the ship's wheel and searched through the blinding wind and rain for a protected cove. Finally, his search succeeded, and the ship hauled up in a small cove. The *Golden Lady* was larger than the doghole schooners that plied the Pacific coast, and she could barely turn around in the cove. It took all the captain's nerve, strength, and skill to swing her stern around so she could weigh anchor and be moored to the rocks with a stout hawser.

The next morning, everyone was pleased that the gale had broken and the sky had cleared, and they were all anxious to be on their way. The captain remained grumpy because he was superstitious and believed that the old adage "whistling up a storm" had arisen from sailors whistling, clapping their hands, and throwing stones in the water, and lady passengers carrying umbrellas. He had seen all those actions since they'd started the trip.

Oliver thought the captain's superstitions were ridiculous, and concentrated on his task of mending torn sails. With the mended sails and the spare sails in the hold, the *Golden Lady* came again to the wind and was soon gliding toward Valparaiso.

Chapter 25
Melted Down

Valparaíso, Chile, was often called The Jewel of the Pacific. It was a major South American city and seaport, and a stopover for many steamers and sailing ships navigating between the Atlantic and Pacific via the Straits of Magellan and Cape Horn. Captain Matthews, Sarah, Oliver, Jack, and the officers and passengers were allowed to go ashore, but the rest of the crew had to remain onboard because the captain feared that some of the sailors might jump ship before they had to make the crossing from the Pacific to the Atlantic Ocean.

Valparaíso was a modern city: it had the first telegraph service in Latin America, between Valparaíso and Santiago; potable running water, streetlights, and the first horse-drawn tram in Latin America.

Oliver, Jack, Sarah, and the captain walked up the hill from the pier to Avenida Pedro Montt, the main street, and the newly created Plaza O'Higgins. There the captain hired a cabriolet, a lightweight two-wheeled vehicle drawn by one horse, to take Sarah and him to see his old friend and colleague, Capitan Vargas, and his lovely wife. The Vargases lived in a beautiful hacienda a short distance outside the city.

While the captain and Sarah visited Capitan and Señora Vargas, Oliver and Jack were allowed to explore the city, but were warned to look sharp and return to the ship before dark because many thieves roamed about, waiting to pick the pockets of innocent foreigners such as they. The pair walked around Plaza O'Higgins, on each side of which were various shops that sold the fashionable new Panama hats. There were also shops that sold ladies' lace-covered parasols, colorful pottery jars and plates, leather goods, piñatas, jewelry, and the usual staples: beans, rice, and corn.

On the streets, vendors hawked fruits and fresh-made tamales. Oliver bought a banana, and Jack a mango, which she peeled with her pocketknife. They continued to amble down the street. On one corner was a foundry and blacksmith shop where metal was melted down and tools and horseshoes were made. Oliver had worked in a foundry at home, and smelled the familiar acrid odor of burning coke from the forge. He and Jack stood in the shade of a nearby pepper tree and watched as the blacksmith hammered the tip of a red-hot rod on an anvil to fashion a hook for hanging cookpots.

A familiar-looking man pushed a wheelbarrow with a large trunk in it toward the foundry. When he showed the foundryman the contents of the trunk, the man's eyes opened wide.

The trunk's owner said, "I need to have this melted down into bars today. Can you do it? I will pay you half now and the other half when the work is done."

"Si, Señor, we melt it down. After siesta, you come back and is ready."

The owner handed some silver dollars to the foundryman, who bit one to see if it was real. "No worry, Señor. Your trunk is safe with me. We close now for siesta."

The man left the trunk with the foundryman and headed to a nearby cantina called *El Libertad*. Oliver and Jack peeked in a window. Several sailors and other travelers stood at the bar. At one of the tables, the man who'd left the trunk was sipping a local Chilean brandy concoction called a pisco sour.

Jack thought, *Pisco sour? Maybe they call it that 'cause it tastes like piss.*"

The foundryman left his shop, looked cautiously around the street, wheeled the heavy trunk inside the courtyard, took off his poncho, and threw it over the trunk. He hung a CLOSED sign over the archway so no other customers would come in, and then walked up the street to his home.

After he had gone, Oliver said to Jack, "That man with the trunk was Sanders. I wonder what he wants melted down," Oliver said.

"Maybe it's 'is wife's silver tea set. If I had to haul that trunk around wherever I went, I'd get rid of some of the junk in it too," Jack said.

"No," Oliver replied. "Don't you remember: his wife said that tea set had belonged to her dear departed mother, and she wouldn't part with it for love or money? His wife would have a fit if that silver teapot was melted down. Wish we could see what else is in that trunk."

"Maybe we can," Jack said, heading toward the courtyard.

"Hey, hold on. What if we get caught?" Oliver said.

"What are ye, Oliver, a man or a mouse? C'mon."

Jack pulled up the latch on the courtyard door. It opened easily. She then crept up to the trunk, lifted the poncho, and tried to open the lid. "Rats! The trunk's locked."

"Maybe I can pick the lock with my penknife," Oliver said.

"Gimme that knife," Jack said. "I been pickin' locks ever since I was a… How do ye think I escaped from that girls' school?" There was a click. Ah, got it!"

Jack opened the lid and they peered inside. Lying underneath a cheap dented silver teapot were three large lumpy sacks with the lettering BANK OF HAWAII printed on them.

"Ah-ha! I knew Sanders was a thief!" Jack said. She grabbed one of the sacks and pulled the drawstring open to look inside. Jack gasped, and quickly clutched the bag to her chest. "There's a bunch o' gold and silver coins in this bag, and the gold coins have an image of a Hawaiian lady on 'em. These must be the coins that detective said was stolen from the Bank of Hawaii. We got to tell the cap'n. Maybe we should take some o' the coins and a sack as evidence. Sanders won't miss 'em once the coins are melted down. If he does, he'll prob'ly think the foundry worker took a couple," Jack said.

"No," Oliver replied. "We'd better not. If Sanders notices that some coins and one of the sacks are missing, he'll be on the alert and the authorities will never catch him."

"I guess ye're right," Jack said. She stuffed the bag of gold coins back in the trunk, slammed the lid, locked the trunk, and put the poncho over it. "Now, no one'll be the wiser. We'd better head back to the ship and tell the cap'n."

"I'm with you, Jack. Besides, I think we've seen enough of this town," Oliver said.

After siesta, Sanders returned to the foundry to pick up the gold and silver bars made from his coins, but he met with disappointment. The foundryman was waiting for him and shook his head. "Señor, I am so sorry. It takes two workmen to make gold and silver coins into bars, and when I arrive at *mi casa*, I discover my brother is very sick. You come back mañana, and maybe we melt your coins."

Sanders shoved the foundryman aside. "Tomorrow is too late! I must have this done today!" Unable to have his coins melted down, Sanders pushed the wheelbarrow with the trunk down the road toward the wharf and the *Golden Lady.*

Chapter 26

The Hacienda

Sarah had never seen a hacienda before, and was awed by the vast estate and home of Capitan and Señora Vargas. To get to the house, they entered through heavy studded wooden doors that led to an interior courtyard. The style of the house was Spanish Colonial. Its thick walls were plastered and whitewashed. The frames around the windows and the doors were painted blue. Over the windows were wrought-iron grates. The roofs of the house and outbuildings were covered with red clay tiles.

The interior courtyard had a garden featuring prickly pear cacti, sunflowers, sage, bird of paradise, climbing red roses, and pepper, olive, and fruit trees. Tiled walkways wound around the garden. There were carved wooden benches to sit on, and in the center of the garden a fountain sprayed sparkling prisms of water that fell into a round basin decorated with blue and white glazed tiles.

A servant girl and boy served Capitan Vargas, Señora Vargas, Captain Matthews, and Sarah a delicious dinner consisting of a corn casserole with meat stuffing; empanadas, cazuela, and a red wine called Carménère, which tasted of berries and a hint of green peppercorn. For dessert they were served a creamy caramel custard called flan, along with oranges, grapes, and goat cheese.

Capitan Vargas said, "Consuela, our cook, is *excelente*."

After the meal, Señor Vargas offered Captain Matthews a fine Cuban cigar and another glass of wine. "Now, shall we all retire to the courtyard?"

"Gracias, Señor and Señora Vargas," Captain Matthews said. That was the best meal I've eaten since we began our journey. Also, I thank you for inviting Sarah and me to your beautiful home."

"Si, Capitan Vargas, it was wonderful! *Muchas gracias,*" Sarah added in her best Spanish.

Señora Vargas just smiled and nodded.

"You must excuse my wife, Señor and Señora. She does not speak much English."

"Neither does my wife speak much Spanish," said Captain Matthews.

While Sarah and Señora Vargas strolled around the garden, the two captains spread several sea charts on a long plank table.

"Capitan, I need to take the fastest route to New York. Having made several stops already, I am behind schedule. Do you think it would be possible to sail my ship through the Strait of Magellan?" Matthews asked.

"No, Capitan. The *Golden Lady* is too big. The strait has many curved channels and unpredictable winds and tidal currents. Only smaller sailing ships and steamships are able to travel through the Strait of Magellan. With such a large ship, you must take the long route through Drake Passage, which separates Cape Horn from Antarctica at the tip of South America. I warn you, Drake Passage is also dangerous at this time of year because of violent seas, uncertain weather, icebergs, and sea ice, but it is the only way you can go. For the safety of your crew and passengers, you must be very careful sailing through the passage, and it may take you several weeks."

Señor Vargas looked at the setting sun. "The sun is almost down. It is time you and your lovely wife were on your way back to your ship. Señora Vargas and I must say adios now, until we meet again. We wish you good luck in all your future endeavors."

Chapter 27

Cape Horn

Having delivered the cargo of lumber and railroad ties to a merchant in Valparaiso, Captain Matthews gave the order to weigh anchor. Jack and Oliver tried to tell him about seeing Sanders at the foundry and about the silver and gold coins, but the captain was in too much of a hurry to get underway and waved them off like pesky flies.

"Not now, Jack! Tell me later. I've a ship to run! Mr. Jones, tide's up! Order the crew to weigh anchor! Mr. Harris, are all crew and passengers aboard?"

"Aye-aye, sir! All accounted for," Harris replied.

"We'll be takin' her along the southern route through Drake Passage."

As they sailed toward the tip of South America, Oliver was awestruck by the many islands, magnificent waterfalls, and the small icebergs afloat in the sea. As the *Golden Lady* neared Cape Horn, the weather grew colder and colder; the men let their beards grow to keep their faces warm. Oliver tried to grow a beard, but only peach fuzz and a few sparse hairs sprouted on his chin.

One morning, frost covered the decks, icicles hung from the ratlines and rigging, and the sails were as stiff as if they'd been dipped in potato starch. The order was given to clear the decks while crewmen climbed the rigging to knock down the ice with hammers. It was a slippery and dangerous job—on a previous trip, two sailors had fallen to their deaths.

When the door to the galley was opened, Frisco raced out on the deck to pee. The deck was slippery with ice, and the dog, unsteady on his feet, fell flat on his belly with his legs and tail splayed out, and spun across the deck until a sailor caught him. The dog whimpered, stood on all four legs, and shook himself as if he'd just had a bath. He seemed to say, *That was fun! Let's do it again!*

Frisco then let out a sharp bark, and half slid across the rest of the deck to the first mate, Mr. Jones, who was standing watch. Frisco sat by him as if waiting for an order. Jonesy had his eye on the approaching storm and ignored the dog. Frisco, wanting his attention, lifted a hind leg and peed against Jonesy's leg.

Jonesy yelped, "What in blazes?! Well, boy, I guess that's one way to warm up a sailor's frozen leg." Even though Frisco knew he had done wrong by peeing on Jonesy, he refused to retreat; he sat right alongside the sailor and stared at the sea.

Looking down at the dog again, Jonesy said, "So, ye're tryin' to tell me ye want to stand watch with me, is that it? I guess I won't mind the company."

Frisco looked up at Jonesy with his sparkling dark eyes and barked twice as if to say, *Aye-aye, sir! Now, keep a sharp lookout for icebergs!* Jonesy laughed at Frisco and did as he was told.

As the ship passed one of the many small islands along the coast, they saw on it the remains of an old seal-hunting and whaling station. On the shore were rusted iron try pots and a couple of dilapidated huts. Smoke curled out of the rooftop of one tumbledown shelter. Dressed in sealskin parkas, two tall, fair-haired men with long beards rushed out of the hut and ran toward shore. They waved a white cloth to signal that they were friendly and not pirates.

"Ahoy there!" the captain shouted from the deck.

One of the seal hunters yelled back, "We are sailors. Come on whaling ship from Norway. Shipwrecked in storm. Only ones to survive. Stay here two years. Eat seal meat, seabirds, moss, heat snow for water. Both good seamen. You take on ship?"

The captain thought, *Hmm! We're still shorthanded. I could use two more able-bodied seamen. They also know the area around Cape Horn.*

"Yes, but I can't pay very much," he shouted.

"Not want pay. Just glad to leave island. You wait—we come soon!"

Lahrs and Jon rushed back to their hut. When they returned to shore, Lahrs was carrying their ship's logbook and an ivory walrus tusk scratched and inked with a drawing of their ship, the name of the ship, the year, and a list of their crewmen who were presumed dead. Captain Matthews recognized the piece as scrimshaw. In Jon's hand was a heavy whaling harpoon. "It was my father's," he said, "so not leave it behind!"

Jones and Harris rowed the cockboat to shore to pick up the two Norwegians. They scrambled into the small boat, and Lahrs said, "We most grateful for taking us!"

As the *Golden Lady*'s trip continued south toward Cape Horn, Jon and Lahrs proved to be true to their word: they were good seamen, and were helpful in advising the captain and crew about the rough seas, icebergs, and the regional flora and fauna.

For three days the weather remained calm and clear; then a very strong westerly wind rose, and black clouds brought rain and hail that pelted the ship. Determined to wait out the storm in a safe haven, Captain Matthews asked Lahrs and Jon if they knew of a sheltered cove thereabouts. Lahrs had heard tell of such a harbor on a small island supposedly a short distance east of Cape Horn. There the ship could anchor in calm water if the inlet wasn't packed with ice. Cape Horn was on Hornos Island, at the southern tip of the Tierra del Fuego archipelago. The scenery was beautiful, and the island and surrounding sea were home to giant petrels, red-beaked penguins, kelp gulls, sea otters, leopard seals, dolphins, and humpback whales.

The captain traced a route to the island on his charts. When the ship arrived at the safe haven, the sea was clear of ice, but the island was covered with snow and ice, and heavy gusts blew from the Andes, causing the ship to rock violently, so he ordered the crew to remain onboard.

Lahrs and Jon were accustomed to the extreme weather and volunteered to go ashore, with the captain's promise that he would not leave them stranded on the island. The Norwegians rowed ashore and climbed to a clifftop where they could get a good view of the sea. There appeared to be open water just beyond Cape Horn.

The rest of the crew, tired, hungry and soaked to the skin, were much in need of a hot meal and some rest. Unfortunately, Stubs was unable to serve anything but lukewarm coffee, cheese, and flavorless porridge, but the crew were grateful for anything that would fill their bellies and warm them up. The four passengers grumbled about the fare and retreated to their cabins.

Stubs mumbled, "To hell with 'em, the miserable wretched landlubbers! If they don't like me food, they shouldn't a come on this voyage."

At about 3 AM, the captain shouted through his speaking trumpet, "All hands and passengers on deck!"

Afraid that the ship was nearing a large iceberg or worse, everyone rushed up on deck. Overhead was a phenomenon rarely seen, except by those who sailed in the Antarctic, the Artic, and Alaska. Across the night sky, a magnificent display of brilliant green, blue, purple, and red lights appeared as curtains, rays, spirals, and flickers. This was the aurora australis, or southern lights. Everyone on deck was delighted by the awesome display. Oliver had read about the auroras known to occur in Alaska and the northern Artic, but was unaware that they occurred in Antarctica as well.

The next day was a bit calmer, and the *Golden Lady* weighed anchor and sailed farther through the Hermit Islands. In the afternoon, Jonesy sighted the mountain-like outline of Cape Horn and shouted, "There she be, Cap'n!"

As the ship sailed south of Cape Horn, the water became shallower, which caused the waves to be shorter and steeper, greatly increasing the danger to the ship. The strong eastward current through Drake Passage met the opposing east wind, which made the waves even higher.

Suddenly, a rogue wave nearly seventy feet high washed over the ship; it poured through the bow ports and hawsehole and over the knightheads, and threatened to wash everyone overboard. Captain Matthews ordered all passengers and crewmembers not needed on deck to stay in the galley, saloon, cabins, or fo'c'sle, or lash themselves to the masts. He told Stubs there could be no fire in the stove because the *Golden Lady,* made of wood, rope, and canvas, would be in grave danger should a fire break out.

By midday a terrific wind was howling, rain and sleet pelted the deck, and the decks were awash. The captain ordered, "I need all able-bodied sailors to go aloft and furl the sails afore this God-awful wind rips 'em to shreds. And may God be with ye!"

In the lee scuppers, the water was up to a man's waist. The crew was ordered to double-reef the topsails and furl all the other sails to protect everything. Oliver was terrified! He had climbed the rigging several times, but it was always in fair weather, not during a raging storm. Eight crewmen, including Oliver and Jack, stood on the footrope and stirrups with their arms wrapped around the yardarm and waited for a squall to subside so they could furl the sails. It seemed like hours before there was a slight calm, but it was actually just a few minutes.

The *Golden Lady* strained against the pounding sea, and the violent williwaw that blew offshore from the freezing mountainous coast was increasing. Slanting sheets of sleet, hail, and ice were thrown against the ship with an angry velocity as the wind clawed and ripped at the sails. The wind was so strong it tore at the backs and collars of the sailors' oilskin coats, tearing the edges to shreds.

Oliver clung for his life to the yardarm along with the other sailors. Suddenly, a huge gust made him lose his footing on the footrope and fall backwards. He nearly fell to his death, but just as he felt himself going down, a hand reached out and pushed him back. The hand was Jack's.

Above the roar of the storm, Oliver screamed, "Thanks!" His words fell on deaf ears due to the howling wind.

After several grueling hours, the crew managed to save the sails: they clewed down, hauled out the reef-tackles again, close-reefed the foretopsail, furled the main, and then hove to on the starboard tack. They could do no more, and the ship was left to the mercy of the wind and rough sea. The ship strained at her cables like a chained wild animal, bucking up and down and heeling over, first to starboard, then to port, over and over again. The captain feared that the ship would be dashed against the rocks and they would all perish.

Finally the wind started to die down. Under bare poles, the ship drifted along the coast. The sea was free of ice along the shoreline, and there appeared to be open water ahead, but farther out the sea was a mess of ice and menacing icebergs. Though worried that they might collide with an iceberg, Captain Matthews was determined to make a passage with the first favorable wind.

The next day, the crew had hardly had time to haul down and clew up when the wind hauled eastward and huge squalls came thick and fast. To leeward were gigantic icebergs. The *Golden Lady* plowed into the teeth of the oncoming storm, as waves the height and flow of Niagara Falls washed over the bow and partially submerged the ship.

As the afternoon wore on, it got colder and colder, and more icicles formed on the rigging. The pale sun was hidden by dark clouds, and the remaining stiff sails cracked loudly like heavily starched sheets on a clothesline.

In the hold, grain boxes and barrels floating in three feet of water collided, causing the ship to list to port and their contents spill out and spoil. The crew had to man the pumps continuously. The few remaining chickens, sheep, and goats were brought up on the quarterdeck and put in pens. The damaged cargo and supplies had to be jettisoned, and the few remaining food supplies were rationed.

The crew and passengers grumbled about having less food, and barely edible food at that, but it couldn't be helped. Rough seas made it impossible for Stubs to light the cookstove, so all were obliged to only eat cheese and biscuits.

"Yuck! These biscuits are stale and crawling with insects, and the cheese is rancid and alive with grubs," Oliver said, disgusted.

"Aah, it ain't so bad, Harris said. I've had worse. Just close yer eyes, boy, and pretend ye're eatin' steak and taters at some fancy New York restaurant, washed down with a pint of ale—that we still got plenty of," he said, stuffing a hunk of rank cheese in his mouth and taking a swig of ale. Harris wiped his mouth on his sleeve and said, "Aah!"

After several weeks of the same rotting food, Oliver swore to himself that he would never eat another stale sea biscuit and cheese crawling with insects so long as he lived.

Jack, Mouse, and Oliver slipped and slid across the deck as they hauled a large pot of coffee to the crew and passengers.

Suddenly, a thunderous rumble was heard as a stack of lumber chained to the deck came loose and washed over the side, dragging with it the boom and part of the mizzenmast, making the entire ship shudder, shake, and roll.

Hearing the loud *boom*, Jack, Mouse, and Oliver let go of the coffeepot, and all three hit the deck face-down. Luckily none of them was hurt. The pot rolled away, leaving a trail of steaming coffee.

The severe swaying of the ship provoked a major uproar, and within minutes the deck swarmed with crewmen and passengers who had come to see what had caused it. The old wooden ship had never been watertight, and the violent rocking made a wave of seawater rush over the deck, bringing with it many live fish and an octopus that tried to scurry across the deck and back into the sea. The foul water leaked through successive floors, to end up in the bilge at the very bottom of the ship.

Jack and Oliver chased after the octopus and scooped it into a bucket, along with several live fish, to bring to Stubs for his stewpot.

Although it was possible for the crippled ship to sail without a boom and mizzenmast, the captain thought it best, with the extreme weather conditions and the nearest major port a long way off, to order a jury rig and sail be constructed.

New spars were brought up from the storage room to replace the mizzen sail and other sails that were ravaged in the wind and now fluttered like flirty eyelashes.

The boys scrambled to retrieve the coffeepot. Luckily, the lid was tight and only a little of the coffee had leaked out. Pot in hand, they headed for the quarterdeck where Mr. Harris and Mr. Jones tried their hardest to man the wheel.

Oliver handed each of the mates a mug of coffee. "Thanks for the c-c-cuppa, lads! This sharp wind and cold rain is like a cutlass slashin' at ye," Harris said through chattering teeth. Though he and Jonesy wore sou'westers, they were both soaked, chilled, and bone tired.

"Perhaps someone can spell ye for a while, Mr. Harris, so ye can get some rest and warm up a bit," Oliver said.

"Not 'til me time's up! Then Cap'n can take over."

Mr. Jones said, "Hey, that dog of yers is one smart little fella. Stayed with me for over an hour while I was on watch. Every time me head started to nod, he'd bark and wake me up."

"See? I told ye Frisco was worth keepin," Jack said.

Suddenly, an albatross swooped toward the ship. Jack and Oliver watched it land on the deck, where it shook its wings and frantically pecked at the single window in the galley. When Stubs opened the door, the bird flew in and landed with a squishy thud on the table. He preened his wet feathers, and then collapsed.

Stubs exclaimed, "Gadzooks! It's me old friend Spike! See, he still has the ring I put on his leg, with his name and the name of the ship scratched on it. He must have flown ten thousand miles followin' us." Stubs turned the exhausted bird over, and the albatross closed his eyes as if asleep.

Stubs picked up the great bird and listened for a heartbeat. "He's still alive! Jack, it's gotta be an omen. I know it's just superstition, but some sailors believe that if they see an albatross, he's carryin' the soul of a sailor who's drowned near Cape Horn. If Spike dies, it might mean one of us may be next. Be quick about it, Jack, and wrap Spike in a towel and put him next to the stove so he can warm up. Then drip some fresh water mixed with some o' that boiled fish into his mouth. We got to save him!" Stubs was almost in tears at the sight of his old friend.

Frisco the dog took one sniff of Spike, sneezed, then whined to be let out.

After a while, Spike revived, shook himself as if to clear his head, preened his feathers, and squawked as if to say, *I'm hungry!* Stubs put a dish of maggot-infested porridge and a small piece of boiled fish in front of the wayfaring bird. Rations were low, and it was all he could spare. Spike gulped down the mush and the protein-rich maggots. He then shook himself again and flew off over the ocean.

"Just like him, the ungrateful wretch!" Stubs said.

Chapter 28
Ghost Ship

Stubs stared after the albatross as it flew out to sea. In the distant haze, Stubs spied what he thought was an iceberg shaped like a sailing ship, but it couldn't be. Perhaps his old eyes were playing tricks on him. Stubs asked to borrow Jonesy's telescope and took a second look. It was a ship!

He immediately alerted Captain Matthews. The captain looked through his telescope at the ship; she was a three-masted barque, and, like the *Golden Lady,* her main and mizzen sails had been down-hauled, presumably to avoid damage during the storm they had just survived. He looked for sailors on deck, but there appeared to be none.

The captain ordered the signal cannon to be fired to alert the other ship of their presence, and to have the *Golden Lady*'s American flag raised so the other ship wouldn't think they were pirates. When the *boom* of the small cannon was magnified by the still, cold air, Oliver put his hands over his ears and Frisco whined. The crew waited for a return signal, but none came.

"Perhaps we should send over a skiff," Harris suggested. "There might still be someone aboard."

The cockboat was lowered, and Jones, Harris, Oliver, and Jack rowed across to the mystery ship. Jones tethered the painter to it, and threw a climbing rope with a hook on the end over the railing. The four sailors shimmied up the rope to the deck.

The ship was silent except for a shrill whistling from the rigging. Jones yelled loudly, "Ahoy there! Anyone aboard?" Still no answer. The silence made Jack shiver.

As Oliver tried to make his way across the icy deck, he slipped and fell to his knees. Picking himself up, he said, "This deck hasn't been swabbed for months, and there doesn't seem to be anybody aboard. Maybe she was abandoned a long time ago."

"I say we take a look around. There still may be a survivor aboard who's scared and in need of our help. Suddenly there was a whir of huge wings, and Spike soared to the ship and tried to land. As the albatross touched down, he slid across the slippery deck and crashed into a bulkhead. "Eh, Eh," the great bird mooed, shaking his head.

Stubs had told Jack many stories about ghost ships lost at sea, and she now imagined the albatross to be the embodied soul of a drowned sailor. She also remembered Stubs saying that it was taboo to harm an albatross, because their appearance was an omen that brought good luck to a ship at sea. She hoped it was the latter.

Jack couldn't get the thought of the albatross being a sailor's soul out of her head. The ship was silent except for the block and tackle swaying and clanging against the rigging. Seeing the bleached block and tackle Jack imagined them to be the skulls of the dead sailors. As they whirled and twisted in the wind, the remaining shreds of sail became ghostly apparitions that would lure unsuspecting sailors to their deaths in the frigid Antarctic waters.

Jack let out a scream: "This is a ghost ship! I'm getting' out of here!" With a look of terror on her face, Jack ran to the rope and climbed down to the skiff below.

Harris yelled down to Jack, "Them ghost stories is just an old tar's way of scarin' nubs. Spike ain't the soul of some dead sailor, and ye know as well as I do that block and tackle ain't the skulls o' drowned sailors, so quit bein' a scaredy cat! Spike's been a good-luck charm for our ship since we set sail. He's followed her near 10,000 miles, and none of us has died. The only bad thing that happened is the mast and boom broke, and that could happen anywhere. I'm orderin' ye to climb back up here, Jack. We need yer help!"

Jack, wide-eyed, was hunched over in the skiff. Looking like she was about to cry, she shook her head.

"Jack, ye can stay there for all I care. It's no skin off my teeth, but Oliver, Jonesy and me are gonna take a look round. There may still be someone onboard in need o' rescuin'."

The three sailors explored the ship from prow to stern. As Oliver neared the galley, he heard what he thought was a sneeze and a hacking cough. A voice then screeched, "Help! I'm a prisoner! If ye don't come now, me hearties, I throw it to the fishes!" Then more sneezing and coughing.

What in heck?! thought Oliver.

The galley door was ajar, allowing a ray of sunlight to illuminate the room. Shrouds of dust-covered spider webs clung to the corners of the room, and a thick film of dust covered the table. Suddenly, a rough voice screamed, "Hands up, ye bloody bastard, or I'll… Help! Help! It's a thievin' pirate!"

Oliver raised his hands. There was another sneeze and an awful squawk and whistle.

Oliver turned around to face his assailant. In the corner of the room was a large birdcage, its door wide-open. On a perch inside the cage sat a beautiful blue-and-gold South American macaw. Its round yellow eyes blinked and stared at Oliver, as if the bird didn't believe there was a live human being aboard the ship.

For two years, the macaw had not seen or heard another creature, human or otherwise, except for an annoying rat, his mortal enemy who, during the night, crept into his cage in search of any tiny morsels left by the bird. The macaw had survived on scraps of whatever rotting food was still on the ship, maggots, which were plentiful, fish that had occasionally washed up on deck, and gnats and flies that happened to come his way.

Curious, the bird hopped down from its perch and onto the table, leaving a pattern of chicken-like footprints in the dust. Oliver noticed previous prints among dishes long ago picked clean. Oliver figured the men who were eating the meal had left in a hurry, and didn't think to take the macaw with them.

Oliver took a closer look at the parrot and noticed his wings had been clipped so that he could not fly. Oliver remembered his mother clipping the wings of their chickens, but after a while the feathers grew back and the birds could fly again. The macaw stared at Oliver and nodded its head, deciding whether he was friend or foe.

Oliver lowered his hands and talked softly to the bird, "Why, you're just some sailor's pet bird. I thought ye was a—you gotta be the only living thing on this ship."

The parrot walked over to Oliver and softly brushed his head back and forth against Oliver's sleeve, a sign of affection. Oliver stroked the bird's head. It continued to blink and nod in an up and down fashion, as if saying, Please, Cap'n, take me with ye! If I have to stay on this ship any longer, I'll soon be joining my dead mates." The exhausted bird then keeled over on the table.

Jonesy and Harris came to the galley to report to Oliver that neither of them had found a single living soul aboard.

Oliver said, "Well I have! A talking parrot. Maybe he can tell us what happened to this ship. I wonder what his name is?"

"A parrot? Ye gotta be kiddin', Oliver! Parrots only mimic their owner's words; they don't understand what they're sayin'," Harris said.

Jonesy said, "I knew a parrot once that could imitate the sound of someone knocking on a door, a cat meowing, and a dog barking. Drove the dog nuts."

The parrot suddenly raised his head, looked at his rescuers, and mimicked someone sneezing, "Achoo! Achoo!" All the three sailors laughed.

"*Gezundheit!*" Oliver said. "Well, Mr. Achoo, since ye can't fly and will eventually die of starvation on this ship, you better come with us," he said, picking up the macaw.

Suddenly, there was a loud cracking noise; it seemed the ship was breaking apart. "Best we be gettin' off this ghost ship afore we become ghosts ourselves," Harris said.

They hurried to the rail and climbed down to the skiff where Jack awaited them. "Ye hear that sneezing, moaning, and groaning? She's a ghost ship, all right, prob'ly stuck on the rocks for months, maybe years," she said.

"Jack, don't let your imagination run away with you," Oliver said. "The only living soul on that ship was this parrot that can't fly. I'm going to give it to Stubs to doctor. The ship started to break up while we were still aboard, so we'd better skedaddle back to the *Golden Lady.*"

Captain Matthews took one last look at the ghost ship through his telescope. A thick fog suddenly rolled in, and like magic the ship disappeared before his eyes.

Chapter 29

Crossing Ceremony

Back aboard the *Golden Lady*, Harris offered to take over the helm, but the captain refused to give up his duty before they crossed from the Pacific to the Atlantic. He was determined to attempt a passage with the first favorable wind.

Three days later, they finally crossed the treacherous waters that linked the Pacific and the Atlantic. The crewmen cheered and tossed their caps into the air. "We've done it again, boys!"

Captain Matthews ordered all hands and passengers on deck. "Gentlemen and ladies, he announced, since we've rounded the Horn with no lives lost, I'd say a celebration is in order. "Jack, Oliver, and Mouse, please pass out the cigars and mugs of ale and rum. Now, good people, we'll pour a bottle of champagne—compliments of Mr. Sanders—into the ocean to thank the Greek God o' the Sea, Poseidon, and his wife Amphitrite, Queen of the Sea, for our safe passage. We'll also pay tribute to all those poor souls who were less fortunate, and lastly, we'll toast the nubs who've rounded the Horn for the first time!" the captain said, holding his mug of spirits aloft and staring proudly at Oliver.

The crew and passengers raised their mugs and cheered, "To the nubs! Hear, hear!"

"Also as a tradition for rounding the Horn, two members of the crew will dress up as Poseidon and Amphitrite and dump pails of seawater over the heads of nubs and passengers," the

143

captain said. The hazing was all in good fun, and the captain allowed it as long as it didn't endanger anyone.

Unfortunately, Mouse, who was dressed as Poseidon, refused to heed the captain's rules. Instead of pouring pure seawater over Oliver's head, Mouse let out a sinister laugh and dumped a bucket of foul-smelling bilgewater, rotting vegetables, scraps, and seaweed. Oliver flinched as the disgusting waste oozed down his face and shoulders.

Seeing what Mouse had done, the captain was not pleased. He yelled, "Damn you, Mouse! That was uncalled for. If it were the old days, I'd have ye flogged for that nasty trick."

Mouse knew the captain's hands were tied when it came to disciplining him, because the captain had made a solemn promise to his first wife, before she died, that he would not harm the boy. The captain gritted his teeth and shook his head.

The captain also allowed another tradition: Once a sailor rounded the Horn, he was allowed to wear a gold loop earring and dine with one foot on the table. Later that evening, while Stubs held a sewing needle under the flame on the stove to sterilize it, Jack sat Oliver down in a chair and held a piece of ice to his earlobe to numb it.

"Many sailors can't swim, and they believe wearin' a loop earrin', they won't drown at sea. Also, it'll make 'em have good eyesight. Ye need good eyesight for navigatin' in rough waters," Jack said.

Stubs blew on the needle, and pushed it all the way through Oliver's earlobe into a cork at the back of his ear. After quickly withdrawing the needle, Stubs inserted the earring through the hole.

"Ouch! That hurts!" Oliver yelped.

Frisco the dog watched the entire procedure. When it was over, he barked as if to say, "Ain't I gonna get an earring too? Oliver wasn't the only sailor to round Cape Horn."

"Sure ye can get one, boy!" Jack said. She placed the piece of ice against the dog's ear to numb it, and quickly pierced it with the needle. She then inserted a loop earring that matched Oliver's.

Frisco just shook his head and looked at Oliver, as if to say, "It was just a little prick and didn't hurt a bit, ye big baby!"

Frisco stared at Oliver, Stubs, and Jack with his glossy dark eyes. He curled his lips as if he were smiling, and looked proud to be a sailor who'd rounded the Horn and crossed from the Pacific to the Atlantic.

Chapter 30

The Sting

As the *Golden Lady* sailed the final leg up the eastern coast of South America and the United States to New York City, the captain thought they'd better come up with a plan to get the evidence they needed to prove that Mr. Sanders had stolen the gold and silver coins from the Bank of Hawaii.

Shipboard life was sometimes very boring, especially during the sailors' slack time. To while away the hours, they played poker, dice, and other games of chance.

One day, while he poured a cup of coffee for Mr. Sanders, Oliver couldn't help but overhear the man complain to his wife about being bored and in need of male companionship.

"Mr. Sanders, I couldn't help overhearing that you are bored. Are you a gambling man, Mr. Sanders?" Oliver asked.

"Uh, I suppose so," Sanders replied reluctantly, glancing at his wife.

"Tell you what, Mr. Sanders: on Friday afternoon, the cap'n and some of the crew are having a poker party in the cap'n's quarters. Maybe I could ask the cap'n if you could join them. The only catch is, they don't use chips or paper money. They only use real coins."

"No problem. I have plenty," Mr. Sanders said.

Overhearing their conversation, the detective said, "Mind if I join you in your poker game? I've also been a bit bored lately."

"I'm sure it would be all right with the cap'n if both of you joined the game," Oliver said with a wink at the detective. Oliver thought, *The fish has taken the bait.* Unknown to Sanders, the detective was also in on the ruse.

"Okay, then, I'll let the cap'n know both of you will be joining him for the poker game. It starts at exactly 2 PM, and Cap'n likes to start on the dot, so don't to be late."

Sanders and the detective both said, "I'll be there."

Unknown to Sanders, the captain, Jack, Oliver, the detective, and other players had been planning the ploy for weeks in order to have him reveal his stash of gold and silver. The coins would be the evidence the captain needed to prove to the authorities in New York that Sanders was a thief and perhaps part of an international gang of thieves.

Captain Matthews had asked all the regular players—Jack, Jones, Harris, Stubs, and the detective—to arrive fifteen minutes ahead of time. Oliver would be the dealer. Jack was told to sit in the first seat to his right, and the rest of the players to choose any other seat other than the one directly across from Oliver. That would be reserved for Sanders. Just behind Sanders's seat was an armoire with a mirror that could reflect the image of his cards; but the captain frowned on cheating, and hoped the players could rely on their own wits to win. Jack was the best player, and the captain and other players were counting on her to win the game.

At precisely two o'clock there was a knock on the captain's door. Oliver opened it and escorted Sanders to the remaining seat.

The captain had ordered Stubs to place a decanter of whiskey, a jug of ale, glasses, and a plate of crackers and cheese on the sideboard. He reached for the decanter. "Well, gentlemen shall we begin? First, a toast to our newest player, Mr. Sanders. May he win big tonight!"

"Hear, hear! Jonesy said, raising his glass.

Before the cards were dealt, Oliver asked each player to ante one or more coins into the pot to start—the required money to enter the game. The detective found that he didn't have enough money to buy in, but he stayed to watch the others play.

Oliver dealt the cards. Mr. Sanders was delighted to win the first two games, as arranged by Oliver's clever sleight of hand.

"Looks like ye're on a winnin' streak, Mr. Sanders. Keep it up and we'll all be broke come tomorrow," the captain said with a chuckle.

Harris and Jones each won a hand. Stubs had yet to win, but managed to stay in the game. Soon, Stubs cashed out, but remained in the room to savor his mug of whiskey.

After an hour of play, Jones and Harris announced that they too had to bow out because they had the watch. That left Jack, Sanders, and the captain in the game.

Jack bluffed on the next hand; Mr. Sanders folded, and she won. Jack smiled and raked in the coins. After a while there was a rap on the door and a sailor yelled, "Cap'n, sir, ye're wanted on the bridge now! Somethin' to do with takin' a readin'."

The captain excused himself and left the room. Now only Jack and Mr. Sanders were left at the table. Stubs didn't count, because he had lost all his money early on, and was now happily smoking one of the captain's expensive cigars and nursing another whiskey. The detective sat quietly, eyes focused on the game.

Oliver dealt one card facedown to each player. Both players looked at their cards. Sanders had an ace of diamonds, Jack, the five of spades. Oliver then dealt each of them the first card faceup. Sanders was dealt the ace of clubs, and Jack the deuce of spades. Sanders, not wanting to give away the power of his hand, checked.

Jack also checked.

The next card dealt to Sanders was the three of clubs. Jack was dealt the four of spades.

Sanders bet half of his money and Jack called.

Sanders's next card was the three of hearts—a pair.

Jack got the ace of spades.

Sanders bet half of his remaining money, and Jack called. She had the five of spades, the ace of spades, and the two of spades. The only ace remaining was the ace of hearts.

The last round of cards was dealt. Sanders got the ace of hearts which gave him a full house.

Jack got the three of spades, giving her a straight flush, which beats a full house.

Sanders bet his remaining money.

Jack raised twice what was in the pot.

Sanders thought he had the winning hand, and told Jack that he had something in his trunk that should cover the bet. He told Oliver, Jack, and Stubs to sit tight while he went to get whatever it was. In the meantime, the captain returned.

"How'd ye do, Jack?" he asked.

"It came down to Mr. Sanders and me! He just now went back to his cabin to get somethin' to cover the bet," Jack said.

"That's my girl!" the captain said.

When Sanders returned, he put several silver and gold coins in the pot. "There, that should cover it!" Sanders said.

"Some o' them coins is mighty shiny," Jack said. "Ye sure they aren't counterfeit or stolen? I only want two of 'em; ye can give the rest to the cap'n to pay yer debt." She picked two tarnished coins from the pot.

Sanders narrowed his eyes at Jack, "You accusing me of being a thief or a counterfeiter? I'll have you know, boy, those shiny gold and silver coins are genuine, and each one is worth up to ten dollars!"

"Don't care if they's worth a hundred. I don't want 'em," Jack said. She knew the gold coins had to have come from the stash of stolen coins, and would be easy to trace, so she scooped up all that remained in the pot and gave them to the captain to keep in his safe as evidence.

Addressing Mr. Sanders, Jack yelled, "Don't ye accuse me of cheatin', ye lowdown dunderhead! I happen to be a good gambler, and I won them coins fair and square!"

Sanders said nothing further. He pushed back his chair, stood up, slammed the door to the captain's quarters on his way out, and retreated to his own cabin.

Chapter 31
The Arrest

After nearly three months' sailing the *Golden Lady* finally made it home to New York City and sailed up the East River to New York Harbor. The ship was guided by a tug past Governor's Island near the mouth of the East River, then Ellis Island, where immigrants were housed for medical quarantine and processing.

All the sailors were in awe as the ship passed Liberty Island where the gigantic Statue of the Lady Liberty stood.

Now green with corrosion, the copper statue had been a gift from the people of France. In her right hand, Liberty Enlightening the World held a torch above her head, lighting the way to freedom and liberty. In her left hand she held a tablet inscribed in Roman numerals with the date July 4, 1776, the date of the US Declaration of Independence. A broken shackle used to fasten a slave's ankles together and a chain lay at her feet to show respect for the ending of slavery. Being a black man, Jonesy was especially in awe. For the millions of immigrants arriving by sea in the United States, the statue was a symbol of freedom and hope.

As the *Golden Lady* docked in New York Harbor, two constables from the New York City Police Department raced up the gangplank and requested to see the captain immediately. Captain Matthews appeared and asked what the urgent matter was.

One of the officers said, "Captain, we've been told on good authority that you have aboard your ship a man and a woman with the surname Sanders. The man sometimes poses as a Hawaiian planter. We believe they may be traveling with another couple using the name of Astor. All four are part of an international gang who stole $50,000 in newly minted gold and silver coins from the Bank of Hawaii. Since Hawaii became a United States protectorate, it is now under the protection of the United States.

"For the past six months, our undercover agent, Detective Byrnes, has been tailing the couple who are believed to be on your ship. Mr. Byrnes has been posing as a passenger on your ship, I believe. Once your ship left San Diego and was in foreign waters, we had no authority to arrest the thieves, and the warrant for their arrest was no longer valid. The Sanderses and Astors are part of an international gang of thieves that we are keeping tabs on. One of their gang members shot and killed one of our agents in San Francisco; he was posing as a Chinese clerk in an herbal shop and using the name Kwon. That makes the Sanderses and Astors part of a conspiracy to commit murder. It's unfortunate that they have managed to give our agents the slip—until now."

Oliver and Jack were shocked to hear that the kindly Chinese man posing as Mr. Kwon, the apothecary clerk, had been killed.

"Now that your ship is in New York City and on United States soil, our warrant is good again. If you will allow my partner and me to come aboard, we will arrest Mr. Sanders and the Astors on the spot."

"Sir, first show me some form of identification and the warrant," Captain Matthews said.

"Yes, yes of course. Here is my badge, an official letter from the Bank of Hawaii, and the arrest warrant."

The captain examined the warrant. "Everything seems to be in order. Permission to come aboard is granted, but please make yer arrest quickly. I don't want any of my crew to panic and think one of 'em is in trouble."

"Thank you, Captain Matthews. We'll do our best not to upset your crew."

At that moment, Sanders, his wife, and the Astors emerged from their cabins. Sanders demanded a wheelbarrow to take their heavy trunks down the gangway.

The constables rushed up and told Mr. Sanders, his wife, and the Astors that they were all under arrest for robbing the Bank of Hawaii and for murdering one of their agents. Before they could handcuff the thieves, Mr. Sanders pulled out a belly gun and fired it at one of the officers. Seeing he had missed, he ran hell-bent down the gangway. Sanders saw two more officers running toward the gangplank, so he jumped into the water and started to swim ashore. Stunned, his wife was left on the deck, and was immediately arrested along with the phony Astors.

Luckily, the cockboat with two oarsmen was waiting just below the ship to take the passengers ashore. Byrnes, the under-cover detective, ran to the rail and yelled, "Stop him! The man is being arrested for bank robbery and murder! He just now tried to shoot an officer of the law!"

Mr. Jones dived out of the boat, grabbed the escapee by the collar, held onto him with his muscular arms, and swam the short distance to the rope ladder that dangled from the ship. He held Sanders's arm behind his back and forced him to climb up to the deck, where the detective quickly handcuffed him.

"If I'm correct," Jack said, "you'll find a good many o' them gold and silver coins in one o' them trunks. While we were in Valparaiso, a crewmember followed Sanders to a foundry where he wanted the gold coins melted down into bars. Fortunately, the ship had to leave afore it could be done."

The captain spoke up, "There are also some of them coins in my safe, won from Sanders in a poker game."

Detective Byrnes shook Captain Matthews's hand and thanked him and his crew for their assistance in solving the crimes. "Perhaps at your convenience, Captain, you'll stop by the New York City Police Department and make a statement. Oh, and there's a twenty-thousand-dollar reward for anyone aiding in the arrest of these villains."

The captain just smiled.

Chapter 32

A Last Goodbye

The *Golden Lady* was beyond repair and had to be sold at auction for scrap. The return to New York City was definitely the last voyage for the old sailing ship. With the money received from the sale of her fastenings and fittings, the captain paid his crew at half wages.

As Captain Matthews said his last good-byes to his crew, he shook hands with Oliver and said, "We've been through a lot on this voyage, you and I. And what an adventure it has been. Jack, Sarah and I will never forget ye. I could not have had a better steward and able-bodied seaman, but now's the time to say goodbye and go our separate ways. And, just to let ye know, Oliver, I sent a telegram to yer folks when we was still in San Francisco."

"You knew I wasn't an orphan all along?"

"Not at first, but after we left San Francisco, Mouse told me about a public notice he'd seen in the newspaper that fit yer description, and I had a friend of mine look into the matter."

Oliver thought, *Probably Mr. Kwon, the unfortunate Chinese clerk.* "And you didn't leave me at the nearest port?"

"No. Why should I? At the time, I was in need of a good steward, and wired yer folks about yer whereabouts. They wired back sayin' they thought bein' a sailor might make ye grow up and be more responsible, which I think it has—'cept maybe for some o' the capers ye and me daughter had.

"Sarah, Jack, and I will be stayin' at a little house in Nantucket, at least 'til the babe's born. And Sarah wants Jack to go back to that fancy girls' boardin' school. Imagine me, a sea captain most o' me life, becomin' a landlubber. Just hope I won't be pinin' for the sea like Stubs always did while he was stayin' at that Old Sailors' Home."

"Congratulations, sir! For becomin' a father again, I mean," Oliver said.

The captain pressed one of the gold commemorative coins saved from the poker winnings into Oliver's hand. Thought ye might like a souvenir o' yer adventures."

Now that the long journey had ended, and they were in New York, the captain was concerned for Oliver's welfare. He put his hand on Oliver's shoulder and said, "Take care of yerself, boy. There may be times when there'll be no one to help ye. Look sharp and keep yer wits about ye. I know ye can!" Finally, he told Oliver to wire his parents for the money to purchase a train ticket back to Washington State.

"Well, lad, good luck to ye. May ye always have fair winds and followin' seas. Perhaps fate will bring us together again someday."

Jack too said goodbye to Oliver and Frisco, and promised to take good care of Achoo.

"Ahoy, sailor! Smooth Sailin! Squawk, Squawk!" the parrot screeched.

Part 2

The Balloonist

Chapter 33
On the Street

After leaving the Matthewses, the first thing Oliver did was wire his folks and ask them to send him money for a one-way ticket back home. He was told that it would be several months before he received the funds. In the meantime, he and Frisco, his dog, were left to make their own way on the menacing streets of New York.

Wandering the streets of the big city, Oliver soon learned that some New Yorkers were quite aloof, and didn't care about a lone boy and his dog. Oliver and Frisco had to resort to sleeping in doorways and begging for money from passersby for food, but Oliver wasn't very successful at begging.

One evening, a gentleman dressed in coat and tails and a top hat, and carrying a cane with a silver knob on top, rushed down the sidewalk. Oliver put out a hand to him: "Please, sir! I'm a poor lad alone in this big city. My dog and I are hungry and cold and have no place to call home. Please, won't you give us a dime?"

"Get out of my way, boy! That's not my problem! And if you know what's good for you, scurry back home to your ma, if ye got one!" With his cane, the man shoved Oliver into the gutter. "Now look what ye've done, ye darn ragamuffin! Ye splashed mud on my coat. The man tried to hit Oliver on the shoulder, and Frisco bared his teeth and growled. The man whacked the dog on his back and hurried off. Frisco whimpered and slunk away.

Next, Oliver tried begging from an old woman. She pinched her nose. "Pee-ew! You and that filthy dog smell worse than a pig! Here, take this quarter and find the nearest bathhouse, then get yourself a bowl of soup from the Salvation Army kitchen." She shooed them away by snapping her umbrella open and shut. Scared of the bumbershoot, Frisco barked at her.

"And put a muzzle on that dog of yours."

Frisco growled at the woman again.

One day, a man offered Oliver a dollar to kneel down in front of him. By then, Oliver had gotten savvy and knew what the man really wanted. Stubs had warned him about men who offered to pay for special favors. Oliver accepted the dollar from the man, palmed the coin, and quickly ran away.

After several days on the streets, Oliver came to a corner where a lad no older than he was riding a unicycle. Oliver watched the cyclist do a bunny hop, throw out his legs, and ride backwards, then stay in one place by pedaling forward and backwards while juggling several red balls. The people watching clapped their hands and threw coins into a box on the ground.

Oliver thought, *Hey, maybe people will throw coins in my hat if I do some magic tricks.* He fished in his pocket for the quarter the old lady had given him, threw the coin up in the air, caught it, and rolled it between his fingers in front of the crowd. Then he made the quarter disappear like magic.

"Ah, a magician!" a man said. "My little boy loves magic. I'll give you a dime if you make that quarter disappear again!"

Oliver made the coin disappear and reappear as if it had come out of the little boy's ear. Oliver removed the red kerchief from around his neck, shook it out, and turned it front and back in front of the crowd. He flipped the bandana in the air and voilà! the bandana disappeared. He then made it reappear, but it was no longer red—it was now blue.

When Oliver whistled the tune *Blow the Man Down,* Frisco danced in a circle on his hind legs, which Oliver had taught him to do while they were on the *Golden Lady.* When Oliver stopped whistling, Frisco stopped dancing, barked, and did a downward stretch, as if bowing to the audience. Oliver held out his newsboy hat, and several people dropped nickels, dimes, and pennies into it. A young couple strolling by dropped in a quarter.

Seeing Oliver earning money, the cyclist came up to him and made a fist like he was going to punch Oliver in the nose, but instead gave him a hard shove.

With an Irish accent, the youth said, "Hey, ye bloodsuckin' thief! What's the big idea o' stealin' me thunder and takin' me corner on the street? You and your mangy cur bug off, afore I call a copper!"

Oliver backed away and retorted, "Sorry, I thought it was a free country. My dog and I are hungry and tired and was just tryin' to make a little dough so we could have a bite to eat and a place to sleep tonight! You can take one of the quarters if ye like."

The cyclist, whose name was Nick, looked at the money in the hat. "I'll be takin' one o' them quarters and that dime too! Then we can call it square."

Oliver let out a sigh. He was so hungry he felt faint. The cyclist caught him before he sank to the pavement.

"Hey, hold on there, lad! There's an Irish pub across the street that serves a free lunch every day if ye plunk down fifteen cents for a glass o' whiskey or ten cents for a pint o' stout. That's how lots of us street performers, immigrants, and beggars survive in New York City. But the manager o' the pub is a friend o' mine, see, and he lets me eat for free when I'm down on me luck. Sometimes he lets me sleep in his storeroom, if the weather's bad. He only asks that I slip him a dime or two under the table when I've got it to spare."

Suddenly, the sky turned dark, then a streak of lightning and a loud thunderclap made Frisco jump. "Come on, lad. We best be gettin' to that pub afore this tempest decides to soak us."

Oliver and Frisco followed Nick across the street to the pub. At the door, a tall burly man with a club that he smacked into in his other hand stopped them and pointed to a sign in the window: No dogs allowed! New York State Sanitation Department.

"Accordin' to a new ordinance, dogs and other animals is excluded from restaurants and saloons for the safety o' the patrons. It's part of the new Food and Drug Act that President Roosevelt recently passed. Leave yer dog outside if ye want to come in. I'll watch 'im for ye, if he don't bite," the bouncer said.

Oliver said, "Thanks, mister. He's a good dog, and he won't bite." He patted Frisco on the head. "Sorry, boy, ye can't come in." Frisco whined, put his paws over his eyes, and lay down near the door.

The pub reeked of spilt whiskey and beer, and it was hard to see through the haze of cigar and cigarette smoke. A crowd was lined up in front of the bar, with men of all classes—clerks, businesspeople, proprietors, drummers, lawyers, street performers, and those down on their luck—trying to get to the bar. Several prostitutes, who called themselves barmaids, wandered among the men and offered their services.

Nick said, "At some o' the cheaper bars, they only serve pickled eggs or sandwiches made from moldy bread. That's why everybody and his brother comes here."

Oliver noticed another rowdy bunch that pushed and shoved to get to the free food at the lunch counter and warm up a bit by a potbelly stove before they went back out in the cold. There were only a few tables in the pub, and most customers ate at long boards set on barrels.

At the bar, four barkeeps wiped dirty glasses with grimy rags without bothering to wash them, then refilled them with whiskey or dark beer for other patrons.

When Oliver and Nick finally reached the bar, Nick slapped down a quarter and a nickel in front of one of the bartenders and said, "I'll have two beers, Fitzpatrick! One for me friend and one for me."

"Hello, Nick. See ye're a payin' customer today. That's a change." The barkeep scooped up the coins. "Ye two better hurry and get in line afore there ain't a lick left in the pot," he advised.

The meal consisted of a hunk of bread, corned beef and cabbage, boiled potatoes, and stewed tomatoes. Oliver wasn't sure if it was worth the price of a pint. The bread was stale, the corned beef too salty and tough, and the potatoes mealy, but Oliver was so hungry he gobbled every morsel. He then went back to fill a plate for Frisco.

Nick and Oliver became friends. They worked the streets together for a couple of months, and continued to eat at the Irish pub. One day, after they'd finished their noonday meal, they strolled over to a bulletin board on the wall that held several fliers for special events, listings of merchandise for sale, rooms for rent, church socials, and jobs available. One job particularly interested Oliver: AERONAUT NEEDED TO RIDE BALLOON, JULY 3–4; APPLY IN PERSON TO PROFESSOR LE STRANGE, CONEY ISLAND AMUSEMENT PARKS, SURF AVENUE, BROOKLYN, NEW YORK.

"Hey, maybe we can get work at Coney Island. We gotta go out there," Nick said.

Chapter 34
The Professor

Two days before the Fourth of July, Oliver, Nick, and Frisco rode the ferry to Coney Island. When they disembarked, they walked along the boardwalk until they came to the Coney Island Amusement Parks. Oliver spotted a ticket-taker's booth where they asked whom to see about getting jobs.

"I'm only the ticket taker. You'll have to see the ringmaster in the big top to inquire about jobs. I'm warnin' you, though, he's in a bad mood today. Too many complaints from the performers, and there's a big show this afternoon."

In the main tent, Oliver and Nick spotted a man dressed elegantly in a black top hat, pink hunting coat with tails, a white cravat, skin-tight buff-colored riding britches, and highly polished black riding boots. A petite lady in a tutu and tights was talking to him. She looked angry. Seeing the boys coming, she shook a fist at the ringmaster and left the tent.

The ringmaster looked Nick and Oliver up and down, and asked, "What you two gophers want? Didn't I tell your boss to handle his own problems?"

"Uh, sir, we're not gophers. We saw your ad for circus performers and want to apply," Oliver said.

"Okay, make it quick, what do you do? And don't tell me ya swallow swords or have three legs. We got enough of them freaks," the man said grumpily.

Nick spoke: "No, sir. I do tricks on my unicycle, and my friend here… well, he can tell ye.

"I want to know where I can find Professor Le Strange. I'm here to answer his ad for a balloonist," Oliver said.

"If you are, boy, you gotta be either one hell of a daredevil or a fool! There musta been two dozen men answered that ad, and not one of 'em brave enough to ride the balloon and put up with that eccentric old man. If I was you, I'd turn tail and run, but if you're serious, you'll find the professor over in the back lot," the ringmaster said, and pointed in the direction of a large field.

"See you later, Nick," Oliver said as he and Frisco headed toward the back lot. Parked in the middle of the field was a black Model T Ford. A man was desperately turning the crank on the auto in hopes of starting the engine. When he saw Oliver coming toward him, he stopped cranking, scratched his backside a few times, and yelled, "Dadburn piece of junk! I never should've…!"

The professor wiped his hands on a rag, then addressed Oliver, "You here for the job, kid? Or just another vagrant looking for a handout? And what's with the dog? I told that damn ringmaster not to send me any more lunatics who are afraid of heights. Last fella panicked and puked all over the gondola. Took me a week to get the stink out!"

The professor had won the automobile in a poker game from a man who couldn't pay what he'd lost. He told the professor that he'd recently purchased an $850 automobile, one of the first Model Ts to come off the Ford Motor Company assembly line.

"It's a good one," the professor said, "and it runs fine once you get her started. Guess Mr. Ford didn't get all the bugs out before he put her on the market." He scratched his backside again and said, "Dammit! Every time I sit in that car, I get bug bites that itch something fierce."

The professor didn't know that the first Model Ts were recalled because everyone who sat in one got chigger bites. It turned out Mr. Ford had used Spanish moss for seat padding, and the same moss for the stuffing in his shipping crates. Both the seats and the crates were ideal nesting places for chiggers.

The professor had accepted the automobile from the gambler because he thought he could attach a belt to one of the axles, and thus deliver the engine's power to a bellows that pumped hot air from a fire into his balloon. He got the idea from looking at the circus organ, whose pipes were filled with compressed air provided by a bellows and blower.

"Guess I'm getting too old to pump air into the balloon by hand. Besides, it takes forever. Using the power of the automobile will make it go much faster. I think it'll work, if I can only get this dang engine to turn over!"

Some kids from town were lighting firecrackers near the edge of the field. The loud bangs frightened Frisco, who took off running to the far end of the field. Oliver raced after him, and when he reached the end of the field, he saw a large half-inflated sphere stretched out on the ground. Attached to the balloon by ropes was a wicker basket. The balloon was tethered with ropes to pegs driven into the ground so that it could go up only so high.

"Frisco! Here boy!" Oliver called, but the dog refused to obey. "Independent cuss!" Oliver said. He hoped Frisco would follow as he wandered back to where the professor was working on the car. The professor was again cranking the automobile. He bent over the engine, touched something that gave him a shock, and whirled around. "Dammit!" he said, sucking his finger.

In his right hand he held a wrench, and his face was smudged with grease and dirt. He took off his hat, pulled a red bandana out of his back pocket, and wiped the sweat from his brow. The man had salt-and-pepper hair, bushy gray eyebrows, and a gray handlebar mustache. He wore wrinkled trousers, a collarless dingy-white shirt with the sleeves rolled up, suspenders, and a misshapen derby hat.

Like Stubs, he sucked on the stub of a cigar that had not been lit. A dirty coffee mug was balanced on the running board of the automobile. Not far from it was a red and yellow gypsy wagon that had seen better days. Painted on its side in flaking gold letters were the words PROF. LE STRANGE, KING OF THE AIR, WORLD'S GREATEST BALLOONIST AND WIRE ARTIST.

"Uh, sir. I saw your balloon at the end of the field. She's really a big one."

"That she is. Made her myself. Aiming to take her up this afternoon if I can get this dang machine to work. So, you're interested in the job? Are you scared of heights? Afraid to be a mile up in the air?"

No, sir, I'm not afraid of heights. I got over my fear when I was a sailor on an old sailing ship. I had to climb the rigging often, sometimes during raging storms."

"Know anything about fixing automobiles?"

"No, sir, but sometimes when the pumps went out on the ship, I worked on them. Also I worked at a foundry before I became a sailor, and people often brought in things to be fixed. Maybe I could give it a try." Oliver was intelligent and mechanically minded, but a great deal of his knowledge was self-taught.

"You think you can help me get Old Betsy here started? Without her, I can't inflate the balloon. Been working on her all morning, but for the life of me I can't figure out why she won't run. There ain't a mechanic around for miles that knows anything about fixing autos. The Coney Island Amusement Parks manager won't pay me a dime if I can't make the ascent at four o'clock this afternoon. Worst thing is, I hate to disappoint the crowd who paid to see the show."

Oliver grinned at the old man. "Mind if I take a look at her."

"Suit yourself. Can't do any harm!"

Oliver went to the front of the Ford and turned the crank. As the engine started to catch, he heard a loud backfire like a gunshot, and a cloud of black soot and smoke spewed from the exhaust pipe, making Oliver and the professor cough. The automobile shuddered, bounced, wheezed, and the engine quit.

When the black cloud had dissipated, Oliver said, "Professor, hand me that rag over there. I think I know what's wrong. If she backfires, it usually means the spark plugs are dirty."

Oliver raised the lid to the engine compartment, removed the spark plugs from both cylinders, spit on them, and wiped them off with the rag. He then screwed the plugs back in.

"Hopefully that'll do it, Professor. Try cranking her again."

The professor turned the crank several times and the Model T started up and purred like a kitten.

"Kid, I could kiss you! You're hired! How'd you know what was wrong?"

"Read an article once about Ford's automobiles in *Popular Mechanics* magazine."

"Now that she's running, we'd better get cracking and inflate the balloon or we won't make the four o'clock showtime," the professor said.

Oliver whistled for Frisco. The dog came, sniffed the old man's pant leg, and lifted his hind leg.

"What the hell?!" the professor said, disgusted.

Chapter 35
Balloon Ride

Just before showtime, the professor handed Oliver a flight jacket, thick cotton twill trousers called jodhpurs, a leather aviator's helmet with fleece-lined earflaps, high-top boots, a wool scarf, leather gloves, and goggles.

"Put these clothes on, boy! The higher you go, the colder and windier it gets!"

A crowd of onlookers had gathered at the back of the lot to watch the ascent. The huge balloon was fully inflated and was tugging at its suspension ropes.

"Oliver, you've got to climb into the gondola, now!" yelled the professor.

At that very moment, Frisco leaped into the basket, put his paws up on the rim, and barked loudly. The crowd thought he was part of the act. Oliver could do nothing about Frisco being in the basket, because Professor Le Strange had already untied the ropes that tethered the balloon. Frisco would have to ride with him.

The balloon immediately rose into the air and gained altitude. It got colder and colder; the temperature dropped to below 50 degrees as the balloon rose higher and higher until it attained an altitude of one mile.

Feeling the chill and wind, Frisco whimpered, shook his entire body, and laid his ears back tightly against his head.

"It's damn cold, isn't it buddy?" Oliver picked Frisco up and stuffed him inside his flight jacket. After a short time the dog poked his head out and seemed to enjoy the ride.

The flight was spectacular and the crowd went wild. Oliver and Frisco stuck to the bag until it would go no higher; then Oliver cut loose his parachute to make the drop. It took the 'chute several minutes to nearly reach the earth, and it was soon apparent that he and Frisco were going to drop into the bay.

When they hit the water, they both started to swim toward shore, but Oliver, bogged down by his heavy clothing, quickly tired. Frisco tugged with his teeth at Oliver's jacket to encourage him to keep swimming. A fog rolled in and the water got colder. Oliver reached out to a nearby floating log and clung to it. Frisco climbed up on the log, shook himself, and barked repeatedly to signal for rescue. After what seemed like hours, a motorboat came into view. One of the men in it dived into the water and swam swiftly toward Oliver and Frisco.

When the swimmer reached them, he yelled, "Take off yer jacket and yer trousers and hand 'em to me, and be quick about it!" The voice sounded familiar. Oliver thought, *It can't be!* He shook his head and did what he was told.

The rescuer flipped the jacket and trousers up in the air and smacked them down on the water to create air pockets. Between the air-filled jacket and trousers and a lifebuoy tossed to the trio, Oliver, Frisco, and their rescuer managed to stay afloat until the boat was near enough for them to climb aboard.

"Whew—that was a close one! Sure glad I spotted ye from the shore when I did," the man said, wiping his forehead.

Exhausted and chilled, and hearing the rescuer speak again, Oliver lifted his head, and through chattering teeth said, "J-J-Jack? That y-you? W-what are y-you doing here?"

"Yes, Oliver, it's me. Sarah's gettin' pretty big now, so Father and I decided to take a little holiday afore the baby's born. This afternoon while Father was tendin' to some business, I decided to take a walk along the beach. That's when I seen a man with a parachute drop into the sea. I didn't know it was ye at the time, but I'm sure glad I ran and got help."

Once Oliver, Jack, and Frisco were back at the professor's camp, Oliver lit a fire, and Jack and he sat with blankets wrapped around their shoulders. They drank cups of hot coffee while they waited for their clothes to dry. Frisco was exhausted and fell asleep at Oliver's feet.

As they sat there, a woman walked up to Oliver and handed him a small piece of paper that read, WARNING – THE STATE HUMANE SOCIETY OF NEW YORK DECREES THAT IT WILL BE UNLAWFUL TO SEND A DOG UP IN A BALLOON. IF THIS WARNING IS NOT HEEDED, THE LAW WILL BE ENFORCED. The woman then left without another word. Oliver read the notice, then wadded the paper into a ball and made to throw it into the fire, but he changed his mind and stuffed it in his pocket.

"Say, Jack, shouldn't you be heading back to meet your father? He'll be putting out a search party if you don't return soon."

Chapter 36

Jack Comes Clean

"Uh, Oliver, I ain't been honest with ye. I didn't come here with me father. I ran away from another horrible girls' school the cap'n and Sarah sent me to, and made me way back to the cottage in Nantucket. At first, that school was okay, and one of the girls even tried to be nice to me. Then they started teasin' and playin' tricks on me to get me in trouble with the headmistress. I felt like I was a doomed ship lost in a storm.

"The headmistress was pure evil, worse than some o' the girls. She carried this ridin' crop and would slap ye on the back with it if ye didn't stand up straight or if ye was late for class. She'd say my whole name, "Jacqueline Fiona Matthews, proper young ladies do not sit with their limbs apart and their elbows on the table. She'd swat me with that crop every time she caught me slouchin'. It was always Jacqueline, do this, Jacqueline, don't do that. It's not proper for a young lady of your stature."

"The first time I sat at table and finished me meal, I belched loudly 'cause Stubs told me it was a way of thankin' the cook for the food. The headmistress like to have a fit. Then, when I wiped my mouth on the back of me hand instead o' the white linen napkin on me lap, she had the gall to say I had manners like a pig. Heck, Oliver, how was I to know not to burp and not to use me hand to wipe me mouth on when they's the only manners

I know. And every time I said, 'Dagnabbit!' the headmistress threatened to wash my mouth out with soap. Then one day I couldn't take it no more; and lit out. I swear, I'll never go back to that godforsaken school! No sir, they ain't never gonna make a lady out of me!"

Oliver couldn't help laughing.

"What's so funny?" Jack asked.

"You! Sorry, Jack, I guess where I come from, wiping your mouth with a napkin is second nature."

Jack quickly gave Oliver a friendly nudge in the ribs.

"Oh, Oliver, I've always been a tomboy and proud of it! I guess I'll never fit in with them scholarly bluestockin's. When I was a little girl, Cap'n used to pat me on the head and call me his boy.

Well, to make a long story short, I made me way back to Nantucket in hopes that the cap'n and Sarah would see their way to lettin' me come back for good."

It was evening when Jack arrived at the cottage. A window was open and she could hear the captain and Sarah bickering. "Captain, I love you, but I've had enough! I'm taking the baby and going home to my mother."

Jack didn't want to be in the line of fire, so she climbed in the window and crept upstairs to her old room, where she stuffed a few things in her knapsack. Achoo was sound asleep in his cage in the corner. He stood on one leg, his head tucked into his neck feathers. Hearing Jack, he woke up, let out a shrill whistle, and squawked, "I'm a prisoner! Take me with you or I'll call the cap'n!"

"Shut up, Achoo! They'll hear you downstairs," Jack said.

"Awk! Take me with you! Take me with you!"

"Okay, ye confounded bird, I'll take ye with me, but ye got to be quiet!" Jack opened the cage door and Achoo flew out and landed on her shoulder. Together they climbed out the window and disappeared into the night.

"Ever since, me and Achoo been on the road, Oliver. Then one day I saw an ad in a paper advertisin' jobs with the circus at Coney Island. I thought maybe ye'd seen the same ad. That's why I decided to come here. It was just a fluke that I seen ye drop from the sky and land in the bay. Oh, Oliver, I've missed ye so much. Ye're like the brother I never had."

"It's okay, Jack, Oliver said, patting Jack on the knee. I ran away from home, too. Where is Achoo, anyway?"

"I left him back at the boardin' house we been stayin' at. As far as ye runnin' away, I know. Cap'n told me. That's why I thought ye'd understand."

"What have you been doing since you ran away?" Oliver asked.

"I had a little money saved up, but that didn't last long. To earn a few cents, I swept out saloons after they closed. Sometimes I got lucky and found a penny or two on the floor. Once I found a fifty-cent piece. Achoo and I ate good that night. Sometimes a barkeep give me a sandwich, a pickled egg, or some oyster stew left over from the free lunches they give customers who buy a pint o' beer."

"I know about the free lunches. That's how my friend Nick and I survived when we were on the streets in New York," Oliver said.

Who's Nick?" Jack asked.

"Oh, just another lad who was a street performer in New York City. We both got jobs here," Oliver answered.

Jack continued: "Mostly, I been on the road, sleepin' in barns and under trees, and fishin' for me supper. Once I was so hungry I stole some eggs from a henhouse. Afore I could run away, a bunch of them chickens made a huge ruckus, squawkin' to beat all hell. A farm lady dashed out o' the farmhouse with a shotgun and blasted the side of the barn. I never was so scared. Near wet me trousers."

Suddenly, a blur of blue and gold circled above Jack and Oliver, then landed on Jack's shoulder. The bird hopped over to Oliver and brushed his head against Oliver's sleeve in affectionate greeting.

"Achoo!" Jack said. "I thought I left ye back at the boardin' house. How in the world?!"

"Get out, you dirty bird! I said get out before I roast you for dinner!" the bird screamed, mimicking a woman's high-pitched voice.

Tied to the parrot's leg was a note from the owner of the boardinghouse where Achoo and Jack had stayed the past week. Oliver untied the paper and read, "Young man, when I let you and your nasty parrot stay here, it was out of the goodness of my heart, and you promised to pay me for your room and board at the end of the week. It's now going on two weeks, and I haven't seen a dime. You and that noisy bird are out of here! And don't think you can come crawling back!"

"Oh, Oliver, Achoo and I have no place to stay now. Can we stay with ye? We won't be no bother. Maybe I could get a job with the circus— be a gopher, do laundry, help with the balloon. I'll do anythin' 'cept… well, ye know what."

"I don't know, Jack. I've only been a here a day myself. Okay, I'll ask the professor if you can," Oliver said, seeing the look of desperation on Jack's face. "Here he comes now, but it looks like it's not a good time to talk to him, 'cause he's talking to the ringmaster who manages the amusement parks."

"I gotta hand it to ye, Professor. That was some show! Just like you promised and more! Here's the pay I owe you, plus a bonus for the boy. Adding that dog to the act and having the lad parachute into the ocean was a real showstopper! The crowd went wild! I look forward to seeing what you have planned for your next performance. Gotta get back to the big top, now," the ringmaster said and walked off.

The professor came over to Oliver and patted him on the back. "Congratulations, son! I knew you had it in you, even if it was one harrowing experience. But if you're willing, I promise to teach you everything I know about ballooning, and pay you a whopping three dollars for each performance." He placed three silver dollars in Oliver's palm.

"Professor, that ride in the balloon was thrilling! Guess I've got the makings of a daredevil after all. And that dip in the ocean was nothing compared to the storms I've been in at sea, so I guess I'll stick it out for a while," Oliver said, smiling.

"Welcome aboard, son!" Looking at Jack, he said, "Say, who's your friend?" He looks like he could use a job."

"His name is Jack and he was on the same sailing ship I was on, so he's not afraid of heights either. He has good balance and climbed the rigging same as I did. I owe him a favor, professor, 'cause he was the one who rescued me when I dropped into the ocean. Do you think you might have a job he could do?"

"Mm! Let me see. He's not afraid of heights, you say? Well, if we have a crowd like we did today, I'll need another lad to help. Or perhaps he might want to learn to be a sky highwire artist. If he agrees, consider him hired."

"It's a deal, sir! Thank ye, sir. You won't regret this!" Jack said, excitedly shaking the professor's hand.

"Ahoy, ye old geezer! Time to feed me!" Achoo screamed at Professor Le Strange.

"It's getting dark, so I think I'll turn in. We've got another performance tomorrow, same time. You two can bed down under the wagon or near the fire. Do what you must to keep that bird quiet. I see you've already found yourselves some blankets and beans," the professor said, and headed to his wagon.

Chapter 37

The High Wire

The professor had the circus prop men set stout poles in the back lot with a strong cable strung between them. Rope ladders, like the ones used on the ship hung from each of the small platforms at the tops of the poles. Under the cable on the ground, the professor placed a hay mound and old mattresses so if Jack fell he'd have a soft landing. Oliver and the professor were Jack's spotters; they wouldn't allow him to practice without one of them present.

In the beginning, Jack practiced every day, walking back and forth along the cable with a long pole or umbrella for balance. Before stepping out onto the wire from the small platform, Jack would calm herself by taking deep breaths and imagining she was back on the *Golden Lady* doing what she loved best—climbing the rigging and balancing on the footrope in a horrific storm while helping her shipmates furl the sails.

Since Jack was a small child, she had loved to climb and balance on the rigging of the ship high in the air; so tightrope walking twenty-five feet in the air was a cinch. Sometimes she would become overconfident, whirl the umbrella around like a baton, hop and skip in the middle of the wire, and pretend to lose her balance, which she thought would make the crowd gasp. One day Nick came to watch Jack practice, and Jack asked if he could teach her to ride a unicycle. Jack learned to ride it, but the professor told her she needed a lot more practice before riding the single-wheel bike across a taut rope.

Three weeks later, Jack told the professor she was ready for her first performance on the highwire.

"You sure, kid? I'd never forgive myself if you fell to your death!"

"I know I can do it, professor! Please? I promise to be careful."

"Well, okay, but none of that juggling stuff, or riding that unicycle yet. Once the balloon reaches twenty to thirty feet off the ground, you lower the rope ladder, climb out of the basket, and climb down 'til you reach the platform. We'll string up an extra rope just above the wire that you can grab if the wind gets too much for you. We don't want you risking a fall. Oliver's next ascent is this Saturday at six PM. We'll bill you as the Lady Aeronaut and Wire Artist!"

"Lady Aeronaut! How did ye know I was a girl?"

"Easy. Your hips sway too much for a man, and you've got no cock showing in your pants!"

"If I'm billed as a woman, can I still wear trousers like Oliver's, or do I have to wear tights and a frilly tutu like the trapeze lady?" Jack asked sarcastically.

"Of course you can wear pants! Go ask the circus prop lady for a pair of jodhpurs or a pair of black tights and red shorts like what Oliver's been wearing lately, even though they make him look like a dang black widow spider clinging to the bag. I'd advise you to wear slippers on your feet so you don't rub 'em raw on the wire.

"I don't really care what you wear as long as it's some kind of costume. If the women in the crowd like what you're wearing, you might start a fashion trend," the professor said, and chuckled as he walked off.

That evening during the performance, the balloon reached the end of its tether, which kept it from going any higher. Oliver readied for the drop in his parachute. At the same time, Jack lowered a rope ladder over the side of the basket and climbed, umbrella in hand, down to the small platform.

As Oliver made his drop in the parachute, Jack gingerly stepped from the platform and made her way out to the center of the highwire, where she twirled her umbrella and bowed to the audience below. Suddenly, a blue and gold parrot landed on her shoulder. Jack nearly lost her balance, but she recovered quickly. A girl on the ground screamed, thinking Jack would fall to her death. Actually, Jack was only pretending to lose her balance to thrill the crowd.

The girl's mother said to her daughter, "That's why I don't want you to do that sort of thing at home."

Jack kept her balance, twirled her umbrella, and waved to the audience, then hopped and skipped her way across the wire to the opposite platform, where she and Achoo bowed again. The audience went wild! Jack thought, *Maybe I can get good enough to ride Nick's unicycle across the wire.*

On the ground, the professor encouraged the crowd to throw coins into a basket. He thought, *This is the most money I've collected in over a year!*

Chapter 38
The Rides

The next weekend, the balloon and aerial act was scheduled for 6 PM, so Jack and Oliver decided to have some fun by riding the roller coaster called the Switchback Railway. The coaster cost a nickel to ride, but the operator knew Jack and Oliver and let them ride for free.

They had to climb stairs to a fifty-foot-high platform that brought them to a train that traveled on a track at the top speed of six miles per hour. The coaster carried the cars to the top of the ride, then, through gravity, picked up speed as it flew along the rails and came to a stop at the opposite end of the track. When the train stopped, the riders could either hop onto another train to go back in the direction they'd came from, or walk down a flight of stairs. Jack and Oliver chose to walk down the stairs because the roller coaster seemed like a leisurely train ride compared to being on a sailing ship in a furious storm.

After the coaster ride, Jack and Oliver decided to ride the carousel. The carved wooden horses were bedecked with sculpted flowers and colorful fake jewels that reminded Oliver of the *Golden Lady*'s figurehead.

"I hope the cap'n saved the ship's figurehead," Oliver said. "She was so beautiful!"

"He did! She's stowed away in the loft of the cottage in Nantucket, waitin' to be put on his next ship—if Sarah will ever let him get one," Jack replied.

Does that mean the cap'n's thinking about getting another ship?" Oliver asked.

"Ye know Cap'n as well as I do. He won't be happy as a landlubber for very long. He told me in secret that he'd like to get one of them ships that has paddlewheels powered by steam. Cap'n promised me I could be a crewman on the steamer once he purchases it. You too, if ye want. Problem is, Sarah ain't too happy about Cap'n goin' to sea again."

The next ride Jack and Oliver went on was the giant Ferris wheel. It was billed as the "World's Largest," but it really wasn't; that was just a gimmick to draw customers in.

The next thrill ride they went on was the Shoot-the-Chutes. This was a ride where you slid down a greased wooden flume and into a lagoon. When Jack and Oliver's flat-bottomed boat hit the water, a huge wave splashed up and soaked them.

After that, they strolled to the arcade to dry off. A carnival barker shouted, "Step right up and win a Kewpie doll! Only a nickel for three chances to knock down the milk bottles and win your sweetheart a Kewpie!"

"What's a Kewpie doll?" Jack asked.

"It's a chalkware figurine made in the shape of a doll. I won one at a fair for my little sister. The figure I won was of Mickey Dugan, you know, the funny-paper cartoon character known as the Yellow Kid in the *New York World* newspaper. The term "yellow journalism" referred to him, because the stories about him were made to shock people so they'd buy newspapers."

"I ain't never heard o' no Yellow Kid or yellow press. Course I ain't read many newspapers or books, and neither has the cap'n. Ye know so much more 'bout things than I do, Oliver. Guess ye think I'm just a stupid jackass. Get it? Jack-Ass," Jack said, with an embarrassed grin.

"Maybe you're an ass once in a while, Jack, but you're no dummy. I think you're just fine the way you are." Oliver said, smiling.

For calling her a jackass, Jack gave Oliver a shove. "Maybe you could win me one o' them plaster dolls."

Oliver plopped a nickel on the counter. On the first try, he knocked down half the bottles.

"Try again!" Jack said excitedly.

On the second throw, Oliver knocked down all the bottles. Jack jumped up and down and clapped.

Quietly, the barker said, "Good goin' young fella! Most folks have a hard time knockin' down them bottles, 'cause I fill 'em half full o' sand to make 'em heavier. Here's your prize."

Jack thought, *What a cheat! Lucky for us Oliver has a strong arm.*

Surprised that Oliver could knock all the bottles down, the barker asked, "Say, young fella, would you be interested in joining the Coney Island Amusement Parks baseball team? I'm the manager and pitcher. We play on Sunday afternoons."

"Thanks, mister, but my friend and I work for Professor Le Strange, the balloonist, and we have to perform on Sunday afternoons," Oliver replied.

"Well, if you ever change your mind, you know where to find me."

Next, Oliver and Jack entered the sideshow freak house and gazed at a petrified mermaid floating in some yucky amber liquid. In a cage was a boy whose wild hair stuck out all over his head and face. Over the cage was a sign: WILD MAN FROM BORNEO. As Oliver and Jack neared the cage, the boy roared and growled at them like a mad dog. They jumped back, then laughed because they knew the boy was a circus performer.

At the next booth was a huge automaton called the Laughing Lady. Jack didn't like the robot—her laugh sounded like a flock of screaming gulls, and she looked like Stubs wearing a wig.

Later, Jack and Oliver strolled down the boardwalk. "Oh, look, Jack! They sell saltwater taffy and ice cream in cones. What flavor would you like? We got a choice of chocolate, strawberry, or vanilla."

Jack hesitated, trying to make up her mind. "I'll have strawberry. I ain't never had ice cream in a cone before."

Oliver put two nickels and a dime on the counter. "We'll have two ice-cream cones, one vanilla and one strawberry."

"Comin' right up! I think ye'll like it in a cone. It's like eatin' ice cream and a waffle at the same time. A vender at the Louisiana World's Fair was sellin' ice cream and ran out of dishes. A man in the next booth was makin' waffles, and helped the vendor out by rollin' waffles into cones that the ice-cream man scooped ice cream into. The fairgoers loved it!"

Jack and Oliver sat on a bench to eat their ice cream and stared at the sea. After they'd finished their cones, they decided they'd had enough fun day at the carnival and returned to Professor Le Strange's camp.

Chapter 39
Water Carnival

In the summer of 1898, Barnum and Bailey's Greatest Show on Earth advertised the "Great Coney Island Water Carnival." The Coney Island Amusement Parks manager wanted to improve the act to draw in the crowds. He approached Professor Le Strange with the idea that Jack, who was by then advertised as a lady aeronaut and wire artist, dress in a swimming costume and dive headfirst into Brighton Bay from a platform attached to ropes that hung from the balloon. Then, the platform would be lowered from the balloon until it reached the water. Jack would swim to the platform and climb on, and would then be hauled back up to the balloon.

P.T. Barnum was known for thrilling acts, and his circus fliers advertised, BARNUM & BAILEY GREATEST SHOW ON EARTH! THE GREAT CONEY ISLAND WATER CARNIVAL; REMARKABLE HEADFIRST DIVES FROM ENORMOUS HEIGHTS INTO SHALLOW DEPTHS.

Jack had dived many times from the deck of the *Golden Lady,* and was not afraid to dive from the balloon. Before doing it for an audience, she practiced the dive several times. It became an instant hit and drew large crowds.

After Mr. Bailey died, the Ringling brothers purchased the Barnum and Bailey Circus from his wife, but kept the two circuses separate. The brothers decided to leave Coney Island by railroading across the continent to California. They were as thrilled with Professor Le Strange's balloon and aerial act as P.T. Barnum had been, and offered to take the professor, Oliver, Jack, Frisco, and Achoo with them.

The professor was ecstatic over the Ringlings' offer to travel with them, and immediately packed up the balloon, the parachute, the Model T Ford, the gypsy wagon, and other equipment.

Nearly a year had passed since Oliver had arrived in New York, and he had not heard from or received any money from his parents to buy a train ticket home, so he too agreed to travel with the circus to the West Coast, in hopes that he would eventually reach his home in Washington State and that his family would welcome him back.

Jack, on the other hand, was worried about what Captain Matthews and Sarah might say about her going out West. She said to the professor, "I don't know if I should go with you. What if Cap'n and Sarah get wind of where were goin'?"

"Don't worry your pretty head about it, young lady. I've already wired the captain as to your whereabouts and what you've been doing, and he's okay with it."

Jack thought, *It may be okay with Father, but what will Sarah have to say? Well, I'm not going to worry about it!*

The circus train stretched nearly a mile in length and weighed close to 6,000 tons. Due to its length and weight, the train had to travel at a much slower pace than the new Transcontinental Railway express trains, and had to follow the Northern Pacific Railroad freight line. To let faster trains pass, the circus train would often be sidetracked and have to wait several hours or even days before proceeding. This made for a very long trip, which could take up to two months or longer to reach California. Some of the states the circus train would cross to get to California were Nebraska, Wyoming, Utah, and Nevada.

The Ringling Brothers' circus train had Pullman palace cars for the ringmaster and special guests. It also had sleepers, dining cars, and parlor cars that were decorated with wood carvings and red velvet hangings. In comparison, the performers and circus workers only had uncomfortable wooden benches to sit and sleep on.

Special stock cars had been added for the elephants, lions, camels, horses, and other animals, and flatcars to transport the circus wagons, steam calliope, big top, and various equipment.

During the day, the cars where the workers and performers had to sit were very hot; the only fresh cool air came from opening the windows. When they were open, black smoke and soot blew back from the smokestack, and the passengers would cough and be coated with soot. The air smelled of acrid smoke, animal dung, and people's sweaty, dirty bodies.

There were separate lavatories for the special ladies and gents on the train, but like a ship's Jardines, the ones for the performers and cirkies consisted of a hole in the floor; the waste just dropped onto the track bed.

The professor warned Oliver and Jack not to drink the water on the train without boiling it first, because the towers alongside the tracks were often supplied with contaminated river or lake water. Some of the passengers did drink the water and got sick, which added to their misery.

During a blinding snowstorm in the middle of Wyoming, the cirkies and performers, including Oliver and Jack, had to spend hours digging the train out of a huge snowdrift.

To an untrained observer the train looked like a gigantic black dragon with smoke and sparks spewing out of its mouth as it weaved through the snowcapped mountains. Oliver could see why the Native Americans called a steam train an iron horse that spat fire.

One afternoon on the desert in Utah, the train engineer invited Oliver and Jack to ride in the cab of the locomotive. This was a privilege, because the only train workers allowed in the cab were the engineer and the boilerman. The engineer ran the train and the boilerman kept the boiler stoked with coal.

Jack asked the engineer, "Do ye think I could operate the train?"

"Sure ya can, son. It's simple, but it'll have to be on the condition that your friend there will spell the boilerman so he can take a break."

Jack looked at Oliver as if to say, *Please, Oliver. I so want to drive the train.*

Oliver felt the heat from the fire and saw how hard it was to shovel coal into the boiler, so he gave Jack a nasty sneer, but he agreed to let her steer the black beast.

Jack did a good job operating the train, but when they had to cross over a high trestle with a river below, she relinquished the controls to the engineer and said, "Thanks, sir, It was fun driving her, but I think I'll let ye take over from here."

The engineer took the controls and the train crossed the trestle with no problem. Then he pulled a cord connected to a lever that opened a valve; this allowed compressed steam to escape through an opening in a pipe, which caused a shrill whistle to sound. Jack enjoyed hearing it and wanted the engineer to blow it again and again. Each time the whistle sounded, Oliver clamped his hands over his ears.

At a crossing about four miles farther down the track was a water tower where the train could take on water. As the train approached it, Jack gasped as she heard a loud explosion and saw the water tower blown to smithereens. Timbers and shards of wood rained down on the train. Within a moment, the huge water tank crashed to the ground and spilled a flood of water and debris everywhere, leaving the place in shambles.

The two men standing near the track wore dark blue denim bib overalls, muslin shirts, and square-toed boots, just like the engineer and the boilerman. The only giveaway was that instead of dark-blue denim hog-head hats, the men wore derbies. They also had red bandanas covering their noses and mouths. One of them had a shotgun, which he pointed in the direction of the train. Unfortunately, the two were too far away for Jack, Oliver, and the engineer to get a good look at their faces.

One of the supposed railroad workers swung a globe-shaped red lantern to signal that there was danger ahead and to stop the train. A short distance down the track from the destroyed water tower, smack dab in the middle of the tracks, sat a railway workman's pedal cycle.

"What in blazes are those two up to? And why in hell did they have to go blow up the only water tower around here for miles in this godforsaken desert?!" the engineer shouted angrily.

Heeding the lantern's warning, he tried to slow the train by pulling the emergency brake lever. "Dagnabbit! How do they expect a train this big, goin' at this speed, to stop? We need at least another mile or two to stop her! Charlie, throw out the anchor and pray she holds!" he yelled to the boilerman.

The brakes squealed and sparks flew as the wheels locked and skidded along the track. The passengers and animals were thrown forward, and the wagons and equipment chained to the flatbed cars shifted, but held fast to the cars.

As the train neared the two men, the one with the shotgun pointed it at the engineer and yelled, "Stop this train or I'll shoot!"

The engineer immediately yelled to the boilerman, "For God's sakes, Charlie, it's a goddam holdup! Pile on more coal and let 'er rip! Even if we was flagged down for President Roosevelt, we ain't stoppin'! Hang onto your hats, boys, this train is goin' through full speed ahead!"

As the boilerman shoveled more coal into the furnace, the train accelerated until it reached the incredible speed of 55.9 miles per hour. It crashed through the pile of splintered timbers from the ruined water tower, and hit the pedal cycle dead on with the cowcatcher. The cycle was thrown high into the air where it exploded, showering the track with bits of metal and wood. One of its tires spun across the desert floor like a Catherine wheel.

As the train passed the debris, Oliver and Jack looked back at the would-be robbers who stood, awestruck, beside the track. Both appeared to be in shock, unable to comprehend what they had just witnessed.

Chapter 40

Podunk Towns

When the circus train pulled into a station, even in a small town, a crowd would gather to watch its arrival. For the circus to make money, the ringmaster insisted that the performers do their acts on the spot. He said he'd pay them when they got to California. Within two weeks the supplies on the train had gotten low and food had to be rationed. After a show, the performers would ask the townspeople for food instead of money, and set their hats on the ground for donations.

At the stations where they were to perform, the circus unloaded the equipment, animals, and supplies and set up the big top in a field at the edge of town. The next morning, a parade was held to attract paying customers. The procession was made up of elaborately decorated gold, red, blue, and white horse-drawn circus wagons, exotic animals, clowns, jugglers, unicycle riders, acrobats, highwire artists, and various other performers all in costume. The steam calliope was always at the end of the parade because it was very shrill and loud, and could be heard miles away. Often, children would put their hands over their ears and scream. Dogs, including Frisco, would howl and bark because the sound hurt their ears.

The calliope's sound came from various whistles attached to a boiler. It was played by a lady who hit keys on a piano-like keyboard. The calliope was the distinctive sound of the circus.

One of the most popular tunes played on it was *The Sidewalks of New York,* a song about life in New York City during the 1890s. It was composed by vaudeville actor and singer Charles B. Lawlor, with lyrics by James W. Blake. The performers sang the song as they marched in the parade.

> Down in front of Casey's old brown wooden stoop,
>
> On a summer's evening we formed a merry group.
>
> Boys and girls together, we would sing and waltz,
>
> While the organ grinder played for us on the sidewalks of New York.
>
> East Side, West Side, all around the town,
>
> The tots sang Ring-Around-Rosie,
>
> London Bridge is falling down.
>
> Boys and girls together, me and Mamie O'Rourke,
>
> Tripped the light fantastic on the sidewalks of New York.

At the back lot, Oliver, Jack, and the professor inflated the balloon and set up the highwire equipment. Fliers were handed out to advertise the act.

The circus would stay a couple of days, and then it was back on the train.

One day Jack said to the professor, "I'm getting' really tired of doin' me act at all these Podunk towns. I thought we'd be doin' it only in big cities. We been travelin' for nearly two months now. How much longer 'til we get to California?"

"I'm not sure, girl. I was just thinking: If we'd gone by steamship to California, we'd be halfway there by now. I believe we'll cross the high desert of Nevada next."

"If that's so, once we cross Nevada, we've only got the Sierra Nevada mountains to go over and we'll be in California," Oliver replied, excited.

Oliver was right. By late afternoon on the next day, the train had arrived at the freight station in Sacramento, California, for a short stop, and then pushed on toward San Francisco.

Chapter 41

Back In Washington State

When the circus train arrived in San Francisco, Jack, Oliver, and Professor Le Strange decided it was time to strike out on their own. Oliver was anxious to return to Washington State to prove to his father that he had become a responsible young man. It had been two years since he'd seen his family, and despite what they'd thought of him when he left, he missed them, especially his little brother Stanley.

With a half-smile, the professor said, "Boy, go home to your folks, and take that mangy cur with you! Every time that dog comes near me, he thinks he can pee on my pants leg.

The Professor said, "We know ye'll miss us, but don't worry about Jack, Achoo, and me. We'll stay with the circus, at least 'til something better comes along. Maybe we'll even pack everything up and come up to Washington ourselves one of these days."

"Or," added Jack, "if we get tired o' the circus, maybe we can get work as sailors on one o' them newfangled steamers that transport goods up and down the coast."

Oliver shook hands with the professor. "Thank you, sir, for everything you taught me about ballooning. I'm sure this won't be the last time we see each other," he said.

Oliver then went to Jack, hugged her, and gave her a peck on the check.

"Dagnabbit, Oliver! I told ye before, I don't like that mushy stuff! Now leave, ye chowder-headed, batter-brained landlubber, afore I do some girly thing like cryin," Jack said, trying her best to hold back tears.

That very afternoon, Oliver and Frisco caught a steamship headed to Seattle, Washington. Once the ship got there, he and Frisco walked halfway to his home in Centralia, then hitched a ride with a farmer who took them the rest of the way in his wagon.

They approached his parents' house, but Oliver hesitated, but then timidly knocked on the door and waited. His mother, Mary, opened the door and stared in awe at her long-lost son. For a moment she was tongue-tied. Frisco broke the ice by barking and dancing around on his hind legs to the delight of Oliver's youngest brother, Stanley, who was standing behind his mother. Mary then reached out and hugged Oliver. "Welcome home, son! Who's your friend?"

"His name's Frisco. I rescued him after I guided the ship into the Port of San Francisco."

"Oh, Oliver, I've missed you so much. I've been worried sick about you, but from the letters and wires we received from Captain Matthews and Professor Le Strange, it sounded like you were in good hands. Well, just don't stand there, son, come in. Supper is almost ready, and we are all anxious to hear about your adventures."

Oliver's sister, Phoebe, and his two brothers, Theodore and Stanley, were delighted to see their brother and his little dog Frisco. Oliver's father was rather standoffish, and didn't say much. Oliver hoped he would come around later.

At the supper table, Theodore said, "Oliver, tell us all about your adventures, especially what it was like going around Cape Horn and being a balloonist?"

Stanley added, "Weren't you scared during the storms and going way up in a balloon? The last storm we had, I hid under my bed."

"I was a little scared, but I soon learned to climb the ship's rigging, which got me over my fear of heights. Eventually I turned out to be an okay sailor. I wasn't a common sailor, because the captain made me his steward, but I still had to be one of the crew if he ordered, "All hands on deck!"

Captain Matthews acted like he was rough, but under that exterior he was actually a kind man. He even taught me some navigation and let me take the wheel sometimes. Once during a violent storm while the ship was rounding the Horn, the other sailors and I were ordered to furl the sails, which means take them down. Eight of us, including a boy named Jack, were balanced on what was called the footrope while we worked. Suddenly a huge wind came up; I lost my balance, and I was swept backwards and almost fell to my death. Luckily, Jack was right next to me, and reached out and caught me. I owe him my life."

To earn extra money before our long trip to New York, we first stopped at Cape Mendocino on the northern coast of California to pick up a load of lumber. Then we sailed to Hawaii, where we picked up a cargo of sugar and pineapples to take to San Francisco. The people there were still recovering from the earthquake; they needed building materials, so we unloaded lumber there too. The next port was San Diego, California, where the captain and his new wife went to a fancy hotel for their honeymoon. From there we sailed to Valparaiso, Chile, then around the Horn and up the eastern coast of South America and North America to New York.

"There, because I wasn't afraid of heights, I got a job at Coney Island Amusement Park with the balloonist Professor Le Strange. The first time I went up in the balloon and parachuted down—"

Phoebe interrupted, "You came down in a parachute?"

"Yes, he did, Phoebe. Let your brother go on with his story," Oliver's father said.

"Yes, Father," Phoebe said.

Frisco was under the table, hoping someone would drop a scrap of food. Phoebe snuck a bit of meat off her plate and dropped it. Frisco gobbled it up and nudged Phoebe's leg for another morsel.

"Well," Oliver continued, "the first time I came down in my parachute I landed in a bay. Frisco was with me, and we hung onto a floating log 'til a boat came to our rescue. One of the rescue workers dived in the ocean and swam to the log. I couldn't believe it—the rescuer was my old friend Jack from the sailing ship. Jack has saved my life twice, so I really owe him."

"Uh, Father, Mother, there's something you should know about Jack. You see, Jack is a girl. The first time I met her she was dressed like a sailor and acted like one, so I thought she was just one of the boys. I later found out Jack was the captain's daughter. She may act like a common sailor at times, but she's really a pussycat and is my best friend. Her real name is Jacqueline. Jack's ma died when she was a baby, and she grew up on the ship. She never knew any other way of life. If it weren't for Jack… well, she was the best sailor on the ship. She taught me a lot and always had my back. I'm truly going to miss her, and I hope to see her again someday," Oliver said, staring sadly at his plate.

Oliver told his parents about Jack because he hoped they would accept her for who she was if she ever came to Washington State.

"Sounds like that gal had spunk and was an all-round good person. I wouldn't mind meeting her someday myself," Oliver's father said, his comment surprising Oliver.

"Oliver, are you in love with this girl? Theodore asked.

"Is girls all you think about, Theo? No, we're just good friends. She had my back and I had hers when we were on the *Golden Lady*."

Oliver said nothing more of how he really felt about Jack. Also, he didn't tell his family about his and Jack's escapade with the bank robbers; he decided to save that story for a later time.

Chapter 42
Back to Work At the Foundry

After a couple of weeks at home, Oliver got back his old job at the foundry. The doors to the foundry were wide-open, exposing the sheet-metal and blacksmith shop. Oliver was at the forge, where he pound the tip of a red-hot rod, twisting and shaping it as part of a wrought-iron fence to be put around a grave in the town cemetery. Oliver's sleeves were rolled up, revealing his tanned muscular arms. He wore a heavy leather apron, goggles, and leather gloves to protect himself from flying sparks. Every so often he stopped pounding the metal and quenched the rod in a barrel of water so the metal would not become brittle and break. Beads of sweat dripped down Oliver's forehead, and his wavy hair was plastered against his forehead.

His brother, Theo, older by two years, leaned against a support post and chewed on a piece of straw while trying to talk with Oliver about a girl. Theo was dressed in a straw boater hat and a three-piece suit with a gold watch fob that dangled from a chain. He worked as a clerk at the Mechanics Bank in town, and preferred to not get his hands dirty. Theo had a high opinion of himself and thought women were supposed to fall in love with him at first sight. He gloated over having more experience with women than Oliver had. The boys were best friends, though they often disagreed on things.

"Hey, Theo, I hear you got a date this afternoon with the town vamp, Viola, or should I say tramp? How did you manage that one, promise to chop firewood for her pa?" Oliver teased.

"Yeah, so what? And for your information, she ain't a tramp, and I didn't have to buy her anything this time. Just used my good looks and charm, old man, which you could use some work on yourself," Theo said smugly. He looked at his right hand, casually blew on his curled fingers, and buffed his nails on the lapel of his jacket.

"So, how much is the gold digger taking you for this time? Bet she wanted to go to that expensive new restaurant in town that would cost a month's wages," Oliver asked with a smirk.

"So what if I promised to take her there. She even said she'd wear a new hat with a white egret feather on it, just for me. It's the latest fashion."

"Yeah, prob'ly some other sap bought it for her," Oliver said. "Theo, where are you gonna get the money to take her out? You know Pa's been out of work for the past six months, and Ma needs every dime we make to feed the family."

"So what if I'm taking a little share for myself. I earn it don't I? Having to stand eight hours a day behind that cage at the bank ain't easy, you know. Wise up, little brother. What Ma and Pa don't know won't hurt 'em. Besides, it's worth it to kiss a girl in the moonlight. But I guess you wouldn't know about that sort of thing, since the only girl you ever took out was your cousin, and she was a real dog."

Oliver wanted to hit Theo, but changed his mind when Stanley and Frisco suddenly burst into the shop. Stanley tried to dash past Theo and get to Oliver, but Theo snagged him on the run.

"Whoa, there, Squirt! What's the hurry?"

Stanley struggled to be released from Theo's grasp. "I got to talk to Oliver. Please, Theo, let me go!" Stanley begged. He wriggled free of Theo's hold and rushed up to Oliver. Frisco, excited by Stanley's shouting, barked sharply.

Oliver yelled at the dog, "Quiet, Frisco!" The dog became silent and slunk away to a corner of the shop where he lay down on the old burlap sack on which he'd spent many an afternoon since Oliver had returned. Oliver threw a horse's hoof trimming to the dog, who greedily chewed it up.

"Okay, Stanley, take a deep breath and start over."

"Oliver, there's a balloonist at the fairgrounds. Says he knows you and will give us a ride in his balloon if you could fix his machine by 4 this afternoon. I told him you worked at the foundry and could fix anything." Stanley tugged on Oliver's sleeve. C'mon, Oliver. Please?"

Oliver thought, *It must the one and only Professor Le Strange. How in the world did he get here?*

"Stanley, was there a girl about my age with him?"

"Yes. She does a highwire act and is a Lady Aeronaut. A picture on a poster showed her with an umbrella tiptoeing on a highwire way up in the air."

Oliver thought, *Jack! How I've missed her!*

"Now, Squirt, you know I can't just up and leave the foundry anytime I want. Old Man Symon will have my hide if I do. Remember the last time I left early? He had a conniption fit and told Pa. I can't afford to lose my job, not with Pa out of work."

Theo looked at his pocket watch. "Oh, go on Oliver," he said. "You got plenty of time. It's nearly the dinner hour, and Old Man Symon won't be back 'til two. He'll just pop in as usual, make one of his nasty comments, and leave again. He won't fire you anyway, 'cause you're the only one in town who can fix things. Go on, you lunkhead. I'll watch the shop while you're gone."

"Oh, please, Oliver?" Stanley begged, tugging on Oliver's sleeve.

"Oh, all right, Stanley, but we've gotta be back before two. I'm only doing this 'cause you're my favorite brother," Oliver said, trying to get a rise out of Theo.

"I'm your favorite brother?! I guess Theo doesn't count 'cause he's the oldest, and Phoebe's a girl," Stanley said.

Oliver laughed, ruffled Stanley's hair, and palmed a nickel from his ear. Here, this is for you to get some cotton candy while we're at the circus. Stanley smiled at Oliver and put the coin in his pocket.

Oliver took off his apron, washed his hands with a bar of homemade lye soap, and dried them on a grimy rag.

"Okay, let's go, Squirt!" As the two headed out the door, Oliver said to Theo, "Thanks, Theo. Once in a while you're okay."

"Don't mention it, old man. Just remember to get back before Symon does, and before I have to leave for my date with Viola. Oh, and, Oliver, you owe me one!"

Oliver thought, *Yeah, and you won't let me live it down, either.*

Oliver and Stanley rushed down the street toward the fairgrounds, Frisco running after them. The storefronts were decorated with red, white, and blue bunting and American flags for the 4th of July. The street was alive with sound: horses whinnied, tack jingled, and the wheels of livery wagons, carts, and buggies clattered.

Suddenly, a black Model T Ford whizzed down the road; it kicked up clouds of dust and left a trail of black smoke in its wake. It continued down the Main Street, wove among the horse-drawn carriages, and backfired when it reached the end of town. The loud *bang!* frightened Frisco, who raced up the road to a field where he lay down and put his paws over his ears.

Oliver got a glimpse of the driver and passenger and thought, *No, it can't be! The professor and Jack? What are they doing here?*

As the auto headed to the fairgrounds, the driver squeezed a rubber blub attached to a horn, which sounded—Ah-ooga!

Ah-ooga!—to warn other drivers and pedestrians to get out of the way.

By the time Oliver, Stanley, and Frisco reached the fairgrounds, it was nearly noon. A rowdy crowd had gathered to listen to a politician who stood on a soapbox and addressed the audience: "Vote for William Howard Taft, the man whose initials, T-A-F-T, stand for 'Take Advice From Theodore,' meaning President Theodore Roosevelt," the man shouted. Taft weighed 300 pounds and hated campaigning. While his wife, Nellie, and Teddy Roosevelt campaigned for him, Taft promised to lose thirty pounds playing golf.

The bars were open early. A drunk staggered out of one, whooped it up, and tried to start a conversation with anyone who'd listen. On the wall of the livery stable was a handbill that advertised the carnival and balloonist at the fairgrounds: Ferguson and Barnes Family Circus, Featuring World-Renowned Balloonist, Professor Zacharia P. Le Strange & Lady Aeronaut on the Highwire. Performance at 4 pm.

"C'mon, Stanley! My lunch hour is half over. If I don't make it back to the foundry in time, Old Man Symon will skin me alive," Oliver said. He took long strides toward the field where the big balloon swayed gently in the wind, causing it to tug at the ropes that tethered it. Stanley held on to his big brother's hand and ran as fast as his short legs could carry him.

The professor saw them coming and waved. "Jack and I arrived here two days ago. Achoo is here too. We just came from town where we were picking up supplies."

"Yeah, I think you passed us in your automobile," Oliver said.

"We were gonna go to your house to surprise you, but we didn't know where you lived. We were gonna ask you to—" Before the professor could finish his sentence, Jack ran up to Oliver and threw her arms around him.

"Oh, Oliver, I missed you so much! I thought I'd never see ye again. Well, we're all here now! And the professor and me was hopin' ye'd become a part of the act again. It just ain't the same without ye."

"I can't, Jack! My ballooning days are over. Jack stepped back from Oliver, appalled to hear his words.

"Jack, you gotta understand, now that I'm home my life has changed. I can't say for the better, but the thing is, my father's been out of work for some time now, and my family needs me to help provide for them."

"I'll pay you four dollars a performance. That's a dollar more than I paid you previously," the professor said, hoping it would entice Oliver to return.

"Hey," Jack said, miffed, "that's two dollars more than I get for doin' just as dangerous an act, maybe more, 'cause I gotta balance on the wire, and that takes a lot more concentration! Oh, to heck with yer family, Oliver. They didn't even come to get ye when ye was left all alone in New York. And what about all them nights ye was cryin' in yer bunk 'cause ye was homesick? Yeah, I heard ye!"

Tears welled up in Jack's eyes; she frowned as she remembered her own loneliness at the boarding school, and now missed the captain. Jack bent down and petted Frisco on the head for comfort and said to him, "Maybe ye could be in the act, and we won't need Oliver."

Frisco looked like he was saying, *If Oliver ain't in the act, I ain't either.*

At that moment, Achoo landed on Frisco's back. The dog barked happily to see his old friend, even though at times the bird bugged the heck out of him.

Turning back to Oliver, Jack begged, "Please, Oliver? We thought ye'd jump at the chance to be a balloonist again!"

"It's not that I don't want to. It's just… oh, to hell with working at the foundry. I was thinking about quitting anyway, 'cause I hate Old Man Symon, the owner. He's always finding fault with me, and he doesn't pay me enough to keep me there anyway. If you still want me in the act, I promise I'll be back here for the four o'clock performance."

"Ye won't regret this, Oliver! I promise you!" Jack said.

"I'd better get Stanley some cotton candy as a bribe, so he won't tell my folks about my quitting. My father can be pretty harsh at times. C'mon, Stanley, let's go! Come, Frisco!"

Chapter 43

The Performance

At precisely 4 PM the professor used a speaking trumpet to address the crowd standing below the balloon. "Ladies and gentlemen and children of all ages, I present to you Oliver, King of the Air, and his dog, Frisco, who will ascend one mile in the sky and then make the drop in a parachute. And the daring and thrilling Lady Aeronaut and her Parrot, Achoo, who will perform an aerial act on the highwire! For the sake of the performers, I ask you to please remain silent during the performance."

Oliver and Jack bowed to the audience, and Oliver climbed into the basket. As part of the act, Frisco raced to the balloon, made a huge leap, and landed in the basket, where he put his paws up on the rim and barked. The professor let loose several of the tether ropes and the balloon rose into the sky. The spectators below shielded their eyes from the sun, clapped their hands, and let out an awestruck "Ooh!"

The balloon rose higher and higher until it reached the end of the stout main rope, a mile in the sky, where it jiggled slightly and settled, held in place by several other ropes anchored to the ground.

Oliver fastened on his harness and parachute, tucked Frisco in his jacket, and jumped over the side of the basket in a freefall toward the crowd. Several cameras clicked. A little boy whooped and clapped, and his mother quickly shushed him as everyone in the audience held their breath. Halfway down, Oliver pulled the ripcord, and the mushroom-shaped parachute opened up and allowed him and Frisco to float gracefully to earth. The audience went wild, cheering and clapping.

Upon landing, Frisco raced to the platform where Jack picked him up and climbed up to the platform. Now it was her turn to perform. Under her costume, Jack wore a harness that she attached to a thin guywire over her head. From the platform, Jack tiptoed onto the highwire, where she balanced for a moment. She then took several steps forward along the wire, bounced up and down, leaped, and, to woo the audience, pretended she had lost her balance. Then she continued to walk to the other end of the cable. From its opposite came a couple of barks and the sound of someone sneezing.

Professor Le Strange announced, "Ladies and gentlemen and children of all ages, here come Jack and Oliver's animal friends Frisco and Achoo! Frisco climbed aboard a small platform on wheels and sat patiently waiting for the parrot. Achoo flew up in the air, circled, and landed on the top of Frisco's head. With Achoo balanced there, the small platform glided across the highwire, drawn by a rope and pulley. At the middle of the wire, Frisco stood on his hind legs and danced to the sailor's shanty *Blow the Man Down,* while Achoo flew in circles above him. Unknown to the audience, the small platform was held in place on the wire by a counterweight that hung below as the platform was pulled along.

Once Frisco and Achoo reached the opposite end of the wire, the dog hopped off the small platform and onto the larger one. Achoo flew up in the air, circled overhead again, and landed on Jack's shoulder. She picked up Frisco in her arms, and together Jack, Frisco, and Achoo bowed. The audience went wild!

Unknown to Oliver, his parents, two brothers, and sister were in the crowd. After the performance, they made their way to Oliver and Jack. Oliver's father shook his hand. "That was some performance, son! I didn't know you were so brave. And, young lady, you are also to be congratulated for your performance," he said.

Professor Le Strange approached. "You can be proud of your son, sir. He has nerves of steel and a passion for what he loves to do. If I were you I would not discourage him."

"Mother, Father, I'd like to introduce you to Professor Le Strange who owns the balloon and runs the show. And this is Jack, I mean Jacqueline, who is my best friend."

"Nice to meet ye, sir, ma'am," Jack said.

The professor handed Oliver four silver dollars, and Jack only two, for their performances. Jack scowled and said under her breath, "It ain't fair. Why does Oliver get four dollars and I get only two? Me act is just as dangerous. The professor's just tryin' to save a buck. If he hadn't billed me as a 'Lady' Aeronaut, I bet I'd get the same pay."

Oliver noticed Jack looking at his four dollars and her two. Oliver clasped Jack's hand, leaving one of his silver dollars in her palm. Jack tightened her fist around the dollar. "Feel better now?" Oliver whispered in her ear. Jack nodded and smiled at him.

Oliver's father also saw the four dollars his son had received. "You get that much for just one performance!"

"Yes, sir. The ringmaster and the professor think I'm worth it," Oliver said.

"He certainly is," the professor said, "and so is Jack. If I could pay them both more, I would."

"Well, Oliver, I can see that you really like this job and have really grown up since leaving home the first time. So, it's okay with me if you quit your old job at the foundry and continue to be a balloonist."

Oliver smiled at his father and at Jack. "Thank you, sir," he said. He quickly raised his eyebrows, then lowered them, and said softly to Jack, "My old man has finally accepted me for who I am."

"Yeah, and did ye see his eyes pop when he saw how much money we was makin'?"

Chapter 44

The Pact

Back at Oliver's family home, there was a knock on the door. Oliver opened it and there stood the professor and Jack. "Your father invited us for supper. Oliver, I missed ye somethin' awful! I was really glad ye decided to join us for the balloon act this afternoon."

"Come in. Come in. You're both welcome," Oliver said with a smile.

A short time later, there was another knock on the door. Jack opened the door and to her surprise there stood Captain Matthews, Stubs, Harris, and Jonesy. "What are ye all doin' here? Father, I thought ye'd be with Sarah and the baby in Nantucket."

The captain lowered his eyes. "I'm sad to say that's all over with, Jack. Sarah and I just couldn't see eye to eye. Her bein' a landlubber and me a devoted seaman just didn't mix. We both knew it. After ye left, she made me her soundin' board. She'd say, "Captain Matthews, don't put your feet on the new sofa. Captain, we do not slurp our soup. Captain, don't talk so loud, you'll wake the baby! It got so I hated to set foot in the house.

"Then one day we had this terrible fight and I couldn't stand it no more. I told her, 'Sarah, ye know the sea is me first love; I can't be happy as a landlubber, so I guess it's goodbye for now,' and I up and left. "Don't worry, Sarah and the baby will be all right. They're with Sarah's mother, and I promised I'd send Sarah money whenever I can, and to check on 'em every so often. Maybe what happened between us is for the best!

"The next day, I looked up Stubs, Jones, and Harris, and the three of us caught the Transcontinental Railroad Express train to San Francisco. Only took us four days, compared to four to six months to get there by sailin' ship.

"It seems Stubs was unhappy about havin' to go back to the Old Sailor's Home; and Harris and Jones, still bein' fairly young, were scared of bein' shanghaied and made to serve under some cruel captain, and not bein' able to come home for years."

Hearing the captain's voice, Oliver came to the door and said to the four travelers, "Come in, come in and meet my family. I've told them all about you." Frisco came to the door and barked, happy to see the sailors again. Achoo flew at Stubs and landed on his shoulder.

With Oliver's family, the professor, Jack, Stubs, Jones, Harris, and the captain, it was a party at the supper table. Having the ship's crew with him again made Oliver feel like part of a big happy family.

After supper, Stubs, Jones, Harris, and the professor said they had to leave. Oliver and his family and Jack and the captain then retired to the parlor. Oliver's father got out his fiddle and played a tune. Oliver asked, "Father do you know the sea shanty *Blow the Man Down?*"

Hearing the tune, Frisco again danced round and round on his hind legs, while Achoo balanced on the dog's head. Everyone clapped and laughed.

Afterward, the captain took Jack and Oliver aside. "I want to show both of ye somethin' I think ye'll like, but ye gotta come with me now! Bring the dog and bird too."

Jack and Oliver were curious. They excused themselves from Oliver's family and followed the captain outside. From there they caught a cab to the wharf, where a steamship with paddlewheels on both sides was moored. The name on the ship was *Aurora.* Stubs, Harris, and Jones waved from the deck.

"Thought ye might want to spend the night on 'er, for old time's sake. Don't say anythin' yet.

"Cap'n, who owns this ship?" Oliver asked.

"Ye're lookin' at 'im. Bought her with the money from the sale o' the brass and fittin's on the *Golden Lady,* and the reward money from turnin' in them robbers. I purchased her first thing when we got off the train in San Francisco. Stubs, Jones, and Harris was just as excited as I was to be goin' back to sea, so the four of us sailed her up here. She was recently refitted and is seaworthy, if ye're worried about that."

The steamer's enclosed paddlewheels could move at various speeds, which made it easier for her to make turns than most schooners, and even allowed her to back up. This made it possible for *Aurora* to enter small ports, called dogholes, where bigger ships like the *Golden Lady* could not go.

"Mm! You say you used the reward money to buy this ship? Then the way I see it, Cap'n, since Jack and I had a big hand in capturing the thieves, we should have half ownership," Oliver said, with a sly look and a wink at Jack.

"Thought ye'd say that. So, what do ye say? Want to join us? Course we won't be makin' any long journeys anytime soon, like sailin' around the Horn. Thought for a while we'd pick up cargo on the coasts of California, Oregon, and Washington, than perhaps head north, maybe to Alaska. I hear some folks decided to stay there after the gold strike, and are needin' supplies."

Jack was taken aback by the offer, "Uh... what about the professor and the balloon act? We'll be lettin' him down if we quit now."

"Oh, I think he'll understand," said Oliver. "Besides, with the money he's made from our acts, he'll get along just fine."

Oliver and Jack stared at each other, and Jack said, "Aye-aye, Cap'n! It'd be a red sky in the mornin' if we didn't say aye! Ye can count on us to be here on the first tide."

Early the next morning, Oliver, Jack, Frisco, and Achoo joined the crew of the *Aurora.*

Achoo squawked at Frisco, "Aye-aye, Cap'n. Don't kill me, ye bloody fool!"

Suddenly an albatross landed on the deck.

Part 3

Aboard the *Aurora*

Chapter 45

The Aurora

Oliver and Jack accepted the captain's offer to be part of the crew of the steamship *Aurora.* Three days later, Oliver, Jack, Frisco, and Achoo headed to the wharf. In the distance they saw a plume of black smoke rising into the air.

C'mon, Oliver, we gotta hurry. I think the ship's on fire!" Jack yelled, and ran toward the dock.

When they reached the *Aurora,* they could see that the plume was coming from her smokestack. Suddenly, they were shaken by a long blast of the ship's whistle. "Whoo-ee!" the whistle sounded, which meant the ship would soon get underway. It reminded Jack of the whistle on the circus steam train.

Frisco whined and put his paws over his ears, and Achoo shrieked, "Bloody Hell! Blow me down with a feather!"

From the dock, Oliver and Jack stared out at the double-paddlewheel steamer. She was a fairly small coastal packet, 169 feet in length, and had two masts, one at the fore and one aft. The space between the masts was reserved for the smokestack and two paddlewheels, one on each side of the ship.

Oliver remembered Captain Matthews saying that the ship had recently been refitted and made seaworthy. She'd had a new steam engine installed to run the paddlewheels, which made it possible for her to travel long distances. The steam also made the whistle blow and drove other mechanical devices on the ship.

The steam was made by boilers—huge copper tubes with two flues and a firebox. The boilers were filled with water, and the fire was stoked high enough to turn it into steam.

The upper sections of the paddlewheels stuck out of the water; they were covered with paddle boxes to keep seawater from splashing up onto the deck. Inside the paddle boxes were the paddles, or buckets, which gave the steamer extra speed when she needed it. Painted on the sides of the paddlewheels in large gold letters outlined in black was the name *Aurora*.

Oliver noticed that the figurehead on her prow was the same one that had been on the *Golden Lady*. It had been repainted. The carved figurehead gave Oliver a warm feeling that made him smile. She had protected the crew of the *Golden Lady* on their long voyage round the Horn, and now she would keep the crew of the *Aurora* safe on their journeys.

On the wharf, several coal trimmers shoveled coal from a huge pile into canvas bags that were then loaded into a sling that slid along a stout wire cable from the dock to the ship and hauled up over the railing onto the deck. Other bags of coal were ferried to the ship by the cockboat; these were loaded into a cargo net and hauled up onto the deck by a boom with a block and tackle. Once onboard, the mass of coal was stored below in bunkers. It was the trimmers' job to make sure it was evenly placed in the bottom of the ship so the steamer would remain level to ensure smooth sailing. In addition to coal and wood, other dockworkers loaded food, barrels of fresh water, and other supplies onto the ship.

When the captain saw Oliver, Jack, Frisco, and Achoo on the dock, he waved from the ship. Through his speaking trumpet, he yelled, "Ahoy there, me hearties! We'll be gettin' underway on the next tide."

The captain ordered the men in the cockboat to row them and their baggage to the ship.

Once on the *Aurora*, Oliver addressed the captain. "What's our first order of the day, sir?"

"Oliver, I want ye to be me steward again, like ye was on the *Golden Lady*. Jack, ye can do as ye please, just don't get into trouble."

Jack thought, *What's he expect I'll do? Start a mutiny or somethin'?*

There was a sudden loud noise that sounded like a gunshot. Both Jack and Oliver hit the deck facedown. Frisco crouched down and, as always, put his paws over his ears, and Achoo squawked, "What in blazes!"

A cloud of smoke drifted across the water from the dock. Lifting her head slightly, Jack yelled, "Gadzooks, Cap'n, I thought ye said this ship was shipshape!" There was another bang and Jack put her head back down.

Oliver spoke to Jack to calm her down: "That was no gunshot. It was a backfire from an automobile."

Through the captain's telescope, Oliver saw a black Model T Ford swerve and skid on the slick planks of the wharf as it raced along the quay. The auto screeched to a halt broadside to the steamer, and shook as if it were a wet dog. The captain recognized the driver as Professor Le Strange, whom he had met at Oliver's parents' house. In the back seat of the auto was a huge basket packed with a mess of ropes, netting, and other ballooning paraphernalia. Tied to the back trunk rack was an aqua-blue wooden seaman's chest with the letters ZPL painted in yellow on the side.

Spotting the captain on the ship, Professor Le Strange coughed from the exhaust smoke and shouted across the water, "Gotta see Jack and Oliver right away! I heard they may be aboard your ship!"

Jack and Oliver heard the professor's strained voice, and got up and ran to the railing. "Professor, what are you doing here?" Oliver called through the speaking trumpet.

The professor cupped his hands and shouted back, "Doing here?! I'll tell you what I'm doing here, you deceitful scoundrels!" he said angrily.

The automobile's engine was still running. It made a terrible racket, so it was hard to hear over its loud rattle.

"Calm down, professor, before you blow a gasket. And turn off that confounded machine of yours!" Oliver shouted.

"Sorry!" The professor said, turning off the engine.

"What'd y say, Professor? Ye want a glass of beer?" Jack yelled.

"No! That's not what I said, you numbskull!"

The captain then ordered that the skiff bring the professor to the ship.

Aboard the *Aurora,* the professor continued his tirade: "What the hell were you two thinking, running off like that without a word and leaving me in the lurch? The ringmaster was hopping mad when you didn't show up for your four o'clock performance yesterday. He had the gall to tell me the only reason he let us travel on the circus train was 'cause your act was the biggest attraction and drew the most money. He said the act wasn't worth a damn without you two and your pets, and told me to pack up all my gear and clear out! I drove to Oliver's parents' house and they told me you were here," he yelled, still steaming.

"Sorry, Professor, but when Jack and I heard that the captain had bought a steamer and wanted us to go to sea with him again, we were so excited we just didn't think," Oliver said.

"You can say that again! I thought you liked ballooning," the professor said, beginning to calm down.

"We *do* like ballooning, Professor, and our earnings kept us from starving, but the sea is Jack's and my first love," Oliver said.

"Well, I guess I see your point. I like the sea too, but now that I'm out of a job, what am I gonna do for money?"

Getting no answer, the professor said, "Say, Cap'n, could you use another sailor on your ship? In my younger days, before I became a balloonist, I was a sailor on a navy frigate. After that, I got a job on a sidewheeler that traveled on the Hudson River carrying passengers and cargo from New York to Albany. Oliver, when you answered my ad for a balloonist and told me you were a sailor on a sailing ship, I knew right away you were the man for the job."

The captain joined in the conversation: "So, ye want to be a sailor on me ship, do ye? Well, I'll have to think about it, Professor, 'cause ain't ye a little old to be a sailor? It's hard work."

"Cap'n, I'm not much older than you or that geezer of a cook you call Stubs, and I've still got my bravery and commonsense!" the professor replied.

Captain Matthews rubbed his chin and thought, *Commonsense, eh? Some of us, like Jack and Oliver, could use some commonsense. Maybe if I hire the old coot he could give me some pointers on how to run a ship with paddlewheels. With a crew of twenty on a ship that normally has thirty-eight, we could use another hand, and with Mouse gone, maybe the professor could help Stubs.*

"All right! All right! Ye're hired, Professor, but don't think there'll be any favors. Ye'll take orders, eat and sleep in the fo'c'sle, and help Stubs in the galley same as the rest of the idlers. The only thing ye won't have to do is stand watch."

The professor nodded. "I accept!" He grinned from ear to ear, showing a black hole where a front tooth was missing.

The captain pointed to the automobile and said, "What ye gonna do with that contraption? Ye can't just leave it on the pier. And what's with the big basket and seaman's chest?"

"The basket is the gondola to my balloon, and what's in it is the balloon, ropes, netting, bellows, and other equipment needed to make her fly. I couldn't leave the balloon behind. Made her myself. And as far as the chest, it was my sea chest during my sailing days. The initials stand for Zachariah P. Le Strange, at your service, sir," the professor said, taking off his bowler hat and bowing.

Captain Matthews rolled his eyes and shook his head, indicating that he wasn't very impressed. "Well, ye gotta do somethin' with that lot soon, 'cause we're leavin' on the next tide."

The professor said, "Aye-aye, sir! Uh… I was thinking per-haps your crew could put a sling under the belly of the tin lizzy and slide her along the same cable they used to load those sacks of coal onto your ship. If the strong man at the circus can pick up the automobile, she can't weigh more than a full load of that coal. Then stow her and the basket and the rest of my gear in the hold. Who knows, the balloon may come in handy someday."

The captain scowled, rubbed his bearded chin, and said, "Hm!" He then gave Mr. Jones the order, "Ready the crane and cargo sling to bring that confounded machine and junk aboard! Then weigh anchor!"

Chapter 46

Underway

Smoke billowed from her smokestack, her paddlewheels churned, and the *Aurora* chugged on the evening tide, out of Puget Sound, near Seattle, and headed through Juan de Fuca Strait and Georgia Strait to Port Hardy. There she would continue on through the Inside Passage to Skagway.

Aurora was a packet steamer; she carried mail, freight, and passengers to the various towns and villages along the Inside Passage. Once she reached Skagway, she would travel 700 miles across the Gulf of Alaska to the Kulak Canning Company, on Kodiak Island, where she would pick up a cargo of canned red sockeye salmon and perhaps some passengers. Then she would head home to Puget Sound.

Though a wireless radio wasn't required on ships until 1910, when an act was passed that all United States ships traveling over 200 miles off the coast must be equipped with a wireless radio with a range of one hundred miles, the captain thought it would be wise to install one anyway.

Aurora passed another steamer as she made for open water. Two short blasts of her high-pitched whistle warned the other ship that she would pass it on her starboard side.

Before heading to Alaska to make extra money, the captain had contracted to pick up a cargo of railroad ties at Crescent City, in Northern California, for the Northern Pacific Railway.

The southward trip went smoothly until the steamer neared the St. George Reef Lighthouse, which stood on a granite caisson six miles off the coast of Crescent City.

Near the lighthouse the wind picked up and the water became a mess of whitecaps. There were also craggy rocks to look out for. *Aurora*'s whistle blew five short blasts to signal that there was danger ahead and to alert the lighthouse keepers that she was passing. No return signal came from the lighthouse.

Through his telescope Captain Matthews saw two men trying to hook a small skiff to a block and tackle to be hoisted up onto the platform the lighthouse stood on. The small boat thrashed about wildly and banged against the platform. Seeing *Aurora,* one of the men waved and motioned to the steamer to keep her distance.

"Ahoy there! Everything all right? Do you need our help?" the captain called through the speaking trumpet.

One of the men shook his head and indicated with his fingers that everything was okay and no help was needed. Suddenly the small boat crashed up against the platform; it broke in two and sent one of the men backwards into the water. The other man quickly swung out the boom. The man in the water was able to catch hold of it, and was hauled up onto the platform. Without a boat, however, the pair were now stranded.

The captain saw what had happened, and shouted to Mr. Jones, "Lower the cockboat. Those men need our help! You and Mr. Harris can row to within a few feet of the platform. The men can swim out to yer boat."

Mr. Jones questioned the order: "But, sir, with these high waves and wind, our own small boat could be swamped and dashed against the rocks."

The captain growled, "Mr. Jones, it's not your job to question my orders. Do as I say. To save these men, we have to take that chance." Jones bit his lower lip and gave the order to lower the small boat. He and Mr. Harris rowed toward the platform.

Suddenly, the wind shifted, the waves calmed, and the skiff was able to come close enough to the men so they could swim to it. Once the two were safely aboard, Jones and Harris rowed swiftly back to *Aurora.*

Once aboard, the men thanked Captain Matthews for rescuing them. The captain then radioed the Crescent City harbormaster that they were on their way. Next, he ordered Mr. Jones to tell the crew, "Head her into the wind. We'll be sailin' straight for the Crescent City Harbor. Oliver, make sure the men we rescued get cups of coffee and blankets."

Oliver learned later that the St. George Reef Lighthouse was built in 1865 after a passenger steamer called the *Brother Jonathan* was wrecked on the St. George Reef during a heavy storm. Of nearly 200 passengers, only nineteen survived.

It was too dangerous for the lighthouse keepers and their families to live at the lighthouse, so they lived on the mainland. They went to the lighthouse only to maintain and light the lamp in bad weather and when heavy fog rolled in.

At the Crescent City Harbor, the cap'n ordered the crew to remain aboard. "We'll only let these lighthouse keepers off and load the ties. We'll then head back north to Puget Sound and up the coast to Port Hardy at the tip of Vancouver Island."

Chapter 47

A Last Goodbye

Back in Washington State, *Aurora* made only a one-day stop to take on drinking water, coal, and food before departing on the morning tide. Oliver was allowed to go ashore and say goodbye to his family. At the noonday meal, Oliver's father raised his glass: "To Oliver the sailor! Oliver, your decision to go to sea again with Captain Matthews is a wise one. We all wish you the best!"

"Hear, hear, brother!" said Theo. "And may you find a girl of your own one day!" Theo said and raised his glass again.

"Are girls all you can ever talk about, Theo?" Oliver asked with a shake of his head.

"All right, Theo," said Oliver's father, "that will be enough talk about girls. Oliver, what did Professor Le Strange say when he found out you and Jack were quitting the ballooning act and going back to sea?"

"He was angry, especially about our leaving without telling him. Also, the circus ringmaster fired him, but he'll get over it. Captain Matthews hired him as a sailor on the steamer. Before the professor became a balloonist, he was a sailor on a steamer out of New York City."

Oliver's father took out his gold pocket watch and looked at the time. "Well, son, we'll miss you, but it's about time you left to get back to the ship. Good luck to you and Godspeed! You'll send us part of your wages as promised?"

"Yes, Father," Oliver said.

Oliver thanked his family for their support and headed toward the door. As he was leaving, his mother ran to him and gave him a tin. "Take care of yourself, Oliver.

"What's this, Mother?

"Oh, just a few cookies to share with your sailor friends. I expect you don't get much in the way of desserts on that ship."

"Thank you, Mother. I know the crew will enjoy them!" Oliver said with a smile.

Stanley ran up to Oliver and clung to his leg. "Oliver, please don't go! I'm already missing you!"

"Squirt, I have to go, but I promise to write you and tell you all about my adventures," Oliver said, ruffling the boy's hair.

Chapter 48

Vancouver Island

On his charts, Captain Matthews showed Oliver the route they would take. Their first port of call would be Port Hardy, at the northern tip of Vancouver Island. From there they would sail to the Inuit village of Bella Bella, then up the Inside Passage through Queen Charlotte Sound, Hecate Strait past Haida Gwaii Island, then on to Kitimat and Prince Rupert. They would then cross Dixon Entrance, and enter Clarence Strait to Ketchikan and Wrangell. Next would be the Russian settlement of Sitka, and the native village on Admiralty Island. They would then enter Frederick Sound, and finally arrive at the new capital of Juneau. From there they would sail up Chatham Strait and Lynn Canal to Skagway. Along the way they would deliver cargo, supplies, and mail and pick up passengers.

The captain then planned to sail the 700 miles across the Gulf of Alaska to Kodiak Island. The Kulak Salmon Cannery was located there, on the south side of the Karluk River, and they could pick up several crates of canned salmon to bring back to Seattle. Whether they would sail to the cannery depended on the weather. If they could, they would then journey back across the gulf to the Inside Passage and head home.

The captain said, "Oliver, I'm askin' yer opinion. Do ye think it's wise to sail across the Gulf of Alaska to that cannery?"

"Sir, in my opinion, going all that way across the gulf, where we could hit bad weather, just to pick up a cargo of salmon seems pretty risky. Wouldn't it be wiser to get salmon at one of the canneries along the Inside Passage?"

"Perhaps ye're right," the captain replied, "but the final decision is mine. I was listenin' to that new radio we got; it said the Karluk Packing Company cannery was closin', and I bet there'll be a lot o' workers wantin' to sail back to the States. We could make a killin' off 'em if they booked passage on our ship."

"Suit yourself, Cap'n, but if it was up to me… uh, I was just thinking about the safety of the crew, that's all. This ship wasn't built yesterday. Even newer and bigger ships have gone down in the gulf.

"Okay, boy, you've made yer point. Now, ye best be gettin' back to the galley, 'cause Stubs and the professor'll be complainin' if ye don't."

Though most of the ship's passenger cabins had been removed to make room for cargo, of the twelve remaining, two had been converted to make one large cabin for the captain. Since Oliver was his steward, the captain wanted Oliver to take the cabin next to his instead of a bunk in the fo'c'sle as he had done on the *Golden Lady.*

Jack protested because she wanted to share the cabin with Oliver, but her father insisted she have her own cabin since she was a young lady now. Each of the small cabins had two bunks. First Mate Jones and Second Mate Harris were assigned to one cabin, and Stubs and the professor opted to share another. That left five cabins for passengers who wanted to board at the various ports. The rest of the crew would have to bunk in the fo'c'sle or sleep wherever space was available.

In hopes of enticing passengers, the captain put an ad in the *Seattle Star* newspaper:

> Ho! For Northwest and Alaska via the Inside
> Passage, book passage on the Good Ship *Aurora.*

> Ports of Call: Vancouver Island, Sitka, Admiralty Island, Juneau, Skagway, Kodiak Island. Stout steamer with two sidewheels; able seamen; expert masters. Five passenger staterooms, two bunks per cabin.

From Port Hardy it was smooth sailing all the way to the former Russian settlement of Sitka on the west side of Baranof Island. Baranof was next to Admiralty Island. They would stop at both to deliver mail. Sitka had been an important fur-trading port when the Russians owned it, and was the capital of Alaska until 1906, when the government decided to move the capital to Juneau.

Aurora anchored offshore at Sitka and a skiff was lowered so the mail sack could be taken ashore. Oliver and Jack noticed several Tlingit tribesmen paddling canoes near the shoreline. Some of the men were fishing for salmon, which was the main staple of the Tlingit. There were also a couple of steamers anchored offshore that had brought tourists to Sitka.

Jack asked, "Cap'n, can Oliver and I go ashore with the mail? I hear other steamships with tourists come to Sitka to see an old Russian Orthodox church that has beautiful religious paintin's in it. We'd like to see them if we can. I'd also like to buy some o' the trinkets, baskets, and wood carvings the natives make."

"Please, Cap'n, could we go?" Oliver chimed in.

"I guess it'll be okay," the captain replied. "But make sure ye come back to the ship before the next tide, when we'll be leavin'."

Jack and Oliver rowed ashore and wandered into the town, where they headed to the Russian church. Though the church was empty when they arrived, Oliver said to Jack, "We'd better be quiet 'cause we're entering a place of worship."

Once inside, Jack turned a slow circle trying to take in everything. "Why ain't there any seats in this church?"

A guide who stood near the entry door answered her question. "There are no seats because the people stand before God. The only time they can sit is during the reading of the Psalms and the priest's sermon. Of course, they make an exception for people who are old and feeble."

"And why does all the pictures look flat, and not one o' them saints is smilin'?" Jack asked.

"They look that way because the paintings have a unique style. Instead of like normal paintings, they are painted in layers. First the artist paints a dark layer of tempera for the background, then the actual picture, and then he adds the white accents. Once the painting is dry, he paints a coat of varnish over it."

Jack looked closely at several of the paintings. "These paintin's got cracks all over 'em."

"Over many years, when the old paint and varnish dries, it cracks, and leaves many fine cracks called craquelure, or crazing, that goes all the way through the varnish down into the paint underneath. If a forger ever tries to duplicate one of these paintings, you can tell right away that it's a fake, because it is very difficult to duplicate the cracks," the guide explained.

Jack looked closely at an icon of the Virgin Mary and Christ child. The Virgin wore a blue dress with a red coat.

The guide said, "The blue dress the Virgin Mary wears means she is human, and the red coat, that she became holy by giving birth to Jesus. The baby Jesus, or Christ Child, is swathed in a red cloth, meaning Christ was born godly. His blue blanket means that Christ became human and suffered the same ills as we humans, such as hunger and thirst. The gold halo-like crowns over their heads symbolize the grace of God shining out from the icon."

Jack had spent almost her entire life aboard a sailing ship, where the majority of sailors put their faith in superstitions and omens instead of acts of God, so the guide's explanation mainly went over her head.

Jack didn't want to sound stupid in front of him, so she said, "Oh, that explains a lot." She looked closer at the painting of the Virgin Mary and Christ Child. "If what ye say about them cracks bein' hard to paint, this must be a fake 'cause it ain't got no real cracks on it, just painted ones."

The guide came over and looked closely at the painting. "Egads! I've looked at that icon a thousand times and never noticed that before. You got a good eye. I must go tell the curator. You'll excuse me."

Soon, an older man with gold wire-rimmed glasses followed the guide out of a back room. In his hand was a magnifying glass. "Sir,' the guide said, "this young man believes the painting of the Virgin Mary and the Christ Child to be a fake." The older man examined the painting with his magnifying glass.

"I don't see anything wrong with it. He must be mistaken," the curator said, then turned abruptly and went back to his office.

Jack whispered to Oliver, "Either that old man's coverin' somethin' up or he needs new glasses. I swear that paintin' has no real cracks."

Jack and Oliver left the church then strolled down the boardwalk to the Indian River where a battle took place in 1804 between the native Sitka Tlingit tribe and the Russians over the destruction of a Russian fur-trading post.

Oliver noticed the sun was starting to set. "Jack, we gotta get back to the ship now, or the Cap'n 'll have us boiled in oil."

Aurora sailed from Sitka to the Tlingit village of Angoon on Admiralty Island. At Angoon, Jack and Oliver were told to deliver the mail sack to the post office at the village store and to be back on the ship before the next tide.

On Admiralty Island brown bears outnumbered the people three to one. The island was also known to have a large population of bald eagles.

Concerned for their safety, Stubs warned Jack and Oliver, "Be careful. Them bears is hungry this time o' year, and if ye see a sow with her cubs, stay clear away, ye hear? If she sees ye anywhere near her cubs, she'll attack. Take this here ladle and pot with ye, and bang on it as loud as ye can to scare the bears away. Wave your arms over yer head to make yerself look big, but don't run or climb a tree. Bears can run faster than you, and can also climb trees."

The professor, who was also sitting in the galley, added, "And yell or sing at the top of your voices when you're walking through the woods, and mind what the cap'n says—after you deliver the mail, you've gotta hurry back."

Oliver and Jack went ashore in the skiff with the mail bag they were to deliver to the Tlingit village post office, which was located in the forest a short distance from shore.

As Oliver and Jack trudged along the path to the post office, they came to a clearing in the woods where several native Tlingit and Haida artisans were selling their trade wares. There were baskets, wood carvings, weavings, cedar boxes, copper, and beadwork.

Jack spied a long-handled wooden spoon with a carved raven on the top of the handle.

"Stubs might like this spoon for cookin'," she said.

"No, Stubs has lots of spoons. How about this cedar wooden storage box for the cap'n? He could store his charts and maps in it," Oliver said. He asked the native the price of the box.

"Too much money for you. Take long time to make, carve, and paint. Only make box for special person, like chief," the artisan said.

Oliver picked up a small dagger made of copper with a carved hilt in the shape of a raven's head.

"You like knife? Knife not sharp, make good letter opener. Make special deal for foreigner."

"How much?" Oliver asked.

"For you, I make trade. Knife for hat with flaps over ears."

"No way! This is the only hat I got left from my ballooning days. It keeps my ears warm when it gets cold. Besides, the professor gave it to me."

"Then I sell knife for one dollar," the native said.

"One dollar? I'll take it!" Oliver said, and laid down a Morgan silver dollar.

The native bit the coin to see if it was real. "Coin make good jewelry," the man said.

Jack bargained for a small cedar trinket box inlaid with mother of pearl.

After leaving the native artisans, Oliver and Jack hurried to the store where the post office was located. A man was just leaving the building.

The man in charge of the post office and village store was just closing for the day when they arrived.

Jack ran up to the man. "You the one who handles the mail?"

"Yeah. Name is Gooch. Mean "wolf" in English. Also run store."

"Mr. Gooch, we're from the steamship *Aurora,* and we brought a mail pouch for your village," Oliver said.

Gooch took the sack. "I close now. Go to village with mail. Today, potlatch in village. Much celebration. Gooch high priest, shaman, medicine man. Okay you come. Speak for entire village. Villagers bring gifts, much food, tell stories, drums, dance, games, gambling. Potlatch already start. Gooch late. So you come now—have good time!"

Hearing that there would be gambling, Jack looked at Oliver. "Please, can we go?"

Not wanting to hear her pleading, Oliver said, "Okay, maybe for a short time, but we promised the captain, Stubs, and the professor that we'd deliver the mail and then return to the ship."

"So kill me with a blunt knife! We won't stay long. C'mon, it might be fun," Jack said, excited at the prospect of a party.

They were about to take Gooch up on his invite, when shuffling, growling, and sniffling sounds suddenly came from the nearby bushes. Gooch put up his hands. "Bear come! We go inside store, wait until bear leave," he said.

Inside, the three of them peered out the small front window. A huge brown bear with two cubs was rummaging through a trash heap near the corner of the building. Jack banged on a pot, and the mother bear stood on her hind legs and roared. The noise scared the cubs and they ran back into the bushes. The sow came down on all fours and chased after them.

They waited a few minutes and then, hearing no more noise, Gooch said, "Bears gone. We go to Potlatch now. Hurry, before bear come back."

Oliver, Jack, and Gooch trudged through the woods to the Tlingit village. The entire way, Jack sang a sea shanty and banged as loudly as she could on the pot. At the entrance of the village were several totem poles, carved and painted with symbolic stylized humans, animals, and supernatural beings that told the status of the clan. At the top of one pole was the head of a bird with a long beak. The bird had human legs and arms and was seated on a throne. Below the bird was the face of a supernatural being with white teeth. Its eyes were lined with black paint, and its carved body was painted blue, red, black, and white. Below the face was an animal with its paws up in front of it. Jack thought it looked like a squirrel.

"What kind of bird is that on the top of the pole?" Oliver asked Gooch.

"Raven and some Eagle. Stand for Tlingit and Haida clan and history. Raven create world. Raven is Trickster. Know how to get food. Change shape. Must hurry. Gooch need to start ceremony." He walked faster, and Jack and Oliver had to run to keep up with him.

They learned later that a potlatch gathering was for giving gifts and sharing wealth, to celebrate births and name children, for marriages, to thank the gods for a good year and the coming year, and to honor leaders and those who had died during the year.

Not far from the totems was a rectangular house with steps that led up to the door. The house was made of cedar planks and had a bark roof. On the entry door, painted in the same colors as the totems, was an image of a large animal. Jack thought it looked like a stylized bear. On each side of the house was a totem representing the clan that lived there. A plume of whitish-gray smoke rose into the air from a hole in the roof of the house. Oliver and Jack could hear the sound of drums, rattles, voices, and feet shuffling as they entered.

Gooch said, "Come. We hurry. Need to start ceremony. Thank gods for good year, give gifts, bless feast." He told Jack and Oliver that the clan made the gifts during the year, to be shared at the potlatch with the tribespeople. It reminded Oliver of Christmas.

Gooch took Jack and Oliver to a bench at the back of the room, built against a wall. "You sit here. Some clan people afraid, think white people bring bad spirits," he warned. They did as they were told and sat on the bench.

The only light in the room came from a firepit in the center. From where Jack and Oliver sat, they saw a raised platform against the opposite wall.

Suddenly, there was the sound of drums and rattles. From behind a panel appeared several dancers dressed in beautiful fringed Chilkat blankets embroidered or painted with stylized designs of animals. Other dancers wore dark blue and red flannel blankets decorated with mother of pearl trade buttons arranged in various designs. Some wore elaborately carved and painted wooden masks made to look like animals and mythical creatures. Others wore headdresses decorated with sea-lion whiskers and bird feathers. A few had circular bone rings in their pierced noses, and iridescent abalone shell earrings hung from their earlobes.

Some of the Tlingit and Haida clansmen wore breechcloths; others wore pants and moccasins. Most of the women wore short skirts made of cedar bark, and only a few wore longer deerskin dresses.

The dancers went behind a screen and a single man stepped onto the stage.

"That must be Gooch," Oliver whispered to Jack.

As the shaman of the tribe, Gooch carried a thick staff with sea-otter teeth on it. To gain everyone's attention, he struck the staff on the stage with a loud *thud!* Jack nearly jumped off the bench at the sound. Everyone watched as the shaman shook a rattle, danced wildly on the stage, and cupped his hands as if he were drinking something. Through his dance he told a story about how raven was born. *Yéil* learned that a beautiful maiden drank from a stream in the morning. One day, Raven watched the girl and turned himself into a tree with needles that floated into her cup. The maiden drank him and became pregnant; Raven was born in human form and was much loved.

In the mythology of Alaskan natives, Raven was known as the creator of the world and bringer of the daylight. He was also well-known as a trickster.

The shaman then signaled to the musicians to beat their drums and shake their rattles again. As he danced, he lifted his arms up and down and made loud animal-like noises as he tried to contact the spirit world. He threw something into the fire that made blue sparks fly up. Awed, Jack grabbed Oliver's arm. Other dancers circled the fire, which cast their eerie shadows on the walls. That gave Jack the goose bumps because it reminded her of the ghost ship in the Antarctic.

The shaman struck his staff on the ground again with a louder thump. The music stopped and the dancers disappeared behind the screen, leaving him alone on the stage. A native woman brought a baby to him. He lifted the child in the air and spoke in their native tongue.

"He must be givin' the babe a name with all that mumbo-jumbo," Jack said.

The shaman handed the infant boy back to his mother, and all the tribespeople nodded and grunted their approval.

Next, the shaman again threw something in the fire, which made sparks fly. He raised his arms skyward and spoke some words. Again, everyone nodded and grunted.

"Perhaps he's asking their gods to give them a good year, and is sending good wishes to those who have died," Oliver said.

After the ceremony, many gifts were shared among the people. A tall olive-skinned man in costume came up to Oliver and Jack and said in a demanding voice, "You come! Give gifts!"

Oliver and Jack didn't want to insult their hosts, and were afraid that if they didn't give a gift they might be harmed or held prisoner.

Regretfully, Oliver pulled from his coat pocket the copper knife he had just bought, and handed it to the dancer. The man nodded his approval. He then turned to Jack, who reluctantly gave the man her newly purchased wooden trinket box.

"Now what are we goin' to give to Stubs and the cap'n?" she whispered to Oliver.

A woman dancer timidly approached Jack and Oliver, her eyes lowered. At their feet she dropped a beautiful woven basket and a carved bone fishing hook and quickly backed away.

"Guess we got some gifts to give them after all," Jack said.

After the gift exchange, several clanswomen spread out blankets on which they placed a huge carved wooden bowl that contained a mess of grayish-looking stew. Trays of dried salmon, halibut, herring eggs, cooked clams, and crabs followed, along with seal, bear, deer, goat, rabbit, and squirrel meat, dishes of berries, roots, and seaweed, and stacks of frybread.

The clan gathered around the feast, and everyone hungrily scooped up the stew with the frybread or their bare hands or carved wooden spoons. Jack noticed that none of the natives bothered to wash their hands; and insects and flies swam and crawled into the food. She thought, *I had worse on the* Golden Lady *when food had to be rationed.*

Gooch came over to Jack and Oliver, pointed to the food, and made eating motions. "You eat! You guests of Gooch. Men hunt meat. Women gather food, cook plenty."

Oliver stared at the communal bowl and thought the grayish mess in it looked like the leftover porridge Stubs sometime served the crew.

"Good stew. Scoop up with frybread. Women make bread, use white flour from store. Mix with water, baking powder, flatten dough with hands, fry in oil or lard. Heat stew with hot stones. Oliver stared at the pile of frybread; he remembered the bug-infested flour in Gooch's store and decided not to eat it.

Jack looked at Oliver and said, "Well, this grub can't be any worse than what Stubs sometimes serves us, so let's dig in. I'm starvin'."

Once they'd helped themselves to some food, Gooch came over and sat next to them on the bench. "You like food? Good, eh? Plenty more," he said. Jack's mouth was full and she nodded yes. She picked up a cooked crab leg, broke off a piece and sucked the meat out. "This cooked crab is delicious! Ye should try some," Jack said to Gooch.

Gooch shook his head. "Shaman not eat beach food. Take away strength, weaken spirit. Mean more food for you and other families, he said with a grin.

"Oliver tasted a piece of salmon. "Hey, Jack, ye gotta try this. It's to die for! I wonder how they cook it."

After stuffing himself, Oliver said, "I can't eat another bite. Thanks for inviting us to your potlatch, Gooch."

Jack wiped her mouth on the back of her hand and burped loudly to thank her hosts. Burping must have been a universal sign, because several of the natives also belched, laughed, and nodded. Jack felt right at home.

After the feast, there was stick gaming and bone games. Jack said, "Oliver, they got gambling games. Maybe if I'm lucky, I could win back your knife and my trinket box."

"No, Jack. We've stayed long enough. The captain will have our backsides if we stay longer, and you know as well as I do that he frowns on your gambling."

"We'll," Jack said defiantly, "you're not my keeper, and the cap'n ain't here, so what he don't know won't hurt him. I'm gonna gamble, whether you like it or not!"

Oliver was annoyed with her and said, "After all that food, my stomach hurts. You go right ahead and gamble, but if you get in trouble with the cap'n, I'm going to tell him I had nothing to do with it."

Oliver knew that once Jack had her mind set on something, there was no stopping her. What he didn't like was when she went against the cap'n's rules. Even if he was innocent of any wrongdoing, he would be accused of being her accomplice and also be punished.

Jack stomped off and joined the gambling. She quickly learned how to play the stick and bone games and won several rounds. After a while, Oliver began to worry that they wouldn't get back to the ship in time. He went to Jack and tapped her on the shoulder. "Jack, ye got to stop now! The captain will have us tarred and feathered and keelhauled if we don't get back to the ship by the time she has to leave. C'mon!" Oliver yelled pulling Jack's arm.

Jack shrugged him off. "Oliver, leave me be! I can't quit now. Can't ye see I'm winnin'? Just one more throw of the sticks and I could win the whole shebang! I promise this will be the last throw, and then we'll leave, win or lose." Jack threw the sticks and won again. Most of the players groaned and got up disgusted. In front of Jack were Oliver's knife, the trinket box, and a pile of native crafts, including a pair of beaded moccasins made of soft tanned deer hide, and a beautiful black, white, yellow, and blue Chilkat blanket woven from cedar bark and mountain goat wool worn only by high-ranking tribe members at special ceremonies.

Jack scooped up her winnings. "Thanks, boys! Gotta go now!" she yelled, smiling and waving to the players as Oliver pushed her in the direction of the door. Some of the players smiled back and waved; others grumbled and nodded. With all the merrymaking going on, no one noticed Oliver and Jack slip out. Once outside they hurried to the skiff.

Just as they were about to shove off, they saw Gooch running hellbent toward them. Several villagers armed with daggers, spears, and warclubs chased him, shouting threats. Quick on his feet, Gooch dodged a spear that landed not far from him.

"Help! Please! Take Gooch with you! Tribe want to kill Gooch! Your fault whole village mad! Gooch make bad mistake invite you to sacred potlatch. Clan say white people bring bad spirits, say white boy cheat at games. Not understand gambling games only for fun. He take gifts meant to share with clan. All blame Gooch."

Seeing Gooch's distress, Jack felt bad that she'd taken the gifts. With the exception of the copper knife and trinket box, she threw all the items she'd won onto the beach. Some of the natives ran to the heap and gathered them up. Still others shouted and shook their weapons at Gooch, Oliver, and Jack. Gooch helped Oliver shove the boat into the water. The three offenders then jumped into the skiff and rowed as fast as they could to *Aurora*.

The tide was rising and it would soon be time to weigh anchor. The captain was hopping mad that Jack and Oliver hadn't returned sooner. Stubs felt responsible for Jack's and Oliver's welfare, and worried that something bad had happened to them. He was also afraid the cap'n would think it was his fault and take his anger out on him.

The captain paced back and forth on the deck; every so often he looked shoreward through his telescope. Seeing the small boat approaching, he shouted, "Here they come now! There are three people in the skiff. Who's the third? Oh, will I give them scallywags a piece of me mind. Take all that time to deliver one sack of mail, then bring another drifter aboard. I should boil 'em in oil, even if one is me daughter and the other me steward."

When Jack, Oliver, and Gooch finally scrambled up the rope ladder, the cap'n said, "Well, it's about time ye showed up! If ye'd been another half hour, we'd a left without ye. Now, what in blazes kept ye so long, and why was all them natives chasin' ye?"

Oliver didn't want Jack and himself to get in more hot water, so he told a half truth: "We're sorry, Cap'n, but there was this mother bear and her cubs… and the postmaster and Jack and I had to shoo them away. Besides being the postmaster, he was the village shaman and invited us to a potlatch. We didn't mean to stay so long, but the time just slipped away. As far as the natives chasing Gooch, they were just giving him a farewell sendoff. You see, throwing spears at a person who's leaving is a tribal tradition."

"My Great-Aunt Matilda's fat arse! Just what kind of story are ye makin' up here, boy? Them natives looked like they meant business," the captain said, growing hotter under the collar. "And who might this person ye brung with ye be?"

Gooch answered, "Name Gooch. Postmaster and shaman of Tlingit village. Tribe make Gooch leave. Work hard if captain take Gooch on ship. Gooch sad to leave wives and children, but wives soon find new husbands."

The captain studied Gooch. "Bein' a native Tlingit, ye must know the language and these waters well."

Gooch lowered his eyes respectfully, then said, "Gooch know waters, good fisherman, know places to find fish, seals. Speak Tlingit and Haida language, also English."

"Well, Gooch, I guess we could make use of yer talents, so welcome aboard. The captain thought, *I just hope he don't turn out to be like that old professor who boasts about bein' a sailor but ain't worth a cent 'cept to keep Stubs company.*

Oliver continued his story: "Once the bear and her cubs left, Jack and I walked along the boardwalk where some natives were selling crafts. I bought a copper letter opener, and Jack bought a trinket box inlaid with abalone shell."

Hoping to appease the captain's anger, Jack handed him the box. "Thought ye might want to use this to keep important papers in." Jack didn't feel it was necessary to tell him that she'd used the box and his envelope opener to gamble at the potlatch.

"Thank ye, daughter, but this don't make up for me worryin' that somethin' happened to ye both, and for yer bein' late. Ye was irresponsible and nearly made us miss the tide. At Bella Bella, I'll have Jones go with ye to deliver the mail, or ye can stay on the ship and I'll find a nasty job for the two o' ye. Now, get yer bony arses back to the galley! he said, laughing under his breath.

To avoid further scolding, Oliver and Jack hurried off.

Chapter 50

The Curator

Unbeknownst to Jack and Oliver, an older man and a younger one whom he identified as his son booked passage on *Aurora* to Juneau, Alaska.

The next morning, as usual, Oliver brought Captain Matthews his breakfast. Then Jack and Oliver made their rounds with a pot of coffee for the crew. As they lugged the heavy urn toward the wheel, Jack spotted an old man wearing wire-rimmed glasses who was standing at the rail. Jack took Oliver aside and spoke in his ear. "When did that old man come aboard? I swear, Oliver, I've seen him before, but I can't put a finger on it."

Jack scratched her head and thought hard. "Now I remember. He's the curator at that Russian church in Sitka. Remember? He come out of his office and inspected the paintin'. Swore it was real after I seen it wasn't."

"I think you're wrong, Jack. The curator didn't have a goatee and was more stoop-shouldered. The only thing that man has in common with the curator is his glasses, so let it go! We're in enough trouble with the cap'n as it is for staying too long at that potlatch," Oliver said.

"I don't care what ye say. I'm gonna find out if he's the curator and if he stole one o' them paintin's from the church. Remember what that security guard said? Each o' them old religious paintin's was worth a thousand dollars or more."

"Jack, you're letting your imagination run away with you. If you want my opinion, which I know you don't, you're just sticking your nose where it doesn't belong. C'mon, now, we gotta get this coffee to Jonesy and Mr. Harris before it gets cold."

"Wait! I'm gonna ask that old man if he wants a cuppa coffee so's I can get a better look at him," Jack said, and jerked the urn out of Oliver's grasp.

Jack addressed the old man: "Good mornin', sir. The cook just made a fresh pot o' coffee and I was wonderin' if ye'd like a cup."

"Why, thank you, lad. A nice hot cup of coffee would be just the ticket this cold morning," the old man said, smiling.

Jack poured him a cup, smiled back, and stared at him longer than necessary. Jack and Oliver then continued toward the ship's wheel.

"Well? Was he the same man or wasn't he?" Oliver asked.

"I'm not sure. With that goatee and them glasses, it's hard to tell. Perhaps ye're right. It ain't none of me business and I should keep me nose clean," Jack said.

Later, as they walked back to the galley, they saw the old man still at the rail, but this time he wasn't alone. A younger man was with him, and they appeared to be arguing. Jack quickly set down the empty coffee pot and approached the two. Seeing her approach, the younger man turned and left.

Jack said to the old man, "Sir, don't mean to pry, but who was that young man ye was talkin' to? As the cook's helper, I'm supposed to know all the passengers so's I can be sure to set a plate for everyone. They'll soon serve the noonday meal in the saloon, and Cook is makin' baked apples for dessert."

"Thank you, lad. I'll be along soon. The young man I was speaking to is my son. He's been a bit seasick and has been staying in our cabin, but he's okay now and will join us for dinner. Say, do you know how long it'll take to sail to Juneau?"

Jack shook her head. "No, sir. Could be awhile, since we got to make several stops along the way to deliver mail and supplies. Cap'n said the next stop is Bella Bella, but I'm not sure how long it'll take us to get there."

"Thanks, lad. Here's a dime for your trouble," the old man said, flipping the coin to Jack.

Jack turned the coin over in her hand and said, "Thanks, mister." She thought, *That old man may be cheap at tippin', but he ain't a bit like that cranky old curator at the church. I guess I was wrong.*

Chapter 51

Mr. Bigmouth

The steamer anchored just off the shore of the Heiltsuk Village at Bella Bella. Captain Matthews warned Oliver and Jack to not tarry on the island, and ordered Mr. Jones to go with them to make sure they got back before the ship had to depart.

Jack didn't like the idea of having a chaperone. "Why does Jonesy have to come with us? We coulda handled the mail ourselves."

"I guess Cap'n still doesn't trust us. Give it a rest, will you, Jack?" Oliver said.

After rowing to the beach, Oliver, Jack, and Jonesy pulled the skiff up onto the sand and headed to the general store, where the post office was located. They were told that the storekeeper was a French-Canadian trader by the name of Bouchard.

For several years, the trader had done good business with the Russians and native people, trading for otter skins and other pelts, but after the otters played out and the Russians had left, Bouchard's business fell off. Still, he decided to remain at Bella Bella, and opened a trading store and post office at the Heiltsuk village.

When Oliver, Jack, and Jonesy entered the store, a nause-ating odor of dried fish, rotting vegetables, moldy cheese, and poorly tanned pelts nearly knocked them over. The three quickly put their neckerchiefs over their noses.

Each time the door opened, a barrage of buzzing flies circled the room and settled on the single smudged window. Toward the back of the store was a makeshift counter made from a plank set on two barrels.

Thinking that the three men had come to rob him, the storekeeper came out from behind the counter and held up his hands. "Messieurs! Please do not shoot!" he said, in fear for his life. "I poor. No money! Deal in trade only. Please do not kill!"

"We ain't come here to rob or kill ye, Mr. Bouchard. We're sailors from the steamer *Aurora* and have brought ye a mail sack. We're hopin' we can buy a few sacks of flour from ye," Jonesy said.

"Yes, yes, pardon me. And as for my name being Bouchard, I have not used that name for many years. The villagers call me Big Mouth, which Bouchard means in French.

Oliver looked into the barrel at the yellowish-gray lumps of flour that teemed with weevils. At the sight of it, he felt like he was going to throw up. *What's going on?* he thought. *This flour looks the same as the flour at Gooch's store.*

"Looks like your supplies are worse than ours," Jones commented. "As a sailor, I've eaten flour before that was infested with insects, but none this bad."

"I am afraid I must leave here. Villagers have no food and take everything in store. Bigmouth not blame them. Government agent to blame. Government ships not bring fresh flour or other supplies over one year. Please take what you want. Soon village move farther up coast. Bigmouth must close store."

Holding his nose and looking at the flour, Jack said, "Uh, Mr. Bigmouth, thanks, but I think we'll pass on the flour."

Bigmouth hesitated, then pleaded, "Please, take me with you on ship. I know waters. Bigmouth good interpreter, work hard for passage. Starve if stay here."

Oliver and Jack looked at Jones as if to say, we can't let him starve. "Okay, Mr. Bigmouth, we'll take you with us, but you'll have to earn your keep like the rest o' the crew," Mr. Jones replied.

Bigmouth gave a toothless grin and retreated to a back room. He returned shortly with a knapsack stuffed with various items, and now wore an old red-and-black-checked jacket and a fur hat with earflaps. "Must deliver mail to village before we go. Will not take long. I meet you at boat."

Bigmouth left for the village, and Oliver, Jack, and Jonesy made for the skiff to await his arrival.

"What's taking him so long?" Oliver complained. "We gotta get back to the ship before the tide rises and it's time to weigh anchor. The captain will never let us go ashore again if we don't leave now."

"Here he comes!" Mr. Jones sang out as Bigmouth ran toward the beach. Three native women and several children followed him.

"What's going on? Who are those women and children?" Oliver asked.

Bigmouth rushed up to the skiff. "Wives and children want go too. Starve in winter if left on island."

"Oh, no, Mr. Bigmouth. That was not part o' the bargain. The women and children will have to stay here! Some sailors think a woman on a ship brings bad luck," Jonesy said, winking at Jack, who he knew was a woman.

Bigmouth noticed Oliver staring at an older Tlingit woman with tattooed lines running from her mouth to her chin. The trader said, "First wife have chin tattooed when become adult. Mean marriage, good cook, many children. Also beauty marks, ha-ha!"

Bigmouth ran back to the women and said something in the Tlingit language. The women and children seemed to understand that they could not go with him, and stayed behind on the beach. Looking sad, they watched Bigmouth hurry to the skiff.

A small boy ran toward Bigmouth and cried, "My father, do not leave us behind!" One of the women took the boy by the hand. She looked like she was about to cry. Their heads down, the women and children slowly walked up the beach and back to the village.

Bigmouth said, "Wives and children sad, cannot go with Bigmouth on ship. Soon, wives and children have new husbands, and forget Bigmouth."

Oliver and Jack got out of the cockboat, and, with Bigmouth's help, pushed it into the water. Jonesy and Bigmouth rowed the 300 yards to the steamer. Some of the villagers tried to follow in their seal-hunting canoes, but the cockboat outdistanced them, and Oliver, Jack, Jonesy, and Bigmouth reached the steamer just as she was about to weigh anchor.

The captain greeted Bigmouth and accepted his offer to become an interpreter and crewmember in exchange for his passage.

Chapter 52

Red Onion Saloon

When the ship finally arrived in Skagway, Oliver and Jack walked through the business district as they carried the mail bag to the building that housed the post office. By 1909, Skagway had a population of 3,000, and the main street, called Broadway, boasted several businesses, including the New West Hotel. One building caught Jack's eye: the Red Onion Saloon, notorious for its classy dancehall and the brothel upstairs.

"How 'bout it, Oliver? Let's go in the joint. I'm game if ye are. I hear they got a piano player," Jack said, trying to entice him.

Oliver remembered what Jonesy had told him about saloons. "Uh, I don't know, Jack. The Red Onion might be one of those dives like in San Francisco, where an unwary sailor is slipped a Mickey and gets shanghaied."

"Aah, don't be such a chicken, Oliver! Tell ye what: if we both go in there, I'll treat ye to a sarsaparilla—you know—one o' them sweet drinks flavored with roots. Stubs bought me one in San Francisco once, in a place called a soda shop."

It was four o'clock, and the saloon was crowded with men who had just gotten off work. When two men left, Oliver sat at their table while Jack wormed her way through the crowd to the bar. She placed two quarters on the bar and said, "Barkeep, I'll have two sarsaparillas, please!"

The barkeep looked at the two quarters. "Sorry, lad, all drinks is a dollar."

Jack said, "A dollar?! Why, that's highway rob… I ain't askin' for no alcoholic drink. So, how much sarsaparilla will ye give me for them two quarters?"

"Half a glass. That's half a dollar's worth. Ya see, normally we don't serve soda pop here, only whiskey, beer, and the rotgut the natives call firewater. But I guess you're in luck. A couple days ago some kids come in here with their Pa, and I found a bottle of sarsaparilla in the backroom." When I told their Pa it'd be a dollar, same as the other drinks, he didn't want it."

I'll take it!" Jack said without hesitation.

The barkeep wiped the dust off the bottle with a rag and poured Jack a single half glass of the sweet stuff. Jack took a sip of the drink and made a face. "This stuff ain't got no fizz and it tastes like lavender soap."

"That bottle of soda is now open, so I ain't givin' your money back," the barkeep said, crossing his arms stubbornly.

As Jack turned to make her way to the table where Oliver sat, the barkeep leaned across the bar, tapped her on the shoulder, and whispered, "Say, young fella, you and that friend o' yours wouldn't be interested in a little…?" The man puckered his lips, whistled, raised his eyebrows, and pointed upstairs. "The Red Onion's got the classiest ladies in town. Just one dollar for a look, another dollar for a feel, and five dollars for a tumble in the… well, ya know what I mean. He looked Jack up and down and continued, "If you're a virgin, it'll be another dollar."

Jack gave him a searing look. She knew exactly what he meant. Stubs had told her all about ladies of the evening.

"No, sir! Are you stupid or somethin'? If I could only afford half a glass o' watered-down sarsaparilla, ye think I got five dollars to have sex with one of yer floozies and get a disease I could die from? I ain't interested, and neither is me friend," Jack replied, disgusted.

"Just had to ask. Company policy, ya know," the barkeep said.

Jack turned her back on him and made her way through the crowded room to Oliver, who looked like he was anxious to leave. When Jack reached the table, she plunked down the glass, spilling a good deal of the contents. "This is all they give me for fifty cents. I hope ye enjoy it!"

"What's got your feathers all ruffled?" Oliver asked, seeing Jack red-faced.

"That no good barkeep, that's what. Ye was right, Oliver. This place is a dive! Let's get out o' here and go back to the ship!"

Oliver downed what was left of the soda, pushed his chair back, and stood, ready to leave. Just then, Jack noticed three men at another table, talking amongst themselves. One of them looked familiar. "Say, Oliver, ain't that the older gentleman who booked passage on our steamer to Juneau? And that younger man with him looks familiar too."

Jack and Oliver studied the third man at the table. "And who's that gent they're talkin' with that looks like he could do with a new suit? Jack asked.

The older man picked up a package he'd been concealing under the table.

Jack and Oliver watched as the seedy-looking man waved two crisp fifty-dollar bills in the old man's face. I'll give ye a hundred dollars for that paintin' and not a penny more. This kinda stuff is hard to resell. I'm just the go-between, and the real fence don't take kindly to bein' cheated. He'll have every bone in yer bodies broke if it ain't real! So, we got a deal or ain't we? I ain't got all day, gentlemen!"

"Yes, yes, we'll take your money," the younger man said, pushing the box across the table.

"Hold it! How do I know you ain't coppers tryin' to trap me?" the middleman said.

"We assure you, sir, the painting is real! This man is the curator of the Russian Orthodox church in Sitka, and I'm a guide there. Here is my card!" The sleazy-looking man took the card, looked at it, and put it in his vest pocket. "Seems legit!" he said, then stood up, the package under his arm, and strode to the exit.

"Glad that middleman swallowed the bait, son! We'd better scram before that boss of his finds out the painting's a forgery. When we get to Juneau, we'll set up our next scheme."

"Thing is, the real icon is worth thousands, and we're only getting a hundred apiece for the fakes. Someone's gonna get suspicious one of these days. By the way, where'd you stash the real one? If we get caught with that thing, we'll spend the rest of our lives in prison."

Don't get your knickers in a knot! I hid it where it's safe and sound," the old man said.

The two conmen left the saloon and headed back to *Aurora.*

After they'd gone, Oliver said, "Well, what do you know, Jack? The icon painting that curator swore was real turned out to be a fake after all, but where do you suppose the real one is? Do you think we should alert the police?"

"No, Oliver! Some sailors believe talkin' about churches brings bad luck, and I guess we're in the thick of it."

"So, we just pretend we don't know anything, and don't tell the police?"

"Ye got that right! If the police get involved, they'll ask all kinds o' questions, and since those two crooks are passengers on our steamer, the police might think the cap'n has somethin' to do with it. Then who knows how long we'll be delayed here. And knowin' the cap'n, he'll take a rod to our backsides for gettin' involved. I say we just keep quiet and let this whole fraud play out," Jack said.

"I guess you're right, Jack. We shouldn't get involved, but we already are! I'm sure those two swindlers saw us in here," Oliver said.

"Well, that's a chance we'll have to take. Let's get back to the ship. It's near suppertime and I'm starvin'."

Chapter 53
Juneau, Alaska

In 1880, gold was discovered by two prospectors who replaced panning with mines that brought in millions of dollars' worth of gold. Juneau boomed, and in 1906 the capital of Alaska was moved there.

As *Aurora* neared Vanderbilt Reef, a dense fog, swirling winds, and high tides buffeted the ship, and Captain Matthews feared she would be dashed against the rocks. His dread became a reality when a loud *crunch!* was heard, and the steamer ran aground, wedged tightly between the rocks. Earlier, the crew had shut down the steam engines to save fuel, and now *Aurora*'s only means of propulsion was her sails.

When it was discovered that the ship had a hole in her side and was taking on water, the captain ordered that the pumps be readied, and radioed the port master in Juneau to send help. Several hours passed with no return signal, and the captain grew concerned. Fortunately, the rift in the hull was repairable, but the ship was so securely jammed between the rocks that there was no way she could move without assistance. The captain hoped a passing tug or fishing boat would see their dilemma and come to their aid.

Frisco and Achoo were frightened by the loud scraping and the shudder of the ship. The dog barked and the parrot squawked loudly, "Cut and run! Abandon ship! We're doomed, I tell ye!"

"Shut up, silly!" Jack said. "Too bad ye're not a carrier pigeon so's ye could take a message to someone. Where's Spike when we need him? We could attach a message to his leg and send him to the nearest village for help."

Circling overhead was the albatross. Hearing his name, the huge bird landed with a *thud!* on the deck. *Did someone call me?* he seemed to say. Spike had been following the ship since it left Port Hardy, and was exhausted. His left wing was injured, and one of his webbed feet had been badly torn, which made it difficult for him to fly and land.

"What happened to Spike? Did one of those territorial eagles attack him, or did he have a fight with his albatross girlfriend?" the professor asked, with a chuckle.

"What are we gonna do if we have no means of sendin' a message?" Stubs asked.

The professor spoke up: "I've got an idea. Maybe we could inflate the balloon. If the wind is blowing in the right direction, we could fly to Juneau and drop an SOS message. Course, it's out of the question if the wind is blowing in the wrong direction, and besides, it could be mighty risky."

"Say, Professor, that's not such a bad idea," said Oliver. I'd be willing to give it a try."

"Me too!" Jack said.

The professor was skeptical. "There's just one problem: I can control our ascent and descent, but we can't steer her without changing altitude; and the only way we can do that is to either add hot air or release it. Releasing, I can do, but putting hot air back in her to rise is another thing. If it gets really cold up there, she'll lose hot air faster and could land anywhere. There's another risk. The balloon only goes in the direction the wind is blowing. If we miss Juneau, the balloon could come down any-where in the Yukon. Are you still willing to risk it?"

"Yes! It may be our only means of getting help. Once we're over Juneau, I'll parachute down and alert the authorities," Oliver said.

"We gotta save this ship for the sake o' the cap'n and all aboard," Jack said. "Also, all the cap'n's money is tied up in *Aurora,* and part of that money is ours. Knowin' the cap'n, there ain't no insurance on her. While Oliver gets help in town, me and the professor will stay in the balloon and try to land it. The question is, once we land, how are we goin' to inflate her again?"

"Cap'n!" Mr. Jones said, We ain't got enough coal left to burn a fire."

"I don't care if ye gotta burn the furniture—we gotta get that stinkin' balloon in the air so's we can get this ship off the rocks!" the captain yelled.

The professor was determined to save *Aurora.* "We can make a fire in an empty oil drum, and use the automobile to run the bellows and fill her with hot air," he said.

Captain Matthews was growing impatient. "Well, whatcha waitin' for? Let's inflate the dang thing! Jones, Harris, order the crew to bring the block and tackle and haul that automobile and balloon up on deck—on the double!"

Once everything was on the deck, a roaring fire was started in a Standard Oil drum. The balloon was laid out the length of the deck, and after several false starts the engine of the automobile started. One end of a belt was put around one of the car's wheel hubs, and the other end was attached to the bellows to pump hot air into the balloon.

Stubs felt it would take hours to fill the huge balloon, and suggested they build a fire in the galley stove and run a pipe from the stove to the balloon to increase the flow of hot air. With both methods combined, the balloon was quickly filled, the basket was attached, and the balloon was kept tethered to the ship. The crew looked up at the balloon in awe—it was taller than the mainmast.

The captain wrote a note telling the ship's dilemma and location, and gave it to Oliver. The needed equipment and a hamper of food and drink were put in the basket, and the three aeronauts, warmly dressed, climbed into the gondola.

"Hurry, untie the ropes! We've no time to waste!" the professor shouted to the crewmen.

Just as the balloon began to rise, Frisco, thinking they were doing a performance, leaped into the basket, put his paws up on the rim, and barked as if to say, *I'm part of this team. You can't leave me behind!*

Chapter 54

Parachuting Into Juneau

Fortunately, the wind blew in the right direction, and the balloon drifted toward Juneau. When the balloon neared the town, the professor let out some of the hot air and lowered the drag rope, and the balloon slowly descended to where Oliver could make the parachute drop. Seeing the balloon and a parachute floating down, a crowd had gathered, including the mayor. After several minutes, Oliver landed unhurt in the midst of the crowd, where he took off his harness and gathered up his 'chute.

"How on earth did you get here?" the mayor asked.

Oliver thought that a silly question, since the mayor could plainly see how he had arrived, but Oliver answered him anyway. He then took the captain's note out of his pocket and handed it to the mayor.

A sudden wind gust pushed the balloon farther from town, and it skimmed over the rooftops toward the Mendenhall River at the base of the enormous Mendenhall Glacier. Jack and the professor were awestruck by the glacier's spectacular blue color. At its base the glacier appeared milky white due to the ice breaking up and creating air pockets, which made rainbow-colored prisms. Jack was afraid that the balloon might land on the glacier, but it continued northward along the shoreline past Lemon Creek toward the town of Dawson. The professor tried to descend there, but the wind seemed to have a mind of its own and drove them northward toward the Yukon Territory. Several hours passed during which they worried that the balloon would never run out of hot air and land.

Finally drained of most of its hot air, the balloon descended toward a small frozen lake. When it landed on the ice, the basket tipped on its side. The professor, Jack, and Frisco, tumbled out onto the ice along with their food basket and instruments. Thankfully no one was hurt. The wind continued to drag the empty basket farther along the frozen lake, until finally the balloon collapsed and lay on the ice like a gigantic beached jellyfish.

Jack and the professor thought they were doomed. Then, Jack noticed, at the opposite end of the lake, four Inuit—a man, a woman, and two children—fishing through a hole they had cut in the ice. In his native language, the boy called to his parents, "Father, Mother, look! Spirits have made the moon fall from the sky onto the lake."

Jack and Frisco ran toward them. The professor followed cautiously behind. Seeing the strangers, the family felt afraid and ran toward shore where their huskies and sled waited. Jack and Frisco continued to run after them.

Frisco got to the young boy first, grabbed his pant leg with his teeth, and hung on until the boy managed to shake him off. Frisco was so happy to be rescued he jumped on the boy, knocked him down, and licked his face. The boy laughed and sat up. Stop! Stop! Please, little dog, your tongue is rough and you are tickling me!" the boy yelled.

Jack caught up to the family. She was so out of breath she had to lean over and rest her hands on her thighs for a minute. She had learned a few Tlingit words and phrases from Gooch. "Please, we need your help! Can you tell us where we are and if there is a village near?"

The father said, "You leave, now! Tribal people afraid of white man! Maybe you witch, make magic, make moon fall in lake. Bring bad spirits! Go away!"

Jack replied: "No bad spirits, no witch, no bad magic. Balloon, not moon, carry us here in sky over glacier," she said.

"You crazy!" the man said, as he struggled to understand what Jack was saying.

"What is your name?" Jack asked him.

"I am Beaver Tail. Wife is Fawn. Live in village not far from lake. Long time ago, work at salmon cannery, learn English words. Wife from Whitehorse Band, no English."

Jack didn't know whether Beaver Tail would understand, but she tried her best: "We are so glad you were fishing on the ice when our balloon went down. My name is Jack, and this is Professor Le Strange. We came in the balloon from a steamship in Juneau where our ship is stuck on some rocks. My father is captain o' the ship, and will pay you big money if you help us get back to Juneau." A tear rolled down her cheek.

Seeing her cry, Beaver Tail said, "Okay. Beaver Tail and Joe Jim help. Take captain's daughter, old man, and dog to Skagway by sled, but Juneau too far, too hard on sled dogs.

"How far is Juneau from Skagway?" the professor asked. "We have to get to Juneau as fast as we can."

"Juneau maybe hundred mile from Skagway. When get there, Joe Jim and Beaver Tail go back home to village. If not come back in six, seven days, wives worry, send out rescue party.

"Like I said, my father will pay you for taking us," Jack said.

"Not want white man's money. Want credit at trade store in Skagway to buy flour, gunpowder, medicine for village. We go in morning. Skagway forty mile. Take two, three days. First we go to village, get warm, eat, sleep. Joe Jim bring balloon, house of woven sticks to village later.

"It's a deal!" Jack said. She thanked Beaver Tail in Tlingit.

Beaver Tail nodded. "You wait here. Must get fishing spear and fish for dinner, left near hole on lake."

"We need to get a few things from the balloon before we go," Jack said. She and the professor hurried back to the balloon.

From the basket, the professor took the logbook and a pencil, telescope, and compass. Jack took her knapsack and the basket of food. They then followed Beaver Tail and his family to their sled.

"Dogs strong. Pull sled with old man, children, small dog. Beaver Tail stand on runners behind sled. Wife and Jack put on snowshoes. Walk. Village not far."

The professor and Frisco climbed into the bed of the sled, and the two small children followed. The six huskies were harnessed in three pairs. The two nearest the sled were the wheel dogs, the middle huskies the team dogs, and the front two the leaders. The wheel dogs were larger than the other four, and provided the pulling power. The dogs strained at their necklines, eager to start for home. Frisco wanted to be part of the team and jumped out of the sled, but Beaver Tail grabbed him and put him on the professor's lap.

"Small dog too little to pull sled, but have big heart," Beaver Tail said.

Beaver Tail yelled to the dogs, "All right," which was the signal to go.

As the sled neared the village, they heard many dogs barking. The village consisted of five square-shaped houses. Their walls were made of stone and sod, and they had peaked roofs made with beams of driftwood. The sod and stone insulated the houses so well they could be lived in all year round. Two of them looked like they had been there for many years.

Beaver Tail stopped the sled in front of one of the houses. "This where family live. You come in, eat, get warm, sleep. We leave at dawn."

Jack, the professor, and Frisco followed Beaver Tail's family into their house. An odor of drying fish permeated the room. In the middle of the house was a firepit. Near it was a rack hung with strips of drying salmon. Wisps of smoke rose upward around the rack and escaped through a hole in the roof. A section of the house was partitioned off with a beautiful screen with a carving that depicted an animal. Around the room were baskets and cedar boxes filled with dried seafood, nuts, berries, and other foodstuffs. On a shelf was an old rifle, gunpowder, and a cedar box with a carving like the one on the screen. Jack remembered similar designs on the boxes and doors of the long-house in the Tlingit village on Admiralty Island.

Beaver Tail noticed Jack staring at the cedar box. "Design on screen and box family crests. Go back many years to time of great-great-grandfather."

Jack and the professor warmed their hands and backsides by the smoldering fire. Fawn fished hot stones from the firepit with wooden tongs, and put them in a pot of stew. Immediately, the food begin to boil. She brought frybread and bowls of the stew to Jack and the professor and made the motion to eat. Jack said, *gunalche' esh,* which means thank you in Tlingit. Fawn nodded in acknowledgment. She lowered her head as a sign of respect, and then fed her family the same simple meal.

After eating, Beaver Tail showed Jack and the professor a pile of furs in a corner of the hut. "You sleep here. Wake early tomorrow. Start journey."

Before she lay down, Jack took Frisco out to relieve himself. Overhead, red, blue, and green lights whirled in the sky, reminding Jack of the lights she and Oliver had seen from the *Golden Lady* in the Antarctic. *This must be the Northern Lights, the Aurora Borealis,* she thought. Jack suddenly missed Oliver, and felt a twinge of sadness that he wasn't with them. She swallowed the thought that she might never see him again. She and Frisco watched the phenomenon until the cold air got to them, and they returned to the house.

At dawn, two sleds with six-dog teams waited in front of the hut. One was piled with furs and robes, the other carried the balloon, their food and supplies, and several baskets of dried salmon and caribou meat for the dogs.

Jack asked, "What are all the furs for?"

"Furs keep people in sled warm, then trade for supplies at store," Beaver Tail replied. "Joe Jim drive sled with balloon and supplies. Beaver Tail drive sled with furs, professor, Jack, and little dog."

Jack and the professor looked at Joe Jim. He was nothing like Beaver Tail, who had dark skin and slit eyes, and was short and round as a pumpkin with all the layers of clothing he wore. Joe Jim should have been named Big Jim—he was nearly six feet tall and had broad shoulders and a scruffy beard. Beaver Tail laughed. "You think Joe Jim Inuit like me. Joe Jim father French trapper from Canada, mother from Inuit village. When father die, mother and boy move to village. Beaver Tail and Joe Jim become good friends. Joe Jim teach Beaver Tail English and French."

"How long to get to Skagway?" the professor asked.

"Maybe six, seven days," Beaver Tail told him.

"At that rate, we could miss the steamer. Is there a faster way?

"Yes, but we not go that way. Much danger this time of year! Ice start to melt, dogs fall in river and drown. Avalanche, lose sleds and dogs. We stay on main trail, or not go! Drive day and night. Dogs run long time without rest, but must eat to keep up power and strength. Stop every few hours to feed dogs. No more questions. We go now!"

Before they stepped into the sled, Beaver Tail handed Jack and the professor traditional parkas made of caribou skin. Each had a hood lined with wolverine fur to keep their faces warm. He also gave each of them a pair of carved driftwood goggles.

"Goggles with slit to see through, so white man not get snow-blind. Fawn make parkas, keep you warm. Also make coat and booties for small dog so he keep warm. The professor and Jack pulled the parkas on over their coats, then put the goggles on. After she fastened the little coat and booties on Frisco, she noticed that Joe Jim also wore goggles.

Chapter 55
Sled Dog

Instead of jumping into the sled, to everyone's surprise, Frisco ran to the front of the team, sat down on his haunches next to one of the lead dogs, and waited for the dogs to start running. Jack called to Frisco to join them in the sled, but he stood his ground. When Beaver Tail tried to pick him up and put him in the sled, Frisco bared his teeth and growled.

Beaver Tail laughed. "Small Dog want to be sled dog. Maybe run with dogs short time, like puppy learn to pull sled. Beaver Tail put harness on Small Dog and hook him up beside lead dog. Small Dog learn commands like lead dog."

Beaver Tail and Joe Jim stood on the runners behind their sleds and yelled, "Hike!" Excited to be part of the dog team, Frisco mimicked the other dogs who straightened, strained at the lines, and readied themselves for the run. Beaver Tail and Joe Jim again commanded, "Hike! All ready!" and the two teams of dogs took up a steady pace. Frisco pulled as hard as he could; he tried his best to keep up with the other dogs, but they ran so fast Frisco looked like he was flying—his feet barely touched the ground.

The sleds skimmed over the ice at a fast pace. As they dashed past snowdrifts, bits of snow and ice stung the professor's and Jack's cheeks. Jack found it more thrilling than any of the rides she and Oliver had been on at Coney Island.

For several miles, Frisco ran as fast as he could. Then Beaver Tail and Joe Jim commanded, "Easy, Whoa!" and the dogs slowed and halted. Worn out, bedraggled and footsore, Frisco collapsed in the snow, his sides heaving. The lead dog that Frisco was hooked to whined and licked Frisco's face like he was her pup. Roused by the licking, Frisco stood up and shook the snow off his coat. He took a couple of steps forward and fell down again.

Beaver Tail said, "Small Dog make good run! Have strong heart, and big desire, but now dogs must eat and rest, gain strength back. Beaver Tail feed Small Dog caribou meat, big dogs eat salmon. After eat, Beaver Tail put Small Dog in sled, wrap in furs, stay warm. Be okay soon." Frisco sniffed the dried meat, took two bites, lapped up some water, and contentedly snuggled in the warm furs next to Jack.

All day and through the night, the sled dogs ran, stopping occasionally to be fed to keep up their strength. Finally on the fifth day, they arrived at Skagway. The townspeople rang a bell to signal that sleds were approaching. The dogs raced down the main street until Beaver Tail gave the command "Easy! Whoa!"

Jack, the professor, and Frisco got out of the sled. Beaver Tail looked at Jack and ordered, "Now, you keep bargain! Pay for take you to Skagway. Go in trade store, ask for credit so Beaver Tail and Joe Jim buy food for families. If not get food and supplies, families in Inuit villages starve in winter. Store owner not want people from tribe come in. Say people are dirty and steal from him. They only take food to feed families because government not give rations of lard, flour, sugar, coffee, canned meat. No one come with rations for many moons. Owner of store say he have too many furs and not want to trade. Will only sell goods to white men for silver and gold coins. You go in store, tell owner to give credit to Inuit people."

Jack said, "But, Mr. Beaver Tail, the owner won't give us credit either. Even if the professor and I pooled our money we wouldn't have enough to pay for one sack of flour; and I do not know when we'll see the captain, if ever again."

"If Jack break promise, Beaver Tail wives get mad. You go, now, ask owner for credit!"

Jack, the professor, and Frisco entered the trade store. The proprietor looked them up and down. Seeing their parkas, he mistook them for Inuit natives. "I told ye before, yer kind ain't welcome in my store. Ye're a bunch o' thievin' varmints that rob me blind, tryin' to palm off yer stinkin' furs for flour, coffee, and sugar. I ain't caterin' to no more natives, so get out of here!"

Frisco bared his teeth and growled. Jack took off her goggles and stared with searing eyes at the storekeeper. "We ain't natives, and I don't like how ye talk about 'em. My father is the captain of the steamer *Aurora,* and the older gentleman with me happens to be the famous Professor Zachariah P. Le Strange from New York City. We're askin' ye to give them tribesmen outside credit in your store so they can buy food and supplies for their families," Jack said.

The owner replied, "I don't care if ye're the King and Queen o' Sheba! I ain't givin' credit to no natives, so scram! And take that mangy dog with ye, or I'll—"

Seated by the stove was a man in a red-and-blue uniform and Mountie hat. Overhearing the exchange between Jack and the store owner, he stood up. "Or, you'll what, Bud? Let those poor natives you've been stealing government rations from starve to death? Don't look so innocent. I've been keeping an eye on you."

The owner looked sheepish. My mistake, Constable. From the way they was dressed, I thought the lad and the old man was natives."

"For your information, Bud, the captain of the *Aurora* and most of his crew have been searching for these two for the past week. Their balloon was last seen headed across the glacier at Juneau. Captain Matthews thought it might have come as far as Skagway or even farther north, so after his ship was repaired he sailed up here. I had to tell him I hadn't seen the balloonists or their balloon. Just a warning, Bud: I'd watch out for that captain if I were you. I hear he's got quite a temper and gets hot under the collar if anyone wrongs him. He and those mates of his are over at the hotel right now."

Hearing that the captain was at the hotel, Jack rushed for the door. Just as she reached it, the captain, Oliver, and Jonesy banged it open and entered the store.

The captain roared, "There are two natives outside sayin' they brung a lad and an old man to town in their sleds, and now they want me to get 'em credit in this store for bringin' them two all the way from their village in the Yukon. What gives here?"

Jack ran to the captain and gave him a big hug. "Oh, Father, ye're here! Me and the professor thought we'd never see ye again, and that we was stranded in this place forever."

Still warming his hands at the stove, the professor nodded to the captain. "Ahoy there, Captain! Sure glad you've come! Thank the Lord you had the foresight to sail your steamer up to Skagway instead of waiting for us in Juneau."

The captain ignored the old windbag and addressed the storekeeper: "Ahem. Sir, I was talkin' just now with them natives out front, and they said their village hasn't gotten their government food rations for several months now, and that ye refuse to trade their furs for food. That right?"

The storekeeper looked up at Captain Matthews, who was two heads taller than he and broader of shoulder. "I wouldn't trade with them natives if they was the last people on God's green earth!" he said.

"What's wrong with you, man?" the captain yelled.

The proprietor squirmed. "Well, ye see, there's been a shortage of supplies lately. When that shipment of government-issued goods come in, I thought I'd—"

"Ye'd what? the captain snarled. "Dip yer hand in the cookie jar and steal the lot, then make a profit sellin' them goods to white folks for high prices and let the natives starve to death? Talk about thievery! Have ye no scruples, man? I expect the Canadian Department of External Affairs would like to hear about this. I think I'll have them natives out front waltz right into that backroom o' yers and load up all them bootleg sacks of flour, sugar, and coffee that rightfully belongs to 'em. And when another shipment for that tribe comes in and they don't get it, I'll make double sure ye're arrested for stealin' government property. Ye got that, storekeeper?"

The Mountie said, "Captain Matthews, will you and your crewmen please pack up all the goods ye can find stamped DEPT. OF EXTERNAL AFFAIRS, CANADA and load them onto those two sleds out front, before this storekeeper gets any more ideas on how to cheat the Canadian government? Since the stamps on those goods prove that they were property issued for the sole purpose of distribution to the Inuit, I'm putting you under arrest, Bud, for selling stolen goods."

The proprietor yelled, "Now, just you wait one darn minute, you red-jacketed Canuck! What gives you the authority to talk to me like that and confiscate anything? If them natives take all my goods, I won't have nothin' to sell to the white folks that come in my store. Them supplies is the only ones that's come here in months. As far as I'm concerned, them natives owe me for all the times they come in here and stole my goods behind my back. What'd they ever do for me 'cept trade their stinkin' furs, which I'm now stuck with since the fur-trading business took a dive? I'm only takin' back what's rightfully mine!"

The captain had heard enough. "I beg to differ. As captain of a U.S. postal steamer that's got a contract with the Canadian and US governments to deliver mail and supplies to native villages here, I'm pressin' charges. I insist ye put this man in irons for cheatin' the natives. Mountie, do your duty, sir!"

Taking the captain at his word, the Mountie slapped a pair of handcuffs on the storekeeper and marched him off to the town jail.

When the crew and natives had cleared the storage room of all the stolen flour, sugar, and coffee, the Mountie came back and posted a sign on the door: Closed Until Further Notice. Anyone Wanting To Purchase Food And Supplies Must See The Constable.

Chapter 56

Karluk Salmon Cannery

After *Aurora* had sailed back to Juneau, the captain learned that the Karluk Salmon Cannery was closing for good, and several of the workers were anxious to sail back home to the United States. The captain hoped he could make extra money by offering a few of them passage.

As a thank-you to the people of Juneau for getting his ship off the rocks, he had Oliver, the professor, and Jack perform a balloon and aerial act that was a big hit. The people of Juneau then bade the master and crew of the *Aurora* a fond farewell, and wished them the best of luck on the treacherous 700-mile journey across the Gulf of Alaska to the town of Homer, Alaska. Homer was known for its coal mines, and Captain Matthews hoped to purchase a lot of it so they could build up enough steam to run the paddlewheels before they sailed south to Kodiak Island where the Karluk Canning Company was located.

It was mid-September when *Aurora* began her journey. There was no telling what the weather would be like. The captain had been told that sometimes there were giant swells, and other times the sea was flat calm. The crew prepared for the worst and hoped for the best.

The farther they sailed the colder it got. They had experienced worse in Antarctica on their trip round the Horn. As they crossed the gulf they saw several icebergs. Some had steep sides and flat tops; others were dome-shaped and had spires. Some of the mountainous bergs reached over a hundred sixty feet above the sea. There were also large pieces of floating ice known as bergy bits, and smaller ones called growlers, chunks that had broken off the many glaciers. The waters of the gulf were haunting, and for two days *Aurora* didn't see another ship. Since most of her coal had been used up, the crew relied on the wind to carry her across the water.

One morning the rigging was covered with icicles and the deck was awash in frost. Jack and Oliver could barely make it to the helm without slipping. While Achoo opted to stay in his cage in the galley, Frisco dashed out to pee—and slid across the icy deck.

Stubs and the professor had purchased some food supplies from the people in Juneau to add to their meager meals, and Gooch's distant relatives had provided them dried caribou and seal meat, dried mushrooms, berries, and seaweed. Oliver found the seal meat chewy, and it had a fishy aftertaste. He remembered the taste of iodine in the liver his mother used to serve when someone in his family felt puny. Mother would soak the liver overnight in milk to lessen the iodine taste, and fried the meat with bacon and onions. Oliver suggested to Stubs that he pound the seal meat to make it tender, and to soak it in milk overnight to lessen the fishy aftertaste. Unfortunately there was no milk, no bacon and not a single onion to be found on the ship, so Stubs ground the meat into patties, added salt and pepper and fried it in lard. Stubs boiled the dried mushrooms in water and made a soupy sauce with them. He then boiled the seaweed like spinach and added salt, pepper and vinegar to the mess. He mixed the dried berries into the porridge. After a while the crew and few passengers ceased to complain about the food, gobbled it down in silence, and washed it down with swigs of liquor. Jonesy said any food tasted better if ye washed it down with whiskey or rum.

After a fortnight, they had crossed the Gulf of Alaska and reached Homer, where they acquired enough coal to fill *Aurora*'s bunkers. They then sailed 140 miles south to Kodiak Island where, the captain hoped, a handful of unemployed workers would want to book passage to Seattle.

In 1882, Karluk Packing Co. was the first cannery to open on Kodiak Island. The cannery was backed financially by the Alaska Commercial Company, and was founded by two former employees, Oliver Smith and Charles Hirsch. Word had spread that there was plenty of sockeye salmon in the Karluk River, and both men made a fortune salting salmon on the Karluk Spit.

Before the steamer arrived at Kodiak Island, the newspaper had advertised:

> Tickets for sale for the good ship *Aurora,* 2 bunks
> per cabin,
>
> $150 per person, $200 for married couples.

When the ship arrived at the old cannery, instead of the expected small group of passengers, more than a hundred men and women anxiously awaited any ship that would take them south. The majority looked like they couldn't even afford a 3×3-foot space on the deck, let alone a cabin. A good many of them looked like they hadn't changed clothes in weeks. Their clothes were in rags and their boots were wrapped with strips of cloth to hold them together. Other than those few who could afford cabins, most had only a small carpetbag or burlap sacks for luggage.

Captain Matthews had a rough exterior, but he had a good heart, and couldn't let all those threadbare people freeze to death during the frigid Alaska winter. But the captain was concerned about where to put them all, how to feed them, sanitation, and the safety of his crew and that of the curator and his son, who were already aboard.

The captain stared at the crowd milling around onshore and announced through his speaking trumpet, "Those who have the money to purchase a ticket with a cabin, please step forward!" Only two out of the crowd of a hundred did so.

Next he shouted, "Those couples who are married now step forward!" Hearing that the price of a cabin was cheaper for married couples, a dozen of the ladies who appeared to be prostitutes paired up with their pimps and any other willing prospects.

"The rest of ye can come aboard for whatever ye can afford or have to trade, but I warn ye, ye won't be comfortable. Dress as warm as ye can, and each of ye'll have to bring enough food for fourteen days and sleep wherever ye can find a space. We'll be leavin' this hellhole on the next tide after loadin' our cargo o' canned salmon."

The remaining passengers in the crowd agreed to the terms, joyful at finding a ship that would take them home. The captain looked at the motley horde and worried: with so many passengers, the ship would ride low in the water.

When the cargo was loaded and the few paying passengers had come aboard, the throng of ragtag folks crammed onto the steamer and found any space they could. As payment for their passage, they gave what little money they had or paid in trade. The growing heap of oddities on the deck included fur pelts, small vials and pokes of what looked like gold, jewelry, various native crafts—four pairs of worn beaded moccasins, a beautifully carved and painted cedar box—a fresh-caught salmon, and a large Italian salami.

What the captain and crew of *Aurora* didn't know was that half the people who boarded were not Karluk cannery workers, but people who'd come down from the goldfields and had been stranded at Kodiak Island for nearly a year, awaiting any ship that would take them to Seattle and San Francisco. Among them were cannery workers, families, shopkeepers, gamblers, prostitutes, and those just down on their luck. After setting sail, the gamblers and prostitutes immediately set up business.

The captain later found out that the supposedly married couples who had bought a ticket with a cabin were selling space in their cabins to make money. The crew, including Jack, also sold space in their cabins and anywhere else on the ship where a person could sleep. The captain tried to stop it, but it was to no avail.

With a hundred passengers and a crew of twenty-three, the main deck, quarterdeck, and every available space was occupied day and night. Captain Matthews ordered Jack, Oliver, Stubs, the professor, Jones, and Harris to give up their cabins and the saloon; they were forced to sleep crammed together with the idlers in the fo'c'sle and galley. The crew and some of the passengers slept in shifts, either in hammocks or two to a bunk. The bedding was never aired, and bedbugs, fleas, lice, roaches, and rats were having a field day. To try to control the vermin, the crew sprinkled salt on the decks and put out dishes of ammonia and vinegar, but the insects and rats still ran unchecked.

Even though the passengers were asked to bring their own food, there wasn't enough to go around. By the end of the second week, the captain ordered that all food be rationed, including that brought by the passengers. The sailors not on duty, including Oliver and Jack, were asked to spend their slack time fishing for salmon to supplement the meager food supply.

Stubs and the professor, who were the cooks, did their best to make the remaining food palatable. Even the giant sausage was diced and added to the split pea soup, which that night created a long line waiting to use the jardines. Drinking water was also rationed to a cup a day.

As the icy wind and cold ravaged *Aurora,* the captain feared she might be trapped by drifting ice from the Bering Sea. As a result, he ordered that the paddlewheels be kept turning the entire way down the Kenai Peninsula and Aleutian Islands, which meant the steamer would use up most of her coal before they reached Seattle. At every stop, the passengers stayed onboard because they feared that if they gave up their space someone else would take it. Finally, after three weeks, the ship arrived at Puget Sound in Washington.

The captain and crew were never so glad to see their passengers disembark. As the curator and his son left the ship, Jack noticed that the curator had a dress box under his arm similar to the one she had seen him give to the fence in the Red Onion Saloon.

"Oliver! That box must have the real icon in it. Let's intercept them before they get off the ship," Jack whispered to Oliver.

The captain, overhearing their conversation, said, "Hold it right there, ye two!" Then, to the curator, he said, "Sir, I'll have that box if ye don't mind! If it contains a paintin' ye stole from the Russian church in Sitka, and ye been makin' forgeries and sellin' 'em to unsuspectin' persons, that's pure sacrilege! By the authority vested in me as the captain of this ship, I have the power to make a citizen's arrest and bring ye to justice. If it was up to me, I'd have ye thrown in the brig, but I guess I'll let the International Police Organization handle it. Now give me that paintin'!"

"Don't give it to him!" the curator's son shouted. "He's just bluffing! He's got no authority!"

"It's okay, son. Here," the old man said, handing over the box.

The captain opened it and was surprised to find only two dirty shirts, a few pairs of socks, and three books.

"I got you this time, Cap'n! I sold that painting to one of those rich couples that first came aboard at Kodiak Island. Got over three hundred dollars for it!"

"The man's son shouted, "It was worth three times that much! Holding out on me, were you?"

The curator ran to the gangway, shoving other passengers aside.

Captain Matthews shouted through his speaking tube, "Ye just think ye got the best of me? Ha! Maybe ye're not so smart after all. Ever since ye left Sitka, the International Bureau of Investigation of Stolen National Treasures has been on your tail. Cuff him, officers!" Two officers of the law ran up the ramp and knocked the curator down.

Later, Oliver asked, "Cap'n, I've never heard of the International Bureau of Investigation of Stolen National Treasures. Is there really any such agency?"

"Hell if I know! It was the only thing I could come up with to stop him, and it sure got the attention of those police officers who were coming to inspect the ship. If there's one thing I hate it's a thief."

The captain, Oliver, and Jack later learned that not only the curator and his son had been arrested for stealing the painting; the couple who bought it from the curator, intending to resell it later at a substantial profit, were also in police custody.

When asked to make a statement at the police station, Captain Matthews, Oliver, and Jack found out that there was a $2,000 reward for anyone who helped the police capture the thieves. The captain took half the money, and gave Jack and Oliver $500 each.

Part 4

The Flying Machine and the Transcontinental Air Race

Chapter 57

An Aeroplane

In the spring of 1911, the professor, Oliver, and Jack were doing their balloon and aerial act at an airshow at Meadows Racetrack near Seattle. The show included an aviator who performed acrobatics in his Curtiss "Jenny" flying machine.

Oliver, Jack, and the professor watched the biplane get a running start on its three wheels, rise into the air, circle the field, and do a loop-de-loop. Suddenly, the engine sputtered, then cut out completely. As the propeller slowed, the crowd gasped. Then, as if by magic, the engine started up again, and the pilot made a smooth landing, taxied a short distance, and stopped.

Oliver approached the pilot. "Sir, what happened? Why'd the engine stop?"

"Not sure. Musta been some gunk in the fuel line. You never know what'll happen with these Jenny's. Thank God she started again. Name's Charlie Olson. Credited with making the first heavier-than-air flight in the state of Washington," he said, extending a hand to shake Oliver's.

"My name's Oliver and I'm a balloonist with Professor Le Strange's Balloon Act. Seeing you pilot that flying machine of yours was so exciting I got goose bumps. Sure wish I could learn to fly an aeroplane like that!"

"You really got the aviation bug, ain't ya, kid? I like you, so tell ye what: If you come back here in an hour or so, old

Charlie'll give ye a ride. I may even teach you some basics on how to fly her."

"Really, sir? I'll be here!" Oliver said, thrilled about going up in an aeroplane for the first time.

Charlie said to Oliver, "Lately, I've been flying this June Bug, which is a Curtiss-Herring No. 1 Reims Racer, at various air shows throughout the Northwest to earn enough money to buy the new Golden Flyer, Reims Racer No. 2. It's lighter in weight, has a more powerful engine, and can fly 175 miles without stopping. Come tomorrow I'll make my last payment, but she won't arrive from the factory for another two weeks.

"I can't wait to get the new 'plane so I can enter a contest sponsored by Mr. William Randolph Hearst, the newspaper magnate. You know who he is, don't ya?"

"Oh, sure, I've heard of him," Oliver replied, with a vague notion of who Hearst was.

"He's offering a prize of fifty thousand dollars to the first pilot to fly across the United States in thirty days or less. For that much money, any flyboy that thinks he can make it that far without crashing is a damn fool not to enter. Guess I'm just a damn fool, 'cause I'm going for it! Already sent in my racing form and entry fee."

"Wow, fifty thousand dollars is more money than most men earn in a lifetime! How much is the entry fee and when does the race start?" Oliver asked, excited at the thought of entering the race.

"Whoa there, kid! The article in the paper said the entry fee is a steep two hundred dollars, and the prize offer expires on October 11, 1911. That's just a couple months from now, but I guess we've still got time. That's if you still wanna buy my old Jenny and enter the contest."

"You said, 'We,' Oliver replied, with a surprised look.

"Yeah. Way I figure it, if you can raise the money to buy this old 'plane we can both enter the race."

"But your new Jenny is supposed to be way faster and will probably outdistance your old one by a long shot," Oliver noted.

"That's a risk you gotta take, but who knows what could happen? Maybe one of the other competitors will break a strut, have engine trouble, get lost in a snowstorm, or crash. So, what do you say? Are you game?"

Oliver lowered his head. "Yes I'm interested, but first I've got to come up with the money to buy your aeroplane, plus pay the entry fee, and learn to fly the thing."

"Well, it may sound like a tall order, but if you're determined, I'm sure you'll figure it all out somehow," Charlie said, trying to encourage Oliver to buy his old 'plane.

"Would five hundred dollars buy your aeroplane? It's all I've got!" Oliver asked, crossing his fingers and hoping it was enough.

"Well, five hundred is a little short. I was thinking more along the lines of fifteen hundred. The Wright Brothers sold their 'plane for a thousand, but that 'plane was lucky to get off the ground. From what I hear, it was stuck together with chewing gum and old bicycle parts."

Oliver thought, *How am I going to come up with that kind of money?*

Seeing Oliver's disappointment, Charlie said, "Tell you what, Oliver, I'll sell her to you for twelve hundred, but no less; and you'll have to come up with the other seven hundred by tomorrow afternoon. That's when I make my last payment on the Reims Racer No. 2. Oh, and then there's the matter of the two-hundred-dollar entry fee, if you plan to enter the transcontinental race."

Oliver really wanted the aeroplane and to enter the race, and said, "Mr. Olson, I'll try to come up with the fourteen hundred dollars by tomorrow! Promise me you won't sell her to someone else in the meantime."

"Okay, I promise, lad. You come up with the money by tomorrow afternoon, the Jenny is yours." Charlie and Oliver shook hands to seal the deal.

Jack agreed to lend Oliver $500 from her share of the reward money on condition that she would be part owner of the biplane and could be the copilot. Next, Oliver got up the nerve to ask the professor for the additional $400. The professor was hesitant, but finally agreed to lend Oliver the money if he would agree to fly the aeroplane in their act. *Doing tricks with an aeroplane could be a moneymaker,* he thought.

Oliver didn't tell the professor that the aeroplane cost only $1,200, that the extra $200 was for the contest entry fee, and that he and Jack planned to leave the act in another month. Oliver wasn't even going to tell Jack they were leaving, until the deal was finally settled.

At 1 PM the next day, Oliver gave Charlie Olson $1,200 for the sale of the aeroplane plus the entry fee for the cross-country air race, which Charlie promised to send in for him.

"Tomorrow, I make my last payment on the new 'plane, but I got two weeks before she'll arrive. In the meantime, how about I teach you to fly this old Jenny. Want your first lesson this afternoon, after my last performance?"

Later that afternoon Charlie was ready to take Oliver up in the Jenny. Oliver walked around the aeroplane. It had three landing wheels, and two large wings, one above the other. Between them was the motor that operated the propeller in the rear. At the back of the fuselage was a small horizontal plane called the tail. It was partially divided by the rudder, which made the 'plane turn left or right by wires connected to the steering wheel. In the front of the Jenny was the altitude rudder, which let the front edges of the wings tip up and down. This was controlled by a long rod connected to the steering wheel. Pushing the wheel forward turned the altitude planes downward. If you pulled the wheel toward you, it made the 'plane go up. The most important thing an aviator had to learn, though, was to get a feel for the air currents, so that without thinking, he could rise or dip according to the conditions.

Charlie explained: "You do this by holding the wheel steady, but not too tight. To keep the 'plane on an even keel, at the outer ends of the main wings are two small hinged planes. They keep the 'plane from tipping over sideways. These planes are operated by arms that stick out from the back of your seat on each side, and they move when you move your body side to side. When the Jenny sags downward on one side, you automatically lean to the other side to regain the balance. That makes the ailerons even out, and the pressure of the wind steadies the 'plane again.

"Some other controls you need to operate: There's two pedals you control with your feet. Press the right one and it short-circuits the magneto, a generator that ignites the spark plugs and also cuts off the spark and stops the engine. That pedal also acts as a brake for the forward wheel, and slows the machine so you can land. Your right foot also controls the pump that makes lubricating oil go to the points faster or slower. Your left foot controls the throttle lever, which controls how much fuel enters the cylinders. The propeller makes an average of eleven hundred revolutions per minute, but with the throttle you can slow it to a hundred. At that speed the prop's not fast enough to keep the 'plane aloft, but it can help if you need to glide."

"Wow!" Oliver said. "That's an awful lot to remember!"

"Uh… once you practice a few times and get the feel for her, it's a cinch!" Charlie said, wanting to reassure Oliver so he wouldn't back out of the sale.

Charlie had installed a jump seat directly in front of the pilot's seat. "That's where you'll sit and watch me operate the machine. It also comes in handy if you ever want to take a passenger with you." Oliver thought of Jack.

Oliver sat in the jump seat in front of Charlie, who said, "Make sure you've got your harness fastened, 'cause we're going up!" With a sudden surge, the 'plane moved forward and ran down the field. As it lifted off, Oliver gasped. Even though he was used to being at great heights in the balloon, he was terrified because the aeroplane moved much faster than the balloon. Oliver listened tentatively as Charlie instructed him. After several takeoffs and landings and circling the field three times, Charlie landed the Jenny, got out of his seat, and put blocks under the front wheels so the 'plane wouldn't roll. "Switch seats with me," he said to Oliver, "'cause it's now or never!"

It was a bit tricky to get the engine to restart, but after a few pulls, the propeller spun. Charlie then shouted, "Contact!" He quickly removed the blocks from the wheels and climbed into the jump seat. Oliver was hesitant to fly the aeroplane, but did as he was told.

Once in the back seat, Oliver asked, "Now what do I do?"

"You take off. First we've gotta taxi down the field. Then you swing her around so we can get in position. Oliver carried out those orders.

"Now, give her some gas and pull back on the wheel. Oliver did so, but as he did, the 'plane lurched ahead and almost made a nosedive.

"I said, "Gentle!" Charlie shouted in Oliver's ear. "Now ease up on the fuel, and try to fly her gentle-like! The aeroplane suddenly shuddered and swooped up and down.

"Pull the wheel toward you so she rises smoothly. Once you reach the desired height, give her a little more throttle, push the wheel forward a bit, and she'll level out. Then give her the full throttle and we're off." Oliver did as instructed, and the Jenny zoomed ahead. Oliver tried hard to control her, but soon learned that flying a 'plane was not so easy; at times it felt tougher than steering a sailing ship in a gale.

"If I didn't know better, I'd swear this 'plane had a mind of its own!" he yelled to Charlie, who just laughed, amused by Oliver's anxiety.

"Now, try to keep her steady and level. To make a right or left turn, turn the wheel in the direction you want to go, just like in an automobile, and lean into the direction you want to turn.

Now, I want you to make several sweeps of the field. Mind you, be alert to any other 'planes that might be in the air."

After making the three sweeps, Oliver said, "Okay, I think I've got it! Now, how do I land the darn thing?" he shouted over the roar of the engine and swoosh of the wind.

"You press your right foot on the lever to stop the motor. The lever also slows the 'plane so we can glide in and land. It's that simple!"

Oliver came in faster than expected, and Charlie shouted, "Pull her up! Cut the magneto! Too late—give her some gas and we'll circle around again. This time, hit the lever with your right foot so the motor stops, and slowly glide her in."

"Uh… yeah!" Oliver followed instructions, and the Jenny made a smooth three-point landing on the grass and taxied to a stop.

It was common knowledge that in the early years of aviation, most pilots flew by the seat of their pants. Most had only a compass to tell them which direction they were flying in, a pocket watch to time the length of their flights, and no lights for night flying. Charlie told Oliver that during the race, the 'planes would follow the Transcontinental Railroad and other tracks in the daylight. There are supposed to be designated fields where we can land just before sunset, eat something, refuel, make repairs, and sleep the night.

"Mr. Hearst and some of the sponsors will travel across the United States in Hearst's private railroad car; they'll set up various stations along the way for some of the sponsored aviators. A man named Rogers persuaded Armour & Company, a meat-packing firm, to sponsor him, pay for a new aeroplane, and pay all his expenses. In return Rogers named his new aeroplane after Armour's grape-flavored soft drink Vin Fiz. Ain't that a kick in the pants? "Vin Fiz! Ha-ha!

"The newspapers will have a field day following our stories. Who knows, the winner of the race could become famous and go down in history as the first pioneer aviator to cross the continent. In my opinion, the entry fee is a little steep for the average Joe, but I guess it's to discourage would-be aviators from entering the race. Do you think you can be serious, Oliver, if you enter the race, and compete against who knows how many fliers?"

Chapter 58

The Aeroplane Race

With Jack as his copilot, Oliver practiced flying the "June Bug" every day when the weather was good up until the time they would have to leave for the race. Oliver also taught Jack to fly the aeroplane. They flew it together as part of the act, and Jack showed off by walking on the wing.

One day Oliver asked Jack, "How would you feel if I told you I signed us up to fly in an aeroplane race across the United States, and the winner gets a prize of fifty thousand dollars? I should have asked you earlier, but I was afraid you'd say no. The drawback is we'd have to reach the East Coast in less than thirty days, and in two days the pretrials start in Sacramento, California, where the race begins. It could be risky. We might crash and die."

Jack's eyes glazed. "Fifty thousand dollars?! Even ten thousand is a fortune and worth the risk. When do we leave?"

"You mean it? You'd come with me on a coast-to-coast aeroplane race, even if it means you might be risking your life?"

"Yes, ye ninny! Ye forget, I've risked me life many times as a sailor, a balloonist, and an aerialist. How much worse could it be to fly an aeroplane across the United States?"

Oliver wiped his forehead, "Whew! That's good, 'cause I already signed us up!"

"Thanks for all the advance notice! I'll do it!" Jack said. "But how's the professor goin' to react to us leavin' the act? Remember when we left to join the crew of the *Aurora?* He like to blow a gasket!" Jack said, laughing.

"He'll get over it if we promise to give him some of our winnings. Besides the grand prize, Hearst is offering twenty thousand for the runner-up, ten thousand for third place, and twenty-five hundred for fourth. With that kind of money, we'd be fools not to enter the race," Oliver said.

At a farewell party given by the captain and the crew of *Aurora,* Jack and Oliver said their good-byes. They told the professor how much the prizes were, and promised to send him a tenth of whatever they won. With that in mind, the professor too wished them good luck.

Chapter 59

Entering the Race

Oliver wanted to improve the Reims Racer No. 1 in hopes of keeping up with at least some of the newer aeroplanes. First he removed the old fuel tank and put in a lighter one. Then he took the prop off and put it back on the other way round. The old pusher prop now became a puller prop. He also added several struts to create more tension, which would make the aeroplane more maneuverable, give the fuselage more lift, and hold the wings level.

Underneath the jump seat, Oliver put his toolbox, in which he placed two brand-new Eveready flashlights with tungsten-filament bulbs. He also put in a small hatchet, a box of quick-strike matches, and various small tools in case they needed to make repairs.

Like the Wright Brothers, Oliver brought along a stopwatch to time the length of their flights, a collapsible telescope, a Veeder engine-revolutions counter, an anemometer to measure wind speed, a compass that Captain Matthews had given him, two gas cans, and maps of the Transcontinental Railroad route from Sacramento to Omaha, Nebraska. Food, water, and medical supplies also went along.

In addition, Oliver had strapped down a sizeable basket on each side of the fuselage. In one of them were two tarps, two puptents, and two bedrolls; the other held extra blankets. Oliver knew the downside: the modifications and extra weight from all the items he'd packed, plus a passenger/copilot, would create more drag, and the faster the 'plane flew, the worse the drag would get, but anything would be an improvement over the slow old Jenny.

The initial flight plan was to fly from Seattle to Sacramento where the inspection and pre-race heat were to be held. Thence they would follow the Transcontinental Railway from Sacramento across to Reno, Nevada, then to Salt Lake City, Cheyenne, and Denver to North Platte, Nebraska. From there they would follow the Union Pacific and Central Pacific Railways east to Council Bluffs, Iowa, then head south to follow the Mississippi River to St. Louis. Then they would follow the route of the Southwestern Limited, a passenger-train service operated by the New York Central Railroad between New York City and St. Louis.

Oliver and Jack weren't sure they could follow that precise schedule, but at least they had a possible flight plan and weren't just winging it like some of the other flyers. As they were leaving, Oliver was handed a U.S. Mail pouch to carry with them to New York. When they got to Sacramento, they learned that a mechanic would follow the route of some of the flyers by train, and would be available at some designated landing sites to perform necessary aeroplane repairs. Jack and Oliver hadn't heard from Charlie Olson since he'd left for Portland, Oregon. They hoped they might meet up with him somewhere along in the race.

Oliver told Jack, "From what I've calculated, as far as the crow flies, with a good tailwind and no mishaps, it should take us about two and a half to three weeks to reach New York City. That's not including our two-day flight from Puget Sound to Sacramento, where the West Coast pilots are supposed to meet up for the pretrials and to start the race. I estimate that if all goes well, we should arrive about sixteen days before the thirty days end on October 11."

On the morning they were to leave for Sacramento, a crowd had gathered to send them off. In attendance were Oliver's parents, brothers, and sister, Captain Matthews, Stubs and the professor. Having heard about the new Eastman Kodak Brownie camera you could hold in your hand and that sold for a dollar, Oliver ordered one so they could take photographs of their trip.

When Eastman Kodak got word of Oliver and Jack's heroic initial cross-country flight, the company offered to sponsor them by releasing a major advertising campaign about their new Brownie camera. Oliver and Jack posed in front of the Jenny, wearing their leather aviator helmets with earflaps, fleece-lined bomber jackets, jodhpurs, laced knee-high boots, white trailing scarves, leather gloves, and aviator goggles. Even though Frisco and Achoo would stay behind with the captain, they didn't want to be excluded from the photograph. Achoo quickly flew onto Jack's shoulder; and Frisco ran to sit by Oliver's side. When the photo was published in the newspaper, underneath it was the caption YOU PRESS THE BUTTON, WE DO THE REST.

After the photo session, Jack climbed into the jump seat, fastened her harness, and waited patiently while Oliver attempted to start the engine. He swung the prop several times before the engine caught; then he pulled out the wooden blocks that held the wheels in place, and jumped into the pilot's seat behind Jack. He gave the 'plane some fuel, and she rose into the air, where they circled the field and waved a final farewell to the spectators. Attached to the tail of the Jenny was a banner with the words TRANSCONTINENTAL AIR RACE OR BUST.

Chapter 60

Stowaways

The weather was good, and they made it to Portland by noon-time, with only one stop along the way. When they arrived, Oliver inquired about Charlie Olson, but no one had heard of him. Jack and Oliver were hungry, so Jack went to one side of the aeroplane to open the basket containing the sack of sandwiches Stubs had given them. Jack noticed that a corner of the cloth cover was slightly open. She opened it further, and a dog's head popped out. Snuggled in the basket next to Frisco was Achoo.

Jack looked at them and called to Oliver. When Frisco saw Oliver, he barked happily and Achoo screamed, "Well, blow me down, if it ain't the pilot!"

"Now, what are we gonna do with these stowaways?" Jack asked.

"Well, I guess we have no choice but to take them with us, 'cause we don't have the time or fuel to waste taking them back to the cap'n," Oliver said.

Achoo flew out of the basket and landed on Jack's shoulder. She noticed that many of Achoo's feathers were rumpled and no longer smooth. Frisco, whose legs had been crossed for some time, was anxious to get out of the basket. Once out, he immediately lifted his leg against one wheel of the Jenny.

Jack laid out the sack of food, and the four of them enjoyed tasty roast beef sandwiches. After they'd eaten their fill, Oliver and Jack decided to catch a few winks underneath the 'plane before starting the next leg of their flight to Sacramento. When they'd caught up on their sleep, Oliver checked to see that everything was secure before taking off again.

Jack put Achoo and Frisco back in the basket. To protect Frisco's ears from the harsh wind, Jack put her old stocking cap on his head. Frisco was content to stay in the basket as long as he could occasionally stick his nose out and sniff the air.

Poor Achoo, on the other hand, had been miserable the entire flight from Seattle to Portland, because the squirmy dog kept climbing on top of him to poke his head out of the basket. Whenever Frisco did that, the strong wind from the thrust of the 'plane would ruffle Achoo's feathers, so he was constantly having to preen himself. Now that the sack of sandwiches had been removed, there was more room in the basket, and Achoo too was content to stay in it.

Chapter 61

Beginning the Race

When Jack and Oliver reached the airfield in Sacramento, Jack spied three other 'planes waiting to be inspected and begin the preheat race. Among the flyers were Charlie Olson in his new Curtiss Reims Racer No. 2; an aviator from Southern California in a Wright Flyer II biplane; and a cowboy from Montana in a homebuilt job. Within an hour, two other aeroplanes landed. A great many pilots had sent in their racing forms and entry fee, but many had lost their nerve and didn't show up. Oliver thought it was to his advantage to have to compete with only a handful of flyers.

The rules stated that after the inspection there would be a preheat race to show the pilots' flying skills. It required them to circle the field three times, do a loop, climb and dip, and then land smoothly. Upon landing, the cowboy's "dragonfly" took a nosedive, and one of its wings was damaged. After a quick fix, however, the 'plane was in the air again. Tex, the cowboy, had hit his head against the steering wheel when his 'plane dived. Tex suffered a bump and a headache, but he claimed he was still able to fly, and he, along with Oliver and Jack, made the pretrial without any further mishaps.

In the preheat race, Charlie Olson's aeroplane, with the new Curtis V8 motor was the fastest; it clocked 47.7 mph. The Wright Flyer II came in second at 44 mph. Another flyer powered down his 'plane in a steep descent, and his machine was stopped by a barbed-wire fence. That pilot was disqualified for reckless flying. Oliver's and Tex's aeroplanes both passed inspection and qualified in the preheat by a slim margin. Oliver tried to make the Jenny go faster, but due to a strong headwind and the extra weight of the equipment, he couldn't get up enough speed to go faster than 20 mph. He and Jack felt like they were standing still compared to the other 'planes, but they did better than the flyer whose aeroplane had five wings and never got off the ground.

The next day, the cross-country race was supposed to begin, but wind and rain delayed the start. For most of the day, Oliver and Jack sat on a log under a tarp in front of a small campfire, sipping cups of coffee and reviewing the route they would take.

Charlie Olson wandered over with a mug in his hand. "Got an extra cup of coffee for a poor flyer?" he asked.

Jack said under her breath, "Poor flyer, me arse! He not only got a boatload of money from us for that old Jenny but he's bragged about winnin' several purses worth hundreds o' dollars."

Charlie poured himself a cup and sat down next to Oliver. "Congratulations, lad, on passing the inspection and preheat! Wasn't sure you were gonna make it, what with a copilot, two pets, and all that unnecessary equipment you brought," he said.

"You have a problem with my bringing a co-pilot, pets, and equipment?" Oliver asked.

"Nothing in the rulebook says you can't, but you won't win any blue ribbons in this race plodding along at twenty mph. If I was you, I'd drop off any gear you don't need, along with those passengers, before you fly over the Rockies. I see you made a few modifications to the old girl—you put in a smaller fuel tank and changed the prop. Good thinking!"

Charlie then addressed Jack: "I'm Charlie Olson, the man who sold Oliver my old Jenny. What's your name, kid?"

Offended by Olson's comment about the extra weight and dropping her and Frisco and Achoo off somewhere, Jack lost her temper. "My name's Jack, and I happen to be part owner of this Jenny. That gives me the right to come along, and as far as the extra equipment is concerned, ye can just bug off, buster!"

"Well, excuse me!" said Charlie. "I was just joking. Didn't mean anything by it."

Charlie turned to Oliver. "So, he's the sucker you tricked into giving you the extra money to buy my 'plane and pay the entry fee, eh? Well, good luck to you both!" Charlie said, then strode off to his own 'plane.

Oliver yelled after Charlie, "I didn't trick him!"

Jack said, "Oliver, somethin' about that guy makes my blood boil. Like Stubs used to say, I wouldn't trust him as far as I can throw an anchor, which ain't very far."

"Oh, Jack, don't mind Charlie," Oliver said. "He's just trying to distract us 'cause we're part of the competition. He probably did the same to the other flyers who qualified."

Unbeknownst to the West Coast flyers, several East Coast competitors anxiously awaited the start of the race in New York City. William Randolph Hearst, sponsor of the coast-to-coast race, was already headed west in his luxury train, which boasted a car designed to carry an aeroplane and accommodations for a skilled mechanic.

Like the West Coast pilots, the Easterners too had to go through inspection and pretrial. Word was that one of them had had to cut his speed upon landing. His 'plane flipped over, which punched a hole in the gas tank and made the 'plane and the pilot's clothing catch fire, but he rolled on the ground to put the fire out, and suffered only minor burns. Glen Curtiss, who was famous for winning the Reims Race in France, was flying a Reims Racer No. 2 with a V8 engine, similar to Charlie Olson's. In the preheat, Curtiss had beat Olson's speed record of 44 mph by reaching a top speed of 50 mph.

Chapter 62

The Air Race

By the morning of the third day, the sky had cleared and the aviators were eager to begin the race. The chairman of the race had each pilot draw a number out of a hat to determine the order in which their 'planes would be allowed to take off. When it was Jack and Oliver's turn, Oliver pulled the prop and the engine caught on the first try. They taxied the Jenny down the field and were soon airborne.

All the 'planes first flew in a line like a flock of geese. Then, as if someone had waved a green flag, they split apart and zoomed off in various directions. Charlie Olson dipped his warped wings and flew south. Another pilot flew north, and yet another headed east toward the Sierras. Oliver and Jack figured they would just keep going in the same direction until they came to the Transcontinental Railway tracks, which they planned to follow across the country.

To make extra money for fuel and necessities, Jack and Oliver thought they might do an occasional air show and display their 'plane in some of the towns along the way. In 1911, not many people had ever seen one before.

Then the aeroplane hit some startling turbulence and dropped in altitude. Oliver quickly pulled the wheel back and the 'plane rose again. Even though Oliver had righted the 'plane, the change in air currents frightened Frisco who barked repeatedly. It also scared Achoo who buried himself deeper in the basket.

As the 'plane passed over a town, several people and their dogs chased after it. Frisco's barking elicited a ruckus from the dogs below.

"Quiet, Frisco! Ye're startin' a dog riot!" Jack scolded.

"Hey, Jack, why don't we land for a short time and do an acrobatics act for the people here? Maybe they'll give us some money for food and fuel."

Oliver landed the Jenny on the edge of a field, and he and Jack got out. Frisco jumped out of the basket and Achoo flew over to land on Jack's shoulder. Frisco stretched his legs and peed against one of the 'plane's tires.

Jack, who was an experienced showman, bowed to the crowd that had gathered, and announced, "Ladies and gentlemen, and children of all ages, I present to you Oliver and Jack, who will astound you with their superb flying and wing-walking act! In addition, Frisco the dog and Achoo the parrot will also amaze you."

Hearing his name, Achoo lifted off from Jack' shoulder, flew around the 'plane, and landed back on Jack's shoulder. Not to be outdone, Frisco raced around the Jenny, stood up on his hind legs, and danced in a circle. Jack announced to the crowd, "Ladies and gentlemen and children, for your own safety and that of the aviators, please clear the field and watch from the sidelines!"

When the crowd had moved off the field, Oliver swung the prop and the engine started. He, Jack, Frisco, and Achoo then climbed back into the 'plane. Oliver raced the 'plane down the field and they lifted into the air!

"It's like magic!" a woman called. An old man said, "It's the work of the devil—man wasn't made to fly!" A younger man shouted in the old man's ear, "You better get used to it, 'cause what we're seein' here today, along with the automobile, is the wave of the future!"

While Oliver piloted the Jenny, Jack climbed onto the wing. She'd practiced wing walking only a couple of times, so Oliver insisted she wear the parachute. Jack made a couple of turns on the wing, did a slight hop, raised her arms above her head, and bowed to the audience.

A sudden severe turbulence made the Jenny drop fast and Oliver lost control of her. Jack slipped and toppled off the edge of the wing. The crowd gasped. Jack thought she would fall to her death. Only by sheer luck was she able to grab hold of the edge of the wing. She clung to the wing, squeezed her eyes shut, and let go. After a short freefall, Jack pulled the ripcord and the parachute opened. She then floated gently to the ground. The townspeople, who thought it was all part of the act, roared wildly.

After their thrilling performance, Oliver and Jack set up camp. The same young man who had said that flying would be the wave of the future came over. "That was one exciting act you two did. My name's Phil Perkins. I have a small homebuilt aeroplane I use for crop dusting. I saw your picture in the newspaper and read that you were entering America's first coast-to-coast race. I thought about entering myself, but I've got five kids and my wife is expecting our sixth.

"If you're thinking about flying over the Sierras, I warn you, it's not safe! Those mountains are close to eleven thousand feet, and your 'plane has a ceiling of sixty-five hundred. It's a treacherous crossing. This time of year, winter can come any day without warning. It could be sunny and dry one day, and the next you could be caught in a blinding snowstorm, freeze to death, and your body not be found 'til spring. I know, 'cause two friends of mine died that way.

"Ever hear of the Devil's Triangle? It's an area in the Atlantic Ocean bordered by Florida and Puerto Rico where some ships and 'planes have mysteriously gone missing and were never seen again. Well, there's a similar place called the Sierra Triangle. Maybe you don't believe in spaceships from other planets, but I swear I saw one there. It was cigar shaped and it glowed orange. One moment it hovered over the desert, and the next it zoomed off faster than any aeroplane."

Jack recalled the eerie ghost ship and looked afraid. "You say there may be snowstorms, and 'planes have gone missin'? What do you suggest we do? We ain't just out for a joyride, mister. We're in an air race, and we gotta get to New York in less than thirty days. Our plan was to follow the Transcontinental Railway across the Sierras and straight on to Omaha. From Omaha we'd fly south to St. Louis, then follow the New York Luxury Express railway route to New York City."

"That's all fine and dandy if you want to risk your lives in the Sierra Triangle with that rickety-looking crate of yours—"

Annoyed by Perkins's talk, Oliver interrupted: "So, which way do you suggest we go?"

"As I was saying, the safest way to avoid the Sierras and bad weather is to fly south along the coast from Sacramento to Los Angeles. Then it's a short hop north to connect with the Atlantic & Pacific Railroad track that'll take you east to Needles, on the border of California and Arizona. From Needles you follow the same track across Arizona to Albuquerque. From there it's a short flight to Santa Fe, New Mexico. From there, you're on your own, 'cause that's as far as I've ever flown. Here—maybe this old railroad map will show you the way," Perkins said, handing Oliver a map of the Transcontinental Railroad lines dated 1880.

"If you can't find your way using the map, you can always swoop down and read road signs, follow the roads, or look for landmarks like bridges and lighthouses to guide you. In some places, people write the name of their town on barn roofs to let aviators know where they are."

Jack nudged Oliver. "Like ye say, mister, as soon as we can get our 'plane in the air we'll head south to Los Angeles."

Oliver was annoyed with Jack for interfering. "Why did you tell that crop duster we'd take the route he suggested without first discussing it with me?"

"'Cause he's right!"

Oliver shook his head and thought, *Stubs was right. Jack can be pushy when she wants to be, and she doesn't care what other people think.*

Chapter 63

The Sharecropper's Route

After they'd backtracked to the coast, Oliver skimmed the Jenny over the ocean waves, sometimes dragging her wheels in the water.

"Hey, this is fun!" Jack said. She noticed two albatrosses following the 'plane. The large birds swooped down toward the water, then caught updrafts off the waves and glided upward. Seeing them overhead, Frisco barked and Achoo flew up to greet them.

"Well, if it ain't Spike and Molly! What are they doin' followin' us, Oliver? Let's land on the beach and find out. Besides, it's my turn to fly the 'plane," Jack said.

Oliver landed the Jenny smoothly on a damp part of the beach so the wheels wouldn't bog down in dry sand. He and Jack hopped out of the cockpit. A moment later, Spike splashed down in the shallow water near shore, rolled over in the waves, then got up and shook himself. Molly looked on and shook her head, then made a perfect ladylike landing on the beach.

Oliver examined Spike for injuries. Tied to his leg was a small oilskin pouch with a note inside. Oliver spread it out on the dry sand and read it aloud to Jack. It's from the cap'n.

> Ahoy there, Oliver and Jack! Stubs, the professor, Jones, Harris, and the rest of the crew and

300

me send our greetin's. If ye're readin' this, Spike and his girlfriend, Molly, musta found ye takin' the south route along the coast bound for Los Angeles. After ye leave there, ye'll head east and follow the railroad tracks. I'm so glad ye didn't try to fly over them dangerous Sierras. Stubs says there's little green men live up there who'll take ye in their space machine and ye'll never be heard from again. Once ye head east, Spike and Molly 'll show ye the rest of the way to New York. Even though Spike can't make a three-point landin', trust me, he'll gct ye there. Well, not much room left on this scrap o' paper, so fair winds and followin' seas.

Cap'n John Sebastian Matthews, Esq.

Of the Steamship "Aurora"

Pacific Northwest

After landing at Dominguez Field, just south of Los Angeles, Oliver and Jack fueled up and took a short break. While Jack stayed with the 'plane, Oliver wandered over to the office of the controller who was in charge of the airport. Oliver inquired, "Any aviators who entered the Transcontinental Race come here yet?"

The controller replied, "Yeah. You're the second one to ask me that. The first was a pilot who'd flown down here from Sacramento. Funny thing, though: Back in January, there was a big meet here in Los Angeles sponsored by William Randolph Hearst to promote the city of Los Angeles and his newspaper the *Los Angeles Examiner.* Several aviators, including Glenn Curtiss, participated. You'd think one of 'em would have said something about a coast-to-coast race, but only that one fella came in here and mentioned it. I ain't seen anything in the newspapers about a race either. You sure it ain't some hoax to get your money? I did hear though, that there might be another race in New York to defend Glenn Curtiss' title, but that won't be for several months."

Worried that the race was a fraud, Oliver returned to the Jenny and told Jack what the controller had said. Jack was taken back as much as Oliver was, and said, "Maybe the controller is mistaken, and publicity about the race hasn't reached Los Angeles yet."

"I doubt that. If Hearst was to sponsor a race with a prize of fifty thousand dollars, he would have announced it back in January when that air meet was going on here."

A cloud hung over Oliver until late that afternoon. He then shook off his depression and said, "Jack, there may not be a coast-to-coast race, and that fake inspection and air race in Sacramento may have been a part of the hoax, but I want to continue the race, even if there's no money involved. I want to prove to myself, my family, and the cap'n and crew of the *Aurora* that I have the guts to stick it out and finish, and if I crash and die doing it, so be it! Are you with me?"

"Ye bet yer arse I am! I got as much of a stake in this race as ye do. Besides, we've come this far, and there'll be no turning back, not now or never," Jack said with a confident smile.

Frisco barked as if to say, *I agree*. Achoo and the albatrosses swooped down from overhead and squawked, "Eh, Eh! Achoo screeched, "To hell with them pirates! Man the guns, boys, and full speed ahead!"

Chapter 64

The Race Continues

After they'd filled the fuel tank, and replenished their food and water supplies, Oliver and Jack followed Spike and Molly northward along the Atlantic & Pacific Railroad track to the town of Needles. There the weather was blistering hot, reaching a temperature of 110. A mild breeze gave them a slight tailwind as the aeroplane ventured farther and farther east over the state of Arizona enroute to Albuquerque. Unused to the heat, Jack imagined she was a crab being boiled alive. Even the broad-brimmed sombrero she wore provided little shade.

Jack crawled out to the basket attached to the fuselage to check on Frisco and Achoo. Frisco was panting, and his tongue lolled out. Achoo, a South American parrot, was better at tolerating the heat. Jack gave both of them some water, then crept back to Oliver and said, "It's mighty hot in this part of the country, ain't it? She held out the canteen and said, "Here, Oliver. Take a swig so ye don't get the heatstroke."

While he tried to keep the Jenny level, Oliver put the canteen to his lips and took a long drink, then wiped his mouth with the back of his hand. He looked at Jack and noticed her sombrero. "Where'd ye get that whopper of a Mexican hat?"

"Bought it at that souvenir store in Los Angeles. Also got ye one," she said, handing Oliver the hat. "The Mexicans wear 'em to keep the sun from beatin' down on their heads and out o' their eyes."

"Good idea!" Oliver said as he placed the hat on his head.

Oliver noticed that the albatrosses flew in wide arcs, swooped down, and then flew higher to catch the updrafts so they could save energy.

At that moment, the wind slowed to under 3 mph and the 'plane dropped several feet. "Hang on to your hat, Jack 'cause we're going down!" Oliver hollered.

Jack quickly mashed the sombrero down on her head, climbed into the jump seat, and buckled her harness.

Frantically, Oliver pulled back on the wheel to raise the 'plane. Within a few feet of the ground the Jenny righted herself, and they could feel the wind whistle past their ears once more.

"Hang on to your hat, Jack, 'cause this wind is fierce." Oliver thumped the gas gauge to see how much fuel was in the tank. "We've only got half a tank left, and we still have to cross those low hills before we can land at Albuquerque."

"We'll make Albuquerque, all right, but we might be comin' in on fumes,' Jack replied.

Oliver watched the albatrosses soar effortlessly, catching a ride on the thermals rising from the ground. He wondered, *Could I do the same in the Jenny to save fuel?*

"What if we cut the engine and glide for a while? Maybe we could save on fuel," he said.

Jack didn't like the idea of not relying on the engine, and said, "I wouldn't do that if I was ye. I think we still got enough fuel to get there."

As they neared Albuquerque, Jack and Oliver spied dozens of colorful hot-air balloons in the sky. "There must be an air show going on," said Oliver. "I hear Albuquerque is big on hot air balloons 'cause it has the ideal weather, air temperature, and wind conditions for ballooning."

"Where are we gonna land?" Jack asked, "There ain't a space available, and it's too dangerous to be among all them balloons."

Oliver handed her the telescope. "On that field over there. Then we can walk to the air show. We'd better take the gas cans with us." Jack, Oliver, and Frisco walked to the field where the balloons were. Achoo rode on Jack's shoulder.

Oliver said, "Maybe we can earn some money by demonstrating the Jenny. Also, if that controller back in Los Angeles was wrong, maybe some of the East Coast aviators are here." He crossed his fingers in hopes that the race was no hoax.

Often skeptical, Jack said under her breath, "I doubt it."

On the field beneath the multitude of airborne balloons, booths had been set up where vendors sold different kinds of food and arts and crafts. Smelling the delicious aroma of red hot tamales, Jack said, "I'm starvin'. We can fill the gas cans later. For now, let's eat."

Frisco barked his agreement, and trotted alongside Jack to a booth where a Spanish lady was selling tamales.

Jack asked the woman, *"Habla inglés?"*

"No hablo inglés," and pointed to a nearby man.

Jack rubbed her stomach, pointed to the dish of tamales, and mimed eating. She then placed a few silver coins in front of the señora, who scooped up the coins and asked in Spanish, "How many would you like?"

Jack counted on her fingers, one each for Frisco and Achoo, and two each for Oliver and herself. "Seis, por favor," she replied in her best Spanish.

Oliver asked, "Hey, where'd you learn to speak Spanish?

"When ye live on a sailin' ship with dozens o' sailors from all over the world, ye pick up a few foreign words here and there."

"Funny thing is, you speak Spanish better than you do English," Oliver said.

Jack gave him a shove, "What's it to ya, ye English-speakin' landlubber!"

Hearing Oliver and Jack speak English, an American cowboy approached them. "Howdy folks! My name's Waco. Come all the way from Brazos River country in Texas to be in this race. You two got a balloon? The one with blue, yellow, and green stripes is mine. My crew's gettin' her readyin' to ascend right now. Say, you two wouldn't want to take a ride, would ya?"

Waco wore a wide-brimmed hat, a long-sleeved shirt that had once been white but was now dingy and yellowed from the dust in New Mexico, a vest, a belt with a big silver buckle inlaid with turquoise, cotton trousers that were partly covered with wooly leather chaps, boots with spurs that reached halfway to his knees, and a red silk handkerchief tied around his neck.

Jack looked at Oliver. They both shook their heads and thought, *What a getup!*

"Thanks for the offer," Oliver replied, "but we can't stay long. We're just here to take a break and fill up our fuel cans. We're in a race of our own. Ever hear of the cross-country race sponsored by William Randolph Hearst, who's giving away fifty thousand dollars to the first aviator to fly his aeroplane coast to coast in less than thirty days?"

"Come to think of it, I seen yer pictures in the *Alamogordo News*. The article was titled AMERICAN AVIATORS ATTEMPT FIRST TRANSCONTINENTAL FLIGHT ACROSS THE U.S. Y'all was standin' next to an old Jenny biplane. Sorry, folks, but I hear that race is just a hoax, made up to sell newspapers, and so some aviator who's in a lawsuit can pay his highfalutin lawyers."

Oliver and Jack looked disappointed. "We figured it was a fraud when we didn't meet any other flyers heading our way, but we're gonna finish the race, even if there isn't any prize money. Somebody's gotta set a record, and it may as well be us!" Oliver said.

Ya mean you're really gonna finish that race just for the recognition? You two are crazy, but I gotta hand it to ya for goin' through with it. I got a friend who's a reporter for the *Denver Post*. Mind if I tell him your story so he can write an article for his paper? Better yet, do ya mind if I take a photo o' y'all standin' next to your 'plane to go with the article? Got my camera right here. Been takin' photos of the balloon race."

"Go right ahead," Oliver said. "A little publicity can't hurt us!"

The cowboy set up his folding wooden camera, put his head under a black cloth, focused the camera and ignited the flash powder in the trough. When the powder exploded and a dense white cloud of smoke escaped, Achoo screeched, "Bloody Murder! He kilt the cap'n!" Frisco whined, and dashed beneath the 'plane for cover.

"Well, good luck to ya both. If I was y'all, I'd keep a keen eye on that old Jenny of yours. Ya never know if there's some scoundrel of an aviator out there mad enough to sabotage your 'plane 'cause he sent in his entry fee and the race turned out to be a sham. Sure you don't want a ride in my balloon?"

"Thanks, Waco," Oliver said, "but we've had enough balloon rides to last us a lifetime! Say, ye wouldn't know where we can get some fuel for our 'plane?"

"No. The only aviation fuel round here is a lot o' hot air. Get it? Hot air! Ha-ha! Pancho Villa, the Mexican revolutionary, confiscated all the fuel to use for his 'planes. Said it was for the cause, meanin' the Mexican Revolution. Before I got my balloon, I had me an old Wright II aircraft. Used her for crop dustin'. Since avgas was scarce, I'd make my own by mixin' kerosene and oil, but I can't quite recall the ratio. Also, I heard from an old aviator friend of mine, if you really got no other choice, ya can pour a bottle of moonshine whiskey in the tank, but the hooch has to be at least a hundred fifty proof to work. Never tried it myself—too scared it might blow up the engine. Like I say, good luck to y'all! I'll be sure to tell my reporter friend about yer adventure."

Chapter 65

The Intruders

Oliver and Jack slept under the Jenny for a few hours. At dawn the next morning, before the heat of the desert sun created thermals and the surface winds started to kick up, the two albatrosses lazily circled above the 'plane, eager to get going. Oliver, Jack, Frisco, and Achoo were also ready to start the next leg of their journey.

Flying north toward Denver, they followed the Atchison, Topeka and Santa Fe Railway tracks. Every so often, Oliver thumped the gas gauge to see how much they had left. The gauge showed a third of a tank. He figured they'd stop at Pueblo in hopes of getting more. If they couldn't get it there, perhaps they could buy some in Denver.

In 1911, the town of Pueblo was known for its ore mines and rich mine owners. Jack was piloting, and landed the Jenny in a field on the outskirts of town. Fortunately, some of the wealthy mine owners had 'planes of their own, and were able to fill the gas tank and the two gas cans. Oliver figured that much avgas would get them the 113 miles to Denver, where he hoped they could fill the tank again. From Denver they would fly to Kansas City, then on to St. Louis.

It was dark when they arrived in Denver, exhausted from flying all day. They pitched their tents. "Good night, Oliver! Don't let the bedbugs bite!" Jack called out.

In the middle of the night, Jack and Oliver were awakened by Frisco's barking and growling. They pointed the Eveready flashlight beams at two prowlers who wore masks and hoods. One of the men had a club and was about to smash the framework of the Jenny. The other had a knife and was trying to slash the fabric on the wings and steal the avgas cans.

Achoo flew at the man with the club and screamed bloody murder: "Stop, thief, 'fore I peck yer eyes out!" The man dropped the club and quickly fled across the field. The intruder with the knife wasn't so lucky. Frisco had sunk his teeth into the man's calf and was holding on tight. The man danced around in a circle, trying to shake the dog off.

To help his friend, Achoo flew at the man, intending to peck his face. The thief yelped in pain. A drop of blood ran down his cheek, and he dropped the knife. Seeing Oliver, Frisco let go his grip on the man's leg. Jack ran up and retrieved the knife. Oliver quickly forced the man's arms behind his back, then asked Jack to get some rope to tie him up. The vandal struggled in vain to get free. Once they had roped him, Jack said, "Let's see who this slasher is," and ripped off the mask. "Charlie Olson? What in hell?!" Oliver roared.

Charlie confessed: "Sorry, I didn't know it was you two. By the time I reached Albuquerque, my fuel was really low, so I asked where I could get some. A friendly cowboy mentioned that a couple of aviators had asked him the same question, so I limped along with the little fuel I had left 'til I reached Pueblo. You can't imagine what it's like flying with nothing but fumes and thinking you might crash any minute."

Oliver and Jack exchanged a look, knowing they had nearly run out of fuel themselves.

"Every so often the engine would sputter and the 'plane would drop so low the wheels dragged on the ground. Luckily, I had a bottle of Daddy's moonshine that he gave me to celebrate with if I won the race. A bit of that white lightnin' in the tank kept her going.

"Funny thing is, other than you two, since I left Los Angeles I haven't seen another pilot who claimed he was in the race."

"That's 'cause there *is* no race! According to the newspapers, it was all a hoax, pulled off by William Randolph Hearst to sell his papers and get people's money!" Oliver said angrily.

Charlie Olson was aghast. "You mean to tell me the race is a hoax, and that rich sonofabitch planned this race just so he could sell newspapers? I don't believe it. You're messing with me so I'll quit the race and you'll have less competition."

Oliver shook his head. "No, it's the truth! If you don't believe me, you can—"

Charlie replied, "I *do* believe you, kid. I'm sorry I tried to steal your fuel, but I was desperate! I thought your 'plane was just a crop duster that belonged to some farmer who'd come to watch the balloon races. I gave that fella who was with me three dollars to help me damage your Jenny and steal the fuel. If I'd known, it was yours, I'd… So, now that there's no race, what do we do?" Charlie asked.

"We continue on to New York," Jack said. "Even if there ain't a real race, and no prize money, don't you want to be the first aviator to fly coast to coast and show the world that it can be done? Maybe we could have our own race. Whoever gets to New York first gets the recognition. Whatta ye say?"

Charlie thought, *Do these lamebrains really think they can beat my new Reims Racer 2 in that old Jenny of theirs? It's a cinch I'll win.* "Okay, I'm game! The only problem is, I've got no fuel left. If it weren't for Daddy's moonshine, I wouldn't have gotten this far."

Jack and Oliver smiled at each other, and handed Charlie one of the full cans of avgas.

Chapter 66
Onward and Upward

When the two aeroplanes took off from Pueblo, Charlie waved and shouted to Jack and Oliver, "See you in New York, suckers!"

Frisco growled his dislike of the aviator.

Instead of taking the same route as Oliver and Jack, Olson opted to fly due north until he reached the junction of Wyoming and Nebraska. He would then make a sweeping right turn so he could follow the Union Pacific railway all the way across Nebraska to Omaha. Then he would continue to follow the Union Pacific across the lower part of Iowa to the Missouri River. Once across the river, it was a straight shot north to Chicago, near the tip of Lake Michigan. From there he planned to wing it the rest of the way to New York.

From Denver, Oliver, Jack, Frisco, and Achoo steadily plodded along in the Jenny. Their plan was to follow the Kansas Pacific Railway across the remaining half of Colorado and the states of Kansas and Missouri to St. Louis, then the Luxury Express line to New York City.

As they flew across Kansas, the weather got hotter and hotter and they saw field after field of corn. Oliver was getting anxious to get to a town because they were getting low on fuel. He and Jack watched the albatrosses glide up and down on the thermals. After a while the two birds touched down in one of the cornfields and began to eat some corn. Achoo flew from the

Jenny and joined them. Oliver was tired from the long stretch of flying, and scanned the area for a place to land. Through the telescope, he spotted a recently plowed field. Close by was a sod farmhouse where chickens pecked the dirt. A tired-looking mule was being led into a barn by an African American farmer. As Oliver passed over the farm toward the open field, the chickens squawked noisily and scattered in all directions. The mule brayed and balked, causing the farmer to hold the reins tightly.

Panic hit Oliver when he saw that the field had recently been furrowed. He was concerned that the Jenny would be unable to taxi and take off again. He searched the area for another place to land, but there was none. "We'll have to risk it," Oliver said to Jack. She cut the engine and glided the 'plane toward the field. The wheels bounced over the ridges, and the nose dipped up and down as the 'plane finally came to a stop in the middle of the field.

"Whew! That was a close one!" Jack yelled.

Immediately, the farmer, carrying a pitchfork, came running across the field. He brandished the fork in the air and yelled, "Git that flyin' contraption off my land! That thing scared my mule, chickens, wife, and kids!" A brown-skinned woman and three children shyly emerged from the soddy. The house was built of thick strips of prairie grass stacked on top of each other like bricks to form the walls. The roof was made of layered branches, hay, and sod.

Jack and Oliver climbed out of the Jenny and walked over the field to the farmer, "We're sorry, mister," said Oliver. "We didn't know you'd just plowed this field. You see, we were desperate for a place to land our aeroplane, and yours was the only field we saw that didn't have corn growing on it."

"Please, sir," Jack said, "we're in a race to be the first aviators to fly across the United States coast to coast, and we've almost run out of fuel and food. We was wonderin' if—"

"Don't think I don't know 'bout them machines. Just 'cause I'm a poor dirt farmer and a Black man don't mean I can't read. I seen pictures and an article in the paper. Ye're one o' them aviators. All I can say is y'all a bunch o' dang fools! Another o' yer kind landed in my field t'other day. Tore it up, and I had to plow it all over again. Was askin' if I had somethin' called avgas. Never heard o' the stuff."

"Oh," said Jack, smiling. "Avgas is aviation gasoline. Know anyplace round here we can get some? All we need is a couple o' gallons to get us to—

"Ye might try over in Perth, 'bout twelve miles from here. It's the biggest town in these parts. Got a bank, two millin' companies, an express and telegraph office, and a general store that sometimes sells gasoline for them contraptions called automobiles. They also sell kerosene and lamp oil. Hear there's a man does crop dustin' out that way—maybe he's got some avgas."

Thanks, mister. We'll leave here as soon as we can find fuel and get our 'plane out of your field."

The farmer relaxed and became friendly. He smiled at Oliver and Jack and said, "Name's Lynwood Perkins. This here's my wife, Grace, and our chillun, Maybelle and John. What's yer names?"

"Oliver and Jack, and our two pets are Frisco and Achoo." Frisco ran to the kids, bowled the boy over, and started licking his face. The boy, John, laughed and petted the dog.

"Since ye didn't treat me and my family like we was slaves, like that other fella that landed here, I'm gonna do you a favor and hook up old Hector, my mule, to yer 'plane and drag it out o' my field. Hector's strong, and can pull yer machine out to the road where ye can take off again. Hearing his name, Hector the mule lifted his head and brayed loudly. But 'fore ye go, my wife just made breakfast and is askin' if ye want to join us. Grace makes the best biscuits 'round these parts."

"Uh… ye don't suppose our dog and parrot could have a little bite, too?" Jack asked.

"I'll have the wife fix 'em a little somethin'," Lynwood said.

With the offer of a good breakfast, Oliver and Jack quickly followed the farmer's family into their soddy, which was one large room. In one corner was a wood-burning stove, and near it was a kitchen table and six chairs. Oliver and Jack were pointed to two of them; Lynwood, Grace, and the children sat in the other four. Jack noticed that Grace was in the family way. Against one of the walls was a piano and a pair of comfortable-looking rocking chairs. Separated by colorful quilts hung from the ceiling was a bedroom. Grace gave Jack and Oliver each a cup of strong black coffee and plates of fresh eggs fried sunny-side up, homemade sausages, grits, and warm biscuits dripping with butter and honey. Jack picked up her fork to dig in.

"Uh… how was y'all brought up? First we gotta thank the Lord for this bountiful food He set before us," the farmer said.

After their ample breakfast, Lynwood hitched up Hector and pulled the Jenny out of his cornfield. Oliver and Jack thanked him and Grace and took off for Perth. As the 'plane lifted into the air, the family waved and the chickens scattered again.

In Perth, Oliver and Jack found the crop duster. He offered to sell them a couple of gallons of avgas at an outrageous price, but they had no choice. The man said, "I seen yer picture in the paper. Hear there's a huge prize for the winner o' the race. That true? With money like that I'd move away from this godforsaken dust bowl and get me a castle somewhere out west," he said, grinning.

"No. There's no money, and no race for that matter. The race was all a hoax. We were fooled, but we want to prove to the world that it can be done, so we've decided to continue on to New York," Oliver said.

"Well, I give ya credit, young man. Most woulda quit by now."

Chapter 67

The Lightning Storm

The farther east they flew the darker the sky got. The albatrosses sensed the change in weather and flew low to the ground. A sudden cold wind whirled around the 'plane; lightning flashed and thunder clapped. Torrential rain assailed the Jenny, and ice formed on her wings. The turbulence made her bounce and shake and dip up and down, nearly tossing Frisco and Achoo out of their basket.

Over the raging wind, Oliver yelled to Jack, "Make sure you're harness is tight, 'cause we're gonna have to make an emergency landing and take cover 'til this storm lets up."

Nearby was an open field where Oliver managed to land, but as they touched down they heard a cracking sound and one of the wheels fell off and rolled away. Frisco jumped out and chased after it. When the lightweight wheel stopped and fell over, he grasped it in his mouth, dragged it back to the 'plane, and dropped it at Oliver's feet. Oliver tossed the wheel into the cockpit and with Jack's help threw a canvas tarp over the Jenny. He hoped she wouldn't be struck by lightning, which, if it hit the engine, could ignite the vapors in the fuel tank and cause an explosion.

Jack looked over the surrounding land. "There ain't a single tree anywhere on this stinkin' prairie where we can find shelter!"

"Good thing there *aren't* any trees around," Oliver replied, "because standing under a tree during a thunderstorm is the worst thing you can do. Remember that thunderstorm on the *Golden Lady* when lightning struck one of the spars? The lightning traveled down the mast and nearly spread to the deck and started a fire. Better we stand out in the open and get soaked."

Soon, as if by magic, the rain stopped and the sun came out and began to dry everything. Oliver and Jack removed the tarp, put the wheel back on the landing gear, and taxied down the field. Spike and Molly flew in an arc around the Jenny, then suddenly disappeared.

Jack looked at the horizon and yelled, "Holy smokes! There's a grassfire comin' our way fast and furious. Hurry, Oliver! We gotta get out o' here afore it reaches us!"

After a running start down the field, Oliver lifted the 'plane into the air. The albatrosses followed. Looking down, Oliver spotted a flash flood that carried rocks, tree limbs, and other debris that swept right past where the Jenny had been.

"Yikes! We got out of there just in time!" Jack shouted.

After flying for some time, Jack landed again so they could put more fuel in the tank. While Jack was tending to the fuel, Oliver lay on the ground, stretched his arms over his head, and watched the albatrosses lazily catching thermals overhead. Suddenly Oliver jumped up. "Jack we gotta do something to lighten our load so the Jenny will go faster. We just can't keep chuggin' along at twenty mph."

"Why should we worry about goin' faster now that we know the race is a hoax? If you really want to go faster, we could pour in some that white lightnin' the crop-duster fella give us."

"No, I was just watching the albatrosses and noticed that they tuck their legs and feet under their bodies to create less drag when they fly. They also lock their wings in place so they can soar like gliders for long distances. The wings on our Jenny are stationary, but maybe I could add an upright board at the tip of each wing that would reduce our drag, increase our speed, give us more lift, and save fuel.

"If I could figure out a way to have the wheels fold up against the fuselage, it might also lessen our drag. As it is now, the framework that holds each wheel is stationary. Maybe I could modify the wheel frames by attaching a hinge so they can bend and fold up. Then, on the end of the frame, weld a long rod with a handle that reaches the cockpit. When we pull the handle, the wheels will fold up to the bottom of the lower wing and be held in place by a self-locking latch. To lower the wheels to land, all we have to do is push the lever down, and gravity will pull the wheels down."

Jack shook her head. "Sounds a little complicated if ye ask me, but like Stubs says, 'Nothin ventured, nothin' gained,' so it's okay with me if ye wanna tinker. But where are you gonna get the materials?"

"We've got all the materials. I packed extra rods, tools, and wood just in case something broke and we were stranded somewhere with no hardware store. Also, I used to work in a foundry."

Chapter 68
Modifying The Jenny

In Kansas City, Oliver, Jack, Frisco, and Achoo walked uptown and found a livery stable where a blacksmith was shaping horseshoes on a forge. Oliver showed him a drawing of the hinge and mechanism he had designed to raise and lower the wheels. He then asked if he could use the man's shop to make them. Oliver explained that he had experience working in a foundry. The blacksmith said, "Come back after the noonday meal and you can use my forge."

Back at the Jenny, Oliver, with Jack's help, dismantled the landing gear and put blocks under the fuselage to hold the 'plane upright. After dinner they took the original landing frames, wheels, and extra metal rods to the livery, where Oliver fabricated the needed improvements. He thanked the blacksmith, gave him a couple of dollars, then took the modified landing gear back to the 'plane and attached it. Jack sat in the pilot's seat and pulled the levers while Oliver stood by to see if the new gear worked. The wheels folded up against the body of the 'plane exactly as he had designed it to do.

"Hoorah, she works!" Oliver called to Jack. "Let's celebrate with some supper in town."

Jack and Oliver ate famous Kansas City steak smothered in sticky sweet barbeque sauce, with baked potato fries alongside.

They couldn't finish the generous meals and asked the waiter for a bag to bring the leftovers to Frisco and Achoo who gobbled the scraps.

After supper, Oliver bought a copy of the *Kansas City Star* newspaper. He opened the paper to the second page where there was a photograph of Jack and Oliver in front of their Jenny at the balloon races in Albuquerque. The photo was captioned YOUNG AVIATORS PROCEED IN COAST-TO-COAST RACE CHALLENGE. Under the photo was the following article:

> Famed newspaper magnate William Randolph Hearst has stated that the Coast-to-Coast Air Race sponsored by his newspaper is not a hoax, and demands that several newspapers, including the *Los Angeles Examiner, San Francisco Chronicle,* and *Chicago Sun Times* publicly announce a correction. Unfortunately, having heard that the race was a fraud, Glenn Curtiss, the "King of Speed," and several other aviators have declined to participate.

> Since the thirty-day deadline has passed with no winner, Hearst is now offering the $50,000 prize to the first aviator to fly coast to coast, regardless of the number of days it takes. In addition, Hearst will award a prize of $20,000 to the first runner-up, $10,000 to the 3rd-place finisher, and $2,500 for 4th place.

> Oliver Turner and his copilot, Jack Matthews, were last seen in their Jenny Reims Racer 1 at the balloon races in Albuquerque. Charlie Olson, in his Reims Racer 2, has yet to report in, and may be missing, along with two other aviators who were last seen crossing the Sierras in Nevada.

Marnie White

Pittsburgh aviator Cal Rodgers, who left New York City in his Wright Model EX biplane, reached Chicago. Learning that the race was legitimate after all, he was determined to continue on to California.

Good luck to all the remaining contestants—they will surely need it!

Chapter 69

Lightening The Load

The next day, Oliver and Jack jettisoned everything they felt wasn't necessary. Oliver topped off their fuel, and they readied the Jenny to fly to St. Louis. From there it would be a hard haul of nearly 800 miles across Illinois, Indiana, Ohio, Pennsylvania, and finally on to New York City.

After they'd lightened their load, modified the landing gear, and added small upright structures to the wingtips, Oliver's design proved true, and the 'plane averaged a speed of 25–35 mph. Oliver and Jack were delighted. They switched piloting every four hours—while one slept, the other flew. Oliver figured if they flew seven to eight hours per day and a few hours per night, they would cut their travel time by at least a week or possibly two.

The tank held only ten gallons of fuel. At an average speed of 35 mph, they thought they might be able to fly an average of 300 miles per day. With a good tailwind perhaps even farther. Besides filling the fuel tank, they also filled two five-gallon gas cans, hoping that if they were conservative with their gas, they wouldn't have to buy as much. In 1911, avgas was expensive and hard to find.

The second night, Oliver wired their flashlights to the front of the 'plane, which gave them enough light to fly for a couple of hours during the night. Jack had brought along extra batteries, but limited their nighttime flying to just two hours to conserve battery power.

At dawn the next morning, they lifted off, and after several hours reached the Missouri River and the town of St. Louis. At the St. Louis Lambert Airport they were surprised to see a crowd of 10,000 waiting to get a glimpse of their 'plane and to wish them well on the last leg of their journey. To thank the crowd for their well wishes, Jack and Oliver did a flyby and circled the field. They had no time for a full aerial performance, but during the flyby, Jack strapped on her harness, climbed out on the wing, and waved her white silk scarf to the crowd, who cheered and whooped.

Oliver landed the Jenny not far from the crowd. A young kid ran up to him and out of respect removed his newsboy's cap. "Please, sir, may I have your autograph?" Remembering his brother Stanley's enthusiasm about the balloon, Oliver smiled at the boy. "Sure, kid. What's your name?"

"Charles Lindbergh." the boy replied with confidence.

"Well, Charles Lindbergh, what do you want to do when you grow up?"

"I want to fly an aeroplane just like you, and become famous for making the first solo transatlantic flight from New York to Paris," Charles said.

Oliver chuckled. "That's kind of a tall order, but maybe someday you'll become an aviator and do just that," Oliver said, smiling at Charles and ruffling his hair. The boy smiled back, thanked Oliver for his signature, and returned to his mother in the crowd.

As Oliver and Jack were greeting the throng, Charlie Olson crept up to the Jenny, bent over as if inspecting a wing, and used a long knife to slash a hole in it. *Maybe this'll slow that damn machine of theirs down,* Olson thought. He then vanished into the crowd.

After a bow to the audience, Oliver and Jack waved good-bye. Once in the air, their next stop would be Tipton, Indiana. Halfway there, Oliver noticed that the Jenny had a lot of drag and was slowing down. Worried, he tried to put her down in a nearby field, but he lost control, and the 'plane nosedived toward the ground where it crashed into a barbed-wire fence and came to a halt. Luckily, Jack, Oliver, Frisco, and Achoo were not badly hurt. Jack suffered a slight bump on the head. Oliver had a scratch on his arm, and the dog and macaw were safe. Fearing that the engine might catch fire, Oliver and Jack quickly exited the 'plane and ran from it. Frisco and Achoo followed, and the albatrosses soared off.

Oliver and Jack waited several minutes. Sensing that the Jenny wasn't going to explode, they inspected it and found several tears in the fuselage caused by their collision with the fence, but nothing that couldn't be patched. One wing also had a long cut that looked like it had been done deliberately.

"I bet it was that no good bugger Charlie Olson made that slash," Jack said.

Several people had seen the 'plane go down and came to their rescue. One man who owned a garage offered to check the engine, and Oliver repaired the damage to the wing with strips of cotton cloth and aircraft dope. Oliver read the instructions on the can: HIGHLY FLAMMABLE. DO NOT USE AROUND FIRE. Oliver knew he had to soften the dope to a consistency that he could easily spread over the cloth strips to waterproof and harden them. He put the can of dope in the hot sun to warm. Soon the goop was soft enough to apply to the patches. He knew he would have to let everything dry thoroughly before taking off again. In the meantime, he took a nap under the 'plane, and Jack went to see if she could get some avgas. The town didn't use much aviation gas, and she was able to get only two gallons, which, along with what was left in the fuel tank, would have to suffice until they got to Bellevue, Ohio.

Three hours later, the Jenny took to the air. Just outside Bellevue the engine started to sputter, then cut out altogether. Oliver spotted an open field, glided toward it, and landed. Another aeroplane circled the field and landed. Jack knew it was Charlie Olson in his Reims Racer No. 2.

"Knew I'd catch up with you again one of these days. I see those two big birds are still following you. If I had my way I'd shoot 'em out of the sky—I've heard albatrosses bring bad luck."

Recalling what Stubs had told her, Jack retorted, "Ye got it wrong! An albatross followin' a ship brings good luck. It's killin' 'em that brings ruin. Besides, we've known Spike since he was a fledgling, and he always brought us sailors good luck. If ye ever try to shoot one o' them birds, I'll shoot ye myself! Ye're the one cut a hole in the wing back in St. Louis, ain't ye?"

Frisco bared his teeth and growled. Jack wanted to hit Olson, but Oliver stepped between them. "Get out of here, Olson, before we tell the race authorities what you've done," he said.

"I ain't through with you two yet!" Olson said as he slumped off toward his 'plane.

Chapter 70

Bellevue, Ohio

At Bellevue another crowd waited to see the aviators. Newspaper photographers flashed photos as they landed. Neck and neck with Charlie Olson and other flyers, Oliver and Jack only had time to fill the fuel tank and gas cans and be on their way again. The crowd cheered as they took off.

They followed the New York Express railroad tracks along the shoreline of Lake Erie, and stopped at several towns for gas and a brief rest. From above the lake, the skiffs and steamers looked like toy boats. Seeing the steamers made Jack miss the captain and crew of *Aurora*.

The next stop was Erie, Pennsylvania, where they refueled before heading to Dunkirk, New York. From there it was a short hop to their final destination, Floyd Bennett Field in New York City. Though bedraggled and tired, Jack kept flying. Suddenly, two 'planes zoomed past the Jenny and dipped their wings in greeting. This would be a race to the finish.

Oliver looked at the other aircraft through his telescope. One of them was Charlie Olson's. The other was a single-wing craft piloted by Fred Brown of Reno, Nevada. The three flew side by side until they reached the East River in New York City, where Olson's aeroplane stalled in midflight, lost altitude, and plummeted toward the murky waters below. Olson crashed on the mudflats; the fuselage of his Racer 2 broke up and partially sank in the mud. Olson, unhurt, managed to stand on top of what remained, and waved to Oliver and Jack for help.

Hoping to win the race, the pilot of the other 'plane buzzed straight on past Olson. Unable to land on the mudflats, Jack lowered a rope with a loop on the end and signaled Olson to catch the rope and put the loop over his shoulders. Olson did that, and hung on as Oliver slowly skimmed over the mudflats to dry land where they briefly touched down and let him go.

To gain speed and make up time, Oliver dumped the last of everything that wasn't needed, with the exception of the parachute and the basket that held Achoo and Frisco. Lighter now, the Jenny picked up speed and flew across the Hudson River to Floyd Bennett Field and finished third in the contest. Fred Brown had already won the second prize of $20,000.

An aviator named Calbraith Perry Rodgers, from Pittsburgh, was the first to make the transcontinental flight from New York City to Pasadena, California, and won the $50,000 grand prize. No other aviators in the race arrived at Pasadena or at Brooklyn. William Randolph Hearst heard that Oliver and Jack could have come in second but opted to rescue a fellow flyer, and decided to give them $15,000. Also, he offered to transport them and their aeroplane back out west on his private train.

Jack and Oliver agreed that once back in Seattle they would repay the professor the $400 he had lent them, with a bonus of $100, since they had both quit the ballooning act. Of the $10,000 that remained, they would give Captain Matthews half, and split the remaining $5,000 between them.

Olson was grateful to Jack and Oliver for saving his life, but extremely angry that he didn't win a prize because his aircraft had failed him at the last minute. Oliver remembered the adage "Whatever one sows, that will he also reap."

Chapter 71
The Proposal

When Hearst's train arrived at the Seattle railway station, a throng waited to congratulate Oliver and Jack for finishing the race. In the crowd were Oliver's entire family, plus Captain Matthews, Stubs, Professor Le Strange, Mr. Jones, and Mr. Harris.

When the speeches ended, and Oliver and Jack had received a special plaque, the crowd dispersed. There remained only a man who was carefully inspecting the Jenny. Oliver approached him and asked, "Sir, is there something I can do for you?"

The man, fascinated with the aeroplane, slowly extended his hand and answered as if he had been daydreaming, "Yes, Mr. Turner. My name is William Boeing of the Aero Products Company, and I'd love to take a ride in your Jenny if you'd be willing." Oliver was taken aback, unused to being addressed as Mr. Turner. Only his father was called that.

Oliver said, "Sure, Mr. Boeing, I'll take you for a ride in my aeroplane, but I warn you, she's a bit slow compared to the newer 'planes. Just let me get the old girl ready and we can take her up. You say you're from the Aero Products Company? What products do you make?"

"We'll, we've only been in business a short time. The factory is located not far from here, in an old boathouse on the Duwamish River. For some time now we've been working on an aircraft we call the Boeing Model 1, a single-engine, float-equipped biplane, but it will be a few more years before she's ready to fly."

That afternoon, Oliver took William Boeing for a ride. Boeing was amazed and impressed at the modifications Oliver had made to the Jenny, such as the retractable landing gear, a lighter fuel tank, and raised tips on the ends of the wings to lessen drag. He even liked the idea of attaching flashlights to the front of the 'plane so it could fly at night. As Boeing and Oliver flew, Spike and Molly followed them.

Oliver said, "Those two albatrosses are friends of mine. They guided this 'plane all the way from California to New York and then followed Mr. Hearst's train to Seattle. I got the idea for the landing gear and wingtips from watching them fly. They're heavy-bodied birds, but they're highly aerodynamic and can fly nonstop for ten thousand miles. When it comes to landing, though, the male is sort of clumsy. Would you like to fly the Jenny?"

Boeing's eyes lit up. "You bet! I've always dreamed of flying an aeroplane, but I think you should give me a few lessons first. Say, would you be interested in working for my company? I could use a good test pilot. I couldn't pay you much at first, but with time..." Boeing hoped Oliver would take the job, because all the aviators he'd previously asked had said a firm no.

"I'd jump at the chance, Mr. Boeing. Before I became a pilot, I was a balloonist, and before that a sailor. I also worked in a foundry," Oliver said excited at the offer.

When Oliver landed the Jenny, Boeing thanked him for the ride. "Okay, then, I'll see you at my factory tomorrow morning about ten o'clock and show you around," Boeing said.

Oliver told Jack about the possibility of working at Boeing's Aero Products Company. At first she looked dejected, then said, "I'm happy for you, Oliver. Don't worry about Frisco, Achoo, and me. We'll be fine workin' for the cap'n on *Aurora,* and I can always go back to bein' an aerialist for the professor."

Oliver stared at her and got down on one knee. "Uh, Jack… I know what you said before about marrying me, but we've been through thick and thin together. I don't care if you dress and act like a sailor, aren't the domestic type, and want to do things men do. I love you, Jack, and I want you to be my wife. Will you marry me?"

"What? Ye numbskull, do I have to tattoo the word "no" on yer forehead afore ye get it? I don't want to marry ye or any other dadblamed fool," she said.

"But with the money we won from the race we could live like royalty—hire a maid, a cook, a butler, a seamstress, even a nanny to take care of our children. I also thought, for appearances' sake, you'd want—"

"Let 'em think what they want, but I ain't gonna marry ye, and that's final. Oh, Oliver, ye just don't get it! We both know it wouldn't work out between us. We'd be fightin' like the cap'n and Sarah within a month. It ain't that I don't love ye. It's 'cause, well, like Stubs says, I've always been an untamed seabird. If I was caught and put in a cage, I'd be unhappy the rest o' me days, wishin' I was free," Jack said.

"I understand, Jack, 'cause that makes two of us. I've been told I'm a dreamer and sort of a wild bird myself, but can we still be best friends?" he asked.

Jack brushed away a tear. "'Course we can, Oliver! Nothin' can change that. "Here's to bein' best mates forever!" she said, raising her mug of coffee and smiling at him.

Early the next morning, Oliver, Jack, Frisco, and Achoo were seen in the Jenny as they flew off to another adventure.

Author's Note

King of the Air and Sea was inspired by the real-life adventures of my grandfather, Henry Oliver Turner, at the turn of the 20th century. As a teenager, he had a falling-out with his father and stowed away on an old sailing ship that journeyed around Cape Horn to New York City.

Like Oliver in the story, Grandfather knew magic tricks, and made an apple disappear before the captain's eyes. Amazed and delighted, the captain made my grandfather his personal steward, much to the dismay of another cabin boy, who swore he would get back at my grandfather. In later years, Grandfather became a professional magician. His stage name was Revilo, which was, of course, his name, Oliver, spelled backwards.

My grandfather was also a balloonist, and worked for the real Professor Le Strange at Coney Island amusement parks and later in Washington State. As part of the act, my grandfather would parachute down from the balloon. Once, he landed in the mudflats where he had to cling to a log till he was rescued. The real-life Oliver loved dogs, and often took his dog up with him in his balloon until the State Humane Society warned him that to do so was unlawful. When my grandfather was a teenager he worked at a foundry. He also loved to tinker and fix things, had to fend for himself on the menacing streets of New York City, and built an airplane that he flew, with his wife seated by his side, around the capitol building in Olympia, Washington. That 'plane hung for many years in a hotel in Olympia.

While I have tried to remain true to my grandfather Oliver, I've taken liberties with certain dates, characters, names, places, and events to fill in what he left untold and to add detail and color to the story. Thus *King of the Air and Sea* is a work of fiction, and most of it stems from my imagination.

Note on Aviation History

In 1909 Glenn Curtiss and Agustus Moore Herring, of the Curtiss Aeroplane and Motor Company in New York, built the Curtiss Reims Racer No. 2 biplane so Curtiss could race in the Gordon Bennet Cup air race in Reims, France. He named the airplane the Golden Flyer No. 2, which featured several improvements over the No. 1.

The manufacturers added a covered stabilizer on the fuselage, increased the wing size, changed the interplane ailerons, and replaced the old 25-horsepower, four-cylinder inline Curtiss OX engine with a lighter, 63-horsepower Curtiss OX V8. They also exchanged the old fuel tank for a lighter one. With less weight and a faster engine, the No. 2 could reach a top speed of 75 mph, fly 175 miles without stopping, and had a ceiling of 6,500 feet. Unlike the Reims Racer 1, the Golden Flyer had dual controls, and its propeller was located in front of the engine, not in back. The Reims Racer No. 2 was used during WWI and later by barnstormers.

The tail of the aircraft was a small horizontal plane. The rudder that directed the airplane to go right or left was split by the tail. The rudder was worked by wires that ran to the steering wheel, which was in front of the pilot. When a pilot wanted to steer the aeroplane right or left, he turned the wheel as in an automobile, and leaned in the direction he wanted the airplane to go.

Glossary

Aficionado – a person who is knowledgeable about something such as fine cigars or wines

Apothecary – a shop where herbs and medicines were sold

Avalanche – when a mass of snow breaks away from a slope and moves downhill fast

Bootleg – illegal

Buffoon – a ridiculous and amusing person

Buona liberazione – Italian for good liberation or setting one free

Canonical hours – set times for Christian prayer

Canuck – slang word for Canadian

Capiche – Italian word for do you understand?

Caisson – a concrete, stone, or metal foundation that a lighthouse rests upon

Catherine wheel – a firework in the form of a flat coil that spins when fixed to something solid and lit

Cazzo – Italian cuss word meaning hell, shit, or damn

Coup – violent overthrow of a government

Curator – a man who oversees a collection of art or artifacts in a museum

Devil's Triangle – Until 1964, the Bermuda Triangle was called the Devil's Triangle

Dither – to be unable to decide

Dope – a lacquer applied to fabric-covered aircraft

"Fair Winds and Following Seas" – a nautical blessing for a safe journey

Flimflam – to swindle or con someone out of something

Fo'c'sle – forecastle, or forward part of a ship below the deck, used as the crew's quarters

Folderal – useless and nonsensical fussy actions or things

Fortnight – a unit of time equal to fourteen days

Gondola – balloon basket

Gooney – an old English name for a stupid or clumsy person

Hail Mary – traditional catholic prayer addressed to Mary, mother of Jesus

Hawser – a thick rope for mooring or towing a ship

Highfalutin – grandiose, overly fancy

Hike! – an old command used prior to "all right" to signal sled dogs to go

Icon – a Russian religious painting, usually on wood

Idlers – common sailors who work during the day and are excused from watch at night

Iodine – a mild antiseptic

Klaxon – a horn first fitted to automobiles in 1908

Molly – the name stems from the Dutch word *mollymauk* for foolish gull

Nautical Times – 1200 hours, 1600 hours, 12:00 noon; 4:00 PM

Nincompoop – dummy

Nipper – slang word for a thief

Nub – non-usable body

Oilskins and sou'westers – a cap with a broad flap covering the
neck; foul-weather gear

Orcas – Killer whales

Painter – a short rope attached to the bow of a small boat for
tying it to a ship or wharf

Phenomenon – a remarkable event or occurrence

Pimps – men who control prostitutes and arrange for their
clients

Puny – small and weak, sickly

Quay – a wharf, dock, or pier

Sacrilege – misuse of what is regarded as sacred

Scruples – a sense of right and wrong; twinge of conscience

Shaman – High-ranking Native tribal leader and medicine man

Shipping the oars – to stop rowing and pull the oars either
inside or alongside a boat

Slop chest – a supply of clothing, boots, tobacco, and other
personal goods aboard ship

Spire – similar to a church steeple

Thermals –in aviation, a column of rising air caused by uneven
heating of the earth

Throng – a large crowd

Whitecaps – when ocean waves break, air and sea mix to form
bubbles that rise to the surface and appear as white patches

About the Author

Marnie White is a native of Northern California. She is a graduate of San Francisco State University where she received a bachelor's degree in English and Creative Writing. An award-winning poet, she is also the author of *Echoes from an Open Space Ranch,* which helped place the Old Borges Ranch, in Walnut Creek, California, on the National Register of Historic Places. Marnie and her husband live in Fort Bragg, California. They have two adult daughters and three grandsons.